The Raging Sea

THIS RAGING SEA

DE ELIZABETH

WALKER BOOKS

First published in the UK 2025 by Walker Books Ltd
87 Vauxhall Walk, London SE11 5HJ

Published by arrangement with Holiday House Publishing, Inc.
 First published in the United States 2025
by Holiday House Publishing, Inc.

2 4 6 8 10 9 7 5 3

EU Authorized Representative: HackettFlynn Ltd
36 Cloch Choirneal, Balrothery, Co. Dublin, K32 C942, Ireland
EU@walkerpublishinggroup.com

This book has been typeset in Adobe Garamond Pro

Printed and bound by CPI Group (UK) Ltd, Croydon CR0 4YY

British Library Cataloguing in Publication Data:
a catalogue record for this book is available from the British Library

ISBN 978-1-5295-3281-4

www.walker.co.uk

FSC www.fsc.org
MIX
Paper | Supporting responsible forestry
FSC® C013604

To anyone looking for something they lost

PART ONE
LOW TIDE

Death has reared himself a throne
In a strange city lying alone
Far down within the dim West
Where the good and the bad and the worst and the best
Have gone to their eternal rest.

EDGAR ALLAN POE, "The City in the Sea"

CHAPTER ONE
BRIAR

Bad news tastes like salt.

It's one of those certainties that Briar knows but can't explain, like the way she can finish her best friends' sentences without thinking. It's as factual as anything in a textbook; it might as well be a law of physics:

When Briar Winters tastes salt between her teeth, terrible things follow.

She swallows the bitterness as she trudges through the dusty beach parking lot, flanked by her three closest friends. They might as well be her family.

Though, lately, it's been hard to call Finn that at all.

Ahead, the ocean reflects a galaxy of rainbow lights. A towering Ferris wheel slices the black sky, and screams haunt the sticky, humid air. The seaside carnival is usually her favorite night of the year, but in just a week, Kai, Astrid, and Finn will be scattered across the country at their respective colleges like little red pins on a map.

And she'll still be here.

In another universe, Briar would snap photos until her battery runs out, drink in every second. The night would become one of those rose-colored memories, forever crystalized in past tense. They'd say, *Remember that time at the carnival?* and think of right now, *this* moment.

Tonight could still be like that.

But if Briar can't heal the wound that's split open between her and Finn, they won't remember it that way at all. Instead, they'll think of a night drenched in quiet regret, each rolling wave like a taunt: *It could have been; it could have been.*

"Bee, what do you think?"

She snaps her gaze to Astrid's as they approach the ticket booth. "What?"

"Nostril or septum?"

Briar blinks. "Huh?"

Astrid angles her face skyward, glossy braids spilling down her back. "I can't decide which piercing to get before orientation next week."

"Careful, your Libra sun is showing," Kai says with a laugh.

Astrid slides a pretend glare toward Finn, who's been silent this whole time. "Did you teach him that?"

Finn shrugs. "Just pierce both."

Briar's stomach twists at the detached clip of his voice, the sadness she knows is only there because of her. He looks so different from the Finn she remembers on graduation night, the last time things felt soft between them. His skin appears pale instead of sun-kissed, and his gold-streaked hair is haphazardly tousled, not styled like it usually is. Two half-moons hang beneath his stormy-gray eyes as though he was awake until sunrise, his desk strewn with math books and graph paper. Briar can easily picture him, glasses on, spinning theories into ink, and her chest aches with everything that's still unsaid.

Kai and Astrid keep talking, but Briar remains silent as they move forward in line, slipping into a pool of ruby light from the sign overhead: ***Loch Creek Summer Carnival.*** In smaller print underneath, the Massachusetts town's catchphrase: ***A haven since 1692.***

Briar's seen the slogan a million times, can trace her hometown's roots to the cries of misunderstood women tied to burning posts. Loch Creek, a safe ground amid a sea of witchcraft hysteria. *A haven.* Some people believe the description still fits, pointing to the summer rush of tourists, the way many are so proud to live in Loch Creek that they never leave.

Her parents are like that. Which is why she can't tell them that, to her, Loch Creek feels more like a trap. A place stained by tragedies no one ever talks about. Loch Creek's sadness lingers beneath the surface, a haunting whisper to anyone who takes care to listen.

But to Briar's ear, it's more like a roar.

Astrid's phone chimes, the name *Ellie* lighting up her screen. Unwanted envy gnaws at Briar's insides. All summer, Astrid has been texting her future Vassar roommate, a gymnast from Kansas City who's planning to major in political science like Astrid. It seems like Astrid's phone buzzes every other minute with a meme, a text, a video. As though her future—the one without Briar in it—is always in the room with them too.

Whatever Ellie sent makes Astrid snort with laughter, her warm-brown skin glowing in the screen's light. Briar watches her reply, gaze lingering on the woven friendship bracelet on Astrid's wrist, identical to the one on hers. And before she can smother the thought, Briar wonders if this is what it's like to be slowly replaced.

Kai notices too, but with a grin.

"Who's got you smiling like that?" he teases, tucking a strand of chin-length black hair behind his ear as he looks. "Damn, I hope Northwestern sets me up with a good roommate. If I get some nasty dude who leaves his socks everywhere, I'm gonna riot."

Briar offers a small smile and swallows the aching reminder that soon, Astrid, Kai, and Finn will be sitting in lecture halls, going to parties, making new friends. It's easy to picture Kai in a film class directing an experimental short, Astrid at a debate podium arguing for a universal healthcare system. Finn in a physics lab, studying equations and time. All while Briar will be stuck in Loch Creek, working at the mayor's office for a year before going to school somewhere close to home. Just like her parents always wanted.

They think they're protecting her so nothing horrible ever touches their family again, but it feels more like being buried. She'll become part of this town, immortalized like one of the statues outside of Old Town Hall. Limestone instead of skin, glass instead of eyes. Frozen in time as Loch Creek High's head cheerleader and straight-A prom queen, a pearlescent picture of hard work and practiced smiling and bullshit bullshit bullshit. No one would ever think to look inside a statue of Briar Winters and see how it's hollowed out, filled with skittering cockroaches that have made a home in the bottomless dark.

"What about you, Briar?" Kai asks.

"Huh?" Another chunk of conversation she missed.

He tips his head, and his curious stare seems to ask, *What's up with you tonight?*

"Think you'll miss anything from high school?" Kai adds.

Briar tries to count the times they walked into Loch Creek High together over the years: hundreds of doorways on hundreds of mornings. Their friendship has always been a constant. Like pi, a number that goes on forever but never changes shape. A connection forged at random when their kindergarten teacher assigned their seats, not realizing she was creating a family.

"I think it'll be stuff like this that I'll miss the most," Briar says, twirling a loose honey-colored curl. "The little moments when it's just us."

And before Briar can stop herself, she silently adds, *Before it's just me.*

"Isn't it strange," Kai says, "how we did so many things for the last time without realizing? Like, I didn't think twice when I finished my last exam. I dropped that blue book on Mr. Halloway's desk and peaced the hell out."

Astrid snorts. "What should you have done? Taken a selfie with Mr. H. to commemorate the occasion?"

"I dunno." Kai shrugs. "Awfully anticlimactic though. Go to class every day, and then *pfft*." He flaps his hands like butterfly wings. "Over. Just like that."

"That's how everything is," Finn counters. "You never realize things are over until it's too late."

Briar's cheeks warm at the rough scrape of his voice, the way his words sound like a coded message only for her. She doesn't have to look to know he's remembering graduation night, how she fled from his apartment the next morning. The way he begged her to stay. The way everything has been wrong since.

"O-*kay*." Astrid laughs. "That's enough existentialism for one night."

Kai's face splits in a smile, but Finn only fidgets with the brass compass looped around his belt, the eighteenth birthday gift they all chipped in for earlier this spring. Briar studies him as he flicks the latch back and forth—and tracks his stare to a dark-haired girl a few paces ahead.

The girl's back is to them, a thick onyx braid with streaks of blue slinking down her spine. She's dressed in all black, fishnets tucked into knee-high boots, and Briar's chest clenches with instant recognition:

Morgan Parker-Blake. A girl Briar has known her entire life. A girl she wishes she could forget.

Just looking at Morgan puts a knot of anxiety in Briar's stomach. It's easier to see her at school, where the rule may as well be written in the student handbook: *Don't talk to Morgan Parker-Blake.* It's part of Loch Creek High lore, like *the D-stairwell is where people go to hook up* and *Mr. Bridges gives pop quizzes on the third Friday of the month.*

No one talks to Morgan. And Morgan doesn't talk to them.

She exists at the periphery of their world—a slab of scenery, silent and still. And Briar likes it that way.

Because if Morgan-Parker Blake is quiet, then she can never tell Briar's most poisonous secret. It remains locked inside. Swallowed whole.

But outside of school, the rules are hazy. And right now, Finn is studying Morgan like he *knows* her. Like he has something he's desperate to say, as if a million things have happened in the two months Briar hasn't spoken to him. Her stomach sours at the possibility.

"*Helloo-oooo*?" Astrid calls, waving a hand in front of Briar's face.

Briar jumps, her flip-flops skidding in the sand.

"Want me to get your ticket? Yes or no?" Her question has an edge, as though it's the third or fourth time she's had to ask.

"N-no, sorry, I've got it." Briar fishes for her wallet before addressing the man working the window. "One please." As an afterthought, she darts another look at Finn. "Two."

Briar offers her hand to the employee, who stamps it with a dark blue crescent wave. She stares at the ink and tries to summon her apology to Finn. *I'm sorry I left. I'm sorry I didn't tell you why. I'm sorry I still can't. Please don't let this ruin us.*

"Show that for reentry," the employee orders. "Need to see yours too, buddy."

"Finn." Kai elbows him. "Finn. *Finnegan.*"

But Finn is somewhere else, eyes cloudy. Briar charts the lines of his face and silently wonders if they've run out of chances to talk about what happened, if time is slipping and slipping like a shell being tugged out to sea.

"Finn, he needs to stamp your hand," she whispers. The first words she's spoken to him all night. Longer, even.

For a moment, Finn looks right at her. Briar sucks in a breath, commanding her face to stay neutral. Because it's *Finn*. The boy she's been friends with for over a decade, years marked with springtime afternoons in tree houses, stretches of endless summer at the beach. Finn, who spent every Christmas at her house since ninth grade with his own stocking on her parents' mantel. Finn, her best friend since kindergarten—the year Briar stopped talking.

Finn, who helped her start again.

She should talk to him now like she did back then, let every painful word spill out. But the thought of telling him what happened after graduation drives a blade of disquiet between her ribs, carving her into a mess of guilt and shame.

She can tell Finn almost anything—but not this.

Briar knows she needs to find another way to mend things. Before he's in another time zone, before his mornings become her afternoons, before he's only a voice on the phone and everything, *everything* topples off-balance.

Finn slides his hand into the ticket booth window, still looking at her.

And Briar silently pledges not to let them say goodbye while they're still broken.

~

Inside the carnival, Kai leads them along the beach, throwing a few careful glances over his shoulder. They shuffle behind a pizza stand, clouds of garlic mingling with the sea air.

"Let's head to the lifeguard tower," he calls. "There's a decent amount of cover there."

"How much did you bring?" Astrid whispers to Briar as they trudge through the sand, fingers intertwined.

"Enough for all of us." Briar peers behind her, as if the crowd somehow knows she's carrying several hundred milligrams of edibles inside her purse.

She can only imagine what her parents would say if they saw her under the bleachers last week, exchanging their cash for a baggie of weed gummies. *Briar*, her mother would gasp, hand splayed over her chest. *What will the Artists' Society think?* Sometimes Briar wonders who her mother would have been without the word *reputation* filling her brain.

The water laps quietly as they walk. Each foam-tipped wave's steady crash feels like the ticking of a clock, sucking away the time they have left together.

"Here," Kai says, once they're behind the lifeguard tower. He glances at his watch. "If we take 'em now, then hit the Ferris wheel, they'll kick in when we reach the mirror house." A grin creases his ivory skin. "And *that* is gonna be badass."

Briar digs her nails into her palms. Kai's been obsessed for weeks with this idea: pop an edible and get lost in the mirror maze. In any other circumstance, she'd laugh and swallow her apprehension, like she does when Astrid makes her watch horror movies or when Finn hits the gas too hard on the turnpike.

But it's been months since Briar has seen her own reflection.

She's learned to avert her gaze when she enters any bathroom or walks past sun-soaked storefront displays. She's even thrown a bedsheet over the vanity in her bedroom and resorted to doing her makeup by guesswork. She's gone to school with uneven winged eyeliner more times than she can count, but it's better than looking in the mirror. She knows what she'll find if she does: The thing that's always waiting for her.

The thing that's waiting for everyone to leave her behind.

Kai turns his palm up. "Let's do it. Briar?"

Briar pulls the baggie of rainbow gummies from her purse. Kai and Astrid reach inside, but Finn studies Briar with a slitted stare.

"Are you gonna take one?" he asks, and Briar nods.

The interaction feels rigid, like a rusted hinge that's forgotten how to bend. Before graduation, they talked a million times a day—shouting over lockers at school, texting beneath desks in class. He used to call her in the middle of the night; her phone would buzz on her nightstand, and Finn's voice would be insistent in her ear. *Do you ever feel like you lost something but you can't remember what?*

But lately, there's been only silence.

Finn is about to eat his gummy when Astrid curls a hand around his wrist.

"We should toast first!"

"With these?" Finn asks, arching a brow.

"What about a promise?" Briar tries. "That nothing changes after next week."

The words taste stale as they leave her mouth—a cruel joke, when so much has already changed.

But Astrid has already latched on to the idea. "Group FaceTime dates every week," she exclaims, flipping her braids over her shoulder.

Briar forces a smile. "Road trips during spring break."

"And every summer, the carnival," Kai says. "No matter where we end up. We'll always come back home."

Briar glances at Finn, who's staring blankly as though he doesn't believe what they're saying. And the more Briar also listens to their pledges, the more they sound like lies. There won't be any video calls or cross-country drives—not if she can't navigate the chasm between her and Finn before it widens too far to cross.

"Summer's not over yet though. We have Briar's birthday next week." Astrid hooks an arm around Briar's shoulders. "Don't worry. We'll take that stuffy old yacht and have the best party this town has ever seen."

Briar forces another smile. Birthdays are supposed to be lit up with glitter and music, but for her, they're only a reminder of what she's lost.

Still, it's easier to twist her face into a mask of excitement than admit she can't stand being surrounded by candles and ribbons. That unwrapping gifts under expectant eyes only makes her bones ache with guilt.

That it hurts to be celebrated when you used to have a twin and you don't anymore.

For six short years, Briar shared her birthday. *Those* were the birthdays she liked. But the ones after have only felt bitter, her stomach turning at the idea of honoring another year on earth when her brother is buried beneath it. This year especially, her party feels like a countdown to the impending day that she's left here alone. Like an unwanted thing, a girl whom time forgot.

Finn clears his throat. "Can we eat these now?"

"Bon appétit!" Astrid quips.

Briar slips the gummy between her teeth, but it doesn't taste like candy. Instead, salt crystals crunch between her molars, and she erupts in a storm of coughs.

"You're supposed to eat it, not choke on it." Kai laughs, whacking her back as Astrid passes her a water bottle.

Briar washes down the rest, running her tongue over her teeth. Out of habit, she reaches into her bag, breathing in relief when her fingers close around her inhaler.

It's always there, but she still has to check. Just in case.

She sips again, staring at the horizon. The shoreline reflects the carnival lights, making the sea beyond it look darker than normal—a rush of endless black. She thinks without meaning to about being underwater, pockets heavy with opal-colored stones. A dream written into the sand, water twisting into red-winged butterflies. A familiar velvety voice seems to whisper on the wind: *Here, here is where you'll sleep one day.*

Goose bumps pebble her skin at the sound. What will it be like, she can't help but wonder, when she's alone with nothing but her own hideous thoughts?

"Briar." Finn whips her name through the salt-bitten air as if she'd spoken aloud.

She swoops her gaze to his, waiting for him to say more. But Finn is quiet, as though he's used up all his questions, every one of them left unanswered in her phone. *Can we talk? What happened? Why are you mad at me?*

Too many thoughts tangle in his silence: The million afternoons they spent together as kids, kneeling in the dirt and trapping ladybugs in glass jars, trading thorn-edged memories that only they could understand. The way somewhere over the years, he started looking at her like she was rare and otherworldly. The reminder of the way time is drifting out toward the tide, how even this moment will soon be past tense too.

"Y'know what? Give me another one of those."

"Finn!" Astrid chides as he grabs the baggie. "You're only supposed to take one, you're—*Fiii-iinn!*"

Kai snatches the bag just as Finn swallows a third, and anxiety shoots through Briar's stomach. That's too many, even for him—

"Dude! Chill!" Kai shakes his head. "What's with you? You've been acting weird since we got here."

"Let's go." Finn's words fall flat. "Don't wanna miss the Ferris wheel."

Astrid frowns. "Finn, what's going on—?"

But Finn has already started walking. Astrid exhales in frustration and lobs a pointed look at Briar that seems to say, *Work your shit out before it ruins all of us*.

Briar swallows a swell of guilt, falling into step with Astrid and Kai. Her thoughts spin with how she could possibly get Finn alone *here*, a place crowded with color and sound. She's still frantically thinking when they reach the line for the Ferris wheel, where the lanky teenager working the control panel sizes them up.

"You're gonna have to go two by two," he says, and the solution unfolds like magic.

Before she can change her mind, Briar grabs Finn's hand—something she's done a million times before. His palm against hers has always been a familiar comfort, something to steady her, to keep her safe. But right now, taking Finn's hand feels like an eleventh-hour act of desperation. Like the fierce grip of a last chance.

"Ride with me?" she asks, and he nods, surprise flashing across his face. As though he didn't ever expect her to talk to him again.

But she will, right now. She'll tell him what she can. Swallow the parts she can't.

And Briar hopes that by the time they're off this ride, everything will hurt a little less.

CHAPTER TWO

FINN

Finn Adler has always been a damn good liar.

He lies the way other people breathe. Without thinking. As a kid, he'd inhale fairy tales and spin them back as something new. He'd scribble in notebooks, weave dream-soaked whispers into stories. Harmless lies. Fiction, really.

But his lies grew as he did. His homework? A coywolf must've eaten it. The bruises on his arms? Got hit with a dodgeball in gym class—don't ask questions.

The only place he's ever told the truth was inside a courtroom. It worked though, setting him free from the wretched woman masquerading as his mother. On his own at sixteen, California-bound at eighteen. UC Berkeley. Physics major.

Like he always planned.

In one week, he won't have to look back at where he came from. A new start is ahead, all palm trees and sunshine. He can't wait.

At least that's what he tells people.

But Finn Adler isn't just a good liar. He's a *great* liar.

He can shrug off his friends and tell them nothing's wrong when there's actually a blade of fear caught in his throat. He can stare right at Briar and tell himself there's still time.

But deep down, he knows, when it comes to her, there will never be enough.

~

The Ferris wheel hasn't left the ground, but Finn's stomach flips like he's in the sky anyway.

It shouldn't be like this—Briar, climbing into the compact car with her teeth tearing her lower lip, mirrored anxiety churning inside him. Finn clutches the compass at his belt and traces his friends' initials on the back, the engraved infinity symbol, and fleetingly wishes they could return to a time before all this. To summers marked by afternoons at Astrid's pool, to the flickering lights of the arcade with Kai. A time when his thoughts weren't weighted with mounting dread, when he didn't look at Briar and only see a girl he's not sure he can save.

But she's barely said a word to him since graduation, all the unspoken things left alone for too long. Astrid and Kai have noticed the shift too—it would be impossible *not* to—but they don't know the reason for her silence. Not the real one.

Even Finn has only threads of a hypothesis. They've been knotted inside him all night, turning him desperate to get Briar alone and compile the right phrase for a warning.

He tightens his hold on his compass, trying to slow his pulse by making a silent list. Somewhere along the line, a therapist gave him that tool. *When you feel yourself panicking, pick a category, and list five things.*

Constellations: Orion. Cassiopeia. Pegasus. Leo. Gem—

The Ferris wheel jerks to life with a rusty squeak. The sound is like a release on a pressure valve, and they both speak at once.

"Finn, I'm sorry—"

"I think you should—"

They fall silent. Finn's practiced speech dissolves at the sight of Briar's expression, her eyes soaked in regret. Behind her, the carnival shrinks smaller and smaller, morphing into a watercolor painting of neon and black.

He should have rehearsed better. He spent all summer unraveling secrets, and now he's finally in front of her without a single good way of explaining them. But it all boils down to the same facts, impossible to swallow, even harder to stomach: There's something rotten in this pristine town. A storm is brewing under the surface.

And the darkest clouds are hovering right over her.

He'll have to lie to soften it. Find a way to tell her without making her hate him forever.

"I'm sorry," Briar repeats, "for what happened after graduation."

Finn meets her gaze, finds her chewing her lower lip again. *Graduation* feels like a swear word between them. A night that started so perfectly, surrounded by the friends he'd chosen as his family. The loaded silence when he was alone with Briar on his fire escape later, weighted by the dizzying way he'd been wanting to kiss her for months. The electricity that sparked between their mouths when he finally did.

The bone-chilling things he heard her whispering into the shadows at dawn.

Briar slumps against the side of the Ferris wheel car. "God, I hate this. Us not talking. Right before you're about to leave Loch Creek forever. It feels like there's a hole—right here." She tightens her fist, brings it to her chest.

Finn swallows the burning confession that going two months without speaking has also hollowed him out, that not hearing her voice has ruined him more than any insults ever could. Instead, he squeezes his compass and summons the words he's been desperate to say for weeks.

"What if," he starts, "you came with me to California?"

Briar tips her head in confusion. "What?"

"You said it yourself. I'm leaving." Finn holds her stare, gaze burning into hers. "You could leave too."

"Finn—"

"I'll help you find an apartment," he barrels on. "We'll figure out flights. I'll change mine if I have to. You could get a job, or go to school, or do whatever you wanted—"

"*Finn.*" Briar's expression only looks pained. "Where is this coming from? You know my parents would never let me."

He grinds his teeth. Briar's parents are practically his family too. Her mom has cooked dinner for him countless times, her dad taught him how to ride a bike—but right now, the mere mention of them snags his carefully threaded plan.

"Briar," Finn pleads, "you're almost nineteen. You don't have to listen to them."

"It's not that simple," she says.

"It is though." He searches her gaze. "Your parents might be upset, but they can't *stop* you. I'll help you tell them, if you want. They can get mad at me instead."

"You know that wouldn't work." She leans closer. "Finn, I was trying to apologize. Can you let me finish—?"

"This is important." He swallows. "Briar, please. Think about it at least?"

She pins him with an incredulous stare. "Finn. Drop it. I can't move away."

"You *can*."

Her breath rushes out. "Why are you doing this? You *know* I can't leave—"

"Briar, you *have to leave*!"

The Ferris wheel squeals to a violent halt as they reach the top, in time with the sudden desperation of his words. Briar stares in stunned silence, and Finn's heart hammers so hard, he's certain she can hear it.

"You have to leave Loch Creek," he says again, quieter.

The seat sways beneath their feet. Her expression is impossible to read. "Why?"

Finn swallows a wave of vertigo. Focuses on her narrowed eyes. "We both know that bad things happen here: the disappearances, the drownings no one talks about, the coincidences." He pulls in a steadying breath. "Thing is, they're not coincidences."

The color drains from Briar's face. "What... what are you saying?"

Forget the Ferris wheel—Finn feels like he's walking a high wire. One wrong word and he may as well be shattered on the concrete below.

"Riley," he says, and Briar's gaze darkens at her dead brother's name.

For a moment they stare at each other, the car rocking in a salt-drenched gust. Briar blinks rapidly like she's fighting back tears, and Finn rushes to get the rest out.

"I know you hate talking about this—you don't have to say anything, okay? Just listen. This whole time you've been ignoring me, I haven't been ignoring you. I've been researching." He sucks in another breath. "What happened to Riley when we were kids? It wasn't an accident."

Briar's jaw clenches as her chest rises and falls with accelerated inhales. Her chin trembles and her lashes flutter. Like she's at war with her body, trying not to break down in front of him. *Shit.* His plan is already threatening to unravel, and he's barely said any of it.

Finn's hands itch to hold her so she doesn't fall apart. But he flattens his palms on his thighs instead, as though she might disintegrate into sand if he were to touch her at all.

"Do you remember," he whispers, "what you said on graduation night? Before you left. Before you stopped answering my texts. You were talking in your sleep. Crying. You said Riley's name. Remember?"

Her nostrils flare, and she shakes her head in a way that tells him she's lying.

"Why did you leave instead of talking to me about it?" Finn keeps trying. "Why did you shut me out for two whole months?"

Briar tightens her lips as if she's fighting to hold words inside. "It's... complicated."

Her answer is a flame between his ribs, igniting the awareness that something scared her into silence that night. Something he can't protect her from if she won't let him.

"Nothing's too complicated for us," he insists. "It's *me*, Briar."

"I know." Her eyes cloud over. "And that's why I can't tell you."

Finn chews over all the ways he could push her to confess before thinking better of it. She's a millisecond away from crumbling, threatening to become a girl of seashell dust and secrets he'll never get to hear.

"That's okay," he forces himself to say. "We'll have plenty of time to talk on a flight to California."

Her gaze drags to his, red-rimmed and aching.

"You're making this hurt so much more than it needs to," she says, and he has to bury his own hurt that rages inside him.

"I'm not trying to be an asshole," Finn says. "I'm trying to keep you safe. Away from this place. Please, consider leaving. We'll figure it out together, like we always do—"

"Why were you staring at Morgan Parker-Blake?" Briar interrupts, and Finn slams into silence, caught off guard. He scrambles for a flimsy lie.

"I—I wasn't."

"You *were.*" Briar scowls. "I saw you. Why were you looking at her like that?"

Finn flips his compass open and shut and thinks of the dozen unanswered DMs he's sent Morgan this summer, all left on Read until she finally blocked him. *Can I ask you something? Does your family know anything about Loch Creek's original founders? Have you ever seen this symbol before? Do you know what this language is? Morgan, hello?*

I need you to answer.

"I was surprised to see her at the carnival," he tries. "Morgan doesn't exactly have friends, you know."

Briar's gaze hardens again, and she turns to stare over the side of the car. Ice floods Finn's veins at her expression, the same one she had by the shoreline earlier. He's seen her features twist a million ways throughout the years; he can predict how her nose will crinkle when she laughs or how her blue eyes brighten when she's going on about her obsessions, like painting or cheerleading or the latest queer pop icon. He loves everything about her face—her long lashes, the freckles smattering her peach-toned skin—but he despises when she looks like this. He wants to fold his hands over her cheekbones, slowly mold her expression into one that doesn't terrify him.

Because when Briar's eyes turn glassy and she stares off into the middle distance, he knows she's listening to something in the water. The same thing that spoke to her before she fled his apartment in tears.

Perhaps the same thing that whispered to her brother thirteen years ago too.

"Briar, I know this is hard to talk about, but—"

"The sea is watching us," she whispers, and he falls quiet.

Fear flattens inside him at the dark, unfamiliar curve of her voice.

He swallows, throat dry, and can only reply with honesty this time.

"I know." He leans closer. "That's what I'm trying to tell you."

She whips her head, and their noses nearly collide.

"You *already* told me," she says, their faces inches apart. "On the phone."

"On the phone?" He frowns. "What do you mean?"

"Why do you always call so late?" Briar continues. "Two, three, four a.m." She lowers her voice in a poor imitation of his own. " 'What's today's date?' 'What season is it?' " Her sigh lands on his mouth. "Why do you always ask that? Do you not have a calendar?"

"Briar." He lets out the tiniest laugh as he remembers the edibles. "You're high."

"Do you think of me when you can't sleep?" Briar asks, nails grazing his neck. "Then you call me so I won't sleep either? That's not very nice."

"I've never called you in the middle of the night," he counters, swallowing an unexpected swell of regret.

Because he wishes he had called her, wishes they'd had this conversation earlier instead of at the last possible second. They should be somewhere quiet instead of the carnival, somewhere safe for her to cry or scream or whatever she needs to when he tells her the truth—whatever it takes to convince her to leave.

"Briar, can we back up?" Finn bites the inside of his cheek so he doesn't give in and kiss her instead. She smells so damn good—orchid, pear, hibiscus—and the world blurs. "I need you to listen. You're—"

Their chair lurches as his words tangle. Briar falls forward, her shoulder smacking against the side.

"Briar." He reaches for her, but she's blurred too, a ghost in the lights. "*Briar.*"

Everything spins as the Ferris wheel makes its descent. The salt-scraped sky is awash with green and black. Below, the crowd swirls and swirls, each person trailing monochrome shadows. Briar holds a hand in front of her face; blue light radiates from her nails, sputtering like a firecracker.

The ride operator unlocks their chair, and he's glowing too. His face is longer than Finn remembers, and his chin droops like putty.

"Time's up," he announces. "You have to say goodbye now."

"What?" Finn asks, blinking.

"To the ride," he clarifies. "Ride's over."

Astrid and Kai appear on the platform, grins too wide and teeth too white. Astrid's braids curl around her smooth brown arms like gold-tipped cuffs; Kai's pale ears are somehow made of glitter, piercings turning into stardust.

"To the mirror house!" Kai yells.

Finn darts a glance at Briar, who is staring at the shore again. As though she's listening to something he can't hear. He grabs her hand, tugging her down the ramp with him.

Five things, he thinks silently. *Category is superheroes: Spider-Man. Batman. Superman. Captain America. The Hulk.*

Finn inhales the salty breeze. Okay. Plan B.

He'll get her alone after the mirror house, ask her if she wants to talk somewhere quieter. He'll try again and again; he won't *stop* trying until they're together, thousands of miles from this broken place. Until he's certain that what happened to Riley thirteen years ago won't happen to her too.

Finn squeezes Briar's hand as they approach the mirror house; the gaping clown mouth at the entrance yawns in the gathering dark. "Stay with me in there, okay?"

To his surprise, Briar shakes her head. "You go ahead. I'm gonna wait outside."

He stops walking, forcing them both to a skidding halt. "For real?"

"Let's gooooo!" Kai yells, already halfway to the entrance. Astrid dissolves into giggles, folding over the metallic railing.

Briar eyes the mirror house warily, and for an instant, they're kids again, her room lit up with nightlights every time he stayed over. *I don't like when I can't see in the dark.*

"I can't go in there," she says in a small whisper.

"Fine," he replies, "I'll stay out here with you."

She shakes her head. "You go ahead."

Anxiety clenches inside him as he imagines Briar sitting on the shore, the breeze clawing at her hair, water whispering in her ear. Beckoning and beckoning until she slips beneath the waves.

Until her body mirrors her brother's, lifeless and blue.

Bile surges in Finn's throat and he squeezes her hand tighter. As if her fingers are the constellation-patterned stress ball he keeps on his desk, as if her touch could do anything to untangle the worry that's been crushing his ribs since June.

"Finn. Please." Briar loosens her grip on his hand as she starts to pull away. "I need to be alone right now. I promise we'll talk after, okay?"

He searches her expression for any indication that she might actually want him to stay, but all he finds is distant sadness in her gaze. His stomach knots with guilt, understanding he's the one who put it there.

Perhaps this time the only way to help her is to let her go.

Finn surrenders her hand with a defeated exhale, reaching for his compass instead. A bite of chilly salt air replaces her warmth, and he pretends not to notice, forcing himself to nod.

"After," he echoes. "Alright. I'll find you."

He wouldn't be able to explain why, but these words taste like his worst lie yet.

CHAPTER THREE

BRIAR

A blade of sunlight pierces the blinds in Briar's basement the following morning, and she isn't sure which is worse—the dull throbbing behind her right eye or the bitter regret in her throat.

She sits up on the couch, curls tumbling around her shoulders. It takes a few blinks through mascara-crusted lashes for her to realize she's alone. The basement is practically silent, save for the soft rattling of the air conditioner. If she listens hard enough, it almost sounds like a familiar voice. *Winters girl*, she imagines it beckoning.

"Guys?" she calls, a note too loud. As if to quiet both the sound and its reminder of the emptiness that waits for her once summer ends.

Briar peers up the stairs. The door is ajar, shadows curling in the alcove.

"Astrid? Kai? Finn—?"

She frowns. Astrid's sand-dusted bag is shoved in one corner. Kai's lanyard is strewn over the coffee table next to his wallet. But Finn's stuff—his backpack, his sweatshirt—isn't here.

As though he got up and left in the middle of the night like she did two months ago.

Briar grabs her phone and scrolls through the notifications: Instagram, email, her reminder for birth control pills, some news headline about washed-up fish on the beach, a text from her mom.

But nothing from Finn.

Anxiety snarls inside her as she remembers her half-formed apology, all jumbled like a puzzle that's been put together wrong. The way Finn cut through her flimsy words to poke at the one truth she can't ever tell.

The way it seemed like he was afraid of something too.

Remorse suddenly grips her. The rattling of the air conditioner becomes a taunt, reminding her that last night was supposed to heal them, but she might have only ripped open the wound instead.

Briar jumps to her feet, wincing at another stab of pain behind her eye. Her joints are stiff too, as if her bones were glued together while she slept and now she has to work them loose.

"Finn?" she calls again, padding across the carpet. "Astrid? Are you guys upst—?"

Briar slows in front of her mother's corny wall collage of family photos and narrows her eyes. One picture is noticeably missing from its frame. Her senior portrait.

She's always despised the photo: the magazine-gloss of her hair, the inhuman smoothness of her skin. Her face had broken out, and her mother paid extra to have the photographer edit her into a porcelain doll. *Perfect, delicate Briar Winters*. There were times she'd fantasized about scribbling ink over her eyes in that picture, adding horns and maybe a forked tongue. It would be worth it to see her mother's expression. And at least she'd look more like herself.

Briar starts up the stairs as she connects the dots of last night's events. After the Ferris wheel was the mirror house. Her stomach turns at the reminder of how she didn't go in—*couldn't* go in. Her friends went without her, while she sat by the water and calculated the dwindling time they had left. She stared at the tenebrous horizon until the roar of the waves drowned out her regrets, turning her numb and cold. And there, in the deepening dark, she gave herself permission to wonder if that was the last sound her brother ever heard.

If the sea was louder than his cries for help. If the water swallowed his voice too.

Briar slams the basement door behind her. She won't think about this now. She needs to find Finn.

Astrid, Kai, and Finn—they came out of the mirror house, *and then what*? Where did they go afterward? What time did they crash here? Briar's stomach twists with fierce awareness that the carnival won't be one of those nights that they'll look back on forever.

Because she can barely remember it at all.

"Guys?" she asks, surveying the silent corridor. "Is anyone here? Finn?" She expels a frustrated sigh. "Where *is* everyone?"

Briar starts up the spiral staircase to the second floor. Maybe, she tries to reason, Finn couldn't sleep and went to her room. She rushes down the hall as if she expects to find him under her thick white duvet. She'll curl up against him, and everything will feel softer, like the jagged edges of last night's conversation weren't as sharp as she thought.

But when Briar opens the door, she finds her bedroom drenched in shadows, the bed made and empty. Fleetingly, she wonders if running out of time ever comes with a warning. Or if most friendships end like this: slowly, quietly, until you're standing in the middle of a mess that can't ever be cleaned up.

Pain bubbles behind her eye and she winces, hissing a breath.

Medicine. Now.

Briar flies into her adjoining bathroom, clutching her temple. Leaving the light off to avoid the mirror, she yanks open a drawer. She shakes out three painkillers, flinging a disparaging glance to the orange bottle of clozapine tucked behind a box of tampons. Out of sight. She thinks about her father counting the little white tablets last year, lining them up like a string of beads. *You're behind*, he scolded, and made her take them in front of him for months after.

She knows this kind of medication can help people, that it's improved so many lives. But those little pills have done nothing but make Briar's head cloudier, that familiar whisper louder. And the idea of her parents monitoring her intake makes her feel caged and small. Like they look at

Briar and see only a helpless child instead of someone grown.

Slamming the drawer shut with a defiant clang, Briar shoves the painkillers in her mouth, swallowing without water. She pulls her phone from her waistband and texts Finn—*Where'd you go????*—before dashing back downstairs, through the long corridor toward the kitchen—

Where she slows to a halt.

Her mother's mermaid painting is hanging crooked on the wall. Briar never liked this one because of how sad the mermaid looks, gazing at a glittering city she can't ever visit. Her face is twisted like she's sobbing, but her cheeks are dry. *A mermaid has no tears*, her mother once explained, quoting Hans Christian Andersen. *And therefore she suffers so much more.*

Knocked askew, the mermaid somehow looks even sadder.

Briar straightens the painting, adjusting the brass frame until it's level. But the second she steps back, it slips again. From this angle, the mermaid seems to stare right at her. Unbalanced and longing to be set right.

Gritting her teeth, Briar presses toward the kitchen, clutching a final thread of hope that Finn will be sitting on the patio with Kai and Astrid, coffee mugs scattered between them. But before she can get there, a scratching noise snags her attention.

She glances toward her mother's craft studio. It's not uncommon for her mother to be inside—Briar's used to hearing the soft clacking of the weaving loom at all hours, a sliver of light spilling under the door in the evening.

But lately, her mother's been spending full weekends embedded in some secret project. Briar has asked about it a few times, wondering if it has anything to do with the incessant PAST DUE envelopes she's seen on the counter, but her mother always smiles coyly, teasing, *Someone's birthday is coming up, you know.*

Her nineteenth. As if she could forget. She wishes everyone else would.

"Mom?" Briar rattles the handle. Locked. She glances at the grandfather clock at the end of the hall—9:30. Her parents should be at the gallery by now.

She presses her ear to the door, but all she hears is her own breath. The house feels especially quiet, her heartbeat echoing in her ears like footsteps.

No. Actual footsteps.

Astrid rounds the corner, practically slamming into her.

Briar startles. "Jesus, Astrid."

"Jumpy much?" Astrid says. "Have you seen Kai or Finn? They were both MIA when I woke up."

"I've been looking for them too." Briar's teeth sink into her lip. "Finn's stuff is gone."

Astrid slumps against the wall dramatically. "Well, he'd better be grabbing bagels because I am in *dire* need of emergency resuscitation. Carbs and caffeine are my only hope now."

"I'll make coffee," Briar says, starting for the kitchen. But she averts her stare so Astrid doesn't see the worry etched into her face. She knows in her gut that Finn isn't going to walk through the door with breakfast, knows that she's the only reason he's gone.

"Do you remember *any*thing from last night?" Astrid asks, as Briar pulls two mugs from a shelf.

Her stomach twists as she recalls Finn's expression on the Ferris wheel, his usually calm demeanor colored with desperation. The way he begged her to leave Loch Creek with him. How badly she wanted to say yes. How much it hurt to know she couldn't.

"Nothing," Briar mutters. "Not after you all went into the mirror house, that is."

"Same," Astrid says. "And I barely remember that. Finn was out of his mind—that's all I know."

Briar gnaws at her lip again as she pops a pod into the coffee machine, slamming the top as if to puncture the silent ache of a last chance.

"I can't believe he took three," Astrid continues. "He needs to cut that shit out, or he's gonna *burn* out."

Confusion stirs inside her. "What do you mean?"

Astrid slides her a glance. "All the excess, you know? He's like a Category Five hurricane waiting to make land. I mean, have you been at his place lately?"

Not since graduation. Briar studies her reddened cuticles, skin ragged from her picking last night. "Yeah," she lies. "I was just there."

Astrid takes the mug from Briar before opening the fridge. She's been to

Briar's place so many times that it's like her own home. They've had infinite sleepovers, a million after-school snacks and stops before cheer practice. Briar's house is Astrid's house, and the other way around. Their history is written here, carved into the bones of this room. This very table was where Astrid came out to her last year. *I don't know if I'm bi like you and Finn or pan like Kai*, she'd said, *but I think I could fall in love with all kinds of people. Maybe I don't need a label, right? Maybe some things don't have to be named.*

"So you saw what Finn's bedroom looked like, yeah?" Astrid asks, head tucked inside the fridge.

A knot forms in Briar's stomach. "I must've missed that. What's up with his room?"

"It was a hot mess," Astrid says, nudging the fridge shut with her foot. "He had papers everywhere, weird math written on his window. He'd pulled those old maps off his walls; they were on the floor, marked up." She pushes a carton of cream into Briar's hands. "And that's not all. I saw empty pill bottles. 'Study buddies,' again."

Briar struggles for a neutral expression. "Did you ask him about it?"

"Yep. But he wouldn't tell me anything."

Briar swallows, guilt like a stone in her stomach. Finn's apartment was normal when she was there last, and she didn't realize he was taking stimulants again. She considers the unanswered texts in her phone, the times she didn't pick up his calls, and the ache inside her deepens. She should have talked to him last night. She tried, she tried, she *tried*—but the words got stuck in her throat like an invisible hand was trapping them inside.

"Actually, I do remember something—" Astrid suddenly frowns, peering at Briar's hair. Her scowl deepens. "What is that?"

"What is what?"

Without answering, Astrid digs into Briar's messy curls, face twisting in confusion as she disentangles something stringy and green.

"Did you go for a swim last night?" Astrid mutters, flinging the offending substance into the sink.

Briar peers into the silver basin. Strands of seaweed encircle the drain, each crusted with gritty sand. She scratches at her scalp and her fingers come away dirty, black grains beneath her half-painted nails. She wipes her hand on her thigh, bewilderment racing through her. She never swims in the ocean.

Not since her brother died there.

She shoves the seaweed into the garbage disposal, flipping the switch a touch too roughly, as though shredding the memories between the blades.

"What were you going to say?" Briar glances at Astrid, who's staring with a hard-to-place expression. "You remembered something about last night?"

Astrid studies her for a moment before reaching into her sweatpants pocket. "Yeah. Or, more accurately, I found something." She tugs out a receipt. "We apparently went to a restaurant after the carnival. Thing is, I've never heard of it at all."

"Seaside Tavern," Briar reads, squinting. She could easily list every restaurant in Loch Creek—and this isn't one of them.

Taking the receipt, Briar scans the list of orders. Fries. Drinks. A milkshake. A burger. The same kind of shit they always get. But . . .

"Who ordered *this*?"

"Popcorn shrimp?" Astrid snaps her a concerned glance. "Maybe it's a mistake. We weren't seriously this high, were we?"

There's no freaking way anyone would have ordered that. They have a pact. It might as well be a blood oath.

They shook on it, after that awful afternoon in seventh grade. They were at Kai's house, eating leftovers from his grandma's Fourth of July barbecue. Tupperware was spread out on the table like a medieval banquet. Nothing was labeled; everything was fried.

It happened so fast. One second, Finn was laughing, and the next, his face was turning red, fingers scratching at his neck. *My throat is itchy*. He pushed back from the table, bent at the waist. The chair tipped with a clatter, and within a single breath, Finn was on the ground.

Where's his EpiPen? Astrid kept screaming, digging through Finn's backpack. Briar attempted CPR, clawing at her memories of health class. How many pumps on the chest? How many breaths? *It's not fucking working! Call 911!*

Kai was the one who dialed, hands shaking, voice cracking on the phone. Briar sobbed, gasping around her inhaler as Astrid continued CPR. She and Kai took turns sending air into Finn's mouth over and over until the kitchen flooded with lights and an EMT plunged a needle into his thigh.

It was the second worst day of Briar's life.

That's when they made the deal. No one orders or serves shellfish. They made their parents promise too.

After that, Briar silently began checking Finn for his EpiPen everywhere they went, scouting out his backpack when he wasn't looking. As soon as she'd spot the red pouch, she'd swallow a mouthful of relief.

It's also why she always checks for her inhaler. Because if she hadn't had it that day, they both would've had to be brought back to Earth.

"Astrid." Briar hands her the receipt. "What if Finn is hurt? Do you think Kai might have taken him to—"

The screen door slides open, and they both whirl. The noise momentarily derails Briar's panic with a burst of familiarity. Her screen door clattering in its frame is the sound of summer. It's the sound of being barefoot on the beach, of staying up until the sunrise, of spilling secrets into the humid ocean air.

Now it's the sound of Kai rushing inside, his dark hair wild and eyes huge. Kai, in a rare panic. Kai, with the worst news.

Salt, salt, salt.

"Guys," he pants. "Finn's gone."

CHAPTER FOUR
BRIAR

"What do you mean Finn's *gone*?" Briar asks, brain flipping through all the possible meanings of the word. "Gone as in—as in what?"

Kai pushes both hands through his hair with a ragged exhale. "I woke up early," he works out between breaths. "I noticed Finn wasn't there. His stuff was missing too. The basement door was wide open; all the lights were on upstairs. And I got this *feeling*—do you ever just get a feeling? Like something's wrong?"

Briar nods, gnawing the inside of her cheek.

"I looked all over the house—nothing. And then I went outside." A knot forms in Kai's jaw. "His car was gone."

"Why would he just take off?" Astrid asks.

"He wouldn't," Briar replies, trying to sound more confident than she feels. As if to prove it to herself, she tugs her phone loose and calls Finn's number. She puts it on speaker, then sets it on the counter. He'll answer for her. He *has* to. He—

"It won't work," Kai says bluntly, and Briar flicks her gaze to his.

"What—?"

The phone spits three fuzzy tones at them, silencing her words. "*We're sorry,*" a robotic voice chirps, "*but the number you have dialed is not in service. Please try again.*"

Adrenaline surging, Briar scoops the phone and swipes to their text thread—and her heart plummets to her stomach.

A red exclamation point sits next to her last message. *Not Delivered.*

But that's not the worst part.

"What?" Astrid asks. "What is it?"

Briar shoves a hand through her hair, electrified with bewilderment. "Finn's messages are *gone*. Look." She turns the phone to show them the slew of bubbles on her side.

As though she'd been talking to herself for years.

"That's what I was trying to tell you," Kai says. "Mine was like that too."

Astrid digs out her phone and taps at the screen, face twisting in confusion. "Same thing. What the hell?"

Briar glances back at her screen, unease flaring inside her as she stares at the last text she sent Finn before all this. Two months ago.

On June 7 at 5:43 in the morning.

The day after graduation.

I'm sorry I didn't stay.

She stares until the letters blur into a mess of blue and black. This was always their code, once bouncing between them easily and without double meanings. *Stay with me.* He whispered it on their fourth-grade camping trip when her flashlight burned out, holding her hand in the dark. *Stay with me.* She said it freshman year when Clara Dalloway broke up with her by DM and it hurt too much to leave homeroom and face her in algebra. So Finn stayed, sat with her in that empty classroom while she cried, getting mascara all over his favorite sweatshirt.

But he said it on graduation night too, and it sounded different then. Kai and Astrid had gone home, and the evening was heavy with sinking awareness that everything was about to change. Neither Briar nor Finn admitted it aloud, but they both knew it.

Nothing would ever feel like this again.

They talked for hours like they always did, huddled on his fire escape while the ocean whispered below. It should've been ordinary, but the air was alive with something new and electric—atoms and neutrons and the *chemistry* of it all. Even Finn's typical ramblings felt charged, every syllable edged with magic.

Do you ever wonder what your life would be like if you'd made a different choice? Do you ever think about how the reason we're all even here is because of a million minuscule decisions and actions, and if one tiny thing had changed, we might not even exist? Do you ever wonder why we do?

Butterfly effect. Chaos theory. Math and numbers and equations. That's Finn.

What would you do, he asked, *if you knew there wouldn't be any consequences?*

Tell you the truth, she thinks now. *I'd tell you everything.*

On graduation night, she would have stayed forever.

But by dawn, she couldn't put enough distance between them, her pulse racing with fear she hadn't felt in years, that too-familiar voice creeping into her skull. Along with a sickening, decades-old reminder of who she really is deep down.

She should have guessed that Finn was planning to leave too. *For every action, an equal and opposite reaction.*

Briar swipes at her lashes, finding them wet. Astrid notices, squeezing Briar's hand.

"Alright," Astrid says. "Let's not panic—when is the last time anyone remembers seeing him?"

"The mirror house," Kai says. "But even that's a blur."

"Me too." Astrid nudges Briar's hip. "Bee?"

She tugs on a curl and shakes her head. "I don't remember anything after."

But Briar avoids Astrid's and Kai's eyes as she says it, worried that they might be looking at her with the same thought that's snaking its way into her brain:

If Briar had stayed with Finn, none of this would have happened.

"Great," Kai mutters, dropping into one of the kitchen chairs. "None of us remembers anything. Freakin' perfect."

"The answer could be simple," Astrid says. "Like, Finn's phone broke and he went to get it fixed. Let's check his place before we jump to the worst-case scenario, okay?"

"And if he's not there?" Briar asks, before she can stop herself.

Astrid slides her a glance, dark eyes solemn. As if deep down, she suspects Finn's apartment will be empty too. "Then," she says, "we'll look until we find him."

~

Driving through Loch Creek usually feels like slipping inside a colorful oil painting, but today the sky is an unfriendly gray. Mist shrouds the road, shadows reaching toward them like bony fingers. Briar presses her forehead to the window in Kai's back seat as they cross the town whose map they could trace by heart.

Most of the streets are lined with old colonial houses resurrected with freshly painted wraparound porches and seashell-lined driveways. The downtown strip is marked with brick roadways and antique buildings, each boasting a historic plaque. Briar's parents work along this street, running the Artists' Society and serving on the Cultural Council board. For as long as she can remember, the Artists' Society's marble lobby has been as familiar as her own living room, but even so, she's not sure what her parents *do* during those Cultural Council meetings. *We preserve the town's history*, her father once explained. *You'll be a part of it when you're older*.

During the summer, downtown Loch Creek is filled with tourists excited to explore the boutiques on Proctor Street before wandering through Old Town Hall. It's where the official Loch Creek deed was signed in 1692, declaring the town a haven during the Salem Witch Trials. *All residents of Loch Creek are immune from persecution of witchcraft*, reads a replica of the document. *There will be no burnings along this corner of the sea*.

Briar eyes the courthouse while Kai slows his car at a red light on Main Street. The historic brick building, with its arched doorway and Roman Doric columns, is typically overflowing with visitors who drove up Route 128 from Boston. But the exterior is noticeably empty today, save for the cluster of orange-clothed workmen inspecting a shattered window on the top floor.

The engine hums as Briar watches them gesturing wildly, as if trying to work out how the damage occurred. Something about their confusion unsettles her, and she averts her stare—

And accidentally glances at the mirror on Astrid's passenger side.

Hissing a swear through her teeth, Briar slams her gaze to her lap. Her pulse spikes as she presses the pads of her fingers to her lashes.

Astrid peeks over the headrest. "You okay back there?"

Briar nods behind a curtain of hair as she clutches her brow. That was close.

She could have seen *her* again.

Briar's teeth threaten to chatter. *Her*, she thinks bitterly. Sure. As if that… *thing* that looms behind her reflection is even a person at all.

But she does have a face. A terrible, nightmarish, poisonous face.

Briar could draw it from memory: Stringy dark hair. Purple-gray skin. Rotting teeth. And her eye—her *eye*.

Briar digs her nail into her thumb until it draws blood. She won't let herself think about it. There's no point anyway. Briar tried to tell her parents once, and they merely responded with more pills, making her brain heavier. But the woman in the mirror—she's never gone away. As if she's attached to Briar, sewn into her reflection like Peter Pan's shadow.

Soon, she'll be the only thing Briar has left.

"Almost there," Kai announces, turning toward the northern beaches.

A knot tightens in Briar's stomach in time with the car's blinker, the apparition momentarily forgotten. Her insides always ache near the beach at Loch Creek's upper border: Sorrow's Shore—a stretch of sand that inevitably feels cold and wrong. It's the one place in town that isn't washed in color, the one corner most people avoid because it's a reminder of things they could lose.

People try to brush it off as a fable, but every time there's a drowning in Loch Creek, it's on that part of the beach. Every time someone goes missing, that's the last place they were seen. Sorrow's Shore has earned its moniker.

Briar might consider it one big coincidence—if it weren't for that day thirteen years ago. The day that's seared into her memory, weighting her blood with shame and guilt. She feels it again now, remembers the car ride with her parents after, how her teeth wouldn't stop chattering. How her pruney hands shook in her lap as she whispered over and over—*I didn't mean to, I didn't mean to, I didn't mean to.*

Those were the last words she said for the entire year that followed.

It's a fitting punishment for Finn to have picked an apartment here. Forcing her to think about the worst day of her life whenever she visits her best friend.

Finn could have moved anywhere when Judge Aguirre granted him freedom from his mother after several afternoons in court. Briar attended every day of the hearing last year, sitting between Astrid and Kai as she listened to Finn recount endless childhood nightmares. More than once, she caught Finn's eye to find his lashes red-rimmed behind his glasses. She fought off her own tears as the lawyer held up photographs of scars and bruises, places on Finn's body that would forever be branded by his poisonous mother.

At least it's quiet there, he justified while paying the inexpensive security deposit with money saved from math tutoring. But Briar heard the real reason in his voice, the part he didn't say: *Nothing could be worse than her house.*

Finn's building is at the end of Rowan Street, a long dusty road not far from Sorrow's Shore. Switchgrass and red fescue line the infinite stretch of dirt, everything overgrown and uncared for. At night, the beach is haunted by crashing waves and low howls of coyotes in the fields beyond the dunes. *Coywolves,* Finn once corrected her.

With no adults keeping tabs on them, his place became an obvious meeting point, a safe zone for when Briar needed a chance to breathe away from her parents' expecting stares. But despite the tranquility of being near Finn, his apartment always filled her with dread. The ocean seemed to idle beneath the window at night, predatory and simmering. As if staring at her beneath the irradiance of the moon and whispering, *I remember what you did.*

She senses it again as she follows Astrid and Kai inside and up the carpeted stairs—the building is watching. Patiently anticipating her arrival. *Winters girl,* the walls seem to hiss. *Winters girl.*

Briar knocks on apartment 2A, shutting out that rattling voice.

"Finn?" she calls.

Silence. Astrid bangs next. "Finn! Are you in there?"

Nothing. Briar's stomach flips as Kai knocks this time.

"*Finn!* Open the—"

The door flies ajar.

And a gasp spills from Briar's lips—because she's looking at Morgan Parker-Blake.

The girl no one, *no one* talks to at school. The girl Finn glared at during the carnival.

Her black-and-indigo hair tumbles over her shoulders, free from its usual braid, as though she's just rolled out of bed. She's wearing a silky robe tied loosely at the waist, and Briar can't help noticing inches of sun-kissed skin beneath the absurdly short fabric.

Did she and Finn—? Are they—? No. No. Not possible.

A discordant combination of possessive anger and blistering insecurity crashes inside Briar, forming the terrible idea that Finn decided he didn't want her anymore. He ran out of patience and chose someone else: the one person Briar completely despises. There'd be no sharper blow than this one, no clearer death knell for what could have been.

Treason, she thinks. *This would be fucking treason.*

"Where the *hell* is Finn?" she demands, wincing at the jealous bite in her own voice.

"Who?" Morgan asks.

But there's a flash of panic on her face before she says it. It's so fast, barely a millisecond, but for an instant, her gold-speckled amber eyes crackle with fear.

Something is wrong.

Without taking a second to think, Briar shoves past Morgan into the apartment.

"Finn!" Briar yells, making a beeline for the bedroom. "*Finn!*"

"Hey!" Morgan shouts. "What the hell are you doing? You can't just barge into someone's apartment—"

Briar ignores her, furious bewilderment coursing through her veins. It feels like just yesterday that Finn's mouth was on hers, his hands exploring her body like he'd been hypothesizing for years what she'd feel like. Just last *night*, he looked at her like she was everything right in the world. Briar storms down the hall and shoves Finn's bedroom door—

She slams to a halt, anger suddenly replaced with dizzying confusion.

And whirls back to Morgan, who is right there—in her face, at her heels.

"*What the fuck?*" Briar rasps. "What the fuck did you do?"

CHAPTER FIVE
BRIAR

The room is spinning.

Finn's bedroom. But... not Finn's bedroom.

Briar has been here a million times, but it doesn't look anything like she remembers. Gone are the leather-bound books, the IKEA desk Kai and Finn built, the Gustave Doré prints framed in brass. There are no crumpled papers, no empty pill bottles in the trash. No maps on the floor, no equations on the windows.

Instead, there are string lights above the curtains, a tapestry covering one of the walls. The bed isn't dressed in Finn's gray comforter but covered with gold-embroidered blankets. A wicker hamper on the floor overflows with heaps of black fabric.

Briar lets out a slow breath, that throbbing ache returning to her eye. It makes absolutely no sense, *and yet*—

There's no sign Finn ever lived here at all.

Clenching her jaw, Briar steps toward Morgan and swallows the realization that Morgan has several inches on her even without shoes.

"Where *the hell* is Finn?" she seethes.

"I don't know what you're—"

"What did you do with his stuff?!"

Morgan just blinks. "Seriously, *what* are you talking about? Get out of my room!"

Briar stares back, fighting the sickening wave of familiar shame that comes with meeting Morgan's golden eyes. She's spent years avoiding Morgan's stare, avoiding *this* exact feeling. It's usually easy, since everyone else avoids Morgan too. *Morgan Parker-Blake is a dangerous girl*, people assert. *She comes from a bad family. She drinks blood. She has sex with the devil.*

But mainly, they say Morgan Parker-Blake is a witch.

Most people wouldn't be able to pinpoint where the rumors started, wouldn't be sure where they first heard the idea. Most people—except Briar.

Because it's a piece of Loch Creek lore she forged all by herself.

Briar didn't mean for it to get so out of hand—in fact, she tried kindness first. Even at six years old, Briar knew the value of keeping friends close and enemies closer. She mailed Morgan an invitation to her parents' Christmas party that year, sealing the envelope with glittery stickers. But Morgan couldn't even be bothered to respond, sending her older sister to shoot down Briar's gesture on the playground instead. *Morgan is not your friend*, she said with such loathing, she may as well have spit at Briar's feet.

So, really, the rumors were self-defense—that's what Briar tried to convince herself through gnawing guilt. Birthed from a desperate whisper, the gossip spread like a virus until it stuck, creating a foul stink around Morgan no other kid could stomach. She was left out on the playground, picked last for every game, and if anyone forgot the rule, Briar had to make sure they wouldn't forget it again—no matter how terrible she felt. She forced herself to be an architect in their lives until Morgan became Other; Morgan became Cursed; Morgan became *Someone to Stay Away From*.

Because if she didn't, Morgan might tell everyone what she saw that day on the beach when they were kids.

Morgan Parker-Blake could *fucking end* Briar.

So Briar had to end her first.

She knows it was wrong; her guilt has grown teeth. She's blushed through countless assemblies about bullying, a sharp twist in her gut every time she's spotted Morgan alone. Last year, when Morgan's mother died from cancer, Briar had five hundred dollars' worth of lilies anonymously delivered in hopes it would ease even a fraction of Morgan's pain, along with Briar's remorse.

It didn't.

But the strange part is that Morgan made herself easy to ostracize. Almost as if she didn't want friends in the first place. Almost as if the rumors might actually be true.

In second grade, everyone in their class fell ill within twenty-four hours of one another—everyone, that is, except Morgan. Sure, it was probably because of birthday cupcakes that Morgan didn't eat because nobody offered her one, but the possibility of witchcraft was more interesting. The following year, Morgan was the only child who couldn't keep a caterpillar alive for most of their butterfly unit. When one finally emerged from its chrysalis, it was different from the rest: all black, with red-streaked wings. Even their teacher couldn't hide her disgust when she realized Morgan's butterfly wasn't colorful or unique.

It was coated in blood.

And while everyone else was gaping at Morgan in horror, Briar's heart raced from the sheer fortune of it all. She looked at that blood-slick butterfly and couldn't repress her satisfied smile.

By middle school, Morgan's fate was written in stone. Their parents fed into it too; Briar's mother whispered about the Parker-Blakes in the grocery store, words burning with accusation. Even when Morgan began hitting back in high school, slipping cryptic notes in Briar's locker or stuffing her gym sneakers full of science-lab crickets, it was too late. It had become one of the many unwritten rules of Loch Creek. Right up there with *don't go to Sorrow's Shore alone after dark* and *don't disrespect the town officials.*

Don't talk to Morgan Parker-Blake.

But now, Briar has no choice.

"This is *Finn's* apartment," Briar says, chasing newfound anger that's easier to swallow than the guilt that's been clawing at her all morning. "Finn Adler. From school. So what the hell are you doing here?"

"I swear to god," Morgan growls back, "if you don't leave—"

"I was here *yesterday*," Kai interrupts from the doorway. "There's, like, three more rooms than there were twenty-four hours ago."

"Kai, what?" Briar pushes past him into the hall.

For a fraction of a second, she panics that they entered the wrong apartment, that they're screaming at Morgan for absolutely no reason.

But no. No, this is *Finn's* home. And yet... it's not.

Finn's apartment is a one-bedroom in the corner of the building: understated, the bare minimum. *I don't need much*, he's always said.

This apartment, it's bigger. Much bigger.

"There was a wall here," Briar insists, staring at the open living area. The wide space is decorated with brass frames and flowering plants, all traces of Finn's presence erased.

"My sister helped me renovate when I moved in," Morgan says, appearing behind her. "When I turned eighteen. Last year."

"What?" Astrid and Kai exclaim at the same time.

"No—that's not possible," Briar insists. "Finn Adler lives here."

"Is this some kind of hazing bullshit? Are you gonna kidnap me and initiate me into your popular-girl cult?" Morgan rakes her gaze over Briar's crop top and leggings. "Gag me with your cheerleading pom-poms?"

"We just wanna know where Finn is," Astrid clips.

Morgan's eyes roll so high, they flash white. "I *lit-er-ally* don't know who you're talking about."

"Yes, you do!" Briar counters. "He sat beside you in AP Physics all year long!"

Morgan shakes her head. "Not ringing a bell."

"We've all been in the same classes since kindergarten!"

"Yeah, and that means what?" Morgan snaps. "We're besties now? We're gonna have sleepovers and do each other's makeup?" She scoffs. "The three of you have some nerve. I finally graduated from that nightmare place, and now prom-queen bitch is in my house at seven a.m.? Yeah, no thank you. Get the hell out."

"No," Briar says, digging her nails into her palms.

"No?" Morgan steps toward her. "You sure you wanna say that to me?"

Briar swallows, refusing to back down, even when Morgan puts less than two inches between them. She thinks of all the whispered rumors:

Morgan and her sister in the woods on Halloween; Morgan slicing into a rabbit's belly with a knife; Morgan's mouth slick with red. Right now, with her undone braid and silky raven robe, Morgan looks exactly like the fictional witch Briar created. Her arched brow holds an unspoken threat, and the widening silence pulses with the weight of their secrets. *I could tell*, Morgan's dark expression seems to say. *I could tell, and then you'd lose everything.*

"Briar." Astrid's voice slices the quiet. "Let's go."

"Listen to your friend, Pom-Poms," Morgan says. "Or I'll put a hex on you."

"Enough of this bullshit, Morgan," Kai interjects. "Finn lives here. I can prove it."

He spins on his heel, stalking back to the bedroom.

"Hey—wait!" Morgan whirls.

"I saw where he hid his pep pill stash yesterday," Kai calls over his shoulder. "He carved a hole in his closet. I'll show you—"

They race after him, floorboards creaking. In the bedroom, Kai flings open the closet and starts rifling through skirts and dresses, everything black or the deepest of jewel tones.

"What the hell?" Morgan growls, grabbing his elbow. "Leave my clothes alone—what are you *doing*?!" She pivots to Briar. "Tell him to stop!"

But Kai doubles down, flinging fistfuls of fabric to the floor. Morgan unleashes a string of swears, clawing to restrain his wrists.

A furious storm is brewing around them, but Briar can only stare as Kai rips more garments from their hangers. Astrid joins Morgan in pulling his hands, their voices overlapping in a crescendo of frustration until finally—

"*Guys*," Briar cries out. Her urgency halts them. "What—what is that?"

A hushed silence swallows the room as they look. Briar drops to her knees, sinking into the heap of silk and tulle. Breath rushes from her lungs.

There's no hole in the back of the closet.

But there is a word, painted on the wall in thin, scratchy penmanship. Finn's handwriting.

The letters, all in red.

"Oh my god," Astrid cries. "Is that blood?"

But Briar can't even comprehend that question, her mind too focused on what it says, the word like a knife to her chest.

S-T-A-Y.

His final message.

And the promise they've now both broken to each other.

CHAPTER SIX
BRIAR

Briar swirls a fourth sugar packet into her coffee and wonders how long it will be before Astrid and Kai realize that this is all her fault.

Beside her in the diner booth, Astrid pushes a forkful of soggy pancakes around her plate. Kai sits across from them, wordlessly staring out the window at the pier, having exhausted every version of *how the hell could this be possible?*

After they discovered the bloody writing, Morgan screamed at them to leave. Paralyzed by confusion, no one could argue. In the car, Briar scraped her inhaler from her bag and shoved it between her lips as Kai and Astrid decided to regroup and plot their next move. The diner was a natural choice, but their usual corner booth feels hollow without Finn. Briar stares at the empty space beside Kai now, her stomach turning with fresh guilt.

"Maybe we should get help," Astrid says suddenly, lowering her fork. "Briar, your parents know everyone. What if we—"

"No," Briar interjects sharply, softening when she catches Astrid's perplexed glance. "I don't want to worry them just yet, okay?"

She buries the rest of it: that she can't deal with her parents' relentless probing stares, the kind that lead to doctors' appointments and more haze-inducing pills.

Or maybe she's not ready to face the cruel truth that Finn's disappearance might only lead back to her. Briar remembers his desperate words on the Ferris wheel, the way he begged her to leave Loch Creek with him. As though he had always planned to disappear and couldn't bear the thought of doing it alone.

And instead of taking his hand, she let him go.

Kai turns from the window, propping his elbows on the table. "Listen, someone has to say it. Finn's apartment was dirt cheap for a reason. No one wants to live near Sorrow's Shore, and we know why. We're watching it happen."

Unease creeps between Briar's ribs. *Again*, she can't help but think. *We're watching it happen again.*

Astrid flinches. "Kai, don't."

"How could we not talk about it? You don't think there's any truth to the stories? The way people just"—Kai lowers his voice—"coincidentally *vanish* there?"

Briar's gaze dips, remembering Finn's warning. *They're not coincidences.*

"C'mon, seriously?" Astrid tilts her head subtly toward Briar, but the gesture is distinct enough to make heat creep across her cheeks.

Her friends' efforts to protect her have been relentless since they were kids. Astrid has always ensured no one mentions certain things in Briar's presence, like twin brothers or drowning. When Briar started kindergarten halfway through the year, it was Astrid who first invited her over for a playdate. Astrid who pulled her into playground games. Astrid who never gave up asking questions even when Briar didn't say a word until the last day of school.

Kai's usually that way too. Like a big brother, surveying the world with a cautious edge to his glare. Because Kai is also familiar with the numbing weight of grief. Briar remembers burying their eighth-grade time capsule at the pier, the photograph he slipped inside of his parents in glittering New Year's Eve attire. *My grandma hates this picture*, he explained. *It was taken the night of the car accident. When I was little, I saw her throw it away.*

I know why she did it—she had to ID them in the hospital that evening. No one wants to be reminded of that. But it's the last picture that was ever taken of them. It didn't belong in the trash.

They didn't talk much about Kai's parents after that, the same way they never talked about her brother, but there's always been a quiet understanding between them, like an invisible thread.

Today, though, his desperation is louder than anything else.

"Nah, I can't do this." He shakes his head. "I can't walk on eggshells when Finn is *missing*. Briar." He leans forward, and her chest clenches tighter. "Do you ever wonder what really happened to Riley that day? No one could ever explain it. And those weird symbols drawn in the sand. What if it's the same thing that—?"

"*Kai!*" Astrid's sandal smacks his shin under the table.

"Ow, what the—?"

"Not the time, okay?"

Astrid slips an arm around Briar's shoulders, but she barely registers the warmth. Instead, her face stings like she's been slapped, Riley's name a curse.

Like when Finn said it yesterday.

But here, under bright daylight, Briar has no choice but to think of that morning thirteen years ago: The way the ocean floor dipped like stairs, the tide luring her in. How it felt like a game, tiptoeing deeper and deeper, stretching the limits of their breath until the squeeze of Riley's hand became an urgent slippery grasp. Salt water flooding her mouth. Her nose, her eyes, her ears. Flailing arms and roaring waves and then—just quiet.

So much quiet.

Briar takes a too-long sip of coffee. There's no mystery to be solved when it comes to Riley. There's no magical key, no answer hidden in folklore. There's only the terrible truth that's lodged between her ribs, the guilt that's made a home inside her bones.

You can never tell, purrs a grinding voice within her. Like two seashells being rubbed together. *I'll hold our secrets, Winters girl.*

Adrenaline spikes in her veins, and she whips around, as though the voice might have come from the booth behind her.

Even though she knows it didn't.

Because it's spoken to her before.

"Shit, I'm sorry," Kai says, oblivious to her hammering heartbeat. He reaches across the table, stilling her fingers as she starts picking at her cuticles. "I shouldn't have said that."

But the gentle warmth in his words only makes her remorse sharpen. Briar clasps Kai's hand and dares to wonder if she could ever tell them everything. If her palm would still fit neatly in his if she did.

Deep down, she suspects that she wouldn't fit anywhere at all.

"Astrid mentioned that Finn's place was extra chaotic," Briar rushes to say. As if changing the subject might silence that guttural hum within her skull. "Could that be a clue somehow?"

"Yeah, it's been a disaster." Kai drops her hand. "When were you last there?"

She averts her gaze. "A couple of weeks ago."

"Hm." Kai studies her.

"It was quick," Briar adds, another lie tumbling loose. "I just picked him up to get ice cream. I didn't go into his room."

"Well, it was a shit show yesterday," he says. "Papers with weird symbols and math equations—intense stuff we never learned in school. And there were numbers all over his window. I actually—hang on." Kai grabs his phone, pulls up his camera roll. "I meant to look this up; I thought it was a phone number. But it's too many digits. I don't know what it means."

"Did he call you guys this year?" Briar asks, as her phone vibrates with their group chat. "In the middle of the night?"

One look at Astrid's face confirms what she should have known—those late-night calls were only ever for her. *Briar. Do you ever wish you could go back and fix something that has already gone wrong?*

"Never mind," she adds, dropping her gaze again. Briar won't say it, but she knows with a fierce certainty: if she had been the one to ask Finn about the strange things in his room, he would have told her everything.

That familiar knot of guilt tightens, and she looks away.

"Do you think Finn went to his mom's new place? In Boston?" Kai asks, and Briar frowns.

"No. No way."

"Where else would he have gone?"

Astrid's eyebrows shoot up. "Uh, literally *anywhere*?"

"We could call her," Kai suggests, drawing another incredulous stare from Astrid. "At least to tell her he's gone."

"We can't." Briar shakes her head. "No, that's, like, a serious betrayal. Finn swore he'd never speak to his mom again."

"*Finn's not here!*" Kai hits the table hard enough that the silverware rattles, and the people at the next booth glance their way. "His phone is disconnected! There's a weirdo witch-girl living in his apartment! Why wouldn't we check with the one family member he's got?"

"'Cause *we're* his family," Astrid says, her voice stern.

"I know," Kai answers, dragging a hand through his dark hair. "I *know*. Finn is blood; he's my brother. I would take a bullet for him. That's why we gotta do something."

"Let's do something *else*, then," Briar counters, grabbing her phone.

"Like what?" Astrid leans over to watch Briar's bitten nails tap at the screen.

"Like... signing into Finn's email," Briar mutters, burying the dread that comes with this half-baked plan. Any answer might only add to the ache growing inside her. "Maybe he took an earlier flight to California."

"Without saying goodbye?" Kai arches a brow. "Are we talking about the same Finn?"

"Yeah, that doesn't make sense," Astrid agrees.

"*Nothing* about today makes sense," Briar says, entering the password she knows by heart, pausing only to remember which letters Finn swapped for symbols. *Asymptote. A line that a function gets closer and closer to but never touches*, he explained once. *It goes on forever.*

"Anything's fair game," Briar continues. "So it can't hurt to..." She frowns at the error message, bright red and taunting.

User not found.

Briar exhales a defeated breath. Next to her, Astrid slumps against the booth. Briar tries it again, but it's the same.

Not found, the screen declares. *Not found, not found, not—*

Briar finally flips her phone face down with a hollow clack that sounds like running out of options.

Kai leans forward, expression softening. "One phone call. Just to rule it out. Okay?"

Briar eyes Kai wearily, swallowing a wave of revulsion as she remembers Rosemary Adler and that crumbling cottage where Finn grew up. Finn never invited them over, but they often found themselves there anyway, dropping off homework if he was sick or picking him up for his shifts as a math tutor at the middle school. Inside, the kitchen teemed with dirty dishes, roaches skittered from under the oven, and rats scratched in the walls. The furniture reeked like stale cigarettes, with holes burned into ratty sofa arms.

If Rosemary was home, she'd greet them with a glass of wine in hand. Sometimes she'd have a man with her, but never the same one for long. Finn's father, once an anthropology professor, had overdosed before he was even born.

But as they got older, Rosemary's boyfriends got scarier, leering at Briar and Astrid through smoke-filled hazes. Briar felt like there were centipedes crawling over her skin; she'd pull at her clothes, hating every curve and inch of exposed flesh that was *there* for them to ogle. She tried to hide her discomfort from Finn, but she couldn't keep quiet after that time in seventh grade, when one man snapped her bra strap. She told Finn about it that night, her face flaming with embarrassment.

The next day, he showed up to homeroom with a swollen gash underneath his left eye. *He's not gonna touch you again*, he said, as he dropped into the seat beside hers.

It was the first time she saw the bruises. But not the last.

"Fine," Briar says, and the word tastes like giving up. "Call Rosemary."

"Put it on speaker," Astrid suggests.

Kai nods, tapping his phone. Briar sits on her hands, flattening her fingers against the cracked vinyl of the booth.

This is a bad idea.

But the phone doesn't ring. Déjà vu seethes underneath Briar's skin at those three ominous tones.

We're sorry. The number you dialed is not in service.

"What the hell?" Kai mutters.

Astrid snatches the phone and starts typing.

"What are you doing?" he asks.

"Googling our darling Rosemary. Maybe she moved or something happened t—" Astrid falls silent. Her face scrunches in sudden confusion, soft lines appearing in her warm-brown skin.

"What?" Briar leans forward, adrenaline spiking. "What is it?"

Wordlessly, Astrid lays the phone down, the screen brandishing a white banner reading *The Law Offices of Rosemary P. Adler*.

And right there. In the middle of the page.

Is a woman who looks nothing like the Rosemary they know.

Gone are her chapped lips and stringy highlights. This Rosemary has silky brown hair and gleaming teeth that aren't threatening to decay. Her complexion is sun-kissed instead of pale, and she's smiling in a way that she never smiled at Finn.

If Rosemary's name weren't plastered above the photo, Briar wouldn't even recognize her.

Briar remembers the first Christmas Finn spent at her house instead of his own, how Rosemary barely bothered to lift her head from the couch when Briar picked him up. She watched Finn later as he stared out of her parents' back seat window in his too-small winter coat, jaw clenched and eyes glassy.

She wondered if it hurt to have so much sadness bursting in his heart, right in that place where love was supposed to fit instead.

"That looks nothing like Ms. A.," Kai says. "But it is her. Look at her face. She's a lawyer now? Since when?"

Astrid frowns. "I'm not sure Rosemary graduated from college, let alone law school."

Briar bites her lip. Something is very, very wrong. The mirror house. Finn's apartment. Riley's hand beneath the water. The whispering in her skull. Guilt tightens her throat. *It's because of me*, she should say. *This is happening because of me.*

She takes Kai's phone from Astrid's hands instead. Maybe the answers will hurt. But the weight of her suspicions is starting to hurt more.

Gritting her teeth, Briar dials the law firm that shouldn't exist.

"Law offices of Rosemary P. Adler," a woman answers.

"Hi, can I please speak with Rosemary?" Briar asks, burying the disgust that comes with speaking her name.

"She's with a client. May I ask what this is regarding?"

"It's about her son." Briar swallows. "It's—it's an emergency."

There's a pause on the other end as the woman's confusion seeps through the wires. Tiny hairs stand at attention on the back of Briar's neck.

"Of course. One moment."

The three of them exchange another glance as piano music trills from the phone.

"I don't like this," Astrid whispers. "Something messed up is going on."

"I know, but let's just—"

"Hello? This is Rosemary."

"Hi," Briar says. "I know it's been a while. It's Briar. I'm with Astrid and Kai."

The silence that follows fills her with prickly fear. A terrible thought pushes into her brain. *Finn isn't just missing. He—*

"I'm sorry, who is this?"

"*Briar Winters,*" she says louder. "Kai Baisho and Astrid Hoffman. We're friends with Finn."

"Finn?"

Icy panic grips Briar as she absorbs Rosemary's confusion at the name of her own child. Bile rises in her throat, adrenaline coursing through her again. That dull ache returns to her right eye, pounding against her skull.

Finn isn't just missing.

"Finn Adler!" Kai's voice is incredulous as he jumps in. "Your *son.*"

Rosemary's next words are like a gunshot, careening them into shocked silence. "I'm sorry, but you must be mistaken," she says. "I don't have children."

He doesn't exist.

And at that, Briar leans over the edge of the booth—and vomits right in the middle of the diner.

PART TWO
RIPTIDE

There shrines and palaces and towers
(Time-eaten towers that tremble not!)
Resemble nothing that is ours.
Around, by lifting winds forgot,
Resignedly beneath the sky
The melancholy waters lie.

EDGAR ALLAN POE, "The City in the Sea"

CHAPTER SEVEN
FINN

The first thing Finn sees when he opens his eyes is his dead father's antique clock.

He lurches to a sitting position. The too-familiar room spins in a whirl of shadows, its contents mocking his bewilderment: Fireplace with a missing brick. Cigarette-burnt green couch. Crooked, dusty blinds. Finn's ears ring, his temple throbs, but he can only stare with wild confusion at the bones of the house where he grew up.

It's not possible.

This place was demolished after his mother moved away. Finn saw this hellhole become a ghost with his own eyes. Yet here he is, sprawled on the living room floor, blinking sleep from his lashes like he simply passed out while watching a movie.

He stands, dizzy and dry-mouthed. Something scratches his bare feet, and he glances to find broken seashells littering the floorboards. Ash clings to the walls and ceiling as though he's been dropped inside a black-and-white movie, holes burning along the edges of the film.

Disoriented, Finn staggers toward the fireplace and lifts the oak clock to his ear. Silent. Hands frozen at 9:30. He stares incredulously at the floral design along the side, the black roman numerals around the face. It's the same one; he's sure of it. The clock his father bought from an antique shop before he died—before Finn was even born.

The same one his mother sold for drug money when Finn was twelve.

He drops it onto the mantel with a clatter. *What the hell?*

A blade of unease sharpens inside him, punctuated by howls in the distance. *Coywolves.* Finn recalls the packs that used to slink along the dunes, how he and Kai always peered into the dark to find yellow eyes blinking back.

He's dreaming, Finn concludes. He has to be. This can't *actually* be real. Finn squeezes his eyes shut like he might somehow wake up in his apartment. He'll drive across town to Briar's house, bring her a coffee with a million sugar packets in the adorably disgusting way she likes it, and *this time*, he'll find the right words to fix what's broken between them. They'll talk it out on her patio, the salty wind biting at her hair.

Her perfect, messy hair. In a ponytail at cheer practice. In a braid with an oversized bow. Undone and tangled in his hands on graduation night.

Plastered to her neck and drenched in blood.

Finn flings his eyes open. Where did that idea even come from? Why the fuck would he think something like that about anyone, let alone *Briar*, the girl he—?

Clattering from the other room snags his attention. Like an object falling to the floor. Followed by a familiar voice, raspy and tinged with pain—

"Finn? Where are you?"

Fresh confusion rattles him, Briar momentarily forgotten. He frowns, peering into the darkened corridor, and whispers a word he hasn't uttered in over two years: ". . . Mom?"

Finn starts down the hallway, feet aching with every step. When he reaches his mother's room, he goes perfectly still.

She's lying in bed, her arm dangling limply over the side, stamped with bruises like storm clouds. Her hand is outstretched, fingers splayed toward the shattered glass on the floor.

Finn's chest clenches at the sight of her cracked lips tinged an alarming blue. And another wave of bewilderment washes over him as he registers her clothing—her work uniform from the convenience store that closed when he was in fifth grade.

This—this already happened.

He remembers this day. Finn had to call 911 because he couldn't wake her up. He sat on his front steps with silent tears as she was strapped to a stretcher, a clear mask covering her mouth. He was filled with clawing numbness, and a silent part of him wished she'd die and get it over with.

The rest of him, terrified she would.

That dissonance wasn't new; Finn spent most of his childhood with a fierce tug-of-war inside his chest. Some days his bones ached under the weight of responsibility: checking on his mother when she'd spend days in bed and stealing packets of powdered electrolytes from the grocery store to slip into her water. *You're such a good boy, Finn*, she'd say.

But when his mother was awake, Finn was a stain on her world; everything he did angered her. Sometimes she showed it with words. Other times, with force: The sting of her palm on his cheek. The burn of her cigarette on his spine. And throughout it all, there were needles and spoons and rubber straps, his mother's addiction like a third person in their family. Finn was stuck on a haunted carousel, years blurring with empty apologies and fresh wounds. As he got older, he started to wonder why he kept his mother alive when she was hell-bent on dying, why he worked so hard to love someone who'd never love him back.

If family could be something he chose instead.

"Mom," he says, sitting on the bed like he did that afternoon. "Mom—wake up."

She doesn't move.

And even though Finn knows how this memory ends—crashing with Kai and his grandma for the entire month his mom was hospitalized—a tiny flame of obligation sparks to life. He grips her narrow shoulders, shaking her.

"Mom," he pleads, a childlike desperation slipping into the word. "*Mom*." Something cracks inside him, a lonely ache that he'd almost forgotten. *Mom. Mom. Mom.*

But the last syllable spirals into a warped scream, and he flings himself off the bed, collapsing onto the floor.

His mother's jaw has fallen open.

And a gush of seaweed and ocean water spills out.

Inky, gelatinous liquid pours from the corners of her eyes, staining her pale skin. Iridescent crabs skitter from her lips, and a discordant keening rattles in his skull, like metal scraping on metal.

"Oh god," Finn manages, scrambling backward across the floor as shells shred his palms. "What the hell—what the—?"

This isn't a memory anymore. This is new and twisted, conjured by his brain and the sea and invisible numbers between the moon and the shore. And he knows, with sinking certainty:

He won't be able to save her. He couldn't the first time; he can't now.

Like Briar, a mocking voice inside him seems to say. *Just like Br—*

Finn grinds his teeth, groping behind him for the doorknob. He pulls himself to his feet and takes one last look at his mother's contorted body, the blackened water soaking the sheets.

"I'm sorry, Mom," he whispers, racing from the room.

He tears through the hall and instinctively reaches for his compass, desperate to feel the cool brass, the comfort of the etching along the edge.

But Finn's belt loops are empty, the chain missing, and he suddenly feels like a little kid who left their favorite teddy bear at the park. Anxiety blooms in his chest.

Five things.

Water deities. Rán. Poseidon. Nammu. Hapi. Lir.

He runs faster.

Oceanic layers. The sunlight zone. The twilight zone. Midnight. The abyss. The trenches.

His eyes fly open. He's back in the ash-covered living room, heart thundering.

Sailing knots. Half hitch. Sheet bend. Reef knot. Bowline. Clove hitch.

But none of these lists are working. Finn's pulse seizes as he casts a glance over his shoulder toward the tunnel of shadows in the hall. What's happening? What the fuck is *happening*?

Setting his jaw, he tries again. Something different. Something real.

Five things he remembers before he ended up here.

One: Graduation night. Sitting beside Briar on his fire escape, electrons and currents raging inside him until he finally worked up the courage to kiss her. The desperate way she kissed back like she'd spent years starving for the taste of his mouth. The way hers was like orchid and pears, a dash of cinnamon and honey, and one brush of her tongue left him certain he'd be chasing that feeling for the rest of his life.

He remembers falling asleep together in a euphoric haze, then waking hours later to find her staring into the shadows with tear-speckled lashes, murmuring about wanting to disappear. *I'll stay until my birthday*, she whispered, voice raspy with sleep and nameless despair. *Then I have to go back to the water. Riley went first. It's my turn, it's my turn, it's—*

Finn did everything he could think of; he shook her shoulders, pressed a cold cloth to her burning skin. He said her name over and over until she dissolved into sobs and tore from his room like the apartment was ablaze. He flew down the stairs after her, begged and begged her to stay.

And when there was nothing left to try, he let her go.

Two*:* A summer of theories, of desperation, of answers. Because something had happened to Briar on graduation night. Something that turned her into a shell of herself the way he remembered her at age six, silent and sullen and choking on unspoken grief.

Like tragedy in Loch Creek was some kind of cycle. A moon phase. A tide.

Like it was coming back around for her.

He tore apart history in his attempt to understand it all. He drowned himself in numbers, in star patterns, in oceanic contour lines. He danced on the outer rims of death, armed with a string of chaos theory and a fraction of hope that he wouldn't be too late.

Three*:* The carnival. Neon lights and salt air. Briar's nonsensical whispers on the Ferris wheel. The way he tried to tell her what he'd learned, to explain his nightmarish hypothesis that was beginning to unfold. *This town will ruin you if you don't leave with me*, he meant to say. *I don't care about our fight. I don't care about anything but you.*

But he never got the chance to say any of it.

Four: Less than a week later. Briar's birthday party—

He drags a hand through his hair. His brain feels crowded, like there's no room to extract this particular memory, but he forces himself to pry it loose.

Briar's birthday party. Her white dress. The cotton-candy sky. Nineteen birthday candles. A flash of silver, a burst of red. The terrible, heartbreaking way she screamed.

The worse sound of her silence.

Finn leans against the wall now, his legs suddenly too weak to hold his weight. He lets himself slide to the floor, broken shells crunching beneath him.

Five: The day after. The cavernous ache in his chest, that gut-wrenching, insurmountable grief. Papers scribbled with perilous equations, stacks of old documents, all tucked into his backpack. A drive across town. A threat, a prayer. And a deal.

A deal he made—with a witch.

Finn's head snaps up as the rest of it rushes back. The black candles, the opal stones. The obsidian dagger in the witch's fist, the string of numbers scraped into the sand. An ancient language whispered on the beach beneath a spring tide. And a promise—a promise it would work. That Briar would be safe. That it wouldn't happen the same way twice.

If—and only if—he agreed to the terms.

For every action, an equal and opposite reaction.

His gaze swings behind him, landing on the warped kitchen of his childhood. *The sea will determine where you wake up*, the witch said. *The In-Between is forged from your memories.*

The In-Between. That's what this place is.

A hidden pocket of time, stretching through space without gravity, without reason. Of course it would take the shape of his mother's old cottage. A house that has roots, buried in nightmares. Refusing to let go.

Finn's temple throbs. If he's *here*, the ritual should have worked. She should be safe. But how—how can he know for sure?

He glances around the decrepit sitting room again, eyeing the fireplace, the mantel, the clock—and this time, his gaze lands on something new: an old black telephone resting atop a cobweb-covered side table. The plastic cord is stripped raw in certain places, buttons rusted over, but he eyes it anyway with the kindling heat of hope.

He has no idea if the phone works, but if it does... he can find out if she's safe now.

The relief he would feel—it might drown him, but he could drown in peace.

Swallowing another jolt of anxiety, Finn crosses to the phone. He snatches the handle. And his breath catches when he hears a faint dial tone. Laced with static, as if underwater.

Hands shaking, Finn dials the number he knows by heart. It rings, and the sound electrifies his pulse with sudden doubt.

Relief? This won't bring relief. Either way, this will ruin him.

Because if the ritual worked, Briar shouldn't know who he is.

No one should.

Finn Adler doesn't exist anymore.

But that's what he wants, right? To know, with fierce certainty, that it worked. That she's safe. That with him gone, it won't happen the way it did, that she won't—

The phone clicks.

"Finn?" Briar's voice slips through, crackling and thick with sleep.

And he crumples at the waist as though he's been stabbed.

She remembers him.

"Finn," she repeats. "It's late."

He tilts the phone so she doesn't hear him fighting not to cry. Panic bursts in his chest like an exploding star. Entire planets burn behind his eyes. It was all for nothing. All that planning, the equations, the research. Her birthday party. All that blood, the churning sea, that thing under the waves. The witch's spell.

It didn't even fucking work.

Hysterical laughter bubbles at the back of his throat, harsh and raw. *It didn't work, it didn't work, it didn't work—*

"Finn." Briar's voice is clearer now. "We have our AP Calc test tomorrow. You need to go to bed."

And at that, he jolts upright.

"Wh-what?" he gasps, swiping at his eyes.

"AP Calc. I don't want either of us to bomb it."

He blinks.

If Briar is talking about their AP test, that means it's . . . early May. Graduation hasn't happened. The carnival hasn't happened.

Her birthday—the worst day of his life—is months away.

The past. He's talking to Briar in the *past*.

Finn scrambles to understand. His brain races through integers and fractions, black hole theory and stellar death. He remembers Briar beside him on the Ferris wheel: her soft breath on his face, the warmth of her whisper.

Why do you always call so late? Do you think of me when you can't sleep?

Realization snaps inside him. He didn't know what she meant at the time, but now—

He does.

And here, in a distorted version of the house where he grew up, clutching a rusted-over phone like a cross, Finn realizes he's holding the remaining threads of the warning he tried so hard to deliver at the carnival. One last chance to protect her. Finite and final, written in blood and sealed with magic.

A fucking Hail Mary. A shot in the dark.

Because otherwise, Briar Winters—the only person he's ever wanted to belong to—is going to die on her birthday.

Again.

"Briar," he says, "do you ever wish you could go back and fix something that's already gone wrong?"

CHAPTER EIGHT
BRIAR

3 Days and 2 Hours Until Briar's Birthday Party

Winters girl.

Briar turns toward the voice, distantly aware that she's dreaming. She scrambles to process the past few hours, thoughts hazy with bewilderment. The diner. Kai driving her home. Astrid tucking her into bed.

But she's not in her room now; she's somewhere else, encased in violet and glass. A steady vibration of EDM thrums in the distance, and fear crystalizes inside her as she realizes her dreams have taken her to the mirror house.

She squeezes her eyes shut, turning her surroundings into shadows. She won't look.

"Astrid?" Briar calls. "Kai? Finn?"

Briar turns a corner quickly—too quickly—and slams into glass, stars dancing along her lashes. She mutters a swear and holds out her hands, fumbling blindly for the pathway out. Anxiety mounting, she moves faster, desperate for fresh air. She turns another corner and smacks directly into something again—but this time, it's not flat like glass.

It's three-dimensional. Spongy and stiff. Like a person.

A vortex of icy wind engulfs Briar's body. Something cold drips onto her feet, but whoever is in front of her remains silent. A faint whimper escapes her. She won't look. She *won't* look. She—

Winters girl.

It's that guttural voice again, like two jagged seashells scraping against each other. She's heard it before, whispering in the thickest quiet. Creeping in at school, at home.

Telling her the rules to a game on the beach with Riley that day.

Open your eyes and let her see you.

The firm command reaches something weak inside her, plucking her obedience like a flower. Briar flutters her lashes—

And bites down on a scream.

She's right there: the nightmarish woman from the mirror. Only this time—

She's standing right in front of her. Tactile and formidable, more dead than alive.

The woman hovers in a shredded white dress amid the lavender haze, her mangled feet barely brushing the ground. She looks like she just emerged from the ocean, with seaweed strewn in her wet hair and murky water dripping from her rotting limbs.

And like every other time, the woman's right eye is completely hollowed out.

In its place rests a ghastly lacuna. All around the sunken hole, her purple flesh is torn, like something ripped her eye out with a vicious bite. Frost floods Briar's veins as she thinks of all the occasions when she's looked in the mirror and found *her* staring back, as if this creature could see Briar more clearly through that shadowed abyss.

"Who are you?" Briar whispers, and the woman soundlessly parts her lips, revealing blackened teeth. Something slithers from her mouth, and Briar stumbles. Her flip-flops tangle, sending her crashing toward the unforgiving concrete.

But instead, she lands in something soft.

Sand.

She's on the beach, waves lapping at her bare legs.

And then that voice slinks back into her skull.

Winters girl, it calls. *I've waited a long time for this.*

"What?" She whips her gaze around.

I knew, eventually, you would need me as much as I need you.

On the periphery of her vision, a flash of silver-white light skitters through the sea-foam, sending a ripple across the ocean's surface—

Then blistering pain sears her calf underwater, like the grip of razor-sharp claws.

This will be over soon, the voice purrs. *Hold still.*

Briar cries out, slapping the waves. Her entire leg burns, drawing an anguished whimper from her. The water around her turns ruby, blood and salt and—

Pain shouldn't exist in a dream.

Wake up, she urges herself. *Wake up, wake up, wake*—

"Briar!"

She sits up with a gasp and lunges for her inhaler. Relief balloons in Briar's lungs as she realizes she's in her bedroom: White-painted bureau lined with cheerleading trophies. The smattering of designer shoes she kicked off without putting away.

And her parents, standing at the foot of her bed.

Copper light spills through the gauzy white canopy, making her right eye throb. She presses her palm to her cheekbone, wincing.

"What time is it?" Briar asks.

Her mother sits on the edge of the mattress. She has Briar's same thick curls, only hers are strawberry blonde. She usually wears them atop her head, pinned with whatever she can find on her studio desk. Today, it's a paintbrush, a few tendrils framing her freckle-covered face. Unfamiliar exhaustion colors her blue eyes, tiny lines that aren't usually there deepening as she checks her watch.

"Five-thirty p.m.," her mother answers. "You've been asleep since we got home."

Panic lurches inside Briar's chest. She needs to call Astrid and Kai, needs to calculate the next steps to find Finn. It's already been too long.

"We need to discuss your birthday party," her mother continues, oblivious. "There are more details to finalize before paying the remaining balance for the yacht."

The word *balance* makes Briar remember the envelopes she's seen lately, the red PAST DUE stamps at the top. Her parents' long nights at the gallery, her mother holed up in the craft room. Briar chews her lip and wonders if this particular party is less about celebrating and more about keeping up appearances. A shiny masquerade to hide what's crumbling beneath.

"The yacht leaves at seven," her mother chatters on, "and I can get you an appointment at Dahlia's salon beforehand, but she needs your input." She tucks a curl behind Briar's ear. "Perhaps pulled back with a bow? You always wore it like that when you were little."

Briar bristles. Her hair was in a bow on her sixth birthday too. Dirty seawater stained the ribbon, dripping down her spine as she sat in the hospital waiting room.

"Mom," she starts, "I don't need a party, you know. We could do something here with Astrid and Kai and—"

Her mother scoffs. "Nonsense! You deserve a fuss."

Briar's stare drops; she's unsure how to tell her parents that that's the last thing she deserves. Candles and presents in honor of turning another year older—something she gets to do but Riley doesn't. Something that Finn might never do either.

"Besides," her mother continues, "the invitations have already gone out to the whole Loch Creek Cultural Council . . . and, oh, practically the entire town."

Briar's gaze snaps up. "But I asked for this one to be small, remember?"

Her mother's sheepish grin only grates on her nerves. "Oops!"

"Mom!"

"We're proud of you, darling," her mother says, nudging her arm. "Graduating with honors, taking first place at the state cheer competition. These are not 'small' accomplishments. We want to celebrate you."

"Or show me off to your snobby friends," Briar mutters, and her mother sucks in a gasp.

The silence that follows is thick, causing Briar's face to flush in bewilderment.

She didn't—she didn't mean to say that out loud.

It's the kind of thing she'd usually think bitterly to herself, not say to her mother's face. It didn't even sound like her *voice*. The words bubbled from deep in her chest, nasty and cruel.

Briar dares to glance at her parents, finding her mother's expression twisted in surprise, her father's pale blue eyes narrowed beneath neatly trimmed blonde hair.

"Briar." He says her name like a warning, his peach-toned skin slack with thinning patience. "Your mother has worked hard on this. A 'thank you' would be nice."

"Mayor Caldwell is attending," her mother adds with a forced smile. "You'll want to make a good impression before you start your job at Old Town Hall next week."

Briar swallows another wave of nausea. Her parents have her whole life planned: she'll take a gap year and work in the mayor's office before going to college close enough to live at home. Briar suspects they'd prefer to clip her wings and keep her trapped so they wouldn't ever have to say they lost a second child too.

If Briar had it her way, she'd put decades between herself and this town until she forgets she ever tried to call it home. But her guilt has become a sedative, turning her obedient and soft. Because if it weren't for her, Riley would still be here and her parents wouldn't spend every day worrying that tragedy might strike their family twice.

But Briar isn't even sure what her job at Old Town Hall will entail; every time she asks, her parents have a different answer, as though they're not sure either.

Under any other circumstances, Briar would wonder why Caldwell would even want to hire someone straight out of high school. Lately, however, he's looked at her in a way that makes her wary of the answer. She's known the bespectacled, white-haired man for her entire life; he's attended all her mother's Christmas parties, been at every art gala. But somewhere between Briar's junior and senior year, he started staring a little too long, a strange, bemused expression on his face. Like she's a gift-wrapped present he can't wait to open.

She could tell her parents about it, but they'd probably say she's imagining that too.

"Are Kai and Astrid still here?" Briar asks, changing the subject.

Her father shakes his head. "We sent them away. You seemed sick."

"I'm fine." Briar glances at the cascading messages on her phone, stomach twisting. They've already lost so much time.

She leaps out of bed—and sudden pain slices up her calf. As if someone carved her skin with a blade. She bends with a startled jolt to clutch her leg, gritting her teeth.

"Briar—?"

She snatches a sweatshirt from the back of her desk chair. "I have to go."

"Astrid told us you threw up earlier, honey." Her mother stands and presses her hand to Briar's cheek. Unfamiliar lines between her eyebrows pinch like soft dough as she frowns. "You feel warm."

"Mom, I'm *fine*." Briar wrenches her face away. Her leg throbs again, but she ignores it this time, chest aching over the reminder of what happened at the diner—and the sudden question of whether her parents have forgotten Finn too.

She bites her lip. Saying the name of a boy who might not exist will send her father straight to her bathroom to start counting pills. Earlier, when Astrid suggested talking to them, Briar couldn't say no fast enough. But that was before the call to Rosemary, before the entire world tipped sideways. Maybe, she reasons desperately, her parents will be different this time. Maybe, for once, they'll believe her.

"Something did happen today though," Briar starts. "We can't find Finn."

"Who?" her mother asks, and Briar's heart sinks into her stomach.

She should have predicted this. It shouldn't hurt this much to see her parents' gazes cloud with confusion, but it's *Finn*.

"You really don't remember?" Briar asks, searching her parents' bewildered expressions. "Mom, you picked us up from school every day for *years*." She knows she's risking an inevitable interrogation, but her panicked urgency is louder than anything else. She turns to her father. "You taught him how to play chess; you helped him buy a *car* last spring. He's part of our family. And he's gone."

But there's no recognition on their faces. Nothing that proves Finn was ever really here.

Instead, they stare at her like she's grown three heads. The gesture pulls at her mother's face, the pale skin around her mouth drooping like wet clay. She seems to notice, pressing two fingers below her ears as if tugging herself back into place. Briar fights the urge to make a snide remark about how the dermal fillers and fancy creams are clearly not working.

"Forget it," she says. "I need to get ready."

Her father, who has been quietly watching, crosses his arms. "Briar," he cautions in a tone that tells her exactly what he's about to say next, "are you behind on your meds?"

She stiffens, forcing herself not to wince at another stab of pain in her calf. "No."

"We made the choice to trust you," he continues. "Do we need to monitor your intake again?"

"No!" Briar inhales sharply as her phone vibrates. "Guys, I really need to call Astrid—"

"What do you expect us to think?" her mother asks. "You're not acting like yourself right now, honey. And that *mess* in the basement earlier."

"I—" Briar narrows her eyes. "What mess?"

"Water and sand—all over the carpet," her father says. "Ring a bell?"

Briar shakes her head, remembering Astrid pulling seaweed out of her hair this morning. *Did you go for a swim last night?* Her mouth dries up.

Her parents exchange a pointed look.

"Honey," her mother starts, "I know your birthday is a hard time of year for you. It's hard for us too."

Briar's shoulders immediately tense. "I'm not—that's not what this is about."

"You've come so far," her mother continues. "If you're hearing voices again, seeing things, sleepwalking—you need to tell us the truth."

"*Stop!*" Something snaps inside her, a distinct pop between her ribs. "There's nothing going on, okay? Look, I need to call Astrid and Kai, and instead I'm talking to you about salon appointments. Tell Dahlia she can shave my head if it makes her happy. I don't give a shit."

Her father's voice sharpens. "*Briar.*"

A defeated sigh whooshes out of her. "A bow is fine. Okay? Can this conversation be over now?"

"No," her mother says. "No, there's something going on with you. The Briar I know would never speak to us like this." She lowers her voice, turning to her husband like Briar isn't even there. "Otto, maybe I should give Astrid's moms a call. Or, I'll be seeing Mika Baisho at the Cultural Council meeting, I could—"

"Seriously?" Briar explodes. "You're gonna call Astrid's *moms*? Talk to Kai's grandma? What is this, third grade? I'm almost nineteen fu—*freaking* years old. I should be moving out, should be—" The room swims in static. She knows it's pointless, but the words spill out anyway. "Sometimes I think about all the things I could be doing. Did you know that Vassar, where Astrid is going, has a killer art history program? I wouldn't even be *that* far away. I—"

"Briar, we've been over this dozens of times," her mother interrupts. "Your father and I think it's best for you to—"

"Stay close to home and continue the family legacy," Briar recites in time with her mother's words.

"Loch Creek is *important* to this family," her mother asserts. "Your father and I have run the Artists' Society for over two decades. My mother ran it before me, and her mother before her. It is an *honor* to work for this town. Right now, our legacy is all we have."

Briar falls quiet at that, thinking again of those unpaid bills strewn across the counter. And she suddenly feels less like a person and more like a pawn.

Winters girl, purrs that voice in her skull. *It's time for them to leave.*

She grinds her teeth, and the voice quiets. Her calf stings beneath her leggings. Her fingers itch to pull up the fabric and look.

"I need to go meet Astrid and Kai," Briar presses.

Her mother sighs. "Is that really the best idea? You've been ill. I think—"

"For the last time, *I'm not sick*. And I need to change. So." Briar reaches for the hem of her shirt, pointedly darting her eyes to the door.

Her mother sighs and turns, but her father takes a step closer, pale eyes icing over.

"Let me make something clear," he says. "You may be an adult by legal terms, but you're always going to be our child. Our *only* child."

"Otto." Briar's mother lays a hand on his arm, the gesture heavy with unspoken words. *Don't bring up Riley. What if our fragile, unstable Briar stops talking again?*

"For as long as your mother and I are alive, we are going to worry about you. Because you are everything to us. You are the future." His jaw tightens. "So show some gratitude. And take your goddamn meds."

Briar glares at their retreating backs before slamming the door shut—hard enough that she feels the rattle in her bones. She finally allows herself to growl in pain, bending to yank her leggings up to her knee—

And bites down on a scream.

A jagged gash is etched into her calf: two inches long with furious puffy edges. Unnaturally dark blood seeps from the corners—nearly black. It trickles down to her ankle, staining her skin, and her mouth dries to cotton as she remembers.

The thing beneath the waves. That silver light. That burst of pain.

Like claws. Like teeth.

There's something in the water.

It was a dream. She *knows* it was a dream.

But this cut on her leg is very fucking real.

CHAPTER NINE
BRIAR

3 Days and 1 Hour Until Briar's Birthday Party

Briar emerges from her bedroom, a bandage plastered over the pulsating cut on her calf, and wrestles with the idea of driving to visit Morgan Parker-Blake.

It's the absolute last thing she wants to do. She'd rather eat those crickets Morgan once put in her sneakers. But her leg is burning from a cut she somehow dreamed into existence, and her world is crashing in a way that feels all too familiar. Riley's playful laugh by the water's edge. Finn's heated stare outside the mirror house. Flickering moments that she didn't realize were goodbyes until it was too late. Both times, near the ocean.

Both times, around her birthday.

And each time, Morgan was somehow right there. As if quietly guarding the answers that Briar's been chasing, waiting for her to catch up.

As Briar reaches the first floor, she eyes the sliver of light from her mother's craft studio. Inside, the weaving loom clacks and hums like a lullaby. The kitchen is swathed in shadows, her father nowhere in sight. Probably back at the gallery.

Just then, a distinct scratching snags her attention. She whirls toward the patio door in the kitchen—

Where the handle is twisting back and forth.

Like someone is trying to get in.

Panic flashes inside her. If the cut in her dream became real, what if that frightening woman did too? What if she's escaped from behind glass? What if she's here *right now*? What if—what if—?

There's no time to think. Briar snatches a frying pan from the wall. She closes a sweaty fist around the handle, prepared to smash that woman's disgusting face, once and for all. Sucking in a breath, she flings open the door—

And screeches when she finds Morgan Parker-Blake crouched on the patio with a knife.

Like she was just picking the lock, trying to work it loose. As if Briar summoned her with her desperate thoughts.

"What the hell?" Briar yelps. "Are you trying to break into my house?"

Completely unfazed, Morgan stands. She tucks her pocketknife into the waistband of her short black skirt and tosses her dark hair over one shoulder.

"Where is it?" Morgan demands coolly.

"Where is *what*?"

"The thing you and your friends *stole* from my apartment today."

Briar blinks. "I don't know what you're talking about."

"Like hell you don't." Morgan's gaze flicks to the frying pan. "You don't strike me as a girl who cooks, Pom-Poms. Better put that down before you hurt yourself."

She pushes into the kitchen, and Briar drops the pan onto the counter with a clatter. Anger bubbles inside her at the determination in Morgan's expression, the confidence with which she's barreled into Briar's home.

"Morgan! What are you doing?"

"Oh, so *you* can storm into my apartment uninvited, but I can't look for my stuff?" Morgan calls, as she sails through the living room, yanking pillows off the sectional.

"What stuff?" Briar races after her. "*Stop!*"

"I know you have it," Morgan snaps, dropping in front of a wicker basket full of art magazines. Her pleated skirt flattens across her thighs, muscles flexing beneath the fishnet stockings tucked into her lace-up boots. Then she grabs the whole damn basket and dumps everything to the floor.

"What the hell is wrong with you?" Briar cries, diving for the mess. "What are you even looking for—? Morgan!"

But Morgan has already moved on, flinging cabinets and tearing through drawers, a storm leaving disaster in her wake. Briar marches after her and fleetingly wonders how she could have even considered seeking Morgan out in the first place. As if they'd be able to sit and *talk,* like there aren't explosives ready to detonate between them at any moment.

"Morgan! You're trashing my house!" she yells, trailing her into the foyer. "*Morgan—*" Briar lunges, snaring her wrist. "My *mom* is home!"

At that, Morgan whirls.

Briar's stomach flips as she realizes how little distance is suddenly between them. She hadn't meant to get this close to Morgan—close enough that she can see the tiny rhinestone in Morgan's nose, close enough to smell her perfume: dark floral, blood orange, amber. Her own rule echoes in her head: *Don't ever talk to Morgan Parker-Blake*. The words are a hollow reminder of every buried secret Morgan could unearth. Yet here she is, inches away, her delicate pulse fluttering in Briar's palm.

Briar drops her hand as though Morgan's touch was scalding.

But Morgan doesn't move. Instead she lowers her voice to a frighteningly soft whisper. "Your scary mommy doesn't scare me."

Briar frowns. "What's *that* supposed to mean?"

"Really?" Morgan crosses her arms. "We've known each other our entire lives, and you're gonna pull that deer-in-the-headlights shit?" Her gold-speckled eyes narrow. "If you're going to fight, fight dirty, Pom-Poms. You know *exactly* what I mean."

Briar chews the inside of her cheek, recalling the stony looks their mothers exchanged over the years. Mrs. Parker-Blake, her scowl always dripping with disdain. Briar's mom, staring back with the icy confidence of someone who knew they couldn't be touched. Briar always assumed

Morgan's mother knew the same awful things Morgan did. That Briar's mother found some way to keep her quiet too.

Yet now she can't help but wonder if the glares that passed between them were about something else entirely. Something worse.

Briar clenches her teeth. "For the last time—I don't know what you're talking about." She huffs a breath. "What are you even *looking* for?"

Morgan only offers the smallest disappointed shake of her head, ignoring her question. *You're pathetic*, her expression seems to say. As if she sees straight through Briar—past her expensive clothes, past the layers of makeup—to the damaged, ugly parts she tries so desperately to hide.

"Fine," Morgan clips. "Keep being the deer." Her predatory gaze rakes over Briar, putting a flush in Briar's cheeks. "Guess that makes me the hunter."

Before Briar can respond, Morgan spins, her boots thudding on the stairs.

"Morgan!"

Briar tears after her. A new surge of anger spikes in her chest as Morgan barges into her bedroom and beelines for her bureau—but Briar is at her heels this time.

"Stop. Stop it! Morgan, *stop*!" Briar bats away Morgan's hands before wedging herself between Morgan and the dresser.

But the motion pulls them into a tangle of limbs and curves and hair, and Briar battles a traitorous warmth inside her as she registers everywhere they're suddenly touching: the metallic studs of Morgan's belt digging into the skin beneath her crop top; rough threads of fishnets grazing her bare thighs. She scrambles to ignore all of it.

"You want to fight dirty?" Briar hisses. "Fine. Tell me why Finn was staring at you at the carnival."

Morgan rolls her eyes. "Didn't we go over this? I don't even know who—"

"You don't know who Finn is, you've never heard of him, blah, blah, blah." Briar raises her chin. "Save it. I know you're lying."

Morgan's nostrils flare. "Well, you'd know a lot about lying, I suppose."

"This isn't *about* me." But anxiety flares inside her anyway, and Briar rushes to continue before Morgan can say anything else. "My best friend vanished into thin air, and the next day, you're living in his apartment? I *saw* him looking at you last night. I saw *your* expression when we showed up this morning. No more bullshit, Morgan. I want the truth."

"The *truth*?" Morgan makes the word sound like a swear. "Like what I saw happen thirteen years ago? That kind of truth?"

A knot twists inside Briar's stomach. Her remaining boldness plummets to the floor. "That's . . . that's not what I was talking about."

"Ah, so it's *selective* truth you're after," Morgan replies. "How convenient. Thing is, I'm not interested in hiding behind lies. I prefer unfiltered, ugly honesty. I know I can take it." She leans in closer, strands of her dark hair skimming Briar's bare shoulder. "Can you, Pom-Poms?"

The room suddenly feels too small, the line of conversation threatening to sew Briar's throat shut in panic. Morgan slowly examines her as if she can tell, making Briar feel like a caged mouse in a lab.

"I didn't think so," Morgan says softly, and there's something new and sad in her voice. Almost like pity. Somehow that stings worse than the heat of Morgan's ire, and Briar scrapes for something—anything—else to say.

"I tried to be *nice* to you," she blurts, cheeks reddening. "I tried to sit with you at lunch in first grade! I invited you to my family's Christmas party that year too! *You're* the one who didn't want to be friends. Not me."

Morgan snorts a surprised laugh. "Yeah, okay. That invitation must have gotten lost in the mail."

Briar scowls. "It didn't! Your sister told me you wanted nothing to do with me!"

"So what?" Morgan presses. "Even if your warped version of history is true—which it isn't—what are you saying? Your delicate feelings were hurt, so you decided to turn me into the world's biggest outcast?" She scoffs. "Yeah, come to think of it, I can see *exactly* why someone wouldn't want to be your friend."

Briar's throat burns with desperation to defend herself, and for a second, she nearly confesses to sending Morgan those bouquets after Mrs. Parker-Blake's funeral. *See?* she could say. *I'm not the monster you think I am. I know what it feels like to lose someone.* Instead, Briar rummages for something that could cut deep, make Morgan bleed until their scars match.

"*I* didn't turn you into an outcast," Briar seethes. "You did that all on your own. You were a bitch to everyone at school, so—surprise, surprise—you were always alone. You did weird shit our entire lives, so—shocker!—people thought you were a witch. But go ahead, blame me for everything. Easier to do that than look at yourself, right?"

Something flashes in Morgan's eyes, and Briar's mouth twitches.

"Dirty enough for you, Morgan?"

With an annoyed exhale, Morgan leans closer, flattening Briar's spine against the dresser. "You," Morgan snarls, "are the most delusional person I've ever met. We both know you never wanted to be my friend. You wanted to make sure I never told a soul about what really happened on the beach that day when we were kids. Isn't that right, Pom-Poms?"

The room spins at her words, and Briar grinds her teeth so hard, her jaw might snap. But she won't give Morgan the satisfaction of seeing her fear or the guilt that's heavy in her stomach like lead. Instead, she summons the calmest voice she can find to reply. "I'm starting to think you don't know my actual name."

"Which would be the worst thing in the world for someone like you, wouldn't it? Pretty little prom queen. High school freakin' royalty." Lashes narrowing, Morgan cages Briar against the bureau with a hand on either side. "But girls like you never leave towns like this one. Everyone's eventually gonna forget who you are. It'll be like you're dead. Worse—like you never even existed at all."

Briar bites the inside of her cheek, grasping for anger to replace the hurt spreading through her chest.

Like you never even existed at all.

"Is that a threat? 'Cause that's exactly what's happened to Finn." Briar dares to press closer, their noses all but brushing. "You know more than you're saying. And I won't stop until I figure out what."

With that, Briar wrenches away to snatch her scissors, pointing them directly in Morgan's face. "Now back the hell off," Briar threatens. "And get out of my house."

If Morgan is shaken by the sight of two blades inches from her skin, she doesn't let on.

"What are you gonna do? Burn me at the stake?" Her crimson mouth curls in a darkly bemused grin. "I dare you." She leans in even closer, the scissors all but kissing her lashes, her whisper edged with something that's not altogether anger. "Go ahead. Light me up, bitch."

Briar's face flushes, and Morgan takes a satisfied step back. A rush of cool air slips between them, replacing the blistering warmth from the press of Morgan's curves against Briar's.

"Seems like we're both looking for something," Morgan says, straightening her clothes. "If you know what's good for you, you'll return what's mine."

With that, she stalks from the room, leaving Briar alone with her pounding heart and the lingering question of what Morgan was so hell-bent on finding in the first place.

A bubble of frustration swells inside her, and she hurls the scissors at her bureau before pulling out her phone and sinking to the carpet. Briar brings her knees to her chest and taps the screen until she reaches Finn's name.

She stares at the space where his photo should be, conjuring the gray of his Berkeley sweatshirt, the glare on his rounded glasses, the lilt of his voice in the middle of the night. The way he'd always ask, *What's today's date?* As though he lost time and gravity in his sleep and needed her to anchor him back to earth.

Those late-night calls started over a year ago, right after Finn moved into his own place. The topics always wandered, as though he'd bring up anything to hear her voice. *You know how people say Loch Creek was founded as a safe haven for the accused during the Salem Witch Trials?* he asked her once. *I think that was a cover.*

But he never spoke about one thing for long, and talk of Loch Creek's history was woven into Finn's other abstract thoughts. Mostly, he'd just ask questions. *Do you ever wonder who you'd be if you'd made different choices? Do you wish you could go back and live a day you already lived?*

Do you ever feel like you lost something?

The calls stopped after graduation.

Or, more accurately, she stopped answering.

But now, Briar wishes she'd picked up every single one. She wishes she'd turned every word Finn ever breathed into ink, because there must be clues somewhere—Finn wouldn't disappear without leaving breadcrumbs, a puzzle piece, a hint.

At that thought, Briar freezes.

There were numbers all over his window, Kai's voice echoes in her ear. *I meant to look this up; I thought it was a phone number. But it's too many digits.*

She gasps and scrolls until she finds the photo Kai sent to their group text earlier. A string of twelve numbers.

Briar fleetingly pictures Finn in AP Calculus, scratching out equations even their teacher didn't understand. *Math is cool*, he once said, *because numbers aren't just numbers. They can tell stories, make predictions. Let you know exactly when and where something is going to happen. Numbers can be time. Numbers can be a place.*

"Oh my god."

Briar swipes into a search engine, fingers flying against the screen before scrambling to her feet with another gasp. She races into the hall and down the stairs, then barrels outside just as headlights flood her vision.

Kai's car.

She runs to meet them, and before he or Astrid can speak, Briar's breath rushes out.

"The numbers you found on Finn's window," she exclaims. "You're right—it's not a phone number. It's *coordinates*." Her heart pounds in time with her next words. "And they lead right to the mirror house at the carnival."

CHAPTER TEN
BRIAR

3 Days Until Briar's Birthday Party

The mirror house looks different on "off" nights.

Loch Creek's summer carnival only runs on the weekends, shrouding the beach in shadows on all other evenings. Endless quiet stretches between metal scaffoldings. Like each ride is its own ghost, waiting for people to fill it with screams.

The clown sign outside the mirror house looms in the hushed moonlight as Kai races up the ramp. Briar swallows the memory of her dream, that ghastly woman looming between darkened glass. The cut on her leg burns, as if it can read her thoughts.

"Locked," Kai calls, tugging at the doors. He inspects the handles. "I could try to pick it."

"Maybe there's a back entrance," Briar suggests.

As they walk to the other side, Briar scans the unpainted portion of the rear exterior, the narrow wooden rafters, the—

"There's something under here," Briar says, tugging her phone loose. She taps the flashlight and bends. "What . . . ?"

Hidden beneath the building is a cluster of opalescent stones arranged in a wide circle. In the center rests a mound of seashells surrounding partially burned candles. Black soot stains the sand, the sight filling her with unease. A dull pain throbs behind Briar's right eye, and she presses it as Astrid kneels beside her.

"What *is* that?"

"I have no idea." Briar studies the stones, the melted wax. "It looks like . . . I don't know, some kind of ritual?"

She angles her flashlight, the silver beam catching a splash of ruby.

"Oh my god," Astrid breathes, noticing at the same time. "Is that blood?"

Kai crawls beneath the rafters. "This has 'Morgan Parker-Blake' written all over it, don't you think?" He turns one of the pale rocks, revealing three symbols scratched into the back. "It has to be her."

"Some girls on the cheer squad saw Morgan and her sister down by the beach last summer. Doing shit that looks a lot like this." Astrid casts a worried glance at Briar. "Do you think this has anything to do with what she was looking for at your house, Bee?"

Biting her lip, Briar hesitates. It was easy to tell Astrid and Kai earlier about Morgan trying to break in, but now, with the sea roaring in her ears, she wishes she could take the words back. Everything is colliding without reason, like galaxies with burning stars getting closer to explosion. The beach and Riley. Riley and Morgan. Morgan and Finn. All the pieces of her life that she's meticulously kept separate—all of her scheming, useless. The crash is inevitable, full speed ahead.

Briar fingers the woven pink and purple strands of the friendship bracelet on her wrist and dreads what it will feel like when she has no one left at all.

"I don't know," she answers, burying the ugly thoughts as she swings her flashlight. "I just—" She narrows her eyes. "Wait."

A black shape slumps beneath the building, and a gasp bubbles inside her as she recognizes it.

"Hold this." Briar hands Astrid her phone and crawls through the sand, coughing against a film of cobwebs until she reaches the backpack.

Finn's backpack.

Briar doesn't even have to peek inside to know it's his—the sailor knot key chain gives it away. She hauls it to her chest like she's five and clutching the stuffed bunny she once carried everywhere. Because it's not just a bag. It's a sign that Finn was here once, that even though he disappeared, he left something behind.

That maybe *lost* doesn't mean *gone*.

"Is that Finn's?" Kai asks, wide-eyed.

Briar nods as they duck out from the rafters.

"Open it," Astrid insists. She pulls out her phone, nestles it beside Briar's in the sand, and extends her hand for Kai's. Their flashlights make a glowing triangle between them.

With shaking hands, Briar unpeels the zipper. Finn's bag is heavier than usual, and when she reaches inside, her fingers close around a thick folder. Her frown deepens as she opens it onto her thighs, shuffling loose pages and documents.

"Shit!" Kai exclaims, leaning forward. "This is the stuff that was in Finn's apartment."

"He left it here for us," Astrid says, and her eyes light up. "He wants us to keep looking."

Briar blinks, recognition fluttering inside her.

From the Offices of Loch Creek County Clerk…

Deposition of…

Town Meeting Minutes…

"These are from the 1690s," Briar murmurs. "When Loch Creek was founded."

Her gaze slips as she pictures Finn on the Ferris wheel, begging her to leave this town with him. The way the thrum of her pulse drowned out his words, all because he'd said Riley's name. Riley, who took his final breaths just a few miles away from where the last traces of Finn linger now. Guilt churns inside her. She should have listened, should have hung on to every word, should have—

"Look at this," Astrid says, tapping a page in Briar's lap. The word DEED is stamped across the top. "A contract for the land of the town. *Agreement between Thomas Abbott and Harper Clay.* Thomas Abbott founded Loch Creek. But who the heck is Harper?"

"You'd think in a town as proud of its history as Loch Creek, we would've heard her name a million times," Kai says. "I've never heard of her at all."

But déjà vu haunts Briar as she recalls Finn's theories on the phone, the way he talked about Loch Creek's origin story like it was a cover for something worse. The name *Harper Clay* echoes in her memory, and for a moment, she's certain she's heard it before.

Briar rifles through the deed and pauses with a frown. "There's a section missing. Look. It jumps from page six to page ten." She flips the document again. "Whatever Finn was looking for—it's something he wasn't supposed to find."

"What if," Astrid adds softly, "someone hurt him because he had this?"

For a moment, they're all silent. A knot of fear tightens between Briar's ribs.

"Wait." Kai points to something Finn wrote in the corner. "'Hawthorne College Department of Anthropology and Religious Studies.' Wasn't Finn's dad a professor? Before he died?"

"All Finn ever said was that his dad got his PhD before the tragic relapse that killed him," Briar says. "Before Finn was even born."

"What if that's not how he died?" Astrid poses.

"Or—what if he's not dead at all?" Kai adds.

They go quiet again, Kai's question simmering between them. Briar drops her gaze to the backpack, registering the weight of it against her thighs. She knits her brow.

"There's something else in here." She tugs a thick book loose, and an unsettling chill greets her. The tome looks old—ancient—with a cracked spine and weathered edges.

"What . . . ?" Kai's breath evaporates in disbelief. "Are those flowers?"

Etched into the dark leather are three looming shapes: perfect circles with six petals inside. Briar narrows her eyes, that déjà vu returning.

"No," she murmurs. "I think they're called 'daisy wheels.'"

"How do you know that?" Astrid wonders, and Briar shakes her head.

"I'm not sure," she muses. "I must have seen one before. Online, I guess. Or in a movie."

Briar opens the book, and her breath rushes out in confusion.

The age-yellowed pages are filled with an unrecognizable language composed of crescent waves and arrows, swirls and triangles. Like the whispers of a secret code. Layered in between the symbols are mathematical equations: square roots and pi, Greek letters and parentheses.

"What the hell? This literally looks like a spell book." Kai narrows his eyes. "And not one you'd find on Glinda's bookshelf, that's for sure."

"Unless Glinda did math," Astrid mutters. She studies one of the pages. "No. Physics. This is the Newton-Girard formula. What's it doing in a spell book?"

"This must be why Finn was trying to solve those equations," Briar mutters, flipping to the last page. The back cover contains three daisy wheels in the center and a set of ominous words—the only ones in English so far—splashed in bold, rough ink.

TO DIE IS TO WAKE.

TO SLEEP IS TO FORGET.

"Jesus," Astrid breathes. "Why would Finn have this?" She slaps the book shut in Briar's lap. "This is terrifying."

"We should have asked him what all this stuff in his apartment was for." Kai drags a hand through his hair. "We should have made him tell us."

"You can't 'make' Finn do anything," Briar points out, and Kai narrows his gaze.

"*You* could." He fixes her with a long stare. "Briar. When was the last time you were at his place?"

Her cheeks redden, instinctively flooded with the memory of graduation night. The silver wash of the moon. The rough warmth from Finn's hands. The way her entire world shifted the second his mouth was on hers.

The way everything devolved into a nightmare hours later.

"I told you," she says, "I was there the other day."

He squints at her in the glow of their flashlights. "Why are you lying?"

"Kai," Astrid starts.

"No, no—we're gonna do this," he says to her. "We need to be real with one another. Be a team. Or else we'll never find him." A muscle tightens along his jaw. "You haven't been there since graduation, Briar. Over two months."

Air rushes from Briar's nostrils. "If you already knew, why did you ask?"

"Why were you avoiding him?" Kai fires back.

She drops her gaze, nails plucking her cuticles. *Because I'm a monster*, she wants to yell. *Because I ruin everything I touch. Because I'll ruin him too.*

"I don't want to talk about it," she says instead.

"We're your best friends," Astrid interjects. "We know when something is wrong." She gently touches Briar's wrist. "You can tell us anything."

The cut beneath Briar's bandage burns, as if Astrid's words were the squeeze of a lemon.

She wishes they were true.

"You really think we don't know what happened?" Kai asks. "C'mon. You and Finn hooked up after graduation. Right?"

Briar chews the inside of her cheek, willing her brain not to conjure the warm taste of Finn's mouth, the fierce, hungry way she kissed him back. How he said they could take things slow, that they'd have all summer, and then set her on fire with the curved shell of his hands. The way his stare seared into hers, like she was the solution to every equation he couldn't solve. *Hooked up*, she thinks bitterly. She can't think of a less fitting phrase for what they did.

"Don't be gross," she says, even though the lie tastes rotten in her mouth. "I don't think of Finn like that. We're just friends."

"Just *friends*?" Kai's eyebrows shoot up. "Briar. Are you serious right now?"

Astrid presses her lips together, sliding her gaze between them.

"Never been more serious in my life," Briar replies.

"I don't get you," Kai says, shaking his head. "We're tearing our hair out trying to figure out where Finn is, and you're gonna waste time lying about something so obvious? You hooked up, and then *you* ghosted. The four of us have been like this"—he crosses two fingers together—"since we met. Finn straight-up *worshiped* you, and you threw that away in our last few weeks together." His nostrils flare. "No wonder he left."

Hurt blooms between Briar's ribs. Her eyes swoop downward.

"Kai!" Astrid cries. "This isn't Bee's fault."

It is though, Briar wants to say. *It is, it is, it—*

"Really?" Kai says, voice clipped. "Have you forgotten what Finn said the night before the carnival?"

Briar's attention darts right back to them. "What are you talking about?"

"God, Kai," Astrid mutters, shooting daggers at Kai across the lights. "We were on the beach. Finn . . . he got a little high. Nothing he said made sense, but in retrospect . . ." She glances down. "He said that you might be in trouble, that there wasn't enough time."

That familiar vine of dread climbs in Briar's throat and summons a memory of Finn's voice on the phone this past year. *Do you remember*, he asked, *when we were in third grade and you drew that picture of the woman with the hole—the hole in her eye?* But Briar didn't want to remember, didn't want to think about her parents' wild stares or those pills that turned her head into a ball of cotton.

I know why you drew that, Finn said. *Please—Briar, don't hang up.*

But she did. She hung up and cried herself to sleep because it was easier than talking. The next day at school, Finn acted like the conversation never even happened. Like maybe he wanted to forget too.

"What sort of trouble?" Briar asks.

"He only said it was good he was leaving. Because you were better off without him."

An ache fills Briar's heart. "He was probably talking about college."

"That's what I thought too." Astrid's voice drops to a small whisper. "Then he was gone the next day."

"Are you saying he disappeared on purpose? Because of me?" Briar struggles for a defense even she doesn't fully believe. "I didn't erase him from time or put a bloody message in his closet, Astrid. How could this be my fault?"

The longer it takes Astrid to respond, the deeper the cavern in Briar's chest grows. As the girls in their group, she and Astrid always had an unspoken agreement to protect each other. Astrid was the person she told when she had her first kiss in eighth grade, the first one to know when Briar came out as bisexual the following year. They understood each other in ways most people never could, sometimes without any words at all.

But right now, Astrid's quiet feels different.

"Tell us the truth," Astrid says. "Please, Briar."

Briar clutches the spell book in her lap. She could talk about the first part of graduation night, how her bones felt like they'd crack under the weight of her final summer with Finn. It was all ending—high school, this parallel stretch of their lives, their shared universe of seawater and stars. The word *last* burned in her brain like crackling candles, and along with it, a terrible, gnawing idea that if she didn't kiss him now now now, she might never get the chance again.

But it was about more than Finn's impending cross-country move. All night, she was fighting an unshakable certainty that staying behind in Loch Creek would drown her. Because eventually, everyone would find out that Briar Winters is a fraud, an imposter of the most nightmarish kind.

And the voice in her skull at the first wash of dawn confirmed it, a reminder of who she really is, the terrible things she's capable of. *Winters girl*, it purred, invisible claws plucking her from sleep. *Don't you want to know how this ends?*

Briar's stomach twists at Kai's and Astrid's pleading faces. She'd rather her friends think she's a coward than a villain.

"Fine," she tries. "We hooked up. It got complicated. Are you happy?"

"Am I happy you just lied to us for the past five minutes?" Kai asks.

Her blood simmers with guilt. She digs her nails into her palms, and when that doesn't help, she rummages around for something to hit back with instead.

"What about *you*?" Briar asks.

Kai shoots her an incredulous stare. "What *about* me?"

Astrid frowns toward the mirror house. "Did you hear that?"

"You said it yourself, that Finn's like your brother." Briar barrels on. "Blood, right? Well, he left you too." She knows she's about to go too far—but it's better than them knowing the truth. "Why couldn't *you* get him to stay?"

Kai's dark eyes flash with hurt. "That's... that's messed up, Briar."

"So you can dish it, but you can't take it?" she clips, swallowing a wave of terrible regret at his wounded expression. "Yeah, that tracks."

He swoops down, grabbing Finn's backpack. "I'm done. Call me tomorrow if the aliens return my actual *friend*."

"I could say the same to y—"

"*Stop*!" Astrid yells. "Both of you, shut up. What is that sound?"

Briar whips her head to the mirror house. For a moment, she doesn't hear anything, except sloshing waves and her own breathing.

But then . . . a series of knocks along the wooden building.

As if they're coming from inside.

"What the hell?" she cries.

"Is someone in there?" Kai calls, stalking to the back entrance. He peers through the darkened window, breath fogging the glass. "Hello?"

Briar freezes. Fast knocks, then slower. Then fast again. Almost like a pattern.

"You guys, I'm getting freaked out," Astrid admits. "Can we go?"

"There's no one in there," Kai says. He holds a hand above his eyes. "This whole back hall is empty. It's—"

More frantic knocks engulf his words. Astrid shrieks, but Briar only stares with rounded eyes at the peeling paint, the shadows moving beneath the rafters. Fast and slow, fast and slow, knocking and knocking and knocking. The walls vibrate with feverish desperation, like whatever is on the other side would stop at nothing to break free.

But just as quickly as it started—silence.

Kai rests his forehead against the door, defeated. In the fresh quiet, Briar pulls her lip between her teeth with remorse.

"Kai," she starts. "I'm sorry, I shouldn't have said—"

"It's fine." But his clipped tone says it's not. He reaches up, twisting his black hair into a bun. "Let's all get some sleep. When you're ready to be real with us, let me know."

Briar casts a pleading look at Astrid, but she only kneels to gather the papers into Finn's backpack. Anxiety roils inside Briar. "Guys, please. Can't we—"

"Kai's right," Astrid says. "Let's hit pause. Divide and conquer. You keep the book, Briar. Kai and I, we'll split the folder. We all need to clear our heads." She slides Briar a pointed look in the dim moonlight. "Maybe tomorrow you'll want to tell us more."

Her voice is optimistic, but dread floods Briar's stomach. Because every hour that passes brings them closer to the day that Astrid and Kai will leave, closer to the inescapable loneliness that waits for Briar here. Closer to the day that no one searches for Finn at all. And as Briar follows Astrid and Kai toward the parking lot, she already sees the crack forming in their friendship. Tiny and jagged, threatening to become a chasm.

Deep enough to swallow them whole.

~

Briar wakes to the tapping of rain.

The hushed gray of early dawn spills through the gauzy canopy. She gropes along the nightstand to check for her inhaler before rolling onto her back—and frowns at what looks like a water stain on the ceiling. Yellow, bloated, and threatening to burst.

Like all her other problems.

Briar bites her lip, considering those past-due bills. As far as she knows, her parents have never missed payments before, have always had more than enough money. Fleetingly, she wonders if she can cover a water-damage repair herself.

To ease the widening anxiety in her chest, Briar closes her eyes and conjures a better memory. A stormy day like this one, in ninth grade. Finn was over for dinner, and they sat on her porch waiting for his mom afterward. But 7:30 turned into 8:00, and 8:00 turned into 9:00, and finally Briar's mother called through the screen door—*Finn, sweetheart, why don't you sleep over? I'll make up the guest room.*

Briar woke constantly from the blaze of lightning, thunder echoing in her teeth. She finally threw off her blankets to tiptoe down the hall, desperate for a sense of comfort, knowing she'd find it next to him. She climbed beneath the heavy duvet as quietly as possible to not wake him, but Finn must've sensed her anyway—

Briar? Have you been awake all night?

She froze, pink creeping into her cheeks. She contemplated saying she'd been sleepwalking, but even in the dim light, his stare drew out the truth. *I was scared of the storm.*

There was a soft quiet. The rain scratched at the glass, and Finn turned to face her in the dark. *Did you know*, he said, *that thunder is just air?*

When lightning strikes, it makes the air hot. But then, as soon as the lightning is gone—bam. The air gets cold again. It contracts and makes a sound. Finn demonstrated with his hands, sending shadows along the walls, and the remaining drops of her fear seemed to slip away. *Sometimes things are less scary once you know what they really are.*

They both drifted off shortly after that, but when Briar woke the next morning, it was to find their fingers intertwined. Finn was still sleeping, and she stared at their joined hands for what seemed like hours. She charted every slope of his knuckles, the stretch of his thumb over hers. The way he held on to her like she was something to keep him safe too.

Briar curls her fingers into her empty palm now, fist cold against the blankets as she recalls her words to Kai. *Finn and I are just friends.* A sickening guilt sours inside her. If no one else remembers Finn, it's up to the three of them to keep his memory alive. Yet there she was last night, erasing one of the simplest truths:

Her heart has belonged to Finn Adler for years.

And instead of trusting him with it, she did everything possible to push him away.

Frowning again at the water stain, Briar sits up and snatches her phone. There's no way she's falling back asleep, not when her friendships with Kai and Astrid are on the verge of crumbling, not when the ache in her chest grows and grows with every echo of Finn's voice.

There must be something they're missing.

Briar slips from her bedroom, ignoring the pain in her leg. She scrolls through her group chat with Astrid and Kai as she descends to the first floor, past yesterday's texts, the coordinates, the—

She freezes, attention snagging on the silver light beneath the craft room door. The steady clacking of the loom drifts toward her. She frowns. It's not even 6:00 a.m.

"Mom?" she calls. She works the handle. Locked. "Mom, are you in there?"

The sound flitters away. The light snaps to darkness.

"Mom?"

She sighs, turning, and stumbles to another halt.

Her mother's ceramic selkie statue, usually perched atop the marble console in the entryway, is on the ground—cracked. Straight down the center.

"Shit," she hisses, diving for it. She must have bumped it when she came home last night.

But on the heels of that thought is a tiny thread of doubt. The mermaid painting. The leak in the ceiling. Her missing senior photo. The red-stamped envelopes. As if her house—her family—is slowly falling apart in time with everything else.

Gritting her teeth, Briar grabs the selkie and shoves it into the umbrella rack before turning back to her phone. She continues toward the kitchen, still scrolling as she reaches for a coffee mug—

Where she pauses, staring at the photo of the restaurant receipt Astrid texted yesterday. Seaside Tavern—the one none of them had ever heard of, the one they somehow visited the night Finn disappeared.

The one they forgot to look up.

Heart hammering, Briar types rapidly, waiting for an address to pop on the screen.

It doesn't.

Instead, there's a singular news article, with a headline that flips her stomach and prickles her skin with fresh goose bumps.

LOCH CREEK RESTAURANT SEASIDE TAVERN BURNED TO THE GROUND AFTER ELECTRICAL FIRE.

And when she glances at the date, the entire room tips on its side.

Because this article isn't recent.

It was written almost twenty years ago.

CHAPTER ELEVEN
BRIAR

2 Days and 12 Hours until Briar's Birthday Party

Briar parallel parks outside a storefront with twinkling string lights draped over displays of hibiscus and sea holly. A hand-painted wooden sign reading *Infinity Florals* sways in the morning wind, rain spilling down the awning.

"Explain it again," Astrid says, as Briar turns off the ignition. "We were at a flower shop the night Finn disappeared?"

"No." Briar shakes her head. "Infinity Florals *used to be* Seaside Tavern. Two whole decades ago." She sucks in a breath before adding, "It burned down eighteen years ago. On May eighth."

"May eighth?" Astrid's gaze swings, fast, to hers. "But that's—"

"Finn's birthday. Yeah." She hands Astrid her phone. "See for yourself."

Astrid skims the article, confusion flashing across her face. Identical confusion filled Briar earlier as she read until the pixels blurred on the screen, until the only thing left to do was send Astrid an SOS emoji and drive across town to visit a building's ghost.

"We should call Kai," Astrid says, swiping on Briar's phone.

"Wait," she says, placing a hand on Astrid's wrist. "I want to tell him myself after we look around. Maybe—maybe we'll find something that leads to Finn."

Briar eyes the flower shop's exterior and swallows the hope that dares to bubble up. Maybe they'll find more than a clue. Something tangible that proves what happened to Finn wasn't her fault, something that could lessen the aching remorse that's threatening to consume her forever.

"I need to make things right with Kai," Briar adds. "After everything I said."

"You guys *both* need to make it right." Astrid hands her phone back, spinning a braid thoughtfully. "I have one question though. Actually—a *lot* of questions. But what's with the shrimp? There's no way we would've ordered that. Not the three of us, anyway."

Briar narrows her eyes. "What's that supposed to mean?"

Astrid slides her a wary glance. "You know how Finn would always make that super-morbid joke? If he knew he was gonna die, his last meal would be all the shit he's allergic to, because it wouldn't matter?"

Briar grinds her teeth, picturing the crinkling corners of Finn's eyes, his lips skewed in a twisted grin. *That's the way I wanna go out*, he once snort-laughed while lying on the beach between them. *A huge seafood platter and eternal fuckin' peace.*

Shoving the memory aside, Briar tugs a notebook loose from Finn's backpack. "I think the bigger question is how did we end up at a restaurant that hasn't existed in twenty years? The night of the carnival feels so fuzzy, but not just 'cause we were high. It's fuzzier than it should be, you know?" She flips through worn graph paper filled with equations in Finn's scratchy handwriting. Square roots and wave functions, Greek letters and fractions. "This isn't just math. This is *quantum physics*. Finn was studying these equations for a reason. It must be connected to that night."

"Quantum physics. Like time travel?" Astrid quirks a brow. "Are you saying we *time traveled* to the past for a single night, and what? Accidentally left Finn behind?"

Briar's gaze drops to the backpack, the clues Finn planted just for them. Her stomach knots. "I don't think any of this was an accident, Astrid."

She glances at Astrid, who's already staring with a serious expression. Neither of them has to say another word for Briar to know they're both thinking it:

Did they leave Finn behind, or did he choose to stay?

Astrid peers out the car window, her expression cloudy. Briar waits for her to offer something else, something comforting, but she only gazes into the fog. Somehow this is worse than anything so far—the sinking awareness that Astrid is losing hope, right in front of her.

But before she can speak, Astrid leans forward, splaying her hands on the dashboard.

"Whoa," she breathes. "Do you see that? That wasn't there yesterday, was it?"

Briar cranes her neck to follow Astrid's stare toward a cluster of construction workers in orange vests, all gathered around something at the end of the street. Her eyes widen at the sight of a colossal sinkhole in the asphalt. Its jagged edges swallow both lanes of the road, as if threatening to devour the entire downtown strip. Her skin prickles as she recalls the cracked window at the courthouse, the crumbling pieces of her own home. *All things are connected*, she can almost hear Finn say. *Everything in the universe is linked.*

"That definitely wasn't there yesterday," Astrid says, answering her own question.

Briar shakes her head. "The whole world is falling apart."

And as if to prove her words true, a tall girl with cropped maroon hair suddenly darts past them on the rain-drenched sidewalk. A girl Briar would recognize anywhere, both from the pointed stride and the invisible storm cloud that swirls around her. Like a warning to stay away.

Nerissa Parker-Blake.

Morgan's older sister.

Astrid sees her at the same time, eyes widening as Nerissa beelines for the front door of Infinity Florals with keys in hand.

And Briar's stomach turns in fresh panic at the awareness that she's led Astrid straight to the cobweb-dusted corner of her life she's spent years trying to hide.

"No freaking way," Astrid exclaims. "Don't tell me Morgan's sister owns this flower shop."

Briar chews her lip as Nerissa unlocks the darkened store, recalling the times she spotted the older girl picking Morgan up after middle school. Unlike Morgan, Nerissa embraced the whispers attached to their family's name: plastering pentagram bumper stickers to her pickup truck, inking her skin with strange symbols and water crests. Every afternoon, her catlike eyes would trail Briar as she walked to her mom's car.

As if to say, *I know who you really are*.

The rain intensifies overhead, rattling on the roof of the car like stones. In the deluge, Briar can't ignore all the warning bells that keep blaring around the Parker-Blakes. Morgan in Finn's apartment. Morgan breaking into her house. Nerissa owning a store they somehow visited in the past.

It's enough to make Briar want to hide—but she doesn't have a choice.

She'll do it afraid.

"Come on," Briar says, adrenaline shooting through her as she pops the door handle.

"What are you doing?" Astrid asks. "The shop's probably closed."

"Exactly." Briar steps out of the car into the smell of rain on asphalt. A blade of pain grips her leg, and she summons every effort not to wince. She pulls her hood up over her curls, warm raindrops pelting the fabric. "We'll get her to open up early."

~

Briar has to bang on the door only once before Nerissa appears on the other side, her delicate features twisted into a scowl. For a moment, it's like Briar's a kid again, staring up at Nerissa on the playground while blinking back tears. *Morgan isn't coming to your pathetic Christmas party*, Nerissa snapped with that same hardened expression. *My sister isn't your friend.*

"We don't open for another two hours," Nerissa calls, pointing at the sign.

"We need to talk to you," Briar musters, ignoring the whirring of her pulse.

Nerissa's face scrunches in confusion.

"We were here two nights ago." Briar raises her voice over the rain. "Do you remember seeing us?"

"Shop wasn't open that night," Nerissa says, starting to turn away.

Astrid slaps the restaurant receipt against the door. "Not here," she says. "At Seaside Tavern."

At that, Nerissa goes very still, her expression impossible to read through the foggy glass. Briar holds back a shiver as the rain intensifies, water soaking through her sweatshirt.

The door clicks as Nerissa unlocks it, peering through the cracked opening. "If this is some kind of prank—"

"It's not," Briar interrupts. "Will you let us in?"

Nerissa stares again, contemplating. Up close, Briar catalogs all the ways she and Morgan are nearly identical: shimmering amber eyes with flecks of gold, razor-sharp cheekbones. But unlike Morgan with her heavy winged eyeliner, Nerissa's face is completely free of makeup. Just dewy sun-kissed skin and fluffed-up brows—currently drawn into a frown. Briar's stomach flips at the awareness that Nerissa could slam the door in her face, that finding Finn now hinges on begging for help from someone who has every reason to hate her.

"Please," Briar adds, and Nerissa huffs a sigh, opening the door.

The flower shop greets them with a gust of gardenia and lavender, sweet pea and peonies. Briar follows Nerissa toward the back counter with Astrid at her side, zigzagging through hanging potted plants and garlands of ivy.

Nerissa slips behind the wooden counter, where she grabs a fistful of roses, nabbing a pair of shears with the other hand.

"I know you kids," Nerissa says, as she starts snipping. "You're in my sister's grade."

"Kids?" Astrid scoffs. "We're, like, three years younger than you."

The shears cut thick stems, raining thorns onto the counter. "You're not very nice to her, are you?" Another harsh snip. "Oh, I've heard about the names everyone calls her. The bullshit rumors. The nasty things people write on her locker." Nerissa moves the handle faster. "Did you know someone once stuffed a bunch of ketchup-covered tampons in her backpack?" She fires a scowl at Briar. "That your handiwork, Winters?"

Yes, because she put a fucking dead mouse in my bag first, Briar almost snaps back. Instead, she grits her teeth, swallowing her shame and desperation to calmly reply, "We didn't come here to talk about Morgan."

Nerissa stills the shears, her gaze flitting to Astrid. "Lemme see that receipt."

Astrid slides it across the counter. Nerissa lifts it with calloused fingers, nails bare, unlike Morgan's long black talons.

"My parents owned Seaside Tavern," Nerissa says, and confusion shivers down Briar's spine.

"Your . . . parents?" she echoes.

"Mama always swore to renovate it after the fire. But then she got sick." Nerissa gestures around the shop. "So it became my project. Never been a fried-food girl. Would much rather surround myself with flowers." She slides the receipt back. "This isn't funny. Maybe Morgan puts up with this shit from you, but not me. I'd suggest you get the hell out of my store."

But Nerissa's harsh words don't sting this time, Briar's brain too busy whirring with this new information. Her thoughts race faster than she can process them, remembering the papers in Finn's backpack, the things he whispered to her on the Ferris wheel. She raises her gaze to Nerissa and summons an unfamiliar confidence.

"Your parents were descendants of the settlers, weren't they?" Briar asks. "Your ancestors were accused of witchcraft during the Salem Trials. That's why they came to Loch Creek. For protection."

Nerissa arches a brow. "You wanna give me a little history lesson? Is that what we're doing here at six-thirty in the morning?"

Briar curls her nails into her palms, pushing down a sarcastic retort. "We're not messing with you," she insists. "We're looking for help. 'Cause we somehow ended up at a restaurant that hasn't existed in twenty years—a restaurant that *your* parents owned. And the next morning, our friend was missing."

"We just wanna find him," Astrid adds softly. "His name is Finn Adler."

Nerissa stares, unmoved, before picking up the shears.

"It's common knowledge that the Parkers and the Blakes can be traced back to the trials," she says, tilting her head as she cuts. "So if you've come here to make some statement about my family's heritage, it's not exactly an earth-shattering announcement. Especially coming from you."

Briar tips her head. Her mouth turns to cotton. "What?"

Nerissa squints. "I'm sorry, are you not the Briar Winters whose family has been running that art society since the days when witches were torched in the streets? Don't come in here with your nose turned up about *my* parents, when you can practically trace our family trees to the same damn forest."

The back of Briar's neck prickles with heat. She thinks again of the tension between her mother and Mrs. Parker-Blake, of Nerissa's watchful stare from the Loch Creek Junior High parking lot. The cut on her calf throbs, and she grits her teeth again.

"I don't know what you mean," Briar starts carefully, "but our families are nothing alike."

A dark smile pulls at Nerissa's mouth. "Well. That's for sure."

Noticing the color rapidly draining from Briar's face, Astrid leans forward. "Can we please talk about our missing friend? All this family stuff feels irrelevant."

"I disagree. My sister's been burned at the proverbial stake for years, so I'd say it's pretty damn relevant. Everyone loooooves a scapegoat." Nerissa lets out a sharp bleating sound—like an actual goat—before dropping the roses into a vase. "So go on. Ask the question."

Briar and Astrid exchange a glance.

"Ask if I'm a witch and I put hex on your friend," Nerissa continues. "That's what you came here for, isn't it?" But she's only looking at Briar as she adds, "I know how much you love your stories."

Briar chews the inside of her cheek, guilt churning over everything Morgan must have told her sister, all the poisonous pieces of history Nerissa holds in her palms. She could fling them across the counter like confetti at any moment—and Briar knows she would deserve it.

"I'm not accusing you of anything," Briar finally says. "I just want answers. There are stories about other disappearances over the years, bad things happening on the"—she swallows the rising discomfort in her chest—"on the northern beach. And a lot of people here... they just look the other way. Loch Creek might be a haven for some, but for others, it's more like this town is cursed."

Nerissa studies her. "And which one are you, Winters? The protected or the damned?"

Briar tongue sticks to her teeth. "I—"

"That was rhetorical. We both know the answer." She folds her arms across her chest. "I think it's time for you to leave."

"Hold on." Astrid points at something behind the counter. "*What* is that?"

Her tone snags Briar's attention. She follows her gaze to the back wall, eyes widening.

There, framed in gold, is a map of what looks like the northeast coast. But most of the canvas is covered with intersecting lines, forming tight spirals. Briar blinks as she realizes she's not looking at a regular map.

It's a nautical chart.

Exactly like the one Finn had in his room.

Nerissa flicks a glance at the frame. "Something I drew."

"You *made* that?" Astrid asks, eyebrows shooting up to her hairline.

"Yeah. It's a hobby. I sell 'em on Etsy and also here." Nerissa gestures to a shelf across the room that displays a collection of framed maps and charts.

Heart pounding, Briar whips her gaze back. "Did you ever sell one to a boy our age? Tall, dark blonde hair, gray eyes?"

"Sometimes wears glasses," Astrid adds.

Nerissa pushes a ring-adorned hand through her short wine-colored hair.

"Before he disappeared, he had a map like this one," Briar continues. "But now—it's like he never lived there at all. *Morgan* lives there. She says she's been in that apartment for over a year—but Finn's lived there since—"

"Hold on. You've talked to Mor about this?" Nerissa asks suddenly.

"Yeah, she tore my house apart looking for something that I don't have."

Nerissa exhales through her nose, her gold-flecked eyes rolling in exasperation. "Of course she did," she mutters. "I'm gonna wring my sister's neck. She sure doesn't do herself any favors."

"Can you answer my question?" Briar sucks in a breath before adding, "Please. Nerissa. We're scared."

Nerissa is silent for a long time. Briar watches her carefully, charting the tiny quirks of her lips as though she's chewing on them from the inside.

“Okay,” Nerissa finally says, “but first, promise to leave my sister alone. She had nothing to do with this.”

Briar hesitates, considering the consequences of making a promise she might have no choice but to break. She swallows and nods anyway. “Deal.”

Nerissa’s mouth flattens into a line. “A boy came in here earlier this year,” she says. “He bought a nautical chart of the Atlantic, circa 1700. He was blonde, like you said. I remember he wore a gray Berkeley hoodie.”

“Finn!” Astrid exclaims, and Briar’s chest clenches. She can easily picture him thumbing through the worn maps, deep in thought. The air in the flower shop turns a touch colder at the realization that he stood right where she’s standing now—like his breath is lingering here, clinging to vines and petals. The thought ignites the faintest hope.

Finn might have chosen to leave, but maybe he wants to be found.

“Do you have copies of the chart you sold him?” Briar asks. “Can we buy one?”

Nerissa nods before striding across the room. She returns with a rolled-up piece of parchment, spreading it on the wooden counter.

“I don’t understand something,” Briar says. “How come you remember him? No one else does—not even his own *mother*. It’s just us.” She narrows her eyes. “And now you.”

Nerissa studies her as she rings up the map. “Well,” she says, a small smile tipping the corners of her lips, “there’s an easy answer for that.”

“And that is?”

Her grin twists into a callous smirk. “I’m a witch, remember?” Nerissa practically shoves the maps into Astrid’s hands. “Now kindly fuck off and get out of my store.”

CHAPTER TWELVE
BRIAR

2 Days and 9 Hours until Briar's Birthday Party

The rain has dissolved into mist by the time Briar and Astrid arrive at the beach near Finn's apartment.

After they left Infinity Florals, Astrid suggested getting coffee and heading to the lifeguard tower at the end of Rowan Street to see if they could make sense of Nerissa's nautical chart. Briar's stomach twisted at the idea of getting so close to Sorrow's Shore, but she let Astrid drive them to the corner of Loch Creek that framed the saddest day of her life.

They crouch between the dunes now, where Astrid unrolls the thick parchment and weighs it down with their iced coffees. She bends over the map, squinting at hand-drawn numbers.

"Alright, time to get into our Finnegan's brain," Astrid mutters. "The day before the carnival, this map wasn't on his wall. It was on his desk, and he'd drawn x's on it. Around here." She taps the swell of the Atlantic, right near the Massachusetts coast.

"That has to be Loch Creek," Briar says, tracing the tip of Astrid's neon nail back to the coastline. "But Finn wasn't just studying the town. He was studying what lies beyond it." She faces down the white-stained horizon, her stomach clenching at the choppy waves. "Out there."

Astrid follows her stare. "I feel like we're close to something. We can put these pieces together. We have a literal *map*." She sits back on her heels. "Do you want to call Kai? He should see this too."

Briar falls silent, unease creeping into her belly. This map might feel like a north star to Astrid, but to Briar, it's another dead end. A spiderweb of a scavenger hunt orchestrated by the smirking Parker-Blake sisters. She knows in her bones that Morgan and Nerissa are at the center of everything, but there's no way to explain it without revealing the pieces she *needs* to keep hidden. But Briar has no other evidence, no smoking gun. Just a weathered map leading them straight to a treasure trove of her worst secrets, the lock ready for picking. X marks the fucking spot.

"I'll call Kai in a minute," Briar says, swallowing a wave of mounting dread. "I just—" She freezes, squinting. "Wait. What the hell is that?"

"What? Oh—ew." Astrid seems to notice them at the same time: milky-pink lumps along the water's edge, lines of little see-through mounds glistening beneath the pale sun. Jellyfish?

No.

Briar stares at the translucent creatures, taking in their beady eyes, their textured fins. There must be fifty of them, all in a row, lifeless and slick in the sand. Briar's memory conjures the headline she saw on her phone about dozens of dead fish washed up on shore, and her skin prickles with goose bumps.

Briar and Astrid approach the shoreline, and Astrid kneels to peer closer.

"Don't touch them!" Briar cautions.

Astrid is quiet as she rakes her gaze over the unmoving creatures. "This is gonna sound absolutely wild," she mutters, "but they seriously look like the fish we studied in my paleontology elective."

Briar swings her gaze to hers. "Tell me you're kidding."

Astrid shakes her head, braids swaying, and snaps a photo with her phone. "We did a unit on early sea-based craniates—animals with a skull, I mean. There was one fish that looked like Jell-O, with a row of six gills and a sloping dorsal fin that merged with its tail." She's quiet for a moment. "Like this one."

A chill rattles Briar's spine as she surveys the shoreline. "Maybe they just look similar," she says hopefully.

"Maybe." Astrid tucks her phone in her pocket. "I can check my notes later."

She sits in the sand, feet from the rotting fish. As though a collection of dead things is hardly worse than everything that's happened so far. Briar slumps beside her.

"A restaurant that doesn't exist. Nautical charts from the past. Fish that died out millennia ago." Briar rakes both hands through her curls. "It's like the universe is imploding, and we're running out of time to put it back together."

Astrid sits back on her palms. "Everything must be linked. There's a throughline we need to find."

Briar grits her teeth and fixes her stare on the waves. She's not sure how to tell Astrid that she might be the throughline, that tragedy clings to her like a disease. That maybe she's infected everyone else. Instead, she watches the water foam against the shore. It reminds her of the weeks after Riley died: she'd dream about the ocean, imagining standing at the water's edge beneath a graying sky like this one.

Once, she woke to find herself lying on the sand beneath the early-dawn light in her nightgown. She had no idea how she'd gotten there; the beach was at least a ten-minute walk from her house, and she wasn't allowed to go alone. She was disoriented, unsure which direction was home, so she stood at the shoreline in bare feet. And listened to the water.

A surfer helped her locate her parents, who immediately called Dr. Fuchs—the psychiatrist she's seen since Riley died.

Sleepwalking, he dismissed. *Common after trauma in young children.*

It was the start of the prescriptions, the appointments, the therapy to get her to talk again.

But what her family doesn't know is that she talked to the water the morning Riley drowned. And for the next six months, she only talked to the water.

Until she talked to Finn.

She curls her fingers into the wet sand and remembers all the ways Finn helped create space for her to find the words she needed back then. Now he's the one who needs to be found.

"Maybe we should talk to our parents," Astrid says suddenly, and Briar's head snaps up. "I mean, your mom and dad run the Cultural Council; my moms are members. Kai's grandma too. They must know something about the town or Morgan's family or—"

"No." An image flashes in Briar's brain of her father with his arms crossed, watching as she swallows a pill. She presses her thumb down on a trickle of blood welling along her shredded cuticle. "We have to leave them out of it."

"Then we need to figure out why Finn was hoarding all this shit," Astrid replies, reaching for the backpack at Briar's feet. She tugs it open, hauling that old black book between them. "He was so excited about Berkeley. He'd need a damn good reason to get *this* obsessed about Loch Creek right before moving away." Astrid gives her a pointed look. "Something he cares about more than himself."

Briar averts her gaze, but she can't help recalling Finn's heated stare on the Ferris wheel. Her ears ache with the desperation of his voice, and the knowledge she's been avoiding slams into her like a tidal wave. Because when everyone already knows the truth, it becomes a lot harder to cling to a slippery lie. Saltwater and guilt seem to clog her lungs until she has no choice but to say it out loud—

"Me," Briar admits. "He left because of me."

Astrid nods slowly, but there's no burning accusations in her stare. "Bee, no one thinks this is *all* your fault," she says carefully. "You didn't erase Finn from existence. But you have to tell us what's going on. Why did you lie about graduation night?"

The question puts a fresh burst of anxiety inside her.

"I..." Briar presses her lips together. She feels like an actress reciting lines from a script, the words stiff in her mouth. "I'm sorry. I shouldn't have. I guess I didn't want to complicate things right before everyone left for school."

Astrid studies her, and the air on the beach suddenly seems too thin.

"It's more than that," Astrid pushes back. "We've never had any issue talking about sex before, so I'm not buying *this*. There's some other reason you won't talk about graduation. You're shutting down in a major way—like you do whenever someone mentions Ril—"

Briar's pulse skyrockets. She slams her gaze to Astrid's.

For a moment, they stare at each other, the ocean clawing at the sand in the background. Astrid's lips skew to the side, as if recalling all the times she silenced anyone who dared to utter a reminder of what Briar lost. As if weighing the consequences of being the one to do it now. Astrid's expression puts an ache in Briar's chest, along with the heavy certainty that she brought this upon herself.

"Just say it," Briar whispers.

Astrid's throat bobs. Her eyes darken with resolution. "*Riley.*"

Briar can only nod bitterly. The silence that follows seems to whisper in her ear: *You're on your own now.*

"Briar, listen to me." Astrid's voice softens. "There's nothing you could tell me that would make me stop loving you."

But her words only worsen the pain in Briar's ribs. Because Astrid's DNA is made up of warm faith and an unshakable belief in everything good. She always sees through her friends' rough parts to the softness underneath, and they do the same for her. Last year, when one of Astrid's moms was diagnosed with breast cancer, they all came each time she visited the hospital. Whenever Astrid's hope crumbled, whenever she reckoned with the possibility that her mom might die, they were there to hold her hand. To remind her that, no matter what, she wouldn't be alone.

They all chose one another. A group of people broken in different places. But together, they were somehow whole.

Briar locks her gaze onto the water and tries to imagine letting every disgusting truth tumble out.

She could point toward the pier and say, *It happened over there.*

She could explain that her parents let them play together in the water because she'd learned to swim that summer. But Riley still didn't know how. She could say that she promised she'd hold his hand, that she *meant* to hold his hand.

Briar could describe how the water fed her whispers, clouding her thoughts until Riley's frantic splashing grew still and quiet, until all that was left was dizzying confusion and the sudden rushing fear that she had done something very, very wrong.

She could tell Astrid how she spun and spun, looking for someone to help.

How the only person in sight was a dark-haired girl by the dunes, her gold-flecked eyes rounded in horror.

She could tell her about the knife of self-hatred that's been lodged in her gut ever since.

And finally, she could tell her about the voice that's never left her alone since that day. The one that's kissed every corner of her mind, the one that crept in on graduation night with a gleeful warning of the monstrous things she'd do next. *Winters girl,* it hummed, invisible claws on her skin, *I'm the only one you need.*

She could, she could, she could. But Astrid—no, she wouldn't love Briar anymore. She tries to see the light in everything, but there must be some places that are too shadowed.

This, Briar knows, is one of those places. Saying the words out loud, it would only feel like giving up her last breath. Like dying.

She drops her gaze, lingering on their matching bracelets. The identical pink and purple strands mock her, a tapestry of all the ways she's breaking their friendship with every unspoken truth.

Briar closes her eyes. "I'm sorry. Astrid. I *can't*—"

A gust of bitter wind swallows her voice. Briar pops her eyes open. The sharp breeze flips open the spell book, its pages crackling in the salty air. And then one sheet blows loose.

"Shit—" Briar lunges, snatching it before it can go too far.

It takes her a second before she understands that *this* paper isn't old. It was tucked inside the spine as though someone had been using it like a bookmark.

A math test, folded up.

She glances at the name on top, and understanding clicks into place along with purposeful anger. She wants to cling to this rage, wants to wrap herself in it. Let it replace the guilt, the sorrow, the shame.

Let it coat her skin in armor.

Because this isn't just a piece of paper—it's the last scrap of evidence she needs.

"What is it?" Astrid asks.

Briar stands and hands her the folded test. *Morgan's* test.

"Come on," she says, casting a stare down the beach. "It's time to hunt a witch."

CHAPTER THIRTEEN

BRIAR

2 Days and 7 Hours Until Briar's Birthday Party

Briar hesitates outside Morgan's apartment, the spell book burning a hole in her bag.

Astrid wanted to come along, but Briar insisted they split up. *I'll deal with Morgan*, she said as they repacked Finn's backpack. *You and Kai should start going through the documents. We'll cover more ground that way.*

What she didn't say was that she needed to have this conversation with Morgan alone, because their shared secret is a time bomb, ticking inside them both. And when the inevitable explosion hits, Briar refuses to have a single witness around to catch fire.

But now that she's here, in front of an apartment Finn once called home, all she feels is consuming nostalgia. If she closes her eyes, Briar can almost convince herself that it's not the end of August but earlier this spring. Before graduation, before Finn was gone.

Briar doesn't know how she spent so many nights at Finn's apartment without kissing him. How she managed to lean against him on the fire escape and pretend her skin wasn't burning everywhere they touched.

Because the truth is, Briar wanted to kiss Finn a million times before it finally happened—in the hallways at school, in the car at red lights, on the beach at twilight. A million wasted chances, all tossed into the sea like glittering dust. A million empty moments tinged with the taunt of *almost*.

There's no scarier haunted house she can think of than this one: a place where Finn used to live but doesn't anymore, each floorboard and beam dusted with the ghosts of all the times Briar *wishes she did*, but didn't.

Swallowing the ache in her chest, Briar raises her fist—but the door swings open first.

"Well, well." Morgan smirks. "Look who's back."

Briar tilts her chin to compensate for the inches separating them. Morgan isn't even as tall as she usually is, having traded her usual boots for sandals, but she still towers like a statue. Briar suddenly feels even smaller, shrinking beneath every unspoken truth between them.

"What do you want, Pom-Poms?" Morgan adds, leaning in the doorframe. She crosses her arms, drawing Briar's attention to the large floral tattoo along her collarbone. Oleanders, she's almost certain. "Spit it out. I have a sacrifice to get to in twenty minutes."

Briar pulls the spell book from Finn's backpack. "Is this what you were looking for yesterday?"

Morgan's smile flutters away. "You *did* have it."

"Not me." Briar holds it out of Morgan's grasp. "A friend. The one whose apartment you've invaded."

Morgan lunges again, reaching around Briar's shoulders. "Hand it over."

Briar retreats, tailbone knocking against the railing of the stairwell. "Not until you answer some questions."

"You get *one*," Morgan bites.

"Three."

"Two."

"Fine." Briar sucks in a breath. "But not out here."

Morgan rolls her eyes, marching inside the apartment. Briar glares as Morgan drops into an emerald velvet settee. There's a half-empty mug on the side table, as if she were casually enjoying a cup of coffee. As if she's not the reason Briar's life has been shredded to ribbons. Briar's stomach knots at the awareness that the one person who might be able to stitch the strings together is this girl who has no good reason to help her at all.

"Alright," Morgan says, already sounding bored. "Hit me with your interrogation."

Briar sits and gathers her courage. "Did you talk to Finn the night of the carnival?"

A muscle clenches in Morgan's jaw. "No."

She quirks a brow. "So you *do* remember him."

"Is that your second question?"

Briar narrows her eyes. "What's in this book you want so badly?"

"Consider it a valuable antique."

"It's a spell book. And that's not really an answer." Briar fights to keep the pleading whine from her voice. "What's *in* it?"

"Danger. Especially in the wrong hands. Which is why *you* need to return it."

"Did you and Nerissa put a spell on Finn?" Briar can't hide her fear when she adds, "Did you hurt him?"

"You're out of questions." Morgan holds out her hand. "Book. Now."

Thunder rolls in the distance as Briar considers the circle of stones in the sand. Finn staring at Morgan in the ticket line, her math test tucked inside a book in his backpack, the fact that she's sleeping in the room that should be his. *Coincidences come in twos*, Finn once said. *Anything over three isn't a coincidence. It's a sign.*

Pressing her tongue to her teeth, Briar works out, "No."

"Are you for real right now?"

"Everything that's happened is connected," she says. "I know you had something to do with Finn's disappearance."

Morgan heaves an exasperated sigh. "I swear on my mama's grave: I don't know where he is."

"Then help me find him."

The words spill out before she can cap them, driven by something desperate and raw. Primal, even. It's not just the aching hunger for the familiarity of Finn's voice, the safe comfort of his hands, but also a sudden need to prove she's capable of something—anything—good. That she's more than a girl who ruins everything she loves.

That maybe she can be the kind of girl who saves someone instead.

"Help me, and I'll give this back to you," Briar emphasizes. "Then I'll never bother or talk to you again."

"That's hilarious. As if you cared to ever talk to me in the first place." Morgan raises her chin. "What makes you so sure I can help anyway?"

"Seriously? Cut the shit. You and Nerissa. You're witches. I'm holding a literal *spell book* with your name in it." Briar gnaws her lower lip. "Whatever happened to Finn, it defies logic. We're not gonna find him driving down Route 128 or combing the beach. But someone with your skills... maybe you could."

"My—*skills*?" Morgan scoffs. "I see how it is. The idea I might be a witch is abhorrent when it suits your mean girl narrative, but when you need my help, it's useful. Tell me, where was this respect for my 'skills' when you were drawing pentagrams on my locker, hmm?"

Briar opens her mouth and immediately shuts it, mind swirling with images of Morgan's locker covered in Sharpie. Remembering her own hands shoved in the pockets of her cheerleading jacket, hiding the marker smudges. The echoes of laughter as Morgan tried to scrub the ink from the shiny blue metal. She eventually gave up and left it there, a scarlet letter designed to keep everyone away.

Briar grinds her teeth. "Well—you put bugs in my sneakers! You hid a dead *mouse* in my backpack, you absolute freak."

Morgan wrinkles her nose. "The crickets, I'll admit, were my finest work. But a mouse? Nah, not my style. You must be confusing me with another archnemesis."

"Enough," Briar snaps, leaping to her feet. "Do you think I *want* to be here, talking to you? Do you think I enjoy asking for your help?" She clutches the book to her chest. "You can forget it—I'm keeping this."

But Morgan stands just as fast, blocking her path. Lightning flashes through the curtains as she leans in, close enough that Briar can feel Morgan's breath on her cheek.

"No, you *hate* asking for my help." Morgan's voice is suddenly a note lower, a touch smokier. "Having to practically beg for my assistance. My 'skills.' " She traces the edge of the book with an onyx talon, a dark smile along her mouth. "It makes you sick to your stomach, doesn't it? And we both know why."

Panicked adrenaline pops in Briar's veins. "*Don't.*"

"But how come?" Morgan searches her gaze. "There's no one else here. Not Mommy and Daddy, not your little posse. It's you and me. And I won't act like you're made of glass just cause everyone else does." Her crimson-stained lips twitch. "You know what, Pom-Poms? I *will* help you. But I don't want your silence in return. I want exactly the opposite."

Trepidation clacks inside Briar. "What?"

"By the time we're done here," Morgan purrs, "you're going to admit the real reason you despise me so much. Right to my face. And you won't stop there. You'll tell your friends too. Your parents. This whole damn town. Don't you have a birthday party coming up? I can see it now: Briar Winters's final confessional, event of the fucking year." That feline grin deepens. "I can't wait to hear those ugly words come out of that pretty, pretty mouth."

Another clap of thunder shakes the room, fierce as the roar of Briar's resentment. It would feel good, she thinks, to slap that smug expression off Morgan's annoyingly beautiful face. March out of here with her precious book and never look back.

But instead, Briar holds her stare and wonders how it would feel to speak the truth to the one person who already knows. The one person who doesn't care about her prom-queen, honor roll, cheerleader bullshit—and instead looks right at the nightmarish beast that's been inside Briar this whole time.

Maybe saying it to Astrid would feel like running out of air.

But saying it to Morgan could feel like taking a breath.

"Do we have a deal, Pom-Poms?" Morgan whispers, extending her hand.

Without giving herself a chance to change her mind, Briar snatches Morgan's palm and shakes. *For Finn,* she thinks. *For Finn.*

Morgan's grin widens, like she's a sea witch who convinced a mermaid to sign away her voice. But then her stare lowers pointedly to the bandage on Briar's calf.

"What—?"

Before Briar can finish the question, Morgan bends down. In one quick move, she grasps the adhesive and tears it off with a sickening rip.

Briar doubles over, the pain white-hot and furious. "What the actual fucking *fuck*?" she screeches, clutching the exposed cut. "What are you *doing*?"

"I said I'd help, didn't I?"

"How is *this* helpful?" Blood seeps between her fingers, and she practically growls in pain. "Jesus *Christ*, what's wrong with you?"

Undeterred, Morgan pries Briar's hands away.

"Morgan, I swear to g—"

Her words evaporate as she absorbs the sight in front of her.

The wound on her leg doesn't look anything like it did last night.

It's no longer a linear scratch but now a pointed oval. Like the shape of a leaf. As though the gash warped in her sleep, folding in on itself to create something new and foreboding. The carved flesh is wet with dark blood, a river of unnatural ruby black dripping down her skin like ink.

Alarm shrills inside her. Knees suddenly wobbly, Briar sinks to the floor. She traces a finger over the petal-shaped cut, barbed dread in the pit of her stomach. She can't help but wonder if whatever vicious monster that's inside her is clawing its way out.

"This cut," Morgan says, "when did you get it?"

"I don't know." Briar clenches her jaw around the lie.

Morgan exhales through her nose and sits beside her. "Okay, Pom-Poms, let's swap. Secret for secret." She sharpens her gaze. "Nerissa and I know magic, but not the kind in the stories *you* like to tell. We don't sacrifice animals or have sex with the devil. The truth is that our magic is connected to the ocean. Tide spells. Salt crystals for healing. We're water witches, not bunny eaters or demon worshipers. Sorry to disappoint."

Briar knits her brow. *Water witches?*

"Most witches who still exist today are the elemental kind—there are four groups of 'em, with sister covens scattered throughout the world," Morgan continues. "A lot of us were extinguished during historic witch hunts—Salem, Würzburg, Valais. So now I'm sitting here with Cheerleader Barbie, because three hundred and something years ago, my great-great-whatever escaped to the 'haven' Loch Creek instead of being burned at the stake. Not sure which is the worse punishment."

Morgan's insult barely lands as Briar's brain scrambles to catch up. The accusation she conjured to protect her own secret—it was true all along.

Morgan Parker-Blake... is a witch.

"If it were up to me," Morgan adds, "I wouldn't be a witch at all. I'd rather dance."

Briar blinks. "Dance?"

"Ballet. Been doing it since I was three. I daydream about leaving this place and joining a dance company. I actually tried once, petitioned my parents with a PowerPoint about how they should let me move to New York. But no, it's more important for me to stay here, to learn tide magic. Continue a legacy I wanted nothing to do with in the first place."

Briar studies her, trying to picture Morgan in a pink leotard instead of her all-black uniform. Raven hair slicked into a bun, pirouetting under stage lights, as if she could possibly spin fast enough to break free.

Something shifts inside Briar as she considers the possibility that she's not the only one who's quietly suffocating beneath expectations.

That maybe Morgan Parker-Blake feels trapped in this town too.

"Category is 'cut the shit,' right?" Morgan's voice flattens with seriousness. "Your turn. I need you to tell me about this wound."

Briar's stomach drops. "You'll think I'm crazy."

Morgan squints. "Try me."

Briar sucks in a breath. "Sometimes, I see things." The truth feels out of place in her mouth. "There's a woman—a *dead* woman. I started seeing her when I was little, in mirrors or windows. There were times I could convince myself it was a shadow, but other times..." She swallows. "I dreamed about her recently. There was this burning smell, like someone was lighting candles. Then something *bit* me. When I woke up, I was bleeding. Dark blood. Almost black." She eyes the cut warily. "It didn't look like that before. It changed."

"When was this dream?"

"Yesterday. The day Finn went missing."

Their gazes meet, and something unnamable flickers in Morgan's eyes.

For an instant, it almost looks like fear.

But then she snaps to her feet, stalking across the room to the kitchen. "You need to treat that with a compound of turmeric, yarrow, lavender, and sage. Sea salt too." Morgan gestures to the island in the middle of the kitchen. "Get up there."

Briar scrunches her nose. "What? No."

"Pom-Poms," Morgan sighs with exasperation. "That cut's infected. Just let me help."

Eyeing her warily, Briar climbs atop the counter, while Morgan dumps herbs onto a shiny brass scale. She tips the contents into a white marble bowl before grinding with a matching pestle.

"I'm just gonna clean it first," Morgan announces, dipping a cloth in water and winding it around her fingers.

Briar nods as Morgan curls a hand behind her knee, extending her leg. Morgan's grip is featherlight, and her nails send a shiver of goose bumps along the delicate skin. In the quiet, Briar's cheeks burn as she realizes that she just gave Morgan Parker-Blake a confession that she's never been able to offer to Astrid. Or Kai.

Or Finn.

Maybe, she reasons, it's because Morgan already despises her. So there's nothing between them to ruin.

"By the way"—Morgan's voice lowers as her cloth-covered hand strokes Briar's calf—"I don't think you're crazy at all."

Briar snaps her gaze to Morgan's, something instantly warming inside her. Finn told her that once too. But it feels different coming from Morgan's mouth, one that's usually dripping with disdain. The affirmation loosens the bolts on her secrets like a coat of oil, and for the first time in a while, she feels a little less afraid.

"When we were in your room, your mirrors were covered," Morgan broaches as she stirs the bowl of paste. "Is it because of her?"

Briar nods, watching as Morgan spreads the composite on a thin strip of gauze. "She wouldn't stop showing up. But earlier this year, I looked in the mirror, and it was *only* her. I wasn't—I wasn't there at all." She curls her nails into her palms, stomach souring at the memory. "I didn't want to see that ever again. So I stopped looking."

Morgan studies her for a moment. Then she unthreads her belt from her shorts before handing it to Briar.

"Bite on this," Morgan warns. "This is gonna sting like a bitch."

Briar sighs but leans forward anyway, arranging the strip of black leather between her teeth. Her breath hitches when Morgan's eyes flutter to her mouth, lingering for a beat too long. The air in the kitchen feels suddenly hazy, the storm cracking against the glass.

"Ready?"

Briar has barely begun to nod before Morgan winds the gauze.

Razor-sharp pain surges through her calf, and she groans loudly around the leather in her mouth. She folds at the waist, watching Morgan's long fingers deftly wrap her wound, too consumed by agony to notice any butterflies from the contact this time.

"Breathe," Morgan demands. "C'mon, it can't be *that* bad, Pom-Poms."

Still hunched over, Briar spits the belt into her lap.

"This should have been done *right* away," Morgan continues. "Use this ointment once daily. If the cut gets worse, call me."

"What *is* it?" Briar asks, breath slowly returning. "Why did it change shape? And how do you know so much about it?"

But Morgan doesn't answer those questions either. Instead, she smooths the bandage over Briar's calf before bending to blow soft puffs of air directly onto it. Her tongue snakes out to moisten her full dark lips between breaths, and Briar can't ignore the unexpected heat that blossoms low in her stomach.

"What does she look like?" Morgan asks, hands still cupping Briar's leg. "The dead woman."

Briar slides her gaze away, that clawing hesitation returning.

"Tell me," Morgan continues softly, as if she can sense it. Her thumb ghosts over Briar's knee in delicate strokes. Coaxing for her answer. "I just want to know."

Briar's pulse seems to spin as she searches for the words.

"She has long hair," she finally says. "Her skin is peeling, gray and purple. She . . . she's missing an eye, and part of her nose. There's a dark hole in her face, but it doesn't go through to the other side—it's an abyss. Like a wormhole under her skin."

Something shifts in Morgan's stare; her throat bobs. But she still doesn't move away, doesn't stop the slow dance of her fingers over Briar's skin. Higher up now, along the outside of her thigh. Like Morgan knows there are more truths she's yet to pull loose.

"Her teeth are black," Briar continues. "She always wears a white dress, but it's covered in dirt and blood. And she's dripping water, like she stepped out of the ocean. She looks like she's from a horror movie." Her voice drops to a whisper. "She's the scariest thing I've ever seen."

Briar absorbs the strange panicked expression woven into Morgan's sharp features. Her full brows are tightly knitted, cheekbones knifelike as she sucks the inside of her mouth. Then, without warning, Morgan steps back. A rush of cold air replaces her hand as she busies herself with cleaning up.

"You know what this vision means," Briar accuses over the sound of rain. "Tell me, Morgan, what is—?"

"It's not a vision," Morgan interrupts, whirling. Lightning flashes, searing the room. "And it's not a hallucination. What you saw is your wraith."

"My—my what?" Briar twists her face in confusion. "What are you talking about?"

Thunder rips through the air, swallowing her words.

"A person's wraith," Morgan finally says, "shows them exactly how they're going to die."

PART THREE
MIXED TIDE

Resignedly beneath the sky
The melancholy waters lie.
So blend the turrets and shadows there
That all seem pendulous in air,
While from a proud tower in the town
Death looks gigantically down.

EDGAR ALLAN POE, "The City in the Sea"

CHAPTER FOURTEEN
FINN

The first time Finn Adler saw Briar Winters, he thought, *this is what an angel looks like.*

It was a silly idea. He didn't believe in God—not even at five—but when Briar walked into his kindergarten class with gold curls down her back, he could only stare like she was something holy.

Her name is Briar Winters, Mrs. Kerrigan said before her arrival around winter break. *She was part of Loch Creek Primary last year, but something very sad happened to her family. Briar doesn't talk much, but she's a sweet girl. Let's make her feel welcome.*

As it turned out, *doesn't talk much* meant Briar didn't say anything. At all.

The other kids didn't mind. Kai and Astrid dragged her into games of tag on the playground, chattered to her constantly. Maybe one day she'd talk back, and maybe she wouldn't. Her presence alone was more than enough for them to call her a friend.

As for Finn, he mostly watched her coloring pictures, combing through books, never uttering a word.

But he knew she had so much to say.

Briar's silence reminded him of all the words trapped inside his own throat. Finn often felt like there was a yo-yo wound up in his chest, one that cinched whenever he dwelled on all the ways he was different. Other kids had moms who remembered to pick them up at school, dads who weren't buried in the ground. That yo-yo pulled tightest at home, pinching with every reminder of his mother's anger until he had no choice but to bury his face in his pillow and let out a scream to unravel the strings.

He wondered if Briar's heart hurt from the tangled knots too.

Finn couldn't explain why, but the idea of Briar choking on silent sadness made his own ribs ache more. He wished they could both tug it loose.

And at recess on the last day of school, he decided to try. He gently took Briar's hand, inviting her up from the blacktop where she was drawing a flower with a fat piece of chalk.

A circle, with six little petals inside.

Blue dust exploded between their palms as he led her around the brick building, where he turned and said, "I think we should be friends."

She blinked at him in a way that seemed to say, *We already are*.

"*Best* friends," he clarified. "Like you and Astrid. You can have more than one best friend, you know."

Briar seemed to consider this before shaking her head, her pigtails swaying.

"Why not?" Finn crossed his arms. "I already know a lot about you. Things best friends would know."

She squinted at him.

"I know you're really good at drawing," he said. "You can jump rope better than everyone. Your favorite color is pink, and your mom always packs celery sticks with peanut butter for your lunch even though you don't like them."

Briar's lips twitched in the smallest grin.

"You live in a big house with a pool and a slide," he continued. "And you used to have a twin brother, but you don't anymore."

At that, her smile vanished. Two pink crescent moons appeared on her cheeks.

"His name was Riley. He had the same hair as you." Finn studied her. "I think you miss him a lot. That's why you're sad all the time."

Briar's chest heaved with shallow breaths. Anxiety spiked inside him.

"It's okay," he rushed to add. "My dad is dead. I'm sad a lot too." *We're the same*, he wanted to tell her.

But Briar's lashes fluttered, eyes glassy and red, and his throat swelled with panic as she started to walk away. This wasn't his plan; he didn't mean to make her cry.

"Wait, Briar, don't go." His pulse raced like a rabbit's. "I know a trick. It helps when you're really sad. Or scared. Or angry. Just—just watch." He swallowed. "I'll show you."

And before he could change his mind, Finn shut his eyes and let out a raw scream.

The trees rustled with startled birds, and shame instantly flooded his chest. He shouldn't have done that. Surely, he'd scared her away. But when he peeked through his lashes, Briar was only staring, and any humiliation evaporated as he realized: She was waiting to see what he would do next.

Sucking in a breath, Finn let out a longer scream, holding her gaze this time. Watching for any signs of apprehension. Briar only continued to study him, unflinching eyes never leaving his face.

In the heavy silence that followed, her eyebrows tightened. Her throat bobbed, lips skewing to the side.

Confidence surging inside him, Finn screamed once more.

But this time—*this time* was different. Because Briar's jaw loosened.

And a high-pitched, keening wail tore from her lungs.

Finn froze. The sound pierced his brain, drenched with something primal and nameless. His hair blew off his forehead at the sheer force of her scream, which seemed to go on and on forever. As if Briar had been hoarding months' worth of blistering grief, and once she let it out, she couldn't begin to stop.

Her scream didn't quiet, not even when several teachers sprinted toward them. It was only when Mrs. Kerrigan's hands clasped her shoulders that Briar fell silent.

"Adler," another teacher snapped, "what did you do?"

Panic gripped him at the accusatory tone. "N-nothing, I didn't do—"

"Finn."

His gaze slammed right back to Briar's. *Did she just—?*

"Finn."

He froze at the tiny rasp of her voice. *Briar's* voice. After months and months of wondering what it sounded like, there it was.

And it was wrapped around his name.

Finn realized he didn't care about getting in trouble. Didn't care about anything except Briar's voice, the way that one word felt more comforting than any others he'd heard in his life. The way even her scream felt like a blanket or a stuffed animal.

Like whatever clawed thing that was inside him might just be inside her too.

Briar disappeared around the corner with their teacher, so she never saw his face. Couldn't see the way he didn't protest the trip to the principal's office and didn't complain when they made him sit on a cold bench for the rest of the afternoon.

She never knew that Finn only smiled.

And silently swore to make sure nothing bad happened to her ever again.

~

The warped version of Finn's childhood bedroom is gouged with numbers, a frantic equation to save the life of a girl he just can't seem to reach.

He's been keeping track of his phone calls to Briar with tally marks on the walls, desperately seeking proof that she survives her birthday. It's how he starts every conversation now: *What's today's date?* But her answer is always rooted in the past, a fraction of moments that have already happened.

The solution, Finn hypothesizes, is in the tides. He's set up a measuring system carved from driftwood, searching for the current that will allow him to talk to her *now*. But she only answers the phone when the sea has receded from the blackened shore.

Low tide, he's certain, is the past.

Which makes high tide the future. *After* her birthday.

Where she's either not speaking to him because of graduation—or because she's dead.

But whenever Finn tries to steer the conversation toward a warning or dares to bring up Riley, Briar hangs up in tears, leaving him alone with his pounding heart. It's not like he can tell her he's calling from an infinite cavern of time. Everything is too precarious for a move like that. One wrong word, and he risks losing her forever.

He needs to find a different way in. Perhaps, in another timeline, he has.

Finn tosses a seashell to the ground, abandoning a sketch of a cube. Block universe theory. *The beginning of time is here,* he can practically hear his physics teacher saying, *and the end of time is here. Inside is every second that has ever or will ever exist.*

"If I return to the past, I become part of the past. Yet the past can never be changed," Finn mutters as he starts for the kitchen. He flings open a cabinet. "But I'm sure as fuck gonna try."

Finn rummages until he finds a warped can of unidentifiable food. The shelves rarely offer more than moldy bread and rotten meat, but sometimes, the kitchen can be more generous. It'll show him other things—fresh fruit or cheese. It varies by the hour, the minute.

Just like the rest of the In-Between.

Nothing is certain here. The cottage morphs with the tide, cracks marring the walls in the morning and disappearing by nightfall. Black moss slithers up the ceiling at noon, receding after a few hours. Outside seems to be the only constant, the shore forever that limitless gray, that red moon tucked against the horizon. It's a place of forgetting and remembering, an infinite loop of time, folded between stars.

At the ritual, the witch warned him that braving the In-Between would be like falling into dream after dream. She told him not to trust his own eyes, that the sea would attempt to wear him down. That the dark thing hungering for Briar on her birthday might be waiting for him too.

That there's a chance he slips into nothingness, and he'll never save her at all.

Snatching a dull knife, Finn works the can open and steps onto the deck. He dumps the contents into a bowl, whistling into the stale air.

Moments later, a coywolf emerges from the dunes.

There must be an entire pack surrounding the beach, but Finn has only ever seen this one—a large male coywolf with a heart-shaped opal patch on his chest. Finn has taken to leaving scraps outside, hoping the routine will help him feel less alone with the weight of his failures.

"You need a name," he murmurs, as the coywolf bounds up the patio. For a fleeting moment, Finn thinks back to second grade when he and Astrid found a stray puppy in the dunes and he begged his mother to let him keep it. *He can be my responsibility*, he lobbied. *You won't have to raise him.*

The unspoken part cracked like ice against his teeth. *The same way you're not raising me.*

But his mother wouldn't allow it, and the puppy went up for adoption instead. Finn spent countless nights wondering where it ended up, if it was sleeping beside a boy who might be able to offer it more than he ever could.

Finn swallows the memory. In the distance, the ocean roils against the shore, as though a sea god is stirring it with a trident. He glances down at the hungry coywolf.

"Neptune," he says. "That's what I'll call you." He bends, daring to give a tiny scratch along the animal's ears, and warmth fills his ribs when the coywolf nuzzles into his hand. "We'll do our best."

Finn leaves Neptune to eat, then heads for the living room before sinking into the torn couch. The walls whisper as he reaches for the rusted phone, glancing out the window at the receding shoreline. Low tide. Briar's past. Maybe this time he'll string the right words together; maybe this time his warning will stick.

Briar answers on the first ring. "Hi."

"What's today's date?"

She sighs. "Finn, it's three a.m."

"How many days until graduation?"

"Fiii-iiin."

Finn's chest swells around a lonely ache. He hates the sound of her voice in this distorted room. Because he could be talking to a dead girl right now, one who's breathing his name and sending echoes of haunted butterflies through his bones.

"Graduation is *tomorrow*," she finally says. "Technically, it's today."

Today? He bolts upright, thoughts racing and racing for the correct thing to say. He has to get it right—he *has* to.

This could be his only chance.

"Briar," he starts. "We need to talk about your birthday."

He can hear her apprehension. "That's over two months away."

"I know, but—" He swallows a burst of unexpected pain in his throat. "I was thinking, instead of that party your parents are planning, what if we did something, just us?"

"I wish," she says, but the phrase isn't lighthearted. It's hollow. The way she sounded on the Ferris wheel, insisting her parents wouldn't let her leave Loch Creek. He clenches his teeth.

"I'm serious," Finn tries. "You and me, Astrid and Kai. No one else. We—" He coughs around something metallic and wet, and it's suddenly a struggle to talk. "We could go—"

"*Finn*. I don't want to think about my birthday right now."

Her clipped tone silences him. It's like a cat's hiss, a snake's rattle. A warning that she's seconds away from lashing out—or shutting down.

Abort mission, he thinks hopelessly.

"Okay," he mutters. Defeat flattens him along with confused fear. Because he could swear a second ago his throat was nearly sewn shut, his warning trapped inside.

Like something didn't want him to say it at all.

A chill shudders up his spine, and the cottage grows darker. He has to keep trying.

"Briar. Will you promise me something?"

"Hmm?"

"If something happens tonight... after graduation. Swear you'll talk to me about it."

He can practically hear the pink creeping into her cheeks. "Like... like what?"

Like we give in to this magnetic thing that's been brewing our whole lives, he wants to blurt. *Like I kiss you and time fucking stops. Like I fall asleep the happiest I've ever been and wake up to you crying that you're going to disappear into the water.*

Like I try to stop it from happening and fail in the worst way you can imagine.

"Just promise," Finn says instead. "No matter what. You're not gonna shut me out." He swallows. "Swear on our friendship. On your life—no, on *mine*."

"Finn," she laughs. "Jeez. Okay. I swear."

He exhales, dragging a hand through his hair. He has no way of knowing if the words will hold, if she's even real, if she's just going to die again and again but—

It's a start.

"Finn," she repeats, suddenly quiet. "I'm scared. I wish you were with me right now."

Too many discordant thoughts jump to life at the idea of being in her room. He can easily picture them at ten, a chessboard resting between them. Thirteen, Briar's textbook splayed over their barely brushing knees. Seventeen, Finn watching her put on lip gloss, suddenly consumed with the question of what she'd taste like if he kissed her.

That year, everything Briar did had new meaning. If she bit her lip while thinking, Finn immediately thought about sinking his own teeth into that exact spot, and every time they'd accidentally touch, it was like an electric shock. He felt delirious, because it was just *Briar*—a girl who used to catch fireflies with him in the humid twilight.

Briar, the only person he'd want for the rest of his life.

And perhaps that was the most terrifying part. The idea that his heart was cracking open, creating space he didn't know existed. The idea that he could offer himself and she might not want him in the same way.

The idea that somewhere, he was still a scared boy in a beachside cottage, wondering if something had malfunctioned in his soul and rendered him impossible to love.

"Scared of what?" A knot tightens in Finn's chest as he races through all the possible things she could say. "What do you mean?"

"It's never going to be like this again." She exhales. "You're *leaving*. And I'll be here."

She's talking about California. Berkeley.

"We'll talk every day," he says, and his ribs crack with the weight of the lie.

But he imagines it anyway: His dorm instead of this rotten cottage, her face lighting up his phone screen. Briar, stepping through the gate at the Oakland airport, kissing him beneath a grid of palm trees. Finn can picture it as though it's a memory instead of a dream, and he swallows the aching awareness that there's so much more they've already lost.

"How many times a day?"

Finn pinches the bridge of his nose beneath his glasses, tries to sound normal, like he's not on the verge of falling apart. "As many times as you want."

"I'm annoying. I'll double text."

Tears dampen his lashes, and he swipes at them. "Well, I'll *triple* text."

A pause lingers. Static along celestial wires. "Promise you won't forget me?"

Finn squeezes his eyes. Her words are knives, scraping and scraping at his heart. Because she sounds like she's right next to him, but she's so far away—light-years and parsecs.

She won't ever be right next to him again.

"Never," he grinds out.

"It doesn't matter anyway." Briar's words slur with sleep. "I'll never get out of Loch Creek."

He freezes at that. "What?"

"I just have a feeling." Her whisper is hazy with exhaustion. "Like I'm gonna die here."

"Hey—Briar, no." Finn snaps the phone closer. "*No.*"

"Sometimes," she murmurs, "I just want to disappear."

"*Stop*. Don't say shit like that. Don't—"

Finn swings his gaze to the antique clock as it hits him.

The hands, forever frozen at 9:30 p.m. The exact time she died.

A biting cold chills his bones as he remembers her blood-soaked sundress billowing in the wind. He presses the phone closer, realizing she's gone silent.

"Briar. Are you awake?"

In the quiet, Finn maps her every inhale and exhale. Signs of life. And then an idea occurs to him. N1 sleep. Alpha waves and the lull of dreams.

"Briar." He swallows. "Can you hear me?"

Nothing. His palms sweat, voice dipping to the faintest whisper.

"I need to tell you something."

Pain blooms in the back of his throat. He swallows, ignoring it.

"The night of your birthday party, you need to stay home." He coughs, trying to rid his mouth of the sudden ache. "Something bad is going to happen. There's something hungry in the water. There are evil people in Loch Creek. People you know. People you wouldn't suspect." Finn's hand shakes as sour liquid seeps through his teeth. The roof of his mouth starts to burn. "These people—they believe in a prophecy about twins. The story is in my backpack. In the inside pocket. Briar—please read it." Tears sting his eyes; his voice breaks. "Don't go to your party. *Stay home.*"

And then Finn drops the phone with a clatter.

Liquid swells inside his throat. He bends, sputtering and gagging as his chest constricts. God, there's something *in* there. He can feel it, slippery, lodged behind his tongue.

Leaning forward, Finn reaches into his mouth. Nausea flips inside him as his fingers close around something soft. He pulls. And pulls. And pulls. *What the f—?*

He stares, horrified, as he tugs loose a string of blackened seaweed.

The flowering plants are knotted together like a chain, and he gags at the slick texture, silently counting. *Six... seven... eight... nine.*

He reaches twenty by the time his mouth is empty, and he flings the lumpy seaweed to the floor. Turning, Finn spits sand and blood, breath heaving. What the *hell* just happened?

Anxiety climbs higher in his chest. The room spins. White lights dance at the corners of his vision. *Five things,* he thinks as he swipes a hand over his mouth. *Category is... deities of death. Hades. Osiris. Hel. Whiro. Plu—*

What's this?

He snaps straight up at the sound of a snarling voice.

Right against his ear.

Shadows consume the walls, sucking the light from his surroundings. The floorboards groan and creak in protest. His blood turns to frost.

A boy who thinks he can tame a wolf.

"No—no," he mutters under his breath, clasping his ears.

A boy who thinks he can save a broken girl.

That *sound.* Grinding. Rattling. Like two seashells being scraped together, sharpened into a blade. Even without ever hearing this voice before, Finn knows exactly what's talking to him.

You can't.

Possessive anger courses through him. "Yes," he bites, "I can."

I sing to her when she dreams, whispers that voice of glass. *I've tasted her blood. Her soul is rotten at its core; her heart is covered in urchin spines and fountain moss. She has always belonged to me.*

Finn palms his ears again, desperate for quiet. But it's pointless. The words aren't being whispered in his ear; they're coming from inside his skull.

Inside *him*.

I will make her mine again, the voice growls. *And I will make you watch.*

CHAPTER FIFTEEN
BRIAR

2 Days and 5 Hours Until Briar's Birthday Party

Loch Creek Artists' Society is washed in shadows. The perfect backdrop for a heist.

Since she left Morgan's apartment, Briar's pulse hasn't stopped racing with fresh determination. She texted Kai and Astrid before she even had a fully formed plan: *Going to see if I can find the missing pages from that town deed.*

But the message made her sound more confident than she feels now, the word *wraith* sucking on her thoughts like a leech. The cut on her leg burns; her eye throbs with renewed purpose. As if *she's* watching, hungrily anticipating the day she and Briar will be the same. Briar averts her gaze from the glass doors as she steps inside the art gallery.

She won't give death a chance to stare back.

The Artists' Society is housed in the city center and shares a basement with Old Town Hall next door. If Briar can reach the stairwell unseen with her mom's key, she can dodge the security guard in the town hall's lobby—and access the archives room on the second floor. Because the missing pages from the deed are more than a clue. Finding them would demonstrate that even if she drove Finn away, she can do something to bring him back.

She'll prove it to Kai and Astrid. And to herself.

Briar checks that no one's watching and darts toward the stairwell—but halts at her mother's favorite gold-framed Fidelia Bridges painting. The one with the sparrows fluttering atop snow-flecked branches.

The one with a menacing crack down the center.

"What?" she murmurs.

It's like someone chiseled it with a hammer. Her frown deepens as she traces the fissure onto the wall, where it climbs up the plaster—splayed like grasping fingers, reaching and reaching for something unseen.

Briar recalls her mother's crooked mermaid painting, the damaged selkie statue. The broken window at the courthouse, the potholes in the street. Little anxious dots cross her mind, connecting like lines on a graph.

If she didn't know better, she'd say Loch Creek is cracking in two.

"Hello, Briar."

Briar whirls, finding Mayor Caldwell standing beside Patrice Weatherstone, Loch Creek's town clerk. Like Caldwell, Patrice was a fixture of Briar's childhood, always appearing at her parents' dinner parties and gallery openings. Others might describe Patrice as sweet and charismatic, but Briar doesn't like how Patrice always tilts her head at her, as if silently clucking, *Oh, you poor thing.* It makes her wonder what exactly she and her mother discuss over their afternoon teas, if Patrice has been spoon-fed fairy tales about a girl made of glass who saw her brother die.

"Good afternoon, Mayor," Briar says, summoning a smile. "Hi, Patrice."

"What brings you in?" Caldwell asks. "Your position doesn't begin until next week."

Briar's throat dries up at the thought. *If I live that long*, she almost spits, but instead she scrambles for an excuse. "I'm here to see my mom!"

"Looking forward to your birthday party?" Patrice grins, and there's something suddenly strange about the shape of her mouth. "Your parents have truly outdone themselves."

"Yeah, it'll be great. . . ."

She grows distracted by how Patrice's lips are drooping, as though her smile has been painted with too-wet watercolors. Briar blinks several times, and when Patrice grins again, she can't be sure whether she imagined it.

Briar flips her gaze to Caldwell to find him leering behind round glasses, as though he's picking her apart.

"It's a funny thing," he says, "to watch a person grow up. I remember when you were a child, coming here with your parents. Now look at you. A blossoming woman."

Briar's cheeks burn as she fights to hold her conciliatory expression, at war with the discomfort ensnaring her. She fleetingly wonders what might happen if she dropped her polite ruse and shoved past him to the records room, removing herself from his patronizing stare. Why, she can't help but wonder, do girls have to wrench their faces into smiles and say *thank you* when someone makes them feel like they aren't a person at all?

"All of Loch Creek has observed your coming of age," Caldwell continues. "It's a true privilege to bear witness to a person becoming who they are. And one worthy of celebration."

Every cell in Briar's body screams to put distance between them. His voice is eerily serene, and he's too close to her. And Patrice is still smiling and fidgeting with that folder beneath her arm—

Wait. Is that…?

Forgetting the mayor's words, Briar narrows her eyes. "Is that a lighthouse?"

Patrice glances down. "Yes. It's an infrastructure proposal for a new lighthouse on the northern shore. In fact, this is a project you'll be assisting with."

Briar peers at the sketch of the lighthouse on the cover, squinting at the windows of the lantern room. It's faint, but it looks like a small circle with petals inside—a daisy wheel.

The same symbol that's etched into the book from Finn's bag.

That icy suspicion returns, dots reappearing in her mind. Her fingers itch with desperation. She *needs* to find the rest of that town deed.

"We can't wait to have you with us at Old Town Hall," Patrice continues, her voice like silk.

"You'll be right at home," Caldwell adds, and this time, his face looks different too. But not his mouth.

His eyes.

The pale skin beneath his lashes is suddenly flaky and withering, as if threatening to crumble off his face entirely. Scabs mar his hollow cheekbones, plum purple and crusting at the edges. He doesn't appear to notice and keeps eyeing her with that hungry smile that makes her want to throw up.

Then, just as she thinks she'll actually vomit on the marble floor, that voice rattles her skull. Seashells scraping against one another. Glass on glass.

Winters girl, it purrs. *Don't be afraid of someone who is far weaker than you.*

A strange sense of calm settles inside her, and with it comes a drive to prove what she's seeing. It's not a vision. Not a hallucination. This is real, *this is real—*

Briar holds up a finger before reaching for her phone.

"My mom's texting," she lies with a feigned roll of her eyes. With the screen angled away from Caldwell, she hits the camera button and snaps a photo.

But when she glances back at the mayor, it's to find his face completely normal once more. Briar shoves her phone into her pocket and forces herself to smile. She knows it was real. She must have gotten the picture in time.

"Gotta go!" she exclaims. "Mom's expecting me."

Before they can say anything else, she sprints down the hall toward her mother's office. She might not be able to reach the records room now, but there must be other answers here.

Puzzle pieces whirl inside her, colliding like bumper cars at the places they don't fit. Cracked paintings and shriveling skin. A daisy wheel on the spell book, a daisy wheel on a lighthouse. Where has she seen that symbol before? She *knows* she's seen it, can nearly conjure the six petals, the perfect circle, the—

"Mom," Briar breathes, flying into her dim office.

"Briar!" Her mother pulls off her reading glasses in surprise. "What are you doing h—?"

Briar snatches a legal pad from her mother's desk and roughly yanks a pen from the adjacent cup, barely registering when the entire thing tips over. Ignoring her mother's surprised cry, she scribbles a daisy wheel in bleeding ink.

"Do you know what this symbol is?"

Her mother knits her brow. "Briar, are you feeling alright?"

She shoves down her bubbling annoyance at *that* question. *Briar, are you feeling alright? Briar, are you ill? Briar, have you been taking your—*

"Mom," she tries again. "What does it mean?"

"Sweetheart, I don't know." She tucks a stray reddish curl behind her ear, itching at her scalp. "Does it mean something to *you*?"

"It's going to be on the new lighthouse in town. But I've seen it before."

"Oh." Her mother skews her mouth to the side. "Well, then it's probably the state flower. You know how patriotic Mayor Caldwell can be."

"A mayflower? No. This isn't a mayflower, Mom."

Her mother sighs. "Briar, I have a scheduled tea with the archivists in ten minutes. Can we talk about this later? But since you're here, I have a question about your party."

Briar exhales a growl of frustration and flops into the chair across from her mother's desk. Her *fucking party*, as if she could stand to put ribbons in her hair while Finn is missing and something hellish is vying for her soul. But sure. Let's launch fireworks off a yacht and pretend that the entire world isn't wrong.

Her phone buzzes at her hip, and she glances down, finding a text from Morgan.

How is it?

The cut, she means. Briar should have changed the dressing before coming here, but her mind has been tangled with everything Morgan shared. Water witches and safe havens. Elemental magic and covens. Wraiths and looming death.

A wraith is your dead self mirrored back at you, Morgan explained earlier. *Many times, people see their wraiths right before they die. They've been known to visit hospitals or places where someone's in the midst of sudden physical trauma, like a car crash. But on rare occasions, a person might see their wraith for years.*

Briar presses her palm to her lashes as her eye throbs again. As if that nightmarish woman is prying it loose from the inside.

"Briar? *Briar*—did you hear a word I just said?"

Briar blinks. "Sorry, what?"

"Your party." Her mother's voice is cut with exasperation. "The caterer wants us to choose between oysters or bruschetta for the appetizers. Do you have a preference?"

Briar glares at her. "Is that a joke?"

"Excuse me?"

"Mom—god!—bruschetta, *obviously*. Finn's allergic to shellfish, how could you for—?"

The words fly from Briar's mouth before she remembers.

Her mother has no idea who Finn is.

Dropping her gaze, Briar works her nail into one of her cuticles. She can feel the heat of her mother's stare as she gouges the paper-thin flesh.

"Briar. For the last time. Have you been taking your medication, yes or no?"

She chews her lip, remembering Morgan's whisper earlier. *You're not crazy.* She peers at her mother through a film of curls and wonders what she'd say if Briar told her that all the terrible things in her head might be as tangible as the room they're in right now.

"If I check the bottles at home," her mother continues, "will I find them full?"

"No."

"If you're fibbing, I'll have no choice but to—"

"I'm taking them." She swallows, throat dry. "I promise."

In the stretch of skeptical silence, Briar recalls being smaller, curled in her mother's lap while listening to a bedtime story. For a moment, she contemplates asking, *Why didn't you ever believe me?* But it would be a pointless question—one she already knows the answer to. Because a girl with otherworldly whispers in her head isn't the daughter they imagined. It's always been easier for them to dress her up like a doll than to admit that something with sharp teeth and talons might have clawed its way inside her a long time ago.

But perhaps the worse truth is that Briar has quietly played the role her entire life to avoid admitting the same thing.

“Alright,” her mother finally acquiesces. “Bruschetta it is.”

She turns to her open leather planner, pushing one hand through her curls—

And comes away with a fistful of hair. Briar’s eyes widen.

“Mom, are you okay?” she asks.

But her mother only smiles. “Fine,” she clips, tucking her hand beneath her desk.

Out of sight, out of mind. Of course. Everything ugly beneath the surface, hidden away.

Like mother, like daughter.

Briar charts the fine lines around her mother’s eyes, the creases along the side of her mouth. Wrinkles and divots that aren’t usually there, thanks to the fillers she’s been getting for the past decade or so. Briar floats her gaze over the spot where her mother’s curls just came loose, and her stomach tightens. A small patch of scalp is visible, seashell white and flaking with dead skin.

“What if we canceled the party?” Briar asks suddenly. “We could have cake at home, you, me, and Dad. Watch a movie. Board games or something. What do you think?”

For a split second, Briar almost thinks her mother will say yes. That maybe she’s tired of pretending too. That she’d be able to accept Briar without all the glittering disguises, that simply being together could finally, *finally* be enough.

But her mother’s face twists in disbelief, a bemused huff escaping her mouth. “Don’t be ridiculous,” she dismisses. “We’d lose our deposit.”

Something cold spills inside Briar at that. She thinks of third grade, the time Finn’s mother neglected to sign his field trip permission slip, the way his face crumbled when he realized he couldn’t board the bus with the rest of them. How he stared at the wall with reddened eyes and muttered, *I wish I had parents like yours*.

Even then, she wanted to take his hand and say, *My mom forgets me too*.

“Right,” Briar says, forcing a smile to mask the hurt. “See you at home.”

Slipping back into the shadowed lobby, Briar casts a look around before grabbing her phone. She clears Morgan’s incessant texts and pulls up Google to type *mayflower*.

She knew it was wrong when her mother said it—because all the mayflower pictures that pop up show a flower with five petals.

Briar rummages through her bag until her fingers close around the spell book. She inspects the daisy wheels on the cover, menacing from each page.

These flowers don't have five petals.

They have six.

CHAPTER SIXTEEN
BRIAR

2 Days and 4 Hours Until Briar's Birthday Party

Briar dashes from the gallery to the duck-lined Jeep Wrangler her parents bought for her last year, rain pelting the top of her umbrella. Once inside, she flings it to the passenger floor and whips out her phone to call Kai.

Her pulse quickens with all the reasons he might not answer. Each ring tightens the knots in her stomach, and when she gets his voicemail, she slumps against the steering wheel in defeat. Briar imagines Kai packing all his books and film posters into cardboard boxes, too busy looking forward to peer back at her. Soon he'll be gone. Astrid too. And all she'll have left are the lies that drove them apart.

"Hey," she tells his voicemail, "I couldn't get the papers. I'm on my way home. Can you and Astrid come over? Maybe there's something we missed." She swallows, digging for the right words. "Kai, I'm so sorry about last night. I—"

A harsh banging on the passenger window jars the stormy quiet. Briar swings her head up—and panic seizes her at the rain-drenched figure beside her car: matted hair plasters her shoulders, obscuring her face.

She's here. Not in glass, not in a reflection. *Outside.*

Briar drops the phone into her lap with a wrenched gasp—and then immediately lets out a rush of air as she realizes—

It's only Morgan.

She fumbles for her phone with one hand, unlocking the door with the other. "Just call me," she mutters to Kai's voicemail. She hangs up and whirls. "Morgan! Don't do shit like that!"

Climbing into the car, Morgan slams the door behind her. "You didn't answer my texts."

"I'm sorry, I didn't realize we were dating," Briar snorts.

"Hilarious," Morgan says. "Somehow I doubt you'll still have your sparkling sense of humor if you're bedridden from an infection." She nods toward Briar's bandaged leg. "How is it?"

Briar huffs, propping her foot to peek inside the bandage. The sight of that petal-shaped cut crusted with pale green pus should turn her stomach. But after everything else, this decaying wound is starting to feel like the least of her problems.

"It's the same as it was earlier," she says, snapping the bandage back. She turns, finding Morgan still staring. And her gaze, saturated with concern, puts a note of bravery inside Briar. Makes her bold enough to say, "Can I ask you something?"

Morgan narrows her eyes. "I suppose."

"Do you ever feel like there's something wrong with this place?" Briar asks. "Things that don't add up? How Loch Creek is sometimes a tourist gold mine, and other times it looks like this?" She gestures across the street to the broken courthouse window. "A town that's so proud of its history but buries its tragedies." She swallows, gritting her teeth. "Even though those are part of its history too."

Morgan shifts in her seat. "What brought all this on?"

"I'm supposed to start working at Mayor Caldwell's office next week. I wasn't exactly psyched about it to begin with, and now . . ." Briar unlocks her phone. "Here, I'll just show you. Look at this. . . ." Her words evaporate as she glances at the photo she took of Mayor Caldwell.

Because his face is completely devoid of markings.

Her heart plummets to her stomach. No. She *saw* it.

"Pom-Poms." Morgan strains to look. "What's going on?"

"No," Briar mutters, tapping the screen. "I didn't make it up. It was *real.* It—"

Her words morph into a startled yelp as she activates the live image.

And Mayor Caldwell's flesh crumbles into the scaly purple scabs that she remembers.

"What the f—?" Morgan snatches the phone, replaying the photo. Again. And again. Until finally, her gaze swings to Briar's. "When was this?"

"Just now," she says, heart pounding. "Something weird happened to Patrice's face too. And my mom—her hair is coming out. The gallery wall is cracked; there's a sinkhole on Abbott Street. Loch Creek is falling apart."

Morgan is silent, mouth drawn in a line—and her quiet rekindles Briar's suspicions.

"You've noticed it too," she accuses. "More than that. You know *why.*"

Morgan looks out the window, jaw tightening. Briar leans forward with urgency.

"*Morgan.*" Briar tugs Morgan's arm, drawing her stare right back. Her rain-slick skin is smooth beneath Briar's palm, and she scrambles not to notice. "Remember our deal. You *said* you would help."

Morgan studies her a moment, as if her brain is racing with some unspoken debate. "Fine," she finally says. "Release your cheerleader death grip, for god's sake."

But Briar clocks Morgan's hand moving to the spot Briar just touched, almost like she misses her warmth. And for a moment, Briar can't help but think about a younger Morgan sitting alone in the cafeteria. How loaded glances always passed between them, as if another universe existed where they might've sat together instead.

Briar squashes the thought immediately. "Out with it."

"Alright." Morgan takes another steadying breath. "Remember how I said there are four main covens for each element? Well, there used to be one more. But their magic wasn't tied to anything terrestrial. They were called aether witches."

Briar's memory lights up, thinking of philosophy class in school. "The fifth element."

"Right—aether, void, quintessence. The general *stuff* that fills the space beyond our universe. That's what fueled their magic." Morgan gestures to the rain outside. "All witches keep parts of nature in balance, right? Water witches regulate tides, ward off tsunamis and hurricanes. But before aethers were pretty much wiped out, *they* regulated time."

At that, the back of Briar's neck prickles. An image of the Seaside Tavern restaurant receipt flutters to life in her mind alongside the memory of Rosemary's confused voice on the phone, not recognizing her own son's name.

Briar fixes Morgan with a pointed stare. "Wait. Could these kinds of witches *change* time?"

Morgan's heavy silence says more than any answer could.

"How is that even *possible*?" Briar adds, bewilderment buzzing inside her.

Morgan picks at a thread on her skirt. Like she knows she's sharing secrets that should stay buried. "Time is a lot more circular than anyone realizes. But people need time to be linear in order to function. So aether witches harnessed celestial energy to create the *perception* of linear time."

Briar's thoughts whirl faster than she can process them. In the quiet static of the rain, she can nearly conjure Finn's whisper. *Time is like a map. The present is where you are. And what you consider the past might be the future to someone else.*

"If time isn't really linear," Briar says, "then Finn is still *here* somewhere, even if mostly everyone has forgotten him. Could we—could we use aether magic to find him? Could you—"

"No. Don't even think about finishing that sentence."

Briar blinks. "But you know magic! Couldn't you—?"

"I don't know *that* kind of magic!" Morgan snaps, and Briar flinches at the sudden bite of her tone. Noticing, Morgan softens her voice, adding, "Look, most aethers vanished in the early 1700s. That's why the other covens convene during equinoxes for a ritual to maintain the straight line of time." She tilts her head. "Not as juicy of a rumor as killing bunnies in the woods, is it?"

"Are there *any* aethers left?" Briar begs, barely noticing the jab. "We need their help—"

"You don't get it—you wouldn't *want* their help," Morgan insists. "There's a reason they aren't in charge anymore—they became totally corrupted. They started dabbling in dark magic, harnessing energy from other worlds in hopes of obtaining longevity and wealth. But there's always a price for that shit. You can't wake an ancient evil and ask it for power without offering something in exchange."

Briar's pulse spikes at Morgan's words. *Longevity. Wealth.* She slides her gaze back to the art gallery in all its pristine marble. Suddenly she can't help but think of its walls like a wilting rose beneath a glass lid, and a million new questions burn behind her teeth.

"Morgan—"

"One more thing," she interrupts, "and this one's personal."

Briar falls quiet. "Alright. I'm listening."

"Right around the time Loch Creek was founded, an aether witch attempted a conjuring ritual that unleashed an evil entity from the oceanic underworld. The remaining covens had to come together to banish it, in a massive spell led by a high priestess water witch . . . named Doris Parker." She pins Briar with a serious stare. "Do you get what I'm saying?"

Briar narrows her eyes. Realization clicks into place. "Your ancestor led that spell."

"She did." Morgan swallows. "To stop anyone from using that dangerous magic ever again. Which is why I'm not about to start. I told you I'd help you—but *not* like that."

Briar slumps in her seat, heavy with defeat. She fleetingly pictures Morgan as a little girl, lacing up her ballet shoes and dreaming of a life that doesn't include Loch Creek. Understanding flattens inside her.

"It must be a lot of pressure," Briar says softly, "having that lineage."

Morgan huffs a dark laugh. "Yeah, tell me about it. Our coven fears that one day, another water witch will have to banish that entity again. That witch would become high priestess and continue Doris's legacy. Luckily for my mama, she had two daughters. Chances were better that at least one of them would be up for the challenge."

"She pit you and Nerissa against each other," Briar says.

"It was never a competition. I didn't want to be a witch. Rissa loved it. We took our places without ever being asked."

But Briar doesn't fully believe her. She recalls Morgan's expression the morning she had those flowers anonymously delivered, how Briar watched from her car to make sure she received them. Morgan's face was awash with surprise, as if she couldn't believe anyone might care about what she'd lost. Briar wonders if Morgan's entire personality—her smirking crimson mouth, her taunting stare—is a fortress to protect her from the taste of the word *failure*. And for the first time, looking at Morgan doesn't feel like staring down a person who could end her—but more like looking right at herself.

Briar shakes off the uneasy sensation, leaning forward. "Wait," she says. "If aethers are gone, how did Finn vanish in time? How is *any* of this happening?"

Morgan's mouth flattens, like she doesn't want to answer.

"*Morgan*," Briar says, her frustration returning. "Come on."

"Promise me something first," she says. "You won't ask me to do magic for you. Of any kind."

Briar narrows her eyes, so hungry for answers that she barely gives any thought to another promise she might end up breaking. "Fine. I promise. Tell me."

Morgan's breath rushes out as she pushes a hand through her hair. "I think there are still aether witches in Loch Creek, quietly scheming to reclaim their power. That spell book—I've been studying it, trying to crack the language. And I'm pretty sure that—"

Morgan swallows her own words, looking apprehensive. Desperation courses through Briar's veins, making her want to grab Morgan's face and shake all the answers loose.

"If aether witches are still here," Briar works out aloud, "then the evil they summoned is still here too. Isn't it?"

Morgan pulls in a breath and nods. "Not just evil," she says, "an *ancient* evil. Something that's being fed, kept alive for centuries." She slides her gaze down to Briar's leg. "There's this belief among witches that there are malevolent spirits caught in the folds of time. They're not fully in our world, but they can find their way in through dreams."

"Like the dream I had?" Briar's pulse hums; she points at her calf. "When I woke up with *this*?"

Morgan leans closer. "The saying goes like this: If one of these creatures draws your blood while you're asleep and your body remembers when you wake—it's a sign. It means you've been *claimed*."

Before Briar can respond, Morgan reaches over, long black nails ghosting over Briar's bare thigh. Inexplicable heat pools beneath her stomach as Morgan's touch slides lower, grazing the edge of her bandage. What Morgan said should drive a knife of fear through Briar, yet her panic is diluted by the warmth of Morgan's fingers, the proximity of their faces in the tight space of the car. The realization that if Briar tipped her head forward, she'd taste Morgan's next words.

"That cut isn't just a wound. It's a *marking*." Morgan's hand stills, eyes hardening. "And whatever gave it to you will ask for something in return."

CHAPTER SEVENTEEN

BRIAR

2 Days and 3 Hours Until Briar's Birthday Party

Briar slams her front door shut and calls Kai for the millionth time.

She's been trying the entire drive home from the art gallery, alternating between him and Astrid, but neither has been answering. A million what-ifs cascade through her mind, all leading to the same dead end: maybe it's already too late to repair what's breaking between them. She flips to their group text and sends an SOS emoji anyway, heading for the stairs.

"Briar? Is that you?"

She freezes at her father's voice from his study. She hadn't realized he was home.

"Can you come in here, please?"

Wincing at fresh pain in her calf, Briar heads down the hall and peeks through the half-open French doors, finding her father filing papers. He regards her with displeasure, and her shoulders instantly tense.

"I want to talk about your medication."

Briar's breath rushes out. "Did Mom call you the *second* I left? Jesus."

"If you're taking them like you say you are, they clearly aren't working."

Her father closes the file cabinet decisively. "Perhaps you're on the wrong dosage. Dr. Fuchs can probably prescribe something over the phone." He strides into the foyer, sharply motioning for her to follow up the stairs. "But he needs to know your weight."

Briar trails behind him. "I don't know. It's around—"

"No," he says, waiting in front of the guest bathroom. "We'll check right now."

Briar freezes, his words sinking in. A white glow spills from the narrow room, and the mirror beckons silently. She has to force herself to keep her eyes on her father's, not to let her stare pull toward the pool of black widening at the mirror's edge.

"I don't want to," she says in a voice smaller than she expects.

"Briar." Her father's tone softens. "I'm not trying to embarrass you. You need help. Talking about boys who don't exist. Irate outbursts. You can't want to live like that."

For a moment, she contemplates telling him she suspects she won't live much longer at all. That her nightmarish fate looms in the glass over his shoulder, leering with blackened teeth and drowned hair. Instead, she shakes her head in refusal.

He glances at his watch. "I have to be at the gallery in twenty minutes, I don't have time for a stand-off."

She chews the inside of her cheek. "Can't you bring the scale in the hall?"

"*Briar.*" He presses his fingers to his temple in a way that reminds her of the year she didn't speak. How frustration seemed to boil behind his eyes at her silence, as though somehow all the words she'd lost were meant as a punishment for him.

"This is ridiculous," he adds, pointing. "Go on, now. Unless you want me to pick you up and put you on that scale myself."

Embarrassment swallows her and she trudges forward, eyes on the tiled floor. She kicks off her flip-flops and steps on the creaking scale.

Winters girl, purrs that familiar voice in her ear. *Wouldn't it be nice to smash this useless thing over his skull?*

Briar sucks in a sharp breath, involuntarily imagining blood trickling down her father's forehead like branches of lightning. And on the heels of that comes an inexplicable memory of him seated on the floor of the playroom she once shared with Riley, his cheeks covered in rosy face paint as they drew flowers into his skin. She flinches, her stomach turning at the dissonance.

No, she thinks back. *I wouldn't hurt him like that.*

Oblivious to her thoughts, her father studies the scale's results. He taps his phone a few times, then nods curtly, like a lieutenant dismissing a soldier. "Was that so difficult?"

Her face burning with too many emotions, Briar starts to dart past him—but skids to a halt when she catches sight of his mouth. "Dad," she says, "you're bleeding."

His hand swings up to check, and Briar's eyes widen. Blood trickles from his top gums, over teeth that are usually unnaturally white but right now appear yellow and almost porous. He hisses a swear under his breath as he inspects his reddened fingers, a muscle ticking on the side of his jaw.

"Dad—"

"I'm fine," he asserts, already halfway into the hall. "Just tooth sensitivity. Listen, I need to head to the gallery—we'll be home late after the Cultural Council meeting, so order takeout for dinner; you can use my card and invite Kai and Astrid if you want. . . ."

His words disappear as the door of his study slams, leaving Briar alone, heart hammering with confusion. She considers her mother's brittle hair, Patrice's drooping smile, the mayor's peeling flesh. An unsettling pinprick of suspicion bubbles up like blood, and she's forced to wonder if her parents are holding back words they're afraid of saying too.

In the silence that follows, the mirror calls to her, a whisper curling in the glass. She darts from the bathroom before she can determine the source of the hissing.

But out of the corner of her eye, she's almost certain she sees her wraith smile.

~

Once in her bedroom, Briar buckles as the wound on her calf throbs. She glances down to find the bandage damp, and her stomach twists.

If it gets worse, Morgan said earlier, *you have to call me. Don't make me keep asking.*

Briar peels back the gauze, and her entire body freezes.

There was one oval carved into her flesh this morning. Now there are two.

All around the connected shapes, her skin is puffy and irritated, and a trickle of black blood snakes its way to the curved bone of her ankle.

Briar clamps a palm to her mouth, inexplicably thinking of slick tentacles raking through seaweed, teeth ripping into scaled flesh. She should call Morgan. She should change the bandage; she should—

Winters girl.

She snaps her head at the scrape of that voice again.

Something new stirs inside her, chipping away at her fear. She's suddenly tired of being a scared girl who contorts herself into tiny shapes for others. Caldwell. Her father. She won't stay small this time.

"Who . . . who are you?" she asks.

That's not a very good question, it purrs. *You know me as well as you know yourself.*

"What do you want?" she tries.

I already have what I want.

Briar closes her eyes, clenching her teeth.

Perhaps the better question is what do you *want?*

With her lashes shut, Briar can almost feel long fingers combing her hair. Gentle nails at her scalp, massaging and soothing. Stroking down the side of her face, knotted knuckles skimming her cheek, the pad of a thumb whispering over her lips.

A calloused palm, curving possessively over her throat.

Her eyes pop open. The room falls quiet, the deep glow of golden hour spilling through the gossamer white curtains. Did—did she imagine that?

She presses a hand to her neck, slides her gaze around—and sucks in a breath.

"Oh no," she whispers, eyeing the water stain from earlier. The yellow mark has grown, bloated and menacing. She guesses there isn't much longer until water starts invading in sheets.

"Shit," she hisses—just as a car horn blares from outside. Tearing her stare from the stain, she rushes to the window, and relief widens inside her.

It's Kai and Astrid.

With the engine still running, Kai leans out of his car. "I've got something," he yells over the rain. "Come down."

Briar nods. Thinking fast, she empties a plastic bin of shoes and shoves it beneath the growing leak, pushing away the image of water spilling down her walls, drowning her home. But as she takes one last look, the sinking knowledge creeps into her bones anyway:

Nothing will be enough to contain the storm that's coming.

~

Briar climbs the ladder to Kai's tree house and sucks in a gasp at what she finds inside.

The crooked floorboards are littered with papers from Finn's backpack, the interior wallpapered with more. *The Deposition of Elizabeth Booth, 1692. The Examination of Sarah Carrier, 1692.* One sheet taped to the window is covered with mathematical symbols—square roots and pi, fractions and infinity. And there are three equations in Finn's scratchy handwriting:

$$dx/dt = 6\ (y - x)$$
$$dy/dt = x\ (\rho - z) - y$$
$$dz/dt = xy - \beta z$$

"Is this what you were doing while I was at the library going through newspaper archives?" Astrid asks, at Briar's heels. "Making a conspiracy wall?"

Kai slides into the tree house behind them, shaking rain from his untamed hair.

"I've spent hours sorting through Finn's stuff," he says, clearing a stack of documents to sit beside Astrid. He turns to Briar, voice warming. "Sorry for not answering your calls. And, you know. For everything else, too."

Briar holds on to the rare slip of solace, as though whatever anger festering between them has since evaporated. Maybe she's not the only one afraid of being buried beneath regret when their time runs out.

Briar nudges his knee with hers. "I'm sorry too."

Kai leans forward, grabbing a pile of papers. "That folder was a mess, so I grouped everything by category. Over here, you have town records.

Depositions from the witch trials, the declaration when Loch Creek was founded. But that's not what I wanted to show you."

He tugs a few sheets loose before handing them to Astrid.

"This is the town deed," Astrid says. "With that random lady's name."

"Harper Clay," Briar says, and the back of her neck prickles with cold.

Kai nods. "Look at the bottom, line item thirteen."

" 'The grantee agrees to maintain a regular pelagic harvest as henceforth outlined by the addendum in section seven-E," Astrid reads. She glances up. "Pelagic harvest? Like, in the ocean? How do you harvest an . . ." She shuffles the pages. "Seven-E. Of course—that's the section that's missing."

"Not anymore," Kai says. "'Cause I found it."

He pulls another paper loose. But unlike the others, this page isn't a photocopy. It's weathered—much older than the others.

Briar's eyes widen. "Kai—where did you get this?"

"After you called and said you couldn't steal the files from town hall, I swiped my grandma's key and took them myself." Kai fixes Briar with a pointed stare. "We're in this together."

Gratitude and disbelief crash inside her. For the first time since Finn disappeared, Briar feels the emerging notes of hope. Because these are more than old papers—they're a reminder that this friendship has always been a safe harbor, a place to land when they aren't strong enough alone.

She springs forward and throws her arms around Kai's neck in a fierce hug, papers crinkling against his hoodie.

"Thank you," Briar says, her words muffled by fabric.

"You would've done the same," he says, but she hears the emotion in his voice too. "Don't thank me yet though. That section? It isn't in English."

"What?" Briar pulls back from their hug, examining the pages. Astrid bends to look as well, her braids spilling between them.

Section 7E. Harvest Addendum. But that's all that's recognizable.

Briar is quiet as she contemplates the symbols—curves and slashes, angles and arrows. She reaches into her bag for the spell book.

"Whatever it is," she says, "it's the same language that's in here."

"*And*," Kai adds, pointing to a slew of frayed notebook pages, "the same language Finn wrote out over and over."

"He was trying to decode it," Astrid concludes, and Briar's stomach knots. *Like Morgan*, she thinks, and that familiar despair creeps back inside her at the awareness that she'll never be able to tell Kai and Astrid about getting help from Morgan earlier today—not without telling them her secret that only Morgan knows. She slides her gaze down and wonders how many lies a person can tell before they choke on them.

"I did some research. Check this out." Kai reaches into his bag for his iPad, all cheekbones in the glow of the screen. "In 1972, a teenager on Revere Beach saw a strange creature in the water. Later, scientists found these symbols drawn in the sand." He flips the tablet, brandishing a pixelated news article. "In 1999, a college church burned down on a Rhode Island campus with no explanation. But when the authorities went to investigate, you know what they found? Bunch of weird freakin' symbols. Whatever code Finn was trying to crack, it's nothing good. It's something dangerous. Ancient." Kai's gaze slips to Briar, his eyes flashing. "Evil."

An uncertain silence drifts between them, and Briar knows what he's thinking. The rumors about that day with Riley. The symbols etched in the sand.

Sorrow's Shore, marked and branded—just like her.

"I have something too," Astrid says, trepidation creeping into her voice. "Those fish we saw earlier today? I was right: They're called Haikouichthys. They're one of the first known vertebrates on earth." She hesitates. "They lived over five hundred and thirty million years ago. On the other side of the planet."

For a moment, they're all quiet, contemplating stretching eons, infinite years stuffed between galaxies. *Time*, Finn once said, *is a single thread. Looped around and around, like this*. He lifted his compass, draping the chain around Briar's fingers. *Past, present, and future—they all exist in space at once.*

"Whatever's happening," Kai says, "it's bigger than Finn. Bigger than us."

"But he left all this behind for a reason," Briar says. "*For* us."

"Wait. Finn had an actual lead, remember?" Astrid says, shuffling the papers. "Here. Hawthorne College, Department of Anthropology and Religious Studies. This *has* to be where Finn's dad was studying. Maybe he was researching the same thing."

"We should go there," Briar says, trying to sound braver than she feels. "Tomorrow."

She looks up to find Kai's mouth twisting in a slow grin as he clicks off the iPad.

"You read my mind, Bee," he says, extending a hand.

Briar smiles back, bumping her fist against Kai's. The gesture is quick, casual, something they've done a million times in the halls between classes. But here in the tree house, it's also an olive branch. A rallying cry.

That's what friends do: they rip at the seams and stitch their bond up tighter. The threads between her and Kai are too strong for any one argument to sever; they'd have to be burned and buried—and even then, they'd find a way to claw their way back to each other.

Maybe alone they wouldn't be able to find Finn. But together, they can. They will.

Something shifts inside her at the realization. An inkling that maybe Briar could tell Kai and Astrid everything, that perhaps they'd emerge stronger. Maybe she was wrong; maybe they *can* follow one another into the darkest places, take turns holding the light.

"Kai," she starts. "Astrid. I have to tell you guys something. It's about Ril—"

But her words are drowned suddenly by something sour and wet at the back of her throat. She corkscrews out a strangled cough and flattens a palm to her clavicle.

"Bee?" Astrid asks, concern sprouting on her face.

Winters girl.

Briar slams her eyes shut. Not now, not *now*. Salt burns in her mouth, stinging her nasal passageway, and she fights back a gag. Her chest heaves, and water trickles from her lips.

I'm the only one you need, the voice purrs. *Don't waste what's left of that pretty breath by spilling our dirty secrets.*

She whimpers, struggling for air around the gelatinous obstruction in her lungs. Panic climbs her spine, and she tips forward onto her knees. She curses herself for not saying it sooner, for waiting until she's about to be left alone with the secrets that are rotting her from the inside out.

In this moment, she's never hated herself more.

"*Shit*," Astrid hisses. "Kai, her inhaler."

Kai snatches Briar's bag, rummaging. "Is your inhaler in here? Briar, where the hell is—?"

Be a good girl, that grinding voice warns, *and stay quiet*.

A pocket of air emerges, and Briar gulps at it, relief flooding her chest just as Kai thrusts her inhaler into her hands.

"I'm okay—" she rasps. "I'm okay."

She swallows the remaining ooze, flinching at the sour taste of seawater, the texture like a mouthful of slippery kelp. She sucks a breath through her inhaler, faintly aware of Kai stroking her back and Astrid's head against her shoulder, but their touches bring no warmth. There's only that ice-laden dread gripping her bones. *I'm the only one you need*. Perhaps that's always been true.

"What were you going to tell us?" Astrid asks, and Briar just shakes her head.

"It doesn't matter."

The words fall flat, that fleeting hope gone for good. Because even if they do save Finn, there will be no rescue for her. You can't save someone who is already gone.

And somewhere inside her skull, she hears that voice laugh.

CHAPTER EIGHTEEN

FINN

The walls of the cottage are bleeding.

Finn freezes, rooted to the kitchen floor. He stepped outside only to feed Neptune—and somehow turned back to find syrupy black liquid leaking from all corners of the ceiling.

As if the entire house is weeping.

The murky substance drips into the room, pooling in broken crevices of drywall. It melts toward the ground with a low rumbling, like thunder in the distance.

Except, Finn knows, it's not thunder at all.

"Shit," he hisses, breaking into a sprint. He tears down the corridor toward his old bedroom, heart hammering in his ears.

He's certain he only has seconds until that voice slinks into his skull, the way it's been creeping in at high tide each day. Forcing him to think about his mother, the bruises, the house that was never a home. Reminding him of all the ways he clings to distraction so he doesn't have to deal with himself. Astronomy. Math. Little orange pills. They all have the same function, really. Something to obsess over instead of dwelling on his failures.

Though mostly, the voice talks about Briar. *His* Briar.

I am woven into her veins, that unseen monster purred the other night, putting a surge of possessive fury inside him. *Our bond was forged in seawater and ash. Tell me, when you kissed her pretty mouth, did you taste my power too?*

Finn has come to expect the jagged insults and baiting taunts. But the bleeding walls—this is new. And it surely means something worse is about to happen.

Unless Finn is able to find the one thing that can destroy this nameless creature first: an obsidian dagger.

In his bedroom, Finn swallows a jolt of fear. That gelatinous liquid oozes from the windows, sucking light from the graying sky. Gritting his teeth, he springs forward, tearing books from their shelves, knocking his mattress askew, trying to picture that old book he stole earlier this summer. Healing spells. Bonding rituals. And a page about magical weapons.

A blade of obsidian, he learned, is the only thing that can protect him against an ancient evil that hovers between worlds—like this one.

Panic consumes Finn as he struggles to imagine what the creature looks like, what it even *is.* A malevolent spirit. A demon unbound by time or space, fed for centuries by an evil faction of Loch Creek. But as hard as Finn tries not to listen to its voice, he suspects that it wants something more than ritualistic offerings. He imagines a clawing beast inside an oceanic cage, longing to stretch its wings across galaxies.

Scheming to break free.

That's why he needs to find that damned dagger. Without it, he doesn't stand a chance.

Finn desperately searches his memories. The night of the ritual, the witch had an obsidian dagger with her. He swiped it when she was reading from the spell book (didn't he?), but he also could've sworn he had his compass—and that's been missing since he got here too.

Anxiety climbing his throat, Finn flings open the closet to rip moth-eaten clothes from their hangers. The room darkens around him. Inky water surges over the floor, and a frostbitten wind turns his exhales silver. Despair lurches inside him. It's not here.

He's out of time, and it's not fucking here.

Nothing makes sense in this place. Everything is an illusion, a trick of the tide, a collection of abandoned things that can never be found.

Then that voice floods his skull. A hiss, a whisper. Glass on glass. Turning him colder with newfound fear.

Such a sad boy, it mocks. *Always looking for something that's missing.*

"Quiet," Finn commands, grabbing a cobweb-covered box. He flings it open. Empty. He hurls it to the ground, moving on to another—

When will he realize, the voice continues, *there's no use searching? There are no magic blades to be found. No broken girls to be saved.*

Finn grits his teeth. "Stop—"

Perhaps he has to know what it's like to lose everything *first.*

"I already have!" Finn shouts, and the static snaps to an eerily thick quiet.

For a moment, there's only the sound of his own breath in the dark. And then a blazing light flashes from outside.

Apprehension grips him. The light snaps off. Then on. Off. Two short flashes. A long one. A short—

If he didn't know better, he'd swear that the lights were almost like—

Morse code.

Finn races to the window and squints through the grimy water obscuring the glass. And all his clenched fear releases in an incredulous tearstained laugh.

Because a younger version of Kai Baisho is standing in the dunes, a flashlight clutched in his fist.

This must be the creature tricking him, readying for a fresh attack. But it's *him*—Kai, from seventh grade. The year they spent hours in Kai's tree house memorizing dots and dashes, spinning their own secret language of light and sound.

That was the summer Briar and Astrid were away at camp in Maine, while Finn and Kai passed the time skateboarding through the abandoned mall off Route 128. Their conversations covered miles of ground, from school to video games to girls. Until Finn blurted out that he also thought about kissing boys, setting the stuck words free.

If Kai was surprised, he didn't show it. *That's cool*, he replied. *Me too.*

They kept skateboarding after that, but it was like they leveled up, reached some kind of friendship holy ground. A celestial plane where Finn could be the realest version of himself, in a world that isn't always friendly to bisexual guys, a world that sometimes makes them feel like they don't fit neatly in any space. Somewhere between heel flips outside a vacant Filene's Basement, both he and Kai knew at least they'd always belong when they were together.

Finn holds his breath now, staring at the younger version of a friend he no longer has. He's certain the voice will return at any moment, but he clings to this vision anyway. A reminder that he still has so much worth fighting for.

Kai's flashlight blinks again. Long, short, long. Short, short, long, long. *C-A-N U C-O-M-E O-U-T?*

Finn presses his forehead against the inky window. "No," he whispers. "I can't."

Kai flicks the flashlight a few times. *F-I-N-N?*

"I'm here," Finn says to the empty walls. "I'm still here."

R U T-H-E-R-E?

"I'm—" Finn's gaze ping-pongs around before landing on the chain hanging from the exposed bulb. Lunging for it, he summons the patterns he once memorized. The room lights up as he tugs on the chain. He pulls again. And again. And again.

.. --

I-M

... - .. .-.. .-..

S-T-I-L-L

.... . .-. .

H-E-R-E

Finn repeats the pattern over and over, ignoring the stinging in his palm. He's faintly aware of blood between his fingers, but he can't stop. Hazy light strobes with dots and dashes, and he fires out the message as fast as possible, as many times as possible. Maybe one of them will be bright enough to cross timelines; maybe Kai will carry this memory with him long after it ends.

Above, the bulb starts to sizzle with electricity. But Finn only yanks harder, his teeth clenched, waiting for Kai to flash back, waiting f—

An ear-splitting pop rattles in his skull. Glass rains down into his hair like snow.

The bedroom plunges into darkness again. Somehow blacker than before.

Five things, he thinks. Five things. But all he can think of is one.

How he's never been lonelier in his whole life, without being alone at all.

Black liquid swallows the window once more, obscuring the beach entirely. Fear creeps into his bones.

Hello again, little lost wolf, the voice purrs. *Are you ready to hear what I have to say? Or do you need another reminder of what's no longer yours?*

Finn freezes, both at the words but also the *sound*, the way it folds over him like a cloak. As if the creature is part of the air he's breathing. He musters the bravery to reply, "Don't call me that."

But why wouldn't I? There's a smile in the rattling response. *I care for you like you do that stray animal. You're a fool to think you can tame your beast, but I certainly will tame mine.*

Drops of sweat roll down his spine. "What are you? *Where* are you?"

Are you saying you'd like to see me?

Finn tightens his jaw. "I don't even know your name."

You never will. Your pathetic mortal tongue couldn't pronounce it.

"Are you a demon?" He narrows his eyes. "A sea god? A king of death?"

Would you like to think of me that way?

Finn huffs a breath through his nose.

Don't you want to know why I'm visiting you tonight?

"You mean it's not for the scintillating conversation—?"

Finn's words evaporate as a set of invisible frostbitten hands seize his wrists. He searches the dark in a panic, and for an instant, he thinks he can make out a face: a man with silvery-white hair and opal eyes, all angles and teeth. Sharp and beautiful and terrifying. But he's only there for a breath—in another, gone. A serrated fear slashes through him, but that death-cold grip only tightens like wintery vines.

I have a present for you.

"Whatever it is, I don't want it."

I think you might. Those hands jerk his wrists, and he lurches to his feet. *Check the closet again. Under the floorboards.*

Reluctant curiosity fills him. The dagger, he can't help but hope. What if—?

Finn lunges for the closet, tripping once on a pile of clothes, and tugs at the floor until he finds a loose board.

Pull it up.

Charged now, Finn dislodges the plank with an urgent pop. He reaches down, closing his fingers over something cold and smooth—and heavy.

It takes Finn a second to realize what he's staring at: a silver pistol, a daisy wheel etched into the handle.

The same one he stole from the safe at Old Town Hall the night of Briar's birthday party.

Finn staggers back. The world spins.

Catching his balance, he frantically points the gun at empty corners.

"I got *rid* of this," he grinds out. "It's at the bottom of the ocean. How did you—?"

The voice is silent now. Waiting to see what he'll do next.

"Are you trying make me kill myself?" he accuses. "I bet you'd love to see me blow my goddamn brains out all over this room. But I'm not gonna do it. I won't give you that satisfaction."

Tucking the gun in his waistband, Finn sprints down the hall toward the screen door. The dark breeze bites at his skin, salt and brine whipping his untamed hair as he races along the onyx shoreline. He snatches the handle and hurls the gun into the blackened sea.

"*Fuck you*," he yells to the nameless, faceless thing.

But when he spins toward the cottage, he slams to a halt.

The gun is *right there*. In the sand, at his feet.

"Oh, what the—?"

Finn whirls in a panic. But the beach is empty save for the crumbling cottage, the shadows of the dunes, and the outline of the blurry Ferris wheel in the distance. Like wet paper in a rainstorm, the ink running and bleeding.

Finn snatches the gun and throws it again. And when he turns this time, at least he expects it. The silver metal in the sand. Waiting. Watching.

He grabs the gun. He hurls it. He turns. Again, and again. Over and over, but it's always the same. The gun at his feet—demanding to be used.

Finn casts the weapon into the sea countless times, until pain shoots up his arm like lightning. He groans through clenched teeth, gripping his shoulder and sinking onto the cold, unforgiving beach.

His head hangs, a surrender.

I decide what you lose and what you keep. Only me.

Finn bites back a terrified sob, head swirling with the memory of Briar covered in blood. He'll never escape it, never know if the spell worked, if any of this was worth it. Maybe he is better off completely dead.

But then, icy fingers caress his injured shoulder from behind.

With a gasp, Finn glances to find a broad pale hand resting atop his shirt. Veins and tendons run from knuckle to wrist, and each finger is adorned with a glittering dark ring. At the tips are razor-sharp talons, flexed and prodding at his collar.

His gaze slides up—

And his breath evaporates.

The creature is right there. Kneeling behind him in the sand.

That ominous presence fades in and out of view like a fleeting comet. Long flowing robes seem to disappear in the shadows, and his wintery hair blends into a fit of starlight looming above.

But that *face*.

It's the same face Finn saw earlier. Piercing opal eyes without any black inside them. A crown of onyx shells resting atop his head. Everything sharp, full of hard lines and angles. Radiating splendor and death.

Finn snaps his gaze to the hushed shoreline, his chest heaving with panicked breaths.

That wound must hurt badly.

He bites the inside of his cheek instead of responding.

Would you like me to make it stop? That hand grips tighter, claws skimming Finn's collarbone.

Swallowing a pathetic whine, Finn nods.

The creature releases a low sound that rattles in his ear.

I want to hear you say it. Out loud.

Humiliation floods him as pain blazes in his arm. But Finn swallows it without a second thought; he's already traded away his life in exchange for

Briar's protection. If it means she'll be safe, he'll hand over his pride too.

"Make it stop." His voice cracks around the words. "Please."

In an instant, a sea of warmth replaces the pain. Finn slumps forward, relief pouring through him as air reaches his lungs. And in the quiet that follows, his head swims with the lonely realization that no one has ever taken care of him quite like this.

That hand at his neck tightens, holding him steady. As though the creature knows that too. Those gem-adorned fingers trail the slope of his throat, caressing in slow, aching strokes.

Would you like to thank me?

Finn squeezes his lashes and chokes it out. "Thank you."

The silver-haired entity slides his hand around the front of Finn's throat, strong fingers splayed across his clavicle. Dipping fully beneath his collar. Claws along bare skin. A foreign, maddening heat spills low in Finn's stomach, and he scrambles to stomp it out, horrified by his body's betrayal. This creature could kill him. And yet—

Words are not my currency, lost wolf. You'll need to try again.

Finn swallows. "I—I don't know what you mean."

A rush of empty air replaces the creature's touch. The beach darkens.

I don't want your whimpers, the voice hums. *I want your guilt. I want your worst secret.*

Finn's stomach turns.

Let's play a game. Who killed the pretty Winters girl?

Terror claws at his spine. "No—not that. Anything but that."

Was it... me?

"Stop, please, I—"

Finn's breath catches as the darkness gives way to flickering gold. The ground sways beneath him, and it takes him a second to realize he's no longer on the beach at all. A briny smell floods his nostrils; a thick breeze rakes his hair.

He's on a boat.

The town yacht, at sundown.

No. *No.*

But there she is. Briar at the bow in a white sundress, curls tumbling down her back. She's rolling her eyes as the crowd sings "Happy Birthday," a cake with nineteen candles glittering below. Astrid and Kai are off to the side, mouths moving as though the memory is being replayed in torturous slow motion.

Another flash of white catches his eye—a boy weaving through guests, his eyes wild.

It takes Finn only a second to realize he's looking at himself.

The Finn who existed on that night. Finn, who figured everything out too late. Finn, who still tried to save her.

Finn, who failed in all the worst ways.

"No," he protests. He tries to close his eyes, but the effort is Herculean, as though invisible fingers are prying them open. Forcing him to live it again.

One look at this terrified version of himself tells him exactly what *this* Finn just found in the basement of the yacht: the hidden hole in the floorboards; the candles surrounding it; the rotten smell pouring from the damp, tenebrous space. The way, at first glance, it looked like some kind of shrine to celebrate Briar's birthday. But the more he stared, the more it didn't look like a tribute at all.

It looked like a memorial.

Finn can see the paper-thin plan emerging as Past Finn races through the crowd: *Briar will come to California*, Past Finn is thinking. *We'll leave right now. Screw plane tickets, we'll drive. I'll get her out of this rotten town, away from danger, away from—*

But Past Finn hasn't slept in days.

And fear is so much louder than logic.

Finn knows what he saw that night—but couldn't say whether it was real, even now. He was *certain* he saw a dark shape on the boat behind Briar, talons reaching toward her. Ready to consume, to devour. To claim.

Tears sting his eyes as he's forced to watch it again—as if he hasn't seen it every minute of every day since. As if he hasn't punished himself relentlessly for his split-second choice, the desperate foolishness of it all. *Obsidian*, he wants to scream. *Not steel! Not a fucking gun!*

Finn sees himself, wide-eyed and feral. He watches himself yell, *Get down! Briar!*

He watches himself reach to his waistband. He watches his own hand, the flash of silver at his fingers, his arm straight and stiff.

"No, please," Finn begs now, tears streaming down his face.

Light flashes against the cotton candy sky. The entire boat erupts into wails.

And then he sees Briar, as he saw her that night, and again and again since.

The blood spouting from the gaping hole where her eye should be, red everywhere, streaming down her neck, the front of her dress, staining her beautiful skin. She stumbles to the side, then back and back—and over the edge of the boat.

While both Finns only stare and stare.

Then, finally, Past Finn screams. The gun falls to the floor as he rushes to where Briar was standing moments ago, her name ripping from his throat in a raw howl of grief.

Finn doesn't have to see any more to remember what came next. The way he dove in after her, choking on inky water, clawing at nothing but the sea. The night he spent at Loch Creek's police station later, shivering beneath a scratchy blanket. *What was in that room at the bottom of the boat? What did you do with the gun, Adler?* The smirking detective who released Finn the next day and told him to lawyer up. How he clapped Finn on the back and spat, *You can kiss that Berkeley scholarship goodbye.*

Kai picked him up, eyes red-rimmed and full of sorrow.

Astrid couldn't bear to be near him at all.

They drove in silence, thirteen years of friendship hanging in the space between them. Infinite car rides filled with swirling secrets, a lifetime of brotherhood.

And then, Kai's final words. The death knell of a friendship that once felt like family. *You're a monster, Finn Adler,* he said. *Get the hell out of my car and never speak to me again.*

Finn chokes on a sob of seawater now, unable to hide from the heart-splitting truth that Briar took her last breaths alone. He should have been there to hold her; he would have cried into her hair, would have begged her not to die. Would have shattered into pieces when he realized she couldn't hold on, would have stayed with her long after she was brave enough to let go.

And in those moments, he would have said it: That he's loved her since the day they met. That he's been hers their whole lives.

That he never wants to be anyone else's but hers.

The secret words burn and burn in Finn's mouth now, turning to ash on his tongue. He'll never forgive himself for not telling her when he had the chance, wishes he told her a million fucking times, ribs aching with the truth that unspoken things can ruin a person more than anything whispered aloud.

And then, the brush of fingers at his hair again—long, lean, cold. Finn goes still, freezing at the unexpected comfort it brings, just as that snarling voice creeps back in.

I'll ask one more time. Who killed the pretty Winters girl?

"I did," Finn whispers, words broken and drenched with despair. "I killed Briar."

PART FOUR
FLOOD TIDE

There open fanes and gaping graves
Yawn level with the luminous waves;
But not the riches there that lie
In each idol's diamond eye—
Not the gaily-jeweled dead
Tempt the waters from their bed.

EDGAR ALLAN POE, "The City in the Sea"

CHAPTER NINETEEN
BRIAR

30 Hours Until Briar's Birthday Party

Hawthorne College's campus sits high above the Boston Common, its brick buildings scattered around the lawn like outstretched arms. Unlike other universities, Hawthorne blends into the city, tucked between apartments and coffee shops. There are no ivy-covered dorms, but the sight of the school's insignia still puts an ache in Briar's chest. As though the crimson-and-white design represents all the memories she'll never get to make.

The Department of Anthropology and Religious Studies occupies a small brownstone on Chestnut Street. In Kai's car on the way, Briar and Astrid practically memorized every professor's name, setting their sights on the department head with summer office hours for prospective students. *He's the one we need to ask about the town deed*, Briar said. *Professor Ryland Quill.*

Briar trails Kai and Astrid along the rain-slick cobblestone now, her calf throbbing beneath its bandage. She grips her umbrella harder with each step, fighting not to limp.

The air conditioner chills them as they enter the building, shaking their umbrellas in the foyer. Briar's bare arms prickle with goose bumps, either from the sudden cold or at the thought of standing in a place where Finn's father might have once stood too. *I wish I had known him*, Finn always said. *I have a feeling, like he would have understood me. Like things would have been easier with him around.*

"Professor Quill's office is on the third floor," Kai says, glancing at his phone. "Remember the plan?"

"Pretend we're prospective students asking about linguistics studies, got it," Astrid recites. "Here's hoping he doesn't kick us out."

Briar gnaws her lip as she follows; each step shoots daggers through her cut. But the wound is somehow less painful than the reminder that she'll never be a prospective student anywhere. She'll never sit in a film-directing class like Kai, or attend lectures on public policy like Astrid. Not while death is tugging on her like a puppet, pulling all resistance from her limbs until she becomes a stiff corpse instead of a girl who dares to imagine a future.

By the time they're upstairs, Briar is dizzy, a film of sweat clinging to her forehead.

"I'll meet you in a sec," she murmurs, then ducks into the restroom at the end of the hall.

Briar leans against the closed door, lungs airless. She rummages for her inhaler before popping it into her mouth. Rain pelts the glass block windows, turning the bathroom smoky with shadows. The rounded mirror above the sink seems to sway, and she shuts her eyes before she can glimpse the pooling dark in the corner.

When her breath returns to normal, she tucks the inhaler in her bag, catching sight of Morgan's homemade treatment. Briar's fingers hesitate against the vial. Morgan said only one application each morning, but the pain is agonizing.

Swallowing, Briar rolls up one leg of her black yoga pants. Clenching her jaw, she unwinds the bandage—and can't hold back her horrified gasp.

Where there were two ovals last night, there's now *four*, wet with dark blood and connected at the center. Her skin is swollen and raw, and a film of green pus seeps from the edges of the wound.

Briar staggers to one of the stalls, bile rising in her throat. She gathers her hair with one hand and retches until she's only coughing up air, tears stinging her lashes. She sinks to the cold floor, struggling to choke back panicked sobs. Hurriedly, she unscrews the vial and dabs the ointment onto the weeping flesh. The wound seethes, and Briar bites the inside of her cheek to stop herself from crying out.

A sudden chill prickles her neck.

Such beautiful pain on such a beautiful face, Winters girl.

Slumping her head against the metal wall, she closes her eyes. Hot, silent tears spill down her cheeks. An idea gnaws at her brain—a blade, curled in her palm, sawing her leg clean off. No more cuts that change shape in the night. No more foul blood that reeks of decay. No more—

An icy whisper sweeps her dampened cheeks, silencing her thoughts. Briar imagines full lips of the palest blue brushing her jaw, then higher, to her cheekbones—where she suddenly feels the soft warmth of a tongue. Licking, lapping at her salty tears.

What if I told you I could make it stop? What if I told you I could take away your pain—forever?

I'd let you, she thinks, but doesn't say. Eyes squeezed shut, she focuses on her breathing. She grounds herself within her body: the cool tile underneath her thighs, the press of her phone in her waistband.

Her phone.

Briar tugs it loose, fleetingly contemplating what it means to keep secrets from her friends but share them with her worst enemy. She's not sure how to explain that it's easier to confess ugly truths to someone who already hates her.

Before she can talk herself out of it, she types out a text to Morgan:

It changed again. I'm scared.

"Briar?" Astrid's voice floats into the bathroom. "Are you sick? What's wrong?"

"I'm fine," Briar calls, adrenaline flaring as she tucks her phone away.

Astrid raps on the stall. "You're *not* fine. You just threw up."

Briar quickly winds the bandage around her calf again before standing. Wiping her mouth with the back of her hand, she opens the door and offers Astrid a tight smile.

"I'm nervous about the plan." The words aren't fully a lie. "What if Professor Quill thinks we're playing a prank? What if this is another dead end?"

Astrid evaluates Briar for a long time. She absent-mindedly twirls the strands of her friendship bracelet, and Briar wonders if she's measuring all the ways everything is falling apart.

"It won't be a dead end," Astrid finally says. "I have a feeling."

But as Briar turns to wash her hands, there's no mistaking the way Astrid narrows her dark brown eyes with suspicion. *You're hiding something*, her face seems to say.

Guilt churns inside her—but maybe it's better this way. Better for Astrid and Kai to move away with a frozen image of how their friendship used to be, their memories like photographs faded to sepia with nostalgia.

Briar's phone buzzes at her hip again, and she tips it just enough to read Morgan's texts. Three of them. Rapid-fire in a row.

Changed how???

Pic???

Pain level? 1-10

Chewing her lip, Briar slides the phone back into her leggings and follows Astrid into the hall. At the end of the corridor, Kai is talking with a tall golden-haired man. The man's back is to her, but her breath catches when she notices Kai's stunned expression.

"That must be Professor Qu—"

The words die on Astrid's lips as the man turns to face them, and Briar sucks in a breath so sharp that she's dizzy with it.

Because they're not staring at a stranger.

They're staring at a man who looks exactly like Finn.

CHAPTER TWENTY

BRIAR

29 Hours and 30 Minutes Until Briar's Birthday Party

"Are . . . are you ladies alright?"

The professor eyes Briar and Astrid quizzically, his thick brows drawn in concern. He's tall—taller than Kai even—with tousled dark blonde hair. It hangs over his forehead, cascading toward gray eyes and sharp cheekbones. The faintest hint of facial hair lines his angular jaw, and he's dressed formally in a long brown blazer, collared shirt, and dark slacks.

If it weren't for the fact that the man is in his early forties, Briar could convince herself that she's staring at Finn Adler.

Astrid finds her voice first.

"Are you Professor Quill?"

"I was just telling your friend, please, call me 'Ryland.'" He slides his gaze to Briar, and she swears his eyes flash with brief recognition. "You're prospective students and had some questions about our ancient language classes?"

"Sort of," Kai replies.

Ryland glances at his watch. "Well, I've got twenty minutes before a meeting, so—"

"This might sound really weird," Briar blurts, "but do you have a son named Finn?"

A muscle tightens in Ryland's jaw in a way that reminds Briar so much of Finn that her stomach flips.

"I don't have children," he says, "but what makes you ask that question?"

"You just . . . you look exactly like a friend of ours," Briar says, heart hammering.

"He's actually missing right now," Astrid adds.

Ryland glances at Kai, narrowing his eyes. "This isn't about a language, is it?"

"It is, actually," Kai replies. "But it's also much more than that." He slips Finn's backpack from his shoulder, opening the zipper. "Look."

Briar's eyes widen as Kai pulls out a polaroid. The four of them at prom, grins flashing beneath string lights. Along the bottom, in Finn's handwriting, is an equation:

$$V-E+F=2$$

"Kai, where did you get that?" she asks.

He shakes his head. "It was in one of the folders."

Ryland's face drains of color as he takes the photo. For a moment, he's quiet as he studies it, absorbing the ways Finn's image looks like his own.

"Hang on." Ryland raises his glance suddenly. "You said this kid is missing?"

"Actually, it's worse." Kai hesitates. "We're the only ones who remember he existed. His own mother doesn't remember him. We called her. She didn't know who we were talking about."

"His mother . . ." Ryland trails off. "What's her name?"

"Rosemary," Briar says. "Rosemary Adler."

And at that, any possibility that this might be some wild coincidence crumbles.

Ryland drags a hand down the side of his face. His eyes briefly close. The air in the hallway turns colder, the rain noticeably louder on the roof. Dread creeps into Briar's stomach.

"Fuck," he mutters. "I was afraid you'd say that."

"Why?" Kai demands.

"You kids from Loch Creek?" Ryland lowers his voice. "That language you wanted to talk about. Is it from the town deed?"

"Yes," Briar whispers, pulse soaring with the satisfaction of suspicions proven right. Perhaps the final piece they've needed has always been here.

A door creaks open down the corridor. Ryland glances in the sound's direction, another muscle twitching along his jaw.

"Let's talk in my office," he says. "That department meeting is gonna have to wait."

~

Ryland has a corner office at the end of the hall, its dark walls covered with framed certificates. Briar sits between Astrid and Kai in front of Ryland's desk, where he's intently studying the papers from Finn's backpack. His concentrated expression looks so much like Finn's that it physically hurts to watch him.

Kai leans forward. "Does this mean anything to you?"

"It does," Ryland says, glancing up. "I've also been studying Loch Creek's history—and this language—for over a decade."

"What?" Astrid breathes. "And you *seriously* don't have children?"

Briar bites her lip. "If you're not Finn's dad, how is it possible you look so much alike?"

Ryland sits back, expelling the longest sigh. "I grew up in Loch Creek," he says. "That town may position itself as an upscale, artsy-tourist gold mine, but it's twenty shades of wrong. Cursed."

Ryland's voice darkens in a way that makes Briar think of Finn on the Ferris wheel, saying almost the exact same thing. Her stomach knots in regret, and she grips Astrid's hand.

"I'm sure you've heard stories about the disappearances, the drownings on the north beach. Coincidences, maybe—but in a town like Loch Creek, where everything seems so polished? That facade starts to feel more like a cover-up." He gestures to the town deed. "If you read this, you know that the Abbotts bought land in 1692 from a woman named Harper Clay and turned it into a safe haven for accused witches. Thing is, Clay wasn't just a businesswoman. She was the high priestess of an extremely powerful coven."

Briar's blood turns icy, Morgan's voice echoing in her memory. *There's a reason that coven isn't in charge anymore.*

"An aether witch?" she asks, ignoring the heat of Kai and Astrid's confused stares.

Ryland throws her an incredulous glance. "How do you know about aethers?"

"Just something I read once," she lies.

He holds her gaze for a moment. As though he doesn't quite believe her.

"The deed contained a bunch of bizarre addendums written in a language most couldn't interpret," Ryland finally says. "The Abbotts signed it without realizing what they were agreeing to, then unknowingly ushered an entire community into the coven's plan—which was to cultivate ancient magic and copious wealth through contact with dark entities from beyond our world." Ryland taps the deed with the back of his pen. "But what they didn't anticipate was that these creatures would want something in return."

"A sacrifice?" Astrid asks.

"No." Briar's stomach drops. "A harvest. A pelagic harvest."

"Loch Creek isn't just a fancy town where bad things happen occasionally," Ryland warns. "Aether witches still live there, reveling in money and youth, all while allowing an ancient evil entity to feast on their own."

Briar recalls Mayor Caldwell's peeling skin, the unsettlingly hungry way he's always staring. As though she's an object to be delivered—but not for him.

For something with teeth and claws.

"So . . . this entity you're referring to," Kai says, "did it take Finn?"

Ryland glances at the photo again. "Couldn't say. But I do think an aether witch might have gotten to your friend with a spell."

Briar snaps her gaze up. She turns his words over, thinking of all the accusations she's hurled at Morgan. If what Ryland's saying is true, then so is Morgan's insistence that she had nothing to do with this—she's no aether witch. She *warned* Briar about them. Remorse swells inside Briar, and she shakes it loose.

"What makes you think an aether witch put a spell on Finn?" Briar asks.

"That woman you mentioned. Rosemary Adler. I know her." He swallows. "We were in love. A long time ago."

A motor whirs inside Briar's chest. "*What?* When?"

"In high school. I thought we'd be together forever." Ryland strokes a hand over his jaw. "But we were bad for each other. Rosemary had a traumatic childhood—and alcohol was her medicine. She'd drink vodka in the bathroom at school, and we both started messing around with harder stuff as we got older. It felt like we were pulling each other down a dark path. Rosemary was everything to me... but she had a cruel side to her. One that seemed to grow harsher with time." He shakes his head. "I could clearly see a future where we made something of ourselves, but it felt like Loch Creek was threatening to drown us both. Especially her. I couldn't explain it, but I knew—if we stayed in Loch Creek together, we'd *decay* there."

Briar swallows, thinking of all the ways Loch Creek is drowning her too.

Ryland forces himself to continue. "I tried to make it work while I completed my studies at Hawthorne—but the more I researched Loch Creek, the more I knew that town was turning her into someone unrecognizable." He sucks in a breath. "I had to end things."

His gaze falls again. Briar's phone buzzes at her hip, and she quickly silences it.

"Last I checked," he continues, "she's got her own law firm. She's doing okay, you know? But I've never stopped thinking about her. She was the love of my life."

"And you let her go," Astrid finishes.

"*She* needed to let go of our life in Loch Creek. I *saved* her," Ryland counters sharply. "Both of us." He leans forward, fixing them with a hard stare. "But here's the thing: Ever since, I've had this dream. Rosemary is pregnant, and we're living in this run-down cottage on the beach. We're *happy*. And she tells me—she says—" His jaw knots. "She says she wants to name our son Finn."

At that, Briar goes completely still. Memories that never existed suddenly taunt her: Ryland in the stands at Finn's math-league championship,

Ryland chaperoning their fifth-grade field trip to the Museum of Science. Briar thinks of Finn as a child, how the fear of being unwanted clawed a hole inside him, and she wonders how it could have felt if he'd never had to question it at all.

"A skill unique to aether witches—and why their power is so incredibly dangerous—is that they can see around corners of time." He glances at Briar. "You ever wonder what would've happened if you'd done the slightest thing differently? Gone left at a traffic light instead of right, stayed home instead of going out?"

Briar nods. Her ribs ache, missing Finn's voice in her ear so much that she's sure she'll burst. "The butterfly effect."

"Right. Chaos theory." Ryland taps the graph paper from Finn's backpack. "That formula Finn was studying—it calculates the rate of change with respect to time. According to mathematicians, it's impossible to predict the future of a chaotic system. But aethers were able to *force* alternate realities to play out with magic." Ryland points to that strange language. "These symbols are derived from Enochian—the ancient language of angels. Aethers put their own spin on it, folding in seventeenth-century mathematics to create uniquely dangerous spells—many of which were meant to bend time."

"Are you saying," Briar starts, "that it's like... like Finn was never born?" She glances at Kai and Astrid. "We're in an alternate universe?"

The words taste bitter as they leave her mouth. She thinks of the stones beneath the mirror house, the spell book, Finn's hushed whisper on the phone—details weaving into a tapestry of guilt. All this time, they've been scrambling to rescue Finn.

But maybe he doesn't want to be saved.

Most everything Finn does has a point to it. A rhyme, a reason, an equation.

Maybe his vanishing was on purpose too.

Why, she wonders for the millionth time, didn't she listen to him the night of the carnival? She would gladly risk the danger of ancient time-bending magic if it meant she could find her way back to that neon-lit sky and get it right.

"Who's to say which universe is the alternate?" Ryland answers. "Where Rosemary and I have a child? Or where we break up? Maybe your reality is the alternate version and now you're back to the original plot."

"No, *no*—Rosemary abused Finn his whole life," Astrid insists. "That happened. *That* was real."

Ryland falls quiet, jaw clenching. "And what about me?" he asks, voice darkening. "Where am I in your story?"

Briar and Astrid exchange a glance.

"Dead," Briar says softly. "An overdose, before Finn was even born."

Ryland glances to the window, eyes cloudy. "I was right, then. If Rosemary and I had stayed together, that town would have poisoned us both."

"Hold on—if Finn was never born," Kai says, "then why do we remember him?"

"*That* is a good question," Ryland replies. "'Cause you shouldn't."

"The night Finn disappeared, I think we went back in time," Briar says. "We don't remember much—but we visited a place that hasn't existed in almost twenty years. Why would that happen?"

"I can't answer that for sure either," he admits. "But it sounds like the three of you got pulled into the spell's magic somehow—probably because of how close you are. Psychic energy rooted in love—platonic or romantic—can sometimes be stronger than time itself, which is actually quite malleable."

Ryland catches their vacant blinks and offers a small smile.

"Quite simply, the three of you love Finn so much that your bond is stronger than any magic," he adds softly. "But it doesn't hurt that whoever cast this spell seems to have done a shit job." He taps at his phone, swinging the screen around. "Saw this article earlier today in the *Globe* and didn't know what to make of it. After talking to you though…"

Briar reads, *PREHISTORIC FISH WASHED UP ON THE SHORES OF MASSACHUSETTS SMALL TOWN*. She darts a glance to Astrid.

"A botched aether ritual could be behind this too," Ryland says. "Someone took apart time with magic. And didn't put it back together correctly."

Unease grips Briar again. Her thoughts race faster than she can process them.

"So, where is Finn *now*? Is . . . ?" She forces out the terrible question. "Is it like he's dead?"

"I don't think so," Ryland says, and relief rushes through her. "If Finn was a victim of this particular spell, he's not dead. He's also not *here*. He's somewhere else—caught between folds of time. In layman's terms, a parallel universe that encapsulates every moment that has ever existed."

"How do we get to him?" Astrid asks wearily.

"You'd need aether magic. Which might prove impossible, since any aether witch who practices today likely does so secretly." Ryland slides a hard-to-read look toward Briar, making confusion and dread creep into her stomach.

"So it's hopeless," Kai concludes, slumping in his chair.

"Not necessarily," Ryland says. "Most spells have a lock on them—a secured loophole to reverse the magic, in case something goes wrong." He taps the thick book on his desk. "It's a matter of finding the key."

Briar's glance drops to the floor, defeat weighing her down. *Swear you'll never ask me to do magic*, Morgan's voice echoes in her mind. She pulls in a breath and silently apologizes for the promise she knew she'd have to break.

"I wish I could assist more," Ryland says, reaching for a business card on his desk. "But here—if anything else comes up, that's my office number."

A heavy ache fills Briar's chest as they stand. Finn's father, a man who could have loved him. In another life, another time. Another series of tides and stars.

Ryland gathers the papers but pauses on the polaroid of Finn, staring as if he's wondering what it would have been like too.

"You can keep it," Briar says. "If you want."

Ryland shakes his head. "This equation he wrote? *V-E+F=2*? It's the Euler characteristic—it describes the topology of a geographical object. The answer is always the same, no matter how much it's bent. Like the friendship you have." He slides the photo back. "This belongs to you."

Briar takes it, and the room blurs through tears.

"Finn is lucky to have friends like you three," Ryland adds.

"We're not just his friends," Astrid says. "We're family."

"I can see that." A shadow falls over his face. "Not everyone gets that either."

"Thanks for your time today, Professor," Kai says, slinging the backpack over his shoulder. "We'll be in touch."

"Wait."

They all turn, but Ryland is only looking at Briar when he asks, "A word alone?"

Briar's chest tightens. Ryland has been silently picking her apart the entire time she's been in his office, like she's the final piece in a puzzle he's trying to solve. Like he somehow knows everything she's kept unspoken, and he's about to say it for her.

Astrid scowls. "Whatever it is, you can tell all of us."

"Please," Ryland says. "It'll just be a moment."

"It's okay," Briar hears herself say, nodding at Astrid. She watches them disappear into the corridor before apprehensively meeting Ryland's gaze.

Ryland's unsettling calm doesn't waver. "Your name Winters?"

"Yeah." She swallows another wave of trepidation. "So?"

"*So.* You're the girl whose twin brother died on the beach." The bluntness of his words lands like physical blows. "Anniversary is coming up, isn't it?"

"Tomorrow." Briar bites the inside of her cheek. "Tomorrow will be thirteen years."

Ryland stares at her for a long, long time. Long enough that Briar counts over ten ticks of the clock. Long enough that she has to look away.

"There's something that I think you should see," Ryland finally says.

Briar's mouth turns to cotton as Ryland crosses to a file cabinet. He rummages for a few moments before producing a paper. And when he hands it to her, she can't hold back her gasp.

Because she's staring at a drawing of a young woman with wild curly hair. A smattering of freckles over her nose. Full lips, high cheekbones, thick lashes.

It's a drawing of herself.

And at the bottom of the page—

Harper Clay, 1692.

"What—?"

"Harper Clay kept a journal that's been preserved over time," Ryland says. "It used to be stored in the archives of Old Town Hall, though someone must have hidden it. I was fortunate to gain access once and took a photocopy of this sketch. It's the only portrait that remains of her."

"But—" Briar swallows, vision swimming. "This is *me*."

Ryland shakes his head. "Harper isn't *you*, Winters. But she's almost certainly your ancestor."

At that, Briar's pulse quickens. The room whirs.

"My parents," she whispers. "Does that mean—are they witches? . . . Am *I*?"

"That's not my place to say," Ryland answers. "I don't know your family. But I do know aether abilities aren't always genetic. Meaning your parents aren't necessarily practicing aethers just because Harper is in your bloodline."

Briar's stare drops to the floor. She thinks of her mother and Mrs. Parker-Blake exchanging stony stares in the grocery store, Nerissa's amused glare over the counter of the flower shop. Fear and bitter guilt knot in her stomach. Her whole life, she's spun rumors about Morgan, sharpened the gossip like blades. Unwittingly, she pictures Morgan's forehead pressed to the school bus window as Briar sent a chant down the aisle. *Witch . . . witch . . . witch.*

This entire time, she was only creating a weapon to use on herself.

"Harper died shortly after Loch Creek was founded, during a conjuring spell," Ryland continues. "The entity she was trying to summon was more powerful than any witch could ever hope to be. A fallen angel. A prince of hell." He cuts his gaze to Briar's, eyes tempestuous. "It destroyed her on the spot. But she'd woken it. And it's still being fed today."

Thunder roars outside, underscoring Briar's mounting fear. "I thought it was banished," she says, recalling Morgan's words. "By a water witch."

Ryland raises his eyebrows. "You know your Loch Creek lore." He walks around to his desk. "You're half-right. Yes, that spell has kept the entity confined between worlds. However, aether witches still cultivate magic and wealth from it through regular harvests." He tugs open a drawer. "By 'harvests,' I do mean 'sacrifices.' Of the human kind."

Briar's head spins with his words. She contemplates all the people who have vanished from Sorrow's Shore, their names in faded newspaper headlines, the absence of Riley's laughter after he died. A live wire ignites in her brain, a combination of grief and rage at the possibility that Riley's life was a gift-wrapped offering too.

Ryland pulls out a chart that rises and dips like mountains. "This is Loch Creek's economy over the past century," he says. "Notice anything interesting?"

Briar takes a ragged breath. "Those fluctuations. They're every thirteen years."

"Exactly," he says, rolling the paper back up. "Loch Creek thrives when it's fresh off a harvest. Money, tourism, new art. But toward the end of that thirteen-year cycle—*bam*—the economy nose-dives. And what else happens every thirteen years? Someone disappears on the northern beach. It's been the same for centuries because—and here's where that banishing spell comes in—no one has been able to offer the entity the required sacrifice to break the spell and free it from the chasm between worlds."

"What's the required sacrifice?"

The second the words leave her mouth, the back of her neck prickles, and Briar realizes she already knows.

"Twins," Ryland answers.

And every ounce of suspicion morphs into terror.

Ryland continues. "If both twins are offered to the entity in the water, it will be set free and supposedly bestow immortality upon the aether coven. That's what aether witches have always sought: Theosis. Becoming godlike themselves."

Briar stares at him. She remembers Riley's fingers sliding from hers, the white gleam of his face as it dipped beneath the waves. Bile rises in her throat.

"Thing is, I've never been able to fully crack the translation." Ryland crosses to the window. "It doesn't make sense to me; why use such an easy-to-solve loophole in a banishing spell? Twins aren't exactly rare. But if you want to know my hypothesis—what happened to your brother when you were children?" He turns, facing her again. "That was no accident."

Briar's face burns. When Finn said those same words on the Ferris wheel, part of her wanted to scream that she knew, because it was *her* fault. But hearing Ryland say it feels different. Because he's talking about something bigger than her.

Like she was merely a cog in the machine that manufactured her brother's death.

Her thoughts hurtle, rapid-fire. The symbol on the spell book. Riley, limp and blue on the shore. The whispered hissing in her brain. Mayor Caldwell's predatory stare. *All of Loch Creek has observed your coming of age.* As though her birthday is less of a celebration and more of a feast.

Like Riley was fed to something beneath the waves, and she's always been next.

"Maybe," Ryland says gently, "you should get out of town for a few days."

The suggestion does her in. Because there's no leaving this place. Not for her, a girl whose feet have all but been nailed to the streets.

Loch Creek, she knows with a sickening certainty, will be her grave.

Tears sting at her lashes, and she turns so he won't see.

"Briar."

She closes her eyes and bites down on a sob. Ryland's voice saying her name makes her dizzy. Like it's Finn in twenty years. Finn as he could have been.

"Do me a favor," he continues. "If you learn anything else, if you're afraid, if anything goes wrong—don't hesitate to call, okay?"

Briar nods, something loosening in her chest. Before she can talk herself out of it, she flings her arms around Ryland in a tight hug. His blazer smells like sandalwood as he pats her shoulders, and the gesture only makes her tears flow faster. Her heart strains with discordant emotions: escalating dread, blistering nostalgia for a man Finn never got to know. It could have been different. *Everything* could have been different.

Briar pulls back, wiping her eyes. "Finn would have wanted to meet you."

Ryland's smile only looks sad. "I'm glad you found me, then."

She feels his stare as she starts for the door. As if he's trying to hold on to what it's like to know her too.

“Winters,” Ryland calls, and she turns, already halfway into the hall. “You’re not bound to this town’s history.” He nods, resolute and guiding. Like a father should be. “Write your own.”

CHAPTER TWENTY-ONE

BRIAR

27 Hours Until Briar's Birthday Party

Kai and Astrid are waiting at the bottom of the stairs when Briar hurries down, face flushed.

"What's wrong?" Astrid asks, expression concerned.

A million possible answers flood Briar's mouth. *My entire existence is a sham*, she could say. *There's something broken inside me, something* evil *in my blood. Riley died because of me. Finn is gone because of me. And everyone keeps telling me to leave this town like I'm not tied to it, like it's not going to drown me no matter how far I run.*

Stay away before I pull you under too.

But saying any of that would mean revealing all the lies she's told—an impossible feat when she's buried beneath them, trapped in the rubble of her own making. What's one more, when her bones are already buckling under the weight of her pathetic deception?

"What did he say to you?" Kai presses protectively.

"He wanted to know more about Finn," Briar says, swallowing her disgust at how easily another lie comes out. But if she's going to follow the threads

Ryland gave her—ones that could lead to her own family this time—she needs to do that alone. "What if we split up again? Divide and conquer?"

Astrid's eyebrows shoot into her hairline. "Split up? *Now?* Are you for real?"

"We're running out of time," Briar insists, and a knot tightens inside her chest. Running out of time because they're leaving. Because she's dying. "If we each take one clue and meet tonight before my party, maybe we can—"

"No," Kai insists. "We're working together. A team, remember?"

"I know, but—"

Briar's hand flies to her hip as her phone buzzes again. *Morgan.*

"Hold on," she scrambles. "I need to take this."

"Seriously? What could be more important right now?" Astrid demands.

"Just a second." Briar darts out the front door, huddling beneath the awning.

"Hi," she pants, casting a glance over her shoulder.

"What the *hell*?" Morgan demands. "What's wrong with you?"

"Excuse me?"

"You text me to light a goddamn distress signal and then ghost for an *hour*?" Her voice softens. "I was worried."

Briar shoves aside the warmth that blossoms in her stomach at Morgan's sudden change in tone. She grits her teeth. "Is there anything you wanna tell me?"

"About what?"

"About my bloodline."

Morgan's surprised laugh is a burst of static. "I have no idea what you mean—"

"Yes, you do, Morgan," Briar interrupts. "We talked for, like, an hour yesterday about aether magic, and you didn't say a *word*. You went on and on about how evil aether witches are, how deadly their magic is—but Harper Clay is my ancestor. My *family descended from that coven*. You knew this whole time."

"Maybe," Morgan says, "I was trying to protect you."

"By lying to me?" Briar snaps, and Morgan falls quiet.

In her silence, Briar considers the dangerous possibility that she's handed her secrets to someone she might not be able to trust.

But she has no other choice.

"I need to learn about aether magic. I need to understand these spells. It's the only way I can figure out what happened to Finn." Briar swallows. "If I come over, will you help me?"

Morgan's breath rushes out. "We went over this. You promised you wouldn't ask—"

"*Please*, Morgan."

The pause that follows deepens the ache in Briar's chest.

"No, Pom-Poms." Morgan's voice almost sounds sad. "I can't."

Despair rages inside her, and Briar races to mask it with anger. "Fine. Then I guess we're finished here. Thanks for the ointment—it's done absolutely *nothing* to help my cut." She barks a laugh. "In fact, you've probably just been poisoning me this whole time."

"Wait," Morgan interjects. "What's going on with the cut? You said it changed—changed *how*?"

"No. Uh-uh. I'm not talking about this anymore. Bye." Briar hangs up and turns—

Smacking right into Kai and Astrid.

Who have been standing behind her the whole time.

"Were you just talking to Morgan Parker-Blake?" Kai demands.

"Instead of *us*?" Astrid adds.

Briar's pulse skips. "Can we just—?"

"What cut?" Kai interrupts. "What ointment?"

"What was that about aether witches and your *family*?"

"How long have you been talking to her about this?"

Not even bothering with her umbrella, Briar flies out into the rain.

"What did she say when you asked her about the magic?"

"Does she—?"

"Stop!" Briar yells over her shoulder.

"No," Astrid counters, spinning Briar to face her. Rainwater drenches them both, plastering their hair and clothes. "No, *you* stop. I've been making excuses for you all week, letting it slide when you lied about graduation, defending you whenever you wouldn't talk about Riley." Astrid's eyes flash.

"But I'm tired of being the only one holding this group together. Do you get what that's like? To be the glue in our group when *both* you and Finn have been hell-bent on ripping us apart?" Her chest heaves. "I'm done. Unless you start answering some questions."

"*You're* the glue?" Anger crackles between Briar's ribs. "You both have been pretty content talking about me behind my back while I try to fix things as best I can!"

"Try to fix things how, exactly?" Kai snaps. "By not telling us anything?"

"Do you think I *want* to keep all this to myself?" Briar yells, spitting rain. "I feel sick to my stomach when I think about what happened on graduation night. And Riley—" She bottles the words. "You guys. *I can't.*"

"You have to this time," Kai insists. "You have to get over yourself and think of someone else first for once."

"You're not the only one who has a hard life, Briar," Astrid adds pointedly.

"I never said I was!"

"We don't have time for secrets," she insists, her voice climbing over the rain. "Kai and I leave for school next week, and—"

"And you'll never have to think about Loch Creek again, right?" Briar snaps.

"That's *not* what I was going to—"

"Well congratu-fucking-lations," Briar continues, voice dripping with sarcasm. "I hope you have a great time in college, Astrid. Maybe you'll find a new best friend without so much emotional baggage!"

"Maybe I will!" Astrid yells back, stunning them both into silence.

The rain pounds harder, turning the brick at their feet into a pool of red.

"There it is," Briar says with a bitter laugh. "You can't wait to get rid of me. Deep down, I think I always knew."

Before Briar can turn away, Kai's hand closes around her upper arm.

"You're not gonna run," he says. "You're not gonna shut down. We're gonna talk this out. We're family, Bee."

"We're *not.*" Briar feels her eyes darken, the scenery around her blurring. "We're not the same. You and Astrid—you have a future. Finn did too, once. But me? I'm gonna be here *forever*. I'm gonna *die here*."

The words rush out faster than she can contain them. She didn't mean to say it, but it's the truth. She's known it since she was little, staring at the endless ocean, inexplicably imagining pockets filled with moonstones and water enveloping her like a blanket. The conviction has been there her entire life. Loch Creek is where she was born, and Loch Creek is where she will die.

She can't escape this town—not tonight, not ever.

Kai's hand tightens. "Briar—"

"No. I'm done." She tries to wrench her arm out of his grip. "Kai, let go."

"Briar, we have to talk."

"Kai, let *go*!"

Caged frustration burns inside her chest, laced with the inexplicable heat of euphoric satisfaction. Because here, on this drenched sidewalk, this anger feels better than anything has for days—better than desperation, better than terror. It's something she can manage.

Something she can wield.

With a growl, Briar twists out of Kai's grasp and shoves him away in one furious motion.

Electricity floods her veins; water roars in her ears. She barely hears Kai's cry of shock as he stumbles backward, careening—faster than humanly possible—into a parked car at the curb. Glass shatters, an alarm wails. Astrid screams, but all Briar can taste is grief drenching her like a rainstorm. She imagines the entire street is suddenly dark as midnight, shrouded with her rage, eclipsing all the remaining sun with the fury of a girl who is tired of being told that everyone else knows better. A girl who is tired of being poked and prodded and studied.

A girl who is just plain fucking tired.

It's only when her breath steadies, only when the wave of anger recedes that she realizes what's happened.

Kai is in a heap on the sidewalk, dusted with glass shards. Astrid rushes to his side, crouching. A low groan floats from Kai's mouth as he struggles to sit.

Remorse instantly consumes her. What did she just do? Kai isn't the enemy. Kai is her *friend*—and she hurt him.

She'll always hurt everyone she loves.

But when Kai looks at Briar, there's no indignation in his eyes—only fear.

Because the entire street *has* gone dark.

The sky is completely black, without the faintest twinkle of stars. And when Briar realizes where the only source of light is coming from, she gasps.

An opal glow seeps from her balled hands, dancing over the jagged edges of glass at her feet. The light mixes with the rain, illuminating each drop with a glimmer.

"Briar—what the hell?" Kai finally asks.

She can't answer; she only uncurls one finger at a time as dozens of translucent blue moths spill from her palms. They bite through her skin as though emerging from a chrysalis before taking flight, glittering wings disappearing into the air. She barely registers the pain, transfixed and horrified at once. Because it's almost like—

Magic.

But she doesn't—she couldn't—

"Briar?" Astrid asks, her eyes wide. "What... what just happened?"

No. Briar's world tilts, the glow and rain blurring into a mix of confusion. Her mind conjures images of pentagrams on Morgan's locker, a bloody butterfly in its cage. *Witch... witch... witch.*

Perhaps this is the most fitting punishment for a cruel girl like her: all her venomous insults melded like glass, forging a mirror that only shows herself.

Panic flashing inside her, Briar staggers backward. Her flip-flops twist over themselves once, but she picks herself up and breaks out into a run, tearing down the dark sidewalk.

Drenched in midnight, in the middle of the day.

~

Briar's heart doesn't stop pounding the entire train ride back to Loch Creek.

It hammers inside her chest when she steps onto the deserted platform, when she climbs into a taxi and stares out the window at the town that's going to end her.

It's still racing as she runs up the path along the Rowan Street shoreline.

By the time she reaches apartment 2A, she's fighting for breath, her pulse alive with electricity. The cut on her leg roars in pain. Her palms are numb now, no traces of moth bites in sight. She shivers in the darkened corridor, knocking over and over and over, her hair plastered to her shoulders, clothes soaked to the bone. She leans her forehead against the wood, surrendering to the rush of terror and confusion. *What the fuck? What the f—?*

The door swings open, and Morgan freezes with bewilderment.

For a moment, neither says anything, the ghosts of their harsh words swirling between them. But then Briar releases her anger, sets free the confession she can't hold back any longer.

"I didn't—" she starts. "I didn't know where else to go."

CHAPTER TWENTY-TWO
BRIAR

25 Hours Until Briar's Birthday Party

For the first time, Morgan Parker-Blake is speechless.

She stares at Briar's drenched form in the hallway, golden eyes flickering back and forth. As if she's not sure what to make of Loch Creek High's most popular girl standing on her doorstep looking like a drowned rat.

"What the hell happened to you?" she finally exhales.

Briar's teeth chatter. "I need your help."

That incredulous expression doesn't budge from Morgan's face as she nods and holds the door open. Wordlessly, she starts for the bedroom, and Briar trails behind, swallowing a wave of nostalgia as she enters Finn's old room. The interlocking lines of a chaos theory graph swell in her mind, and Briar wonders if another version of herself is buried beneath the floorboards, whispering all the things she wishes she'd said when she had the chance.

Morgan dips into the adjoining bathroom and emerges with a towel.

"I'm gonna get you something dry to wear," she says, "and then you're gonna tell me what's going on."

Briar nudges the towel around her shoulders, still shivering. And then, out of the corner of her eye, something shifts in the standing mirror.

Something dark, like the hem of a blood-soaked dress.

Briar squeezes her lashes together, but not before spying the decaying feet in the glass. Those purple-gray toes hover above the floorboards, dripping inky water onto the wood. Fear grips Briar's chest as she contemplates how few hours she has left.

By tomorrow night, they'll be the same.

"The mirror—Morgan." Her right eye throbs, voice a terrified whisper. "*She's here.*"

She half expects Morgan to sigh with exasperation, but instead, a sudden scraping fills the room. When Briar dares another peek, Morgan has turned the mirror to face the wall. Briar deflates, letting out a breath.

"Clothes," Morgan says, shoving an oversized black sweatshirt and leggings into her arms. "Now start talking."

Morgan averts her gaze as Briar peels off her soaked crop top, tugging the warm hoodie on in its place. Briar flushes at the faint whisper of Morgan's perfume—blood orange, amber—and she's suddenly consumed with the urge to gather the fabric to her nose and inhale.

"Pom-Poms," Morgan clips, "out with it."

This time, Briar doesn't try to keep the words locked inside. Instead, everything tumbles loose—the town deed, Professor Quill, Kai. She talks and talks as she pulls on the rest of Morgan's clothes, leaving her rain-drenched ones on the floor. Morgan trains her stare downward the entire time, concern etched on her face.

Concern—and fear.

"There's one more thing," Briar says. She steps toward her. "On the train back to Loch Creek... I noticed this."

And then, she uncurls her fingers to show Morgan what's happened to her hands.

Jagged violet lines have erupted down the middle of Briar's palms, splintering off toward her fingers and wrists. They weave around the backs of her hands like twisted ivy, crawling over tendons and knuckles. As though her veins exploded beneath her skin.

Morgan's stunned gaze snaps to hers. A terrible prolonged silence fills the space between them.

"Say something," Briar whispers.

Instead, Morgan marches into the hall.

Briar races after her. "Morgan, where are you going—?"

"Come with me." She snatches her keys. "Now."

Grabbing her own bag, Briar trails her out the door and down into the rain, all while shouting her name. Morgan doesn't answer, just flings open the passenger side of her sleek black car and practically shoves Briar inside. Finally, upon climbing into the driver's seat, she announces, "We're going to Nerissa's house."

"Why? Morgan, wh—?"

"I can't fix this, okay?" Morgan blurts, starting the engine. "I don't know how. But my pain-in-the-ass sister might."

Briar falls quiet as they tear down lonely Rowan Street. Behind them, the ocean seems to claw at the shore—at her.

"I'm dying, aren't I?" she whispers.

Morgan's jaw tightens. Her throat bobs in a swallow. "Not if I have anything to say about it."

Something inside Briar warms at that. She suddenly thinks of the Morgan she knew all those years in school, always shooting suspicious glares over her shoulder. The girl everyone used as their collective punching bag, a girl who took shot after shot and never complained. A girl who, if she wanted to, could have ended all her enemies with a single word.

A girl who could have ended *Briar* but never did.

She gives herself permission to watch Morgan drive, one palm curled around the steering wheel while the other guides the gearshift. Briar's gaze drifts higher, charting the sharp lines of Morgan's face, the fullness of her dark red lips.

And for one second, she allows herself to wonder what Morgan Parker-Blake's mouth would feel like pressed against hers.

Morgan slows at a red light and turns to catch her staring. Briar braces herself for the snappy tone, the clipped *what are you looking at, Pom-Poms?*

But Morgan says nothing. Instead, she holds Briar's gaze, golden eyes hazy with unfamiliar softness. Briar's breath hitches, but she doesn't look away, and for a foolish moment, she questions if Morgan is thinking about kissing her too.

The light turns green. The car lurches as Morgan slams the pedal, and Briar bites down on her only smile in days. Perhaps, she thinks fleetingly, dying might hurt less if she stitches together enough moments like this first.

~

By the time they reach Nerissa Parker-Blake's house on the southern shores of Loch Creek, Briar is consumed with all the ways this plan might fail.

Briar sits nervously at the kitchen table while delicate antiques stare back, mocking. Paintings of water crests whisper that she's in enemy territory; colorful fish in a six-sided tank swim in a frenzied taunt. Reminding her that even if Nerissa can help, she might not want to. This cottage stuffed with water lilies and crystals might be the last place she visits.

But she tells her story anyway, clocking the way Nerissa's face shifts from confusion to suspicion to terror. In the silence after, Briar tucks her plum-veined hands under her thighs, shame coursing through her. Her throat stings, unaccustomed to telling so many truths.

"Do you know what's happening to me?" she finally asks.

Nerissa fixes her with a stern stare. "Your body," she says, "has learned aether magic."

"*What?*" Briar and Morgan unleash at once.

Morgan leans forward, brows drawn together. "Rissa, that's impossible. Mama always said—magic can't be taught, it's—"

"She must have been selected," Nerissa interrupts, pushing her chair back. "That cut on your calf, let me see it."

Briar rolls up her pant leg, bracing herself for what vile sight might be underneath. But when Nerissa unwraps the bandage, it's to reveal the same four ovals, swollen and crusted with green. A briny, putrid odor drifts from the wound, and Nerissa's face twists as she wraps it again.

"I'm gonna be blunt." Nerissa crosses to the counter.

Briar's heart pounds. "Okay?"

"That wound and your newfound magic are connected. For centuries now, aethers have harvested power from dark forces—creatures that lurk within hidden corners of the earth, like the deepest part of the ocean. One of those entities marked you for a reason and gave you magic." Nerissa flattens her mouth into a line. "Not as a gift. As collateral."

A cold understanding snaps into place as she recalls Ryland's words. *A fallen angel. A prince of hell.* Briar pictures that voice, those invisible cold hands in her hair, molding her to host an unseen beast. Her parents called her unstable, kids at school probably thought she was a bitch, but Briar always knew it was something worse. It was always a monster, laughing silently as she pretended to be a normal teenager who went to cheer practice and took math tests. Waiting for the day it would sink its teeth into her and never let go.

Briar stares at her latticed hands, feeling more like a ghost than a girl, and realizes that being right doesn't matter if you're simply too damn late.

"Collateral," she grinds out, balling her fists. "How do you mean?"

"There's only one way that cut heals," Nerissa says, voice muffled as she rummages through the wooden hutch. "And it's not from my sister playing medwitch. In all honesty, Mor, you probably made the poor girl worse."

Nerissa pulls several vials from the cabinet, then dumps spoonfuls of dried herbs into a tea strainer. Light purple. Pale green. Deep red.

"This won't cure you either," she adds, reaching for the kettle atop the stove. "It's just to take away the pain."

Briar swallows. "What's the cure?"

Nerissa stares, the faucet running behind her. "The entity that marked you," she finally says, "is the sole thing that can heal you."

A solemn quiet hangs between them. Briar is sure the creature is smiling somewhere with cruel, unseen satisfaction. She wonders what it would be like to yield to the empty dark, to curl up in the lap of a monster and let it lick her wounds. Maybe giving in would feel better than running. Maybe surrender is her only choice now.

"You said I was selected," Briar says. "Why?"

"One of two reasons," Nerissa says, placing the kettle on the stove—but she doesn't turn on the burner. Instead, she wraps one ring-adorned hand around the ceramic base, her fingers lighting up blue.

Heating the water with her magic.

"Did you happen to make any deals with a demon?" Nerissa continues as Briar stares. "Bargain your soul to be prom queen, that sort of thing?"

"What—? No, of course not." Briar slides Morgan a look of disbelief.

But Morgan won't meet her gaze, and Briar's stomach flips with confusion.

"Option two." Nerissa folds her arms. "Aether witches aren't extinct. There are still some right here in Loch Creek, walking among us. Biding their time."

"Waiting for the right sacrifice," Briar remembers. Dread slips back in. "Me."

Nerissa narrows her eyes. "Perhaps. But most sacrifices are ultimately pointless because a demonic entity only cares about its own survival. It doesn't keep promises. It's selfish. Lustful. Sadistic." Steam rises behind Nerissa's back, but her attention remains fixed on Briar. "This creature chose you," she continues, "because you have something that it needs."

Briar studies the fish tank and chews the inside of her cheek. *Had something*, she wants to say. *I had a twin, but I don't anymore*. She thinks of Riley's soaked curly hair beneath the rush of sea-foam, the salty wind roaring, the way he reached and reached and reached for her but—

"So you're saying this *is* my fault," Briar blurts, desperate to squash the images.

Morgan flings her a curious glance. "No one is saying that."

"You're thinking it though, aren't you?" Briar demands.

"What? *No*." Morgan's voice dips. "Pom-Poms. Stop blaming yourself."

Her soft tone only makes the pain in Briar's chest worse, and she musters hot anger to replace it.

"You know what?" she bites. "I liked it better when you were being mean to me."

She holds Morgan's gaze, silently begging her to lash out. Draw blood. Leave a scar. Make her feel *some*thing other than this terrible, endless fear.

But Morgan only leans forward, her voice infuriatingly calm. "Did anyone ever tell you that you're a shitty liar?"

"Enough, both of you," Nerissa barks, her order punctuated by the scream of a teakettle.

Morgan sits back, jaw tightening, and Briar crosses her arms to look the other way. The walls of the kitchen suddenly feel too small as she realizes all her old tricks for silencing her panic aren't working.

Soon, she'll be alone with it.

"Here," Nerissa says, carrying a steaming teacup to the table. "Just a couple of sips will do."

Briar raises the cup, sniffing the maroon-colored liquid. A pungent floral scent pierces her nostrils. "What's in this?"

"It's a homegrown blend." Nerissa dunks the strainer. "Lavender. Feverfew. Mostly poppy. It'll ease the pain better than anything you can get at the pharmacy." She cuts Morgan a glance. "Used it when Mama was sick."

Morgan sits up straight. "Rissa, no, this stuff is too strong, I don't think you sh—"

"*You* don't get an opinion," Nerissa says, her tone clipped like an exasperated mother's. "I'll deal with you in a minute." She pulls the strainer from the cup and flings it into the sink. "Winters. Drink. But not too much."

Briar takes a careful taste of the tea. Her stomach turns, and she stares down at the ruby liquid. Her reflection shines back, distorted and shimmering. Her *reflection*—she can't look, she—

Her breath skips as she realizes that the Briar in the tea is smiling, while she is not.

The Briar in the tea, with blackened teeth and rivers of blood on her cheeks.

The Briar in the tea with only one eye.

Choking down a cry, Briar raises the cup to her lips. And throws her head back.

Briar is vaguely aware of Morgan's voice—"*Pom-Poms! Not the whole thing!*"—but she ignores that too, draining the searing tea until there's nothing left to reflect her nightmares. She'll extinguish all light from the world, turn her surroundings black as her wraith's lacuna, to never see her hideous death-washed face again.

With a pained gasp, Briar drops the empty teacup onto the floor. Her shoulders heave as she violently gags. A sudden wave of dark blue calm flattens her, coupled with the grip of Morgan's palms on her back.

"Oh god," Morgan breathes, but her voice sounds far away. "Is she okay?"

"She's fine," Nerissa answers, as she collects the cup from the floor. "No thanks to you."

Briar's lashes flutter. She imagines the drink rushing through her veins, swirling with her blood. Her pulse pounds in her ears, lulling her toward sleep.

"Hey. Listen." Nerissa's voice fights for her attention. Briar's eyelids feel heavy as concrete. "There's one more thing you need to know about aether magic. A lot of people want it. Bad people. Good people. But no one can *take* your magic from you, Winters. You'd have to give it. Willingly." Nerissa gives her a long, hard look. "Be careful who you trust."

Fear seizes her belly. Briar opens her mouth, questions bubbling behind her teeth. But only a groan comes out.

"She needs to rest," Nerissa declares.

Morgan sighs. "I can take her back to my—"

"No. She'll sleep here."

Briar slumps against her arm, listening to the clanging of glass as the older girl cleans up.

"I'll make up the guest room," Nerissa continues.

"Okay..." Morgan hesitates. "I guess I can pick her up tomorrow—"

"You'll be staying too," Nerissa orders.

"What?"

"If she dies on my watch, I'd like a witness." Nerissa says it flatly, as if she were talking about what to make for breakfast the next morning. As if death is just another possibility, something that could happen at any time.

But Briar knows it will come for her tomorrow.

"Come on," Nerissa mutters, circling Briar's waist. "Let's get you to bed."

~

Briar can barely stand as Nerissa carries folded towels into the dimly lit guest room. She leans against the carved oak bureau, dizziness closing in. Morgan lingers in the doorway, arms crossed.

"Here," Nerissa says, placing the towels atop the bed's white comforter. "There are sleep clothes in the bureau, and the guest bath is fully stocked with anything you might need."

"What room am I supposed to sleep in?" Morgan asks, an edge to her voice.

Through heavy lids, Briar catches the slow smirk that tugs on Nerissa's lips. "You're standing in it."

"But..." Morgan's eyes narrow into gold slits as she studies the layout. "There's only one bed in here."

"Hmm." Nerissa shrugs in a way that can only be described as cruel.

"No." Morgan crosses her arms. "Absolutely not. I'm not sleeping in there with her."

A surge of unexpected hurt hits Briar right in the stomach at Morgan's words. It takes her a moment to place it, for her to understand—

Tonight is her last one alive. She doesn't want to spend it alone.

"Don't worry. The feeling's entirely mutual," Briar mutters to drown out her own thoughts, but it doesn't sound the least bit convincing. "I'd rather sleep outside."

Morgan whirls, rueful anger shattering her expression. "Why don't you, then? This weather really suits your glowing personality."

"There it is," Briar manages. "I've been waiting for your shitty insults to return."

A muscle feathers along Morgan's jaw. "Just keep to your side."

"No problem." Briar forces a snide smirk. "I don't cuddle with witches."

Morgan scowls. Shadows hollow her cheeks like she's biting the inside of her mouth, searching for something cold-hearted to say.

But when Morgan finally responds, her voice only sounds sad. Like she's exhausted every strike, like all that's left is a truth neither of them is ready to admit.

"I guess," she says, "I could say the same to you."

CHAPTER TWENTY-THREE
BRIAR

20 Hours Until Briar's Birthday Party

Winters girl.

Even in Briar's dreams, that voice finds its way in. There's nowhere she can run to escape it. Because it's part of her, claiming every breath, every thought.

Tomorrow, she thinks distantly, it will claim her life.

Sleep has returned Briar to the shore, icy water lapping at her ankles. The sky is pure white, casting a glare over the gray waves. The only color comes from the moon, a pulsating ball of crimson amid translucent clouds.

"You can't catch me!"

The high-pitched, childlike tone slashes Briar's ears like a knife. She whirls. And her chest clenches at the sight of Riley wading into the water.

He's wearing the same green-striped swim trunks as *that* day, his narrow back patchy with sunblock. Water climbs his sides, luring him farther into the ocean. For a moment, Briar is frozen with shame, her white dress like a cape of lead, anchoring her to the sand.

"It's too deep!" she forces herself to scream, edging into the sea. The waves are bitter cold; seaweed ensnares her legs. "You can't stand!"

He goes still at that, the water like a sheet of glass around his shoulders. Heaving a breath, Briar catches up to him and snatches his hand. Her heart aches at his palm in hers, still so small, forever frozen at six years old.

"Riley," she whispers.

He won't face her, his gaze lost somewhere over the horizon. All she can see is the back of his head, his messy curls identical to hers. For a fleeting second, she imagines how it could have been: The two of them celebrating every birthday together, blowing out candles in tandem. Mirror images connected by an invisible, unbreakable thread.

But they'll never get to do any of that.

Instead, Riley is only a memory. Instead, Riley will never grow up. Instead, Riley's tiny body is decaying in the earth, becoming dirt and moss, *all because of what. She. Did.*

"Riley, I'm sorry," Briar says, her cheeks suddenly wet. "I'm so, so sorry, I'm—"

A terrible creaking sound smothers her words as Riley turns toward her. Moving his head a single degree at a time, closer and closer . . . until she sees his face.

Briar sucks in a raw, petrified gasp.

Riley's skin is a distorted purple-gray, his lips the color of a bruise. The way he looked when they pulled him from the water—with a single nightmarish difference: his eyes are milky white. No irises. No pupils.

Briar tries to pull back, but he tightens his grip, fingers ice-cold and stiff. His unseeing gaze bores into hers. *Your fault*, his silent rage accuses. *Your fault.*

"I know," she whispers, tears hot against her skin.

Then, without warning, Riley slips beneath the surface. Still clinging to her. Just like that day.

This time, though, she'll hold him. *This time*, she'll save him. But it's useless; his body is so heavy, as though his pockets are filled with moonstones. The waves engulf his curly head, wrapping him up, swallowing him whole.

"Riley," she cries. "Get up!"

Let go, Winters girl, hisses that glass-on-glass voice.

Just like it did that colorless morning when Riley took his last breath. Same words. Same command.

Let go and count to one hundred. Show me how good you can be.

"*No*," she growls to the beast in her brain. Briar whips her gaze behind her. She'll stop it, somehow, from happening twice. "Someone, help! Help, please, h—"

And then Briar goes perfectly still.

The day Riley died, Morgan stood feet away by the pier, gold-flecked eyes rounded in horror. Something wordless and terrible passed between them that morning. An understanding of what Morgan had seen.

But in this dream, it's not Morgan standing by the pier.

It's Finn.

Finn as she remembers him at the carnival, white button-down shirt and ripped jeans, gold compass swinging from his pocket and winking in the pale sun. Finn, the boy she's silently loved for her entire life.

Finn, gaping at her like she's a monster.

"What did you do, Briar?" he cries. "What did you *do*?"

"Finn," she calls. He backs away, terror on his face. "Finn! Please, wait! I didn't mean to, I didn't—"

But Finn turns and runs. Like Morgan did that day. Briar chokes on a sob. Everyone runs from her; everyone will vanish. They'll leave her alone. Alone, alone, alone—

"Why did you disappear after the carnival?" she pleads with Finn's retreating back. "Was it because of me? Because of *this*? Finn—please come back, *Finn*—"

She starts toward him, but something snags her ankle and yanks her straight under the waves. She glances down, horrified to find a black snake ensnaring her wounded calf, its silver eyes glowing as it reveals a forked tongue.

I will take the fight out of you. I will break you and make you whole again.

Tomorrow, you're mine.

Briar's lungs flood with salty liquid. If you die in a dream, she wonders distantly, do you ever wake up?

She claws at the water, fingernails making contact with something soft. Adrenaline rushes through her.

"*Stop!*" Someone new is yelling, but she's wild, oblivious, desperate to break free.

She scratches again. *Again.*

"Pom-Poms! Stop!"

A cold grasp encircles her wrists, pinning them over her head. She screams again, but this time her vocal cords produce sound, and when she gasps, she inhales cold air instead of seawater.

Briar's eyes fly open to find Morgan above her, face inches away.

Chest heaving, Briar rapidly gathers her bearings. Guest bed. Rain. Nerissa's house.

Morgan's braid has come loose, and her indigo-streaked hair falls over them both like a curtain. One strap of her nightgown hangs halfway down her arm, and her knees are planted on either side of Briar's hips. Her gold eyes simmer as she wrestles Briar's struggling wrists, a trail of scratches along her cheek and neck.

"What the *hell?*" Morgan hisses. "You're *that* mad at me?"

Briar opens her mouth, but her airway tightens. Panic flashes white-hot in her chest.

"Nothing to say?" Morgan demands, as she pushes Briar's wrists deeper into the mattress. "Not gonna answer?"

Briar jerks her chin toward her bag atop the nightstand. Her lungs feel too small, the breath she's struggling to find, too big. The room swims. Inhaler. She needs her inhaler. She's supposed to have one more night; she's supposed to—

"What—? Oh shit." Morgan's anger dissolves as she processes Briar's constricted throat. She releases her wrists. "What's happening? Are you—?"

Briar lets out a strangled sound and stretches toward her bag, but her fingers fall short. Catching on, Morgan lunges for it too. In a second, she produces the inhaler—in the next, she plunges it right between Briar's lips.

Briar finally manages a deep breath and unclenches the blankets, fists relaxing as her airway loosens. But as the oxygen reaches her blood and the panic subsides, she's forced to confront the heat sparking at all the places their bodies are touching, only thin layers of clothing separating their skin.

"I didn't know you had asthma," Morgan admits.

"Since I was a kid." Briar wipes her mouth with the back of her hand. "There's a lot you don't know about me."

Morgan drops the inhaler onto the bed without averting her gaze. " 'Gee, Morgan, thanks for saving my life.' " She rolls her eyes. "God! You're impossible."

"Me? You're the one who—"

Whatever Briar was about to say evaporates as Morgan's fingers fold around her jaw, nails digging into her cheeks. "You scratch the hell out of my face while I'm sleeping, and then you go and almost die on me?"

"I didn't mean—"

"You have the *goddamn nerve* to almost die," she continues, closing the space between them, "before I can do *this*?"

And Briar's heart slams into her chest as Morgan leans in the rest of the way—and fuses their mouths together.

She tastes like blood orange and coconut, her lips full and soft, and a swell of warmth bursts inside Briar at the contact . . . and the realization that she's kissing Morgan Parker-Blake.

But then Morgan tears away, her mouth hovering over Briar's in a cruel taunt. Her breath is soft against Briar's skin, and she smiles in a way that only feels like an insult. *I dare you*, her eyes seem to say. *If you want it, take it.*

Letting out a low sound, Briar reaches around to the nape of Morgan's neck and hauls her back down.

The action snaps a cord in them both, releasing something hungry and feral. Morgan's teeth snare Briar's lower lip. Her fingers tug on her jaw, forcing her open, and Morgan swirls her tongue along Briar's in slow, fire-soaked brushes. Briar matches her rhythm, bringing one leg around her waist, clawing at her hair. They kiss as though they're still fighting, spitting scornful words and poisonous curses.

"For the record," Morgan whispers into her mouth, the hem of Briar's nightgown in her fist, "I still can't stand you, Pom-Poms."

Briar lets her lips curve in a dark smile against Morgan's before grasping her upper arms and flipping her onto her back in one smooth motion.

Smug satisfaction flashes inside her at the surprise on Morgan's face, and Briar leans down, reversing their positions.

"And I still think you're a total bitch," Briar says, warmth kindling low in her stomach at the press of Morgan's thigh slotted between hers.

"Good," Morgan replies, arching to kiss her again, palms burning as they slide up from her waist. "On the same page for once."

Briar growls her agreement, surrendering to the pull of Morgan's mouth, the eager grasp of her hands. She pushes out everything else—the guttural voice in her skull, the sour guilt over Riley, the aching loneliness in her heart ever since Finn vanished from time. With each sigh that leaves her throat, Briar expels all her fears into the sea, living only in Morgan's dangerous lips and the threat of this coiling heat. Briar could drown in the sharpness of Morgan's kiss, her teeth like jagged edges of moonstones. She could let Morgan fill her lungs with seawater and darkness until the world turns black, and this time, she'd only thank her.

CHAPTER TWENTY-FOUR
BRIAR

9 Hours Until Briar's Birthday Party

The next day, Briar wakes to the pounding of rain. For a moment, she lies perfectly still and wonders how people are supposed to feel on the morning of their death.

It takes her a second to register the empty bed beside her, the faint sound of a sink running in the adjoining bathroom. Briar sits up, wincing at the dull pain that throbs behind her right eye. Her lashes are sticky at the corners, and she rubs them before reaching for her phone.

Briar's stomach flips at a text notification from her mother. On her way to Morgan's, Briar fired off a message about sleeping at Astrid's—a lie that could easily be disproven with a call to Astrid's moms—and she gnaws her lip.

But worse than an angry message about catching her in a fib, her mom's text is about her party—oblivious to the way her daughter's life is crumbling into nothing.

Your appointment at Dahlia's is at 5. I told her you wanted an updo with a bow. ;)

Briar pushes a hand through her tangled curls and contemplates asking her mother if she'll still enjoy seeing Briar's hair in a bow when she's lying on a fucking metal table in the morgue.

Shoving the thought aside, she swipes to her group chat with Astrid and Kai.

The one that's been noticeably silent since yesterday.

Her bitten nails tap the screen. *Are you still coming tonight?* She smashes the Delete button. *Can we talk?* Delete, delete, delete. *I-m s-o-r-r-y.* The blinking cursor seems to mock her, taunting that her worthless apology is too little, too late.

Briar flings her phone at the mattress and kicks off the blankets—but stills when she notices the bedsheet tossed over the mirrored vanity.

She blinks, trying to remember if she did that last night, if avoiding her own face has become so second nature that it's simply part of her bedtime routine. Before she can recall, the door creaks open, and Morgan slips inside dressed in her clothes from yesterday. When she registers Briar's expression, she nods toward the mirror.

"I did that when I got up," Morgan says. "Just a precaution."

A rush of emotions balloons between Briar's ribs: The airiness of relief. The swell of gratitude.

The comfort of simply being believed.

"Thank you," Briar works out.

Morgan sits on the edge of the mattress, cautiously snaking a hand over the comforter to grasp Briar's. As if part of her expects Briar to pull away.

But the warmth from Morgan's skin unleashes memories from last night: Morgan's tongue tracing along Briar's throat, hands moving under Briar's nightgown, Morgan's fingers their own kind of magic. The way Briar took her time learning the shape of Morgan's body, finding out how she liked to be touched too. How they stayed tangled together afterward, Morgan's arm hooked over her waist as if they'd slept that way a million times before.

Briar stares at their joined palms now, and a cord of guilt snaps inside her. It wasn't too long ago that Finn's mouth was on hers, his hands doing the exploring. Maybe, Briar reasons, there are places inside her heart that can only be reached by him. And Morgan has found a different way in.

Lighting up new corners, leaving the ones that belong to Finn untouched.

"Was last night real?" Morgan asks.

Briar studies her. "Do you want it to be?"

Morgan hesitates, and insecurity flares inside her. Briar retracts her hand, retreating within that impervious shell she so quickly discarded.

But before she can say anything else, Morgan nods.

"I don't think," she confesses, "I've ever wanted anything more."

Warmth spills inside Briar at the sudden smoky edge to Morgan's tone, and she leans forward to close the space between them.

"Wait," Morgan says, shifting on the mattress. "I need to ask you something." She rethreads their hands, a knot forming in her jaw. "What were you dreaming about? Before we—before everything that happened."

Briar's mouth turns to cotton. Her palm grows slick against Morgan's. But when she raises her gaze, she sees it in her solemn expression: Morgan already knows the answer.

"You said his name," Morgan adds softly. "Riley."

Briar's face flushes reflexively, but she finds that her pulse doesn't immediately jolt with panic. She doesn't dig at her cuticles, doesn't feel her throat lock up with bitter shame.

Instead, she stares at Morgan and wonders if her bones would feel lighter, if everything would hurt less, if she pried loose the truth that's been stuck for years. Before she can stop herself, before she can worry about the consequences, before that hissing voice can demand she *stay quiet and be good*, she lets the question tumble out—

"Did you see what it looked like?" Briar's voice drops to a whisper. "In the water?"

Morgan's eyebrows draw together. "What?"

Briar sucks in a breath. "The creature Nerissa was talking about. It was there that day. The day—" She swallows, throat burning. She'll get it out. She *has* to get it out. "The day Riley died." She holds Morgan's gaze. "And you were there too."

Morgan tightens her hand, bewilderment crowding her expression. As if she can't fully believe Briar is finally admitting it out loud, the source of the hatred that's festered between them all these years.

But maybe it wasn't ever hatred. Maybe it was always fear. Fear of this exact moment, of Morgan staring straight at the vilest thing Briar has ever done. She's lived her life in a bubble of pretenses, and Morgan Parker-Blake has always been the one person who could pop it. But there's only so long someone can hide behind a shiny mask threaded with venomous lies. All snakes exorcize old scales, and Briar Winters is past due for a shedding.

It was always going to come to this.

"Did you see it?" Briar repeats, and her heart plummets when Morgan shakes her head.

"All I saw was you."

"Right. Me." Briar's gaze drops. "Because I was the only real monster that day."

"No."

"You looked at me like I *was* one."

Morgan's eyes flash. "That's not even close to what I thought."

Briar attempts to disentangle her hand. "You ran *away*."

"To get *help*!" Morgan insists, grasping Briar's fingers tighter. Not letting her move a single inch. "Who do you think called 911?"

Briar's gaze slips away as she recalls the paramedics pulling Riley's body from the water. Seaweed clung to his blue limbs. Shells knotted in his hair. While Briar sat by the shore with a blanket over her shoulders, staring at the sun until her vision turned white and her ears hummed with guttural praise. *You and I are going to change the world, Winters girl.*

"That morning," Morgan continues, "I was there with my mother and Rissa, practicing tide spells. I kept messing it up. But Rissa was perfect, and my mother actually asked me, 'Why can't you just be more like your sister?' " She scowls. "My mom always said the inside thoughts out loud. Anyway, I took off. Thought I'd show them what it was like without me there at all." Her laugh is bitter. "Ironic that I went to the north beach to escape witchcraft and ended up so much deeper in it."

"Because of me," Briar finishes, untangling her fingers from Morgan's to study the warped lines on her palms. Her curls fall forward, and Morgan quietly brushes them back, returning Briar's stare to hers.

"To this day," Morgan says, "I don't think I could fully explain what happened that morning. I knew something terrible had transpired. I knew you were in trouble. I knew your brother was in worse. But I *never* thought you were a monster." Her golden eyes spark with something unnamable. "I thought you were the saddest, prettiest girl I'd ever seen. And I was always gonna take that to the grave. Along with what I saw to make me think it."

Briar's heart lurches with regret and confusion. "So why did you avoid me back then? Why didn't you come to my Christmas party?"

"Isn't it obvious?" Morgan raises a brow. "I never got that invitation, Pom-Poms. My mother wouldn't let me go near you. At the time, I thought it was because of what happened. Some people act like tragedy is contagious. But I understand now—it was because of your family. You're Harper Clay's bloodline." Her jaw tightens. "That made you the enemy."

Briar shuts her eyes, overcome with fatigue. She contemplates all the glares they've exchanged over the years, the fossilized anger that feels Herculean to chisel away, even now. The damage has already been done. Her cruelty may as well have been sewn into Morgan's skin with needle and thread, all because she was afraid of a secret that Morgan never intended to tell.

Morgan wasn't ever going to reveal Briar to the world as a monster.

Briar's doing that all on her own.

"I'm not a sad girl," Briar finally says. "I'm a bad one."

"Pom-Poms." Morgan pokes a black-talon-tipped finger against Briar's thigh. "Come on."

"I'm serious, Morgan. I'm not a good person. There's nothing—literally *nothing*—in my life that I'm proud of. Everything that's happened—it *is* my fault. You can say it's not all you want, but I know the truth. I drove Astrid and Kai away. Finn is gone because of me. Riley is dead because of *me*."

Morgan leans forward. "Stop—"

"It's always been like this," Briar barrels on. "There's this perception of me that other people have. But I can't ever live up to it, so I'm always failing." She clenches her vine-covered hands. "It's impossible to explain that you feel like a fraud when everything looks so pretty from the outside. You come off as obnoxious. Ungrateful. A bitch." Her gaze falls. "It becomes easier to play pretend."

Morgan is silent. The rain grows louder against the glass.

"It's the most suffocating thing," Morgan finally says, "to know everyone wants you to be someone you're not. My parents always acted like witchcraft was a gift, but I hated it. Hated them too, for making me like this. Hated Rissa for thinking it was fun. I was alone at home and alone at school."

Briar raises her head. "I know. I'm sorry, Morgan. I'm—"

"It wasn't just because of you," she interrupts. "How do you make a friend? No one showed me. My parents were too busy teaching me magic that I didn't want to learn." She laughs, the sound rough and dark. "Add on that I'm queer? Forget the pentagrams on my locker; I wasn't ever gonna fit in. I was *different*. The only thing that made me happy was imagining myself at the Paris ballet instead of trapped in Loch Creek." Morgan's jaw knots. "It was easier for me to play pretend too."

Briar holds her stare. "You don't have to hide who you are with me. I mean, I'm bisexual." She pauses. "Not like it's always so easy to be."

Morgan arches a brow.

"People see the long hair, the cheerleading uniform, and they assume I'm straight. I have to find ways to tell them I'm not. Sometimes, that part of me feels the most invisible." Briar rakes a hand through her curls. "It's exhausting, setting yourself against some kind of imaginary default. Finding ways to declare that you're *this*, not that. Because you're proud, and you want people to know. But you also just want to be seen as who you really are." She tips her head thoughtfully. "Why didn't you just tell everyone the truth about your magic?"

Morgan's stare instantly hardens again. "Right, 'cause that would've gone over *so* smoothly with kids who believed I literally had sex with the devil on Halloween." She rolls her eyes. "I'm never gonna hold hands with your homecoming court, Pom-Poms."

"What about holding hands with me?" Briar asks, before she can stop herself.

Morgan's lips twitch into a smile. "I'll consider it," she says. "But we have to do something about those cuticles of yours. Haven't you heard of—?"

Briar grabs Morgan's braid and pulls until their mouths collide, swallowing her words. She tastes Morgan's surprise at first, but in the next moment,

Morgan's palms burn against Briar's waist. Their hands clutch at fabric and curves, a push and pull that ends with Briar coaxing Morgan back on the mattress and kissing her like she doesn't know how to stop.

But this isn't last night's relentless desire—this kiss is tinged with the bitter edge of lost time. Years' worth of pointless anger crackles between their mouths, and every swirl of Morgan's tongue feels like a reminder that she's someone who could have understood all along.

And now it's too fucking late.

Briar breaks the kiss, pressing her forehead against Morgan's. Without saying a word, Morgan seems to understand, stroking her hair. In the quiet that follows, Briar's phone vibrates, and her skin prickles at the thought of another text from her mother, asking about oysters in a universe where Finn isn't there to die from them.

A universe where Briar's going to die next.

Unless she does something about it first.

Maybe, she thinks desperately, she *can* write her own history. Maybe there's a reason she's kissing her worst enemy on her last morning alive.

Maybe survival, like time, has its own equations.

"What if I stay with you tonight?" Briar asks suddenly.

Morgan goes perfectly still. "What about your party?"

"I've just decided. I'm not going."

They stare at each other for a moment, something hard to place shifting in Morgan's eyes. Finally, she plants a kiss on Briar's forehead and sits up.

"Brilliant idea. Screw the party." She extends a hand to Briar, hauling her upright. "Let's go to my place right now. You can stay as long as you want. You'll be safe with me."

But there's something empty about her words, almost like she doesn't believe them.

Like they both know Briar won't be safe anywhere.

Morgan starts tossing things in her bag—phone, lipstick, keys—while Briar twirls the strands of her friendship bracelet and thinks about Astrid and Kai. There's no room for them in this plan. Just like there's no room for her in their future. She's not sure how to say goodbye without breaking what's left of her heart.

Perhaps it's better if she says nothing at all.

Morgan catches sight of Briar's expression and pauses. "You know what? Let's have coffee first." She offers a small grin. "I'm a total bitch without caffeine."

Briar forces a smile. "So, you haven't had any coffee since the carnival, then?"

"So funny." Morgan pauses by the door. "Wait for me here. Rissa isn't nearly as friendly as I am in the mornings."

The door clicks shut, leaving Briar alone in the quiet with wild hair and her nightgown askew.

Her gaze drops to her palms, and her throat tightens at the sight of those gnarled violet lines marring her skin. She rubs at them as though she could erase them, but they only seem to get darker instead.

Out of the corner of her eye, she spies Morgan's bag, tipped on its side. Her wallet and phone are spilling out, and Briar crosses the room to fit the contents back in their rightful place.

But as she gets closer, she spies a glint of gold at the bottom of the bag.

A wave of familiarity crashes over her. Glancing at the door, Briar slides her hand inside before closing her fingers around something round and cold.

For a moment, she can't absorb what she's staring at. Can't process the brass rim, the slim needles, the etching on the back.

But then . . . the gasp that slips between Briar's lips is so loud that she instinctively slaps her free hand over her mouth to muffle the sound. Confusion and despair collide inside her as her mind races to catch up, to connect the dots, forming a constellation of fury. Her teeth grind together; her ribs crack under the weight of this wretched, *inconceivable* betrayal.

Because she is holding Finn's compass.

Which has been tucked inside Morgan's bag this entire fucking time.

CHAPTER TWENTY-FIVE
BRIAR

8 Hours and 40 Minutes Until Briar's Birthday Party

White. Hot. Anger.

That's all that flashes behind Briar's eyes as she flings open the bedroom door and storms into the kitchen, where Morgan is pouring cream into a coffee mug.

"I thought I told you to—"

The mug slips from her hands and shatters on the floor as she stares at the compass dangling from Briar's fist. Scalding coffee and ceramic shards explode beneath their feet, but Briar barely registers the pain as she flies toward Morgan.

"You lied to me," she seethes.

Morgan takes a step back, toward the table. "I didn't exactly lie."

With an exhale that crescendos into a growl, Briar snatches a knife from the counter—but Morgan only arches a brow.

"Easy, Pom-Poms," she says, holding up a hand.

"You *lied*," Briar says again, closing the distance between them. "You said you didn't know where Finn is."

"I *don't* know where Finn is."

"You said you didn't know those kinds of spells."

"I don't!"

"Then why do you have *this*?" Briar's voice rises, and she leans in, close enough that Morgan backs up against the table. "Finn had his compass the night he went missing. So start talking, or I swear to god, I *will* stab you."

Morgan studies the long blade, dangerously close to her neck now. "I can't tell you."

Another wave of rage ignites inside her. "Do you think I'm fucking *bluffing*?"

"I guess we're gonna have to find out."

Briar fumes between clenched teeth and fits the blade against the soft curve of Morgan's throat. She swallows the realization that just minutes ago, her lips were there instead.

Morgan's body tenses against hers, as if she's fighting to hide her fear. As if recalling Briar's blank stare on the beach that day while Riley ran out of air. As if a part of her expects Briar to drive the knife through her neck and end her too.

"Morgan," she says, "I *need* to know where Finn is."

"I told you, I—"

"You and I both know," Briar continues, "that whatever is happening to me can't be stopped. I saw it on your face. On Rissa's face too. I'm dying, and there's nothing anyone can do about it." Her pulse whirs. "I have to find Finn first. I have to get at least one thing right." Her hand shakes around the knife. "Please, Morgan."

Morgan's nostrils flare with unnamable emotion. Her chest heaves like she's fighting to keep words inside.

"For the last time," she grinds out, "I don't know where he is."

Briar's vision whitens with opal light; stars of rage and despair explode behind her eyes. "You're *still lying*!" She presses the flat part of the knife harder, and Morgan's knuckles tighten around the table's edge. "Right to my fucking face. After kissing me like it actually meant something."

"It did," Morgan whispers, raising her chin. "It meant something to me."

But Briar shakes her head. "You're exactly who I thought you were."

Something shifts behind Morgan's stare—a cloud of sadness that settles into hard anger. "Then do your worst, Pom-Poms."

Briar holds her gaze, palms sweaty around the handle of the knife. Adrenaline courses through her as she imagines twisting her wrist and puncturing Morgan's smooth skin until her throat is slick with blood. Until there's a fucking lake of it at Briar's feet, staining her white nightgown ruby—

Careful, Winters girl.

Briar stiffens at that rattling voice in her skull, its ice chilling the dim kitchen.

So beautiful with such bloodlust. But you're wasting your time.

"Quiet," she whispers.

Morgan's pained expression twists into confusion. "What?"

You won't find what you're looking for so far from home.

At that, Briar abruptly drops the knife. Morgan jumps at the sound, eyes round in bewilderment.

Without another word, Briar glides toward the door as if in a trance. Home. She needs to get home.

"Wait—*wait*!" Morgan calls, as Briar continues down the corridor, back to Nerissa's guest room. "Was something just talking to you?"

But Briar ignores her, peeling off the soft nightgown and yanking on last night's borrowed clothes. She snatches her belongings, half noticing the flurry of texts from her parents. And her heart briefly soars—because there's one from Astrid too.

We're worried about you.

Briar shoves her phone into her bag and flies from the room.

"Let me drive you," Morgan begs, chasing her down the hall. "You're not safe out there. Please let me—"

Ignoring her, Briar flings open the door and dashes out into the rain.

"Pom-Poms! Wait, please—"

Finally, she whirls. "You can stop acting like you care about what happens to me."

"I *do* care."

"You don't. And I'm leaving. We can go back to hating each other's guts." Briar spits a dark laugh. "Actually, we can go back to not talking at all."

"No, hold on—"

She turns instead.

"Wait!"

Briar gets halfway down the front path before Morgan finally says it—shouts it, untethered, into the blistering wind.

The truth makes Briar slam to a halt in the rain, paralyzed.

"Finn killed you."

CHAPTER TWENTY-SIX
BRIAR

8 Hours and 20 Minutes Until Briar's Birthday Party

Rain hammers down as Briar stares at Morgan, her words hanging between them.

"Finn Adler killed you," she repeats, stepping closer. "He *shot* you."

Shocked confusion roars through Briar's veins. Morgan is speaking, but the sentences don't make sense.

"It was an accident," she adds, yet the phrase does nothing to close the wound in Briar's chest.

Because Morgan is using past tense. Something that *happened*. But if Finn killed her, does that mean—

"Are you saying I'm . . . dead?" Her right eye throbs at the question, and she presses a hand to her rain-slick lashes.

"No." Morgan flattens her lips together. "You died at your birthday party, and Finn and I—we brought you back."

"My *birthday* party?" Briar spits rain. "But . . . that hasn't even happened yet."

"It did. But it's happening again. I—I fucked up the spell."

"What?"

"I wasn't lying when I said that I didn't know aether magic!" Morgan insists. "But Finn showed up at my house with a book I'd never seen before and waved *a gun in my face*, and I—" She clenches her teeth. "I didn't have a choice."

"I don't understand," Briar says. Nerissa's house swims before her; her eye pounds beneath the cascading rain. "Finn shot me? I—died? A spell—oh god."

"Shit," Morgan says, as Briar staggers. She rushes forward, holding Briar at the waist. "Do you see why I couldn't tell you? This kind of information would be too much for anyone."

But Briar pushes her away, stumbling down the path around the side of Nerissa's house.

Morgan follows. "Hold on—wait."

Images whirl inside Briar's brain: a pink sky over unnaturally still water; a rectangle of gold candles; Finn, holding a gun, the silver gleaming in the moonlight.

What does it mean, she wonders distantly, to die twice?

Desperate for dry air, Briar ducks inside a shed in Nerissa's backyard, Morgan right at her heels. She pulls the heavy door shut, the rain like a halo of static around them.

Chest heaving, Briar sinks to the dusty floor and hugs her knees against her torso. Her whole body shakes as she rocks forward and back, vaguely aware of Morgan kneeling in front of her. Behind her are rows of shelves holding jars of floating starfish and sea urchins, all seeming to stare and stare as Briar drops every last defense and allows herself to come apart.

"Pom-Poms," Morgan whispers, a tentative hand sliding over her knee. "I'm—"

Briar bats her hand away without looking up. Her teeth chatter. "Tell me—tell me what happened."

"Are you sure?"

She raises her head, letting Morgan see her flushed face, her reddened eyes. She nods.

"Okay." Morgan whooshes out a breath and sits beside her. "Okay. So, all summer, Finn had been sending me DMs, asking weird questions about

Loch Creek and my family. I ignored them. But then—" She swallows. "The day after your birthday, I was in my apartment—my *real* apartment, not Finn's place—and he called me. I wasn't invited to your party, so I didn't know the details. All I knew was that you'd been shot." Morgan bites her lip. She turns, ghosting her fingertips over Briar's cheekbone, her lower lashes. "Here."

Briar's stomach lurches. Her eye aches as Morgan lowers her touch, something sticky and wet gathering in the corner like syrup. If her wraith is nearby, she's surely laughing. All these years avoiding her reflection, silently choking on fear.

And this entire time, it was Finn's hand that would turn her into her worst nightmare. A hand she once clung to beneath a thundering sky, an anchor to keep her safe.

"Finn asked to come over, talk about magic." Morgan's voice turns cold. "He sounded like he hadn't slept in weeks. He said he figured out all these secrets about Loch Creek, that what he did was an accident. Said he was trying to protect you from something unspeakable—but the whole plan turned to shit."

"Because he shot me," Briar says.

"Yeah." Morgan's jaw knots. "He showed up at my place. Said he needed my help, that he found an aether spell that would restore a person's life if it was performed within twenty-four hours of their death. He said I was the only one he knew who could do it."

"Why you?"

"Because everyone says I'm a witch?" Despair crowds Morgan's expression. "I *told* him I didn't know aether magic, but he said that didn't matter, that he had a book, he figured out the pronunciations of the symbols. That I could just *read it*, like this was French class or something. I tried to tell him—a spell like this, there's always a trade. For every action, an—"

"An equal and opposite reaction," Briar finishes, letting out a rush of air.

A heavy quiet falls over them; outside, the storm howls.

"There had to be balance," Morgan explains. "In order to reverse time and bring you back, something else had to be erased."

"Finn," Briar realizes, and despair roils inside her along with the truth she's always known:

She's the reason why Finn disappeared.

There's never been any other answer.

Briar isn't sure how anyone can live with the kind of guilt that's threatening to explode inside her. It must eventually corrode a person's insides, turn them into a withered husk. Until they're unrecognizable. Good as dead.

Then again, she already is.

"Finn agreed to the trade." Morgan stares toward the vials of kelp and algae. "I told him that he'd end up somewhere *between* time. Here, but not here. Lost, but not gone." Morgan slides a glance her way. "He didn't care. Said he would kill himself right there if I didn't do the spell. The gun he had with him—it wasn't ever for me."

The ache in Briar's chest widens as she imagines Finn's fingers wrapped around the handle, the muzzle kissing his forehead. His horrible, desperate expression as he threatened to pull the trigger.

"We chose the carnival, the mirror house specifically, as the site for the spell," Morgan continues. "It was Finn's idea—something about heightened metaphysical energy. But I must have done something wrong." She rakes her hands through her hair. "*No one* was supposed to remember him. It should have been like he was never born. But I woke up the next day in his apartment. Like some evil force was punishing me for meddling. *Laughing* at me. Whatever alternate reality I created, I was suddenly at the center of it." She points to the windows. "Those dino-fish washing up on shore? The fire that burned down my parents' restaurant? All because of me. *Everything* is out of balance." She drags her gaze to Briar's. "That's why I made you promise to stop asking about aether magic. I sure as hell wasn't gonna do this twice."

Briar just stares at her. "Why didn't you tell me the truth from the start?"

"What was I supposed to say? Finn killed you, and I erased him from existence to bring you back, but—oops!—I threw the entire world into chaos?"

"What was Finn trying to protect me from?" Briar fires on. "At my party."

But the second she asks, she realizes she already has the answer.

The whisper inside her skull. Glass on glass. Purring in her ear since she was a little girl and standing alone in an ocean that had swallowed her brother whole. She wonders what Finn would say if he knew that creature has been part of her forever.

"He never would have been able to save me from that," Briar whispers. Her entire body threatens to shut down at this new awareness: Finn sacrificed everything he had to rescue a doomed girl who is only destined to die again.

All this was for nothing.

Morgan studies her. "Pom-Poms, there's something else you should know. That type of aether spell—it required more magic than any witch could possess. In order to bring you back, I had to borrow from something... inhuman."

A cold chill works its way up Briar's spine. "Morgan. What are you saying?"

"Someone... some*thing* talked to me during the spell." Morgan shudders. "Said it would help, wouldn't ask for anything in return. Somewhere I knew it had to be a trick, but I was so scared and disoriented. The aether magic, it messed with my head. Made me see horrible things, like a nightmare I couldn't wake up from." She lowers her head. "By the time I realized what I'd done, it was too late. You and this creature—you were irreversibly bound."

"*Morgan.*" Briar grinds her teeth. "You bargained with the exact thing the aether witches are trying to set free! The thing that wants me as a sacrifice!"

"I know."

"No wonder it didn't ask for anything in return! You were handing me over on a silver platter, you absolute asshole!"

"Pom-Poms. I *know*. I fucked up—supremely."

Briar snaps to her feet. "You *damned* me."

Morgan stands just as fast. "You and I both know," she says quietly, "you've been damned since the day you were born. But not because of me."

Fury simmers inside her—not just because of Morgan's words, but because of the weight of their truth: Briar's never had a choice in any of it.

Then a new terrible question creeps into her thoughts. If this creature wanted her as some kind of sacrifice, why would it help Morgan restore her life at all?

Unless, Briar realizes, it needs her for something worse.

Cold sets into her bones, and she has no choice but to remember the morning on the beach with Riley. The instructions that echoed in her ear, forcing her limbs into obedience.

The nightmarish things that voice told her on graduation night, what it promised she'd do next. *Who* she'd hurt next. Briar studies her latticed hands as though they're not her own, before curling her fingers inward. She's been a pawn her entire life.

She won't become a weapon too.

"What did you borrow?" Briar demands through clenched teeth, desperate for every last truth. "How did this . . . this *hell prince* bring me back?"

Morgan's gaze drifts, stalling. As if she knows the answer will be the final nail in the coffin of what could have existed between them.

"Blood," she finally says. "He gave you his blood."

Briar's breath rushes out. "What?"

" 'Blood as black as midnight,' " Morgan recites, " 'to match a soul that's newly dead.' That's what the spell said I needed."

Chilled, Briar considers her cut: the scarlet-onyx substance that's been leaking from the wound. As if she's merely a shell of a girl, now a vessel for a beast.

"There's one more thing," Morgan says, dragging Briar's gaze back. "This part of the spell—it wasn't a recipe. It was a tether."

"What?"

"His blood—his *inhuman* blood—is your sole connection to the living world. It's like you're on life support." Morgan closes her eyes briefly before delivering the final blow: "The only thing keeping you even half-alive now," she says, "is him."

Briar stares at her for a long time. Just a few hours ago, Morgan was starting to change shape to her. Her mouth wasn't a ticking time bomb threatening to explode with secrets, but something soft and sweet. Her body was once enemy territory, but last night, Briar kissed her like she could grow to love the taste of treason.

How foolish she must be to believe she could hold Morgan's hand on a fire-scorched battlefield and try to build a haven of their own instead.

Swallowing a bubble of shame and regret, Briar holds up Finn's compass. "You still haven't told me why you have this."

"I kept it," Morgan says flatly. "As an amulet. In case I needed to go after him."

Briar studies it, contemplating their engraved initials, the infinity symbol on the back. *Because friendship goes on forever.* And with a jolt, Briar unhooks the clasp of the compass and fastens it against the nape of her neck.

She might be damned, but Finn isn't.

If she has any time left, she sure as fuck knows how she's going to use it.

Morgan seems to realize it at the same time.

"No—no, wait," she says. "Only a witch can use an amulet to travel between worlds."

"Don't I have magic now?" She starts for the door. Morgan blocks it. "Out of my way."

"You don't know how to *use* your magic," Morgan points out. "Please, trust me, don't—"

"*Trust* you?" Briar practically spits it, and her tone slams Morgan into silence. "Don't you dare ask me to do that again."

"Hold on," she insists. "Remember when you came to my apartment and there was shit written in the closet in blood?"

Briar's jaw clenches around the word. *Stay.*

"I peeled back the wallpaper after you left. That wasn't all Finn wrote." Morgan's eyes flash. "There was more to the message. He said, 'On your birthday, stay home.'" She reaches for Briar. "Pom-Poms, you can't go to that party. Come back to my place like we talked about. Let me try to keep you safe—*please*."

Briar searches Morgan's gaze for more lies, but all she sees is the desperation of a girl who's laid all her cards on the table. A girl who expects to get burned anyway.

"Do you want to know something, Morgan?" Briar asks. "After your mom died last year, all those lilies that arrived on your doorstep without a card? *I* sent them. I told myself it was because I didn't want you to feel alone—and I didn't—but I also wished so badly that things had been different between us." She takes a steadying breath. "I hate that I was right all along about you. I should have stayed the hell away."

For a second, Morgan doesn't say anything. Her eyes turn glassy like she might cry. But then, in the smallest whisper, she offers, "I always knew it was you who sent them."

Briar huffs a breath out her nose and storms toward the door. "I'm leaving."

"Wait—" Morgan lunges for her wrist. "Listen to me. The original thread is trying to right itself. You're going to die again. *Tonight.*"

Briar freezes and drags her stare to Morgan's. Her words should put a blade of fear inside her, but all she feels is resolve.

"I know," Briar says. "But before I die, I'm going to bring Finn home."

CHAPTER TWENTY-SEVEN

FINN

As night falls, something begins to scream.

Finn jumps, turning away from the half-shattered mirror where he had been studying his unrecognizable reflection. His too-long hair and unshaved jaw are instantly forgotten as he whips his gaze around the bedroom, trying to locate the source of the keening wail.

It takes him a second to realize it's a telephone. The one he's been using to call Briar in the past.

But it hasn't rung once since he got here. He's only ever dialed out.

Finn sprints down the corridor without a second thought. He barrels into the living room and snatches the receiver before fully registering the black waves licking the switchgrass outside the window. High tide. The time of day when Briar never answers his calls—the time after her birthday. But what if? What *if*—?

Nonsensical hope surges inside him, and Finn squeezes his eyes shut in silent prayer as he answers. "Hello?"

"Hi, is this Finn?"

For a moment, Finn's breath catches at the sound of her voice, familiar and warm and right in his ear. Wild happiness pours through him, and he leans against the wall for support, unsure if his body can hold the weight of this relief. It's high tide, and Briar is talking to him. Briar is alive, she's alive, she's—

But then she adds, "Do I have the wrong number?" and unease snaps his joy in two.

Her tone, he realizes. It's clipped. Formal. Briar, but not *his* Briar.

A chill flies up his spine.

"Hello—?"

"No, it's me," he answers. "Briar? Is that you?"

A breeze rustles the phone with static. "It was really nice meeting you this morning, but I have to reschedule. Or cancel. I have to cancel."

Her words rattle in his brain, an equation he can't compute. "What did you say?"

Briar pauses, and wind floods the airwaves again. "I have to cancel our—"

"No." Finn swallows. "The first part."

"Oh. It was nice meeting you."

"Meeting me?" he echoes, pulse thrumming. His breath shallows as he races through all the possibilities of what she could mean.

"At the bookstore?" Briar's confused tone almost matches his now. "This is Briar Winters. You gave me your phone number. Do you remember? You asked me to—"

"The bookstore... I gave you my..." Finn drags a hand through his hair, bewilderment consuming his entire body. "What's today's date?"

"Um. August twenty-first."

Her birthday. His blood pressure climbs with fear. "What—what year?"

She releases a small laugh, like she's not sure if he's kidding. "It's 2038."

Finn whirls so fast that the base of the phone clatters on the floor. He doesn't even bother to pick it up. "I'm sorry, did you say '*2038*'?"

His mind races faster than he can possibly form a single thought. She's calling from the future?

Briar is *alive.*

But 2038.

That's—

Thirteen years from now.

Thirteen.

Panic grips his entire core as he turns to the window again, as if anything on the pale foggy beach could help explain what the fuck is going on. If that creature didn't claim her on her sixth birthday, and it somehow didn't claim her on her nineteenth, then—

"Yeah, um." she says. "I know we had plans to meet tonight, but I can't."

Finn paces as he tries to piece together what's happening. *Briar is alive*. This fact should be louder than anything else, but... but why is she acting like they just met? For as much as he's studied, as many numbers as he's crammed inside his skull, he can't understand this. Can't understand why Briar would be calling him from the beach thirteen years from now, not knowing anything about him other than his name.

"Briar—"

Before he can say anything else, a low rumbling rocks the cottage. The walls creak, floorboards shifting beneath his feet. The air grows cold enough that Finn's exhales turn ghostly, and he doesn't even have to look to know there's a black mass gathering in the corners.

He's almost out of time.

"I'm sorry," Briar says. "There's something I have to do. I shouldn't have made plans—"

"*Wait*," Finn urges, finding his voice as a wisp of black smoke curls around his throat. His breath corkscrews as he fights desperately for one more chance, one last shot in the dark, one—

"Briar," he works out. "*Briar*. Do you ever feel like you lost something, but you can't remember what?"

Finn hears her whispered answer, but he doesn't get to say anything else to her.

The line goes dead, and the room turns to ash. As if sucking the light from every future Finn ever imagined with Briar. Because in one timeline, it's thirteen years from now, and they're holding hands under palm trees and stars.

In another, she doesn't remember him at all.

Unable to grasp any of it, Finn casts a grief-stricken glance across the room—and finds the Death King already waiting for him.

This is no longer the whisper of a face or the hint of a fang. The Death King is three-dimensional, alive with chilling splendor. Power radiates from him in a swirling fog that kisses his silhouette. He turns the entire room to ice with his presence alone.

Fighting to steady his pulse, Finn peers into the shadows. "What do you want?"

For a moment, the Death King is silent. He sits perfectly still in a high-backed wooden chair, clothed in dark robes, black armored gloves, and a hooded cape drawn over his wintery hair. His long legs stretch languidly in front of him, as if he's on a throne, and his sharp pale eyes are fixed on Finn. Glowing from beneath the hood.

Finally, he smiles, his teeth glimmering white. *I've come to collect your debt.*

Finn bristles at that familiar voice. There's something disorienting about such a nightmarish sound coming from a creature so alluring, and he's suddenly dizzy at the dissonance.

But then Finn narrows his eyes. He can feel Briar's voice slipping away with every second, and stubborn anger coils inside him. He won't let this monster keep taking what belongs to him.

"I don't owe you anything," Finn clips.

I healed that shoulder, didn't I? The Death King studies him. *Perhaps we can continue to help each other.*

Trepidation creeps into his stomach. "How?"

The Death King's eyes are two orbs in the dark. *I can offer you freedom. Escape. You won't have to remain stuck in this place.*

Finn blinks. There's no way this creature will help him at zero cost. "And what do you get in exchange?"

A vessel. His smile tips higher, razor teeth gleaming like a barracuda's. *Did it ever occur to you that I, too, am trapped?*

Finn skews his mouth to the side, considering. This beautiful human face he sees right now—that can't be his true form. Creatures like this, they seduce. They entice.

They corrupt, in order to possess.

"You want to use *me* as a vessel," Finn counters. "My body. For what, exactly?"

Three centuries ago, the Death King says, *I was awoken beneath your filthy sea and promised unfettered access to the world above in exchange for my magic. Instead, your kind has turned me into a fed prisoner, a beast in an underworld cage. In order to obtain the true power I am owed, I must take matters into my own hands. But without a bodily form, my foothold in the mortal world is merely fleeting. Do you see?*

"Power," Finn echoes. "That's all you want. And at any cost." He drags his thoughts to the history he studied over the summer, the town documents, the spell book. "Loch Creek has been sacrificing their own people to you for years, thinking that setting you free will grant them your godlike magic. But that's not the case, is it?"

Becoming a god, he says, *is not achieved through bargaining.*

"That's a riddle, not an answer." Finn rakes a hand through his hair. "I know what you are. You're a demon. You'd destroy the world if you got the chance. I'm not going to help you do it."

Not even, the Death King says, *if you could see her again?*

Shadows swallow the room as Finn's breath rushes out, defeated. He hangs his head, strands falling in front of his eyes. He doesn't have to look to know that the Death King's grin has deepened. Because Briar is Finn's most vulnerable weakness. Her name alone can convince him to do anything. Claw his way through time. Point a gun at a monster. Let a witch whisper an ancient language and exile him to a world of dreams.

But maybe it's not weakness. Maybe it's strength.

Finn has spent his whole life worrying that his heart would harden like his mother's, that he'd one day fill his world with numbers and pills until there's no room for love at all. He wasn't sure his mother's heart was even capable of love, and it made him wonder if it was genetic, stamped into his DNA before he ever got the choice.

But if this isn't love—this fierce, unrelenting ache to do anything for someone even if it means ruining yourself—he's not sure what is.

Maybe, at the end of all this, he won't be able to say he protected her.

But he will have tried everything.

Maybe, eventually, that will be enough.

Finn raises his gaze. "If I agree—and I mean *if*—I have one condition."

I'm listening.

He clenches his teeth. "I need to know that you won't hurt Briar. *Ever.*"

The Death King is quiet for a moment. Red moonlight seeps through the window, painting the hollows of his cheekbones a glittering ruby. *Consider it an oath.*

Finn squints. "Why should I believe you? Your banishing spell can only be broken with a sacrifice of twins. You were already given Riley. Briar's all that's left."

Our bond can only hold if you trust me, the Death King says. *I won't hurt her.*

Finn stares into the shadows and wrestles with what it means to strike a deal with a creature of the dead. There's a trick in this vow, he's sure of it. A loophole stitched between syllables, a catch hidden beneath that slippery forked tongue. Because if the Death King is so readily agreeing not to hurt Briar, it can only be because he doesn't need to.

Or because he's planning something worse.

Finn would do well to come up with a trap of his own.

Flattening sweaty palms against his flannel pants, Finn starts across the room. "Alright." His voice sounds detached to his own ears. "I'll do it."

A slow smile splits the Death King's face.

There's just one thing first. His fangs glow in the shadows. *If you're to think of me as a king, you should be on your knees.*

Finn exhales through his nose, humiliation consuming him as he lowers before those long folded legs.

The Death King rises and takes a few silent steps toward him. Finn freezes as his gloved hand rests on his shoulder before sliding to the back of his skull.

Empty your thoughts. Think only of midnight, of the sea. Think of death. Finn can hear the smile in the Death King's soulless words. *Think of me.*

Finn squeezes his lashes shut. His teeth clack together; his breath hisses loose. He digs his nails into his palms so hard that his skin becomes slick with blood.

Then his spine burns with a fiery ache. He cries out—a raw, wounded sound that silences the second he opens his eyes.

Because the world around him is bleeding with color.

Bright, brilliant, beautiful color.

Gone are the peeling walls, the crumbling floor. The windows shimmer with sparkling glass, and white-tipped candles line the entire room. That tattered sofa is now a plush velvet one, draped in expensive blankets. The Death King's rickety chair has now become a true throne with pointed black spears carved from shells and sapphire-encrusted arms.

The realization strikes him: with the Death King inside him like this, he won't have to remember what this place really looks like. Won't have to think about where he came from.

He can be someone new.

I told you, the voice rattles, as if reading his mind. *I can give you anything you want. I can make all your pain disappear. Look.*

In a trance, Finn crosses to the hall mirror, and his throat constricts.

His too-long hair is slicked away from his face in a smooth knot. Where his body had begun to look malnourished and weak, his reflection shows hard lines across his torso and arms corded with muscle. Suddenly desperate to see more, Finn pulls his T-shirt over his head to inspect his defined chest.

When he twists to peer at his back, it's to find his skin perfectly smooth, devoid of cigarette-burn scars. For a moment, Finn can only stare, thinking of the way his cheeks would flare with anxiety in the locker room, how he'd change with his spine pressed against metal so no one would see. The embarrassment that later hardened into anger at the thought of spending the rest of his life branded by his mother's rage.

But now it's as though she never hurt him at all.

We're more alike than you could have ever imagined, the Death King purrs inside him. *Both of us, confined to predetermined paths. Restricted from our true potential. But there is strength in suffering. In fear. In pain.*

Finn's stomach warms, still transfixed by his reflection—until he notices his eyes.

They've turned wholly black, no whites visible, no gray. An empty stare for an empty boy.

Don't you see? the Death King continues. *Together we can change the world.*

Those words are like cold water drenching Finn's skin. Trick, he reminds himself. It's a trick. Malignant creatures like this one, they offer the *illusion* of bargains. Anything Finn agrees to will only serve one of them—and it isn't him.

Tearing his gaze away, Finn closes his eyes and concentrates on the memory of that obsidian dagger—the one item that could kill the Death King. He traces the scars on his palm from the ritual. Remembering the slice of the blade through his flesh.

And his breath stills as he pictures the weapon clearly for the first time. Not tucked in his belt like he thought, but strapped to a girl's smooth thigh.

Morgan Parker-Blake.

Morgan still has the obsidian dagger.

He never took it at all. It's still there, in the world above.

But instead of surrendering to despair, he allows the seeds of a desperate plan sprout to life in his mind. He could let the Death King take him back to the mortal world. Let him use Finn as a vessel. Find that dagger—and then slit his own damn throat, taking that godforsaken creature with him.

He'd die—but the Death King would be gone forever too.

Finn's heart races. His palms grow clammy. Dying, he thinks, would hurt a lot less than everything else that's happened so far.

It's a perfect plan, except for one glaring hole:

The obsidian dagger only responds to magic.

In order to pull it off, he'd have to acquire magic of his own. Finn squeezes his eyes shut. The spell book had a bonding ritual, didn't it? One that transferred a witch's power to a mortal. Morgan? Could he convince her to . . . ? No. That's too much. No way *Morgan* would agree to something that intimate, not after everything she's already done for him, not—

A sudden pain bursts in Finn's ears, and he cries out, his palms flat on either side of his head.

Don't be a fool, the Death King hisses from inside his own throat. *If I wanted a mess of your blood on this floor, I'd do it myself.*

Finn's eyes pop open at the realization that the Death King was reading his mind.

But as he turns over the words, something else clicks.

"You can't," he says, "or you would have killed me already. You need me—my body—for something. You're *planning* something. What is it? Wh—?"

He stumbles to his knees as his ears start to ring—a terrible, keening sound.

"Get out." He grips at his hair, his temples. "Get *out*!"

Finn's head tips back as deep laughter bubbles from within his larynx, and he clasps his hands around his throat, trying to smother the sound. Pain engulfs his lungs, shooting like blades behind his eyes, and he folds at the waist in defeat.

When he raises his head, the room is tenebrous and frostbitten once more, the ground littered with shells. But he barely has a moment to absorb the transition before the Death King hauls him to his feet.

Finn's spine crashes into the wall, and the room darkens, shadows spreading out behind that towering figure's back like widening wings. Or fins. The Death King's leather-covered hands hold him at the shoulders, digging into Finn's bare skin so hard, they'll leave behind violet bruises. But then he leans in, bringing his mouth just below Finn's ear.

I claimed you alive. And you will remain alive until I say otherwise.

The words inspire a jolt of fear, but that rough whisper fills Finn with an infuriating warmth. As if he can sense the change, the Death King unfurls a low, rumbling growl that vibrates down the length of Finn's throat straight to his core. Heat pools low in his stomach, and he scrambles to battle this maddening contradiction of wild terror laced with traitorous wanting.

You are nothing without me. A broken boy. Unwanted. Cast aside.

Finn's teeth grind together; he wrestles against the gloved grip. "Stop."

Rejected. Unloved.

His chest heaves in anger. "Not true."

But these are not my words, my little lost wolf. One large hand slides up the column of his throat, his fingers reaching to Finn's jaw. That mouth splits in a smile, fangs glittering. *They're yours.*

Finn's breath spirals. His vision blurs at firm strokes of leather against his skin.

And then, the Death King's touch travels to his lips. Running a broad thumb possessively over the seam of his mouth, back and forth, until Finn opens for him.

I hold every idea of yours, the Death King whispers, thumbing the flat of his tongue, the bottom row of his teeth. *Every secret, every sin. Every ugly thought you've ever had is mine.*

Finn battles another unwelcome blaze of heat, at war with the pain filling his ribs. He hates each second of the Death King's touch, despite being suddenly desperate to feel those hands elsewhere. Wanting to live forever in the arms of a fallen god just as monstrous as Finn believes himself to be.

But then the Death King lowers his hand to Finn's throat again and asks, *Are her desires as impure as yours?*

And the tempting heat disappears, replaced only by the icy reminder of what this creature ultimately wants: Briar.

"You will *never* find out," he warns, twisting free of the gloved grasp.

Perhaps not, the Death King says. *As long as you hold up your end of our bargain.*

Finn glares at him, dark and stormy.

It was a pleasure entering your soul this evening, the Death King purrs. *But by the time we're done here, you'll invite me in yourself.*

~

Finn is hauled awake by a girl yelling. The sound splits his eardrums, tearing through his blood. Straight down to his rib cage to crack his heart in two.

Because it's not just any girl. It's a voice he'd recognize anywhere: Calling his name across the hallway. Whispering a secret in his ear. Crying through broken telephone wires.

"*He didn't just leave me!*" the girl shouts. "*He left you too!*"

It's Briar.

Finn scrambles to his feet in the dark and immediately staggers—he's not in the cottage. He's somewhere else, murky and claustrophobic. And when his eyes adjust, his breath rushes out to find that he's staring at himself.

Dozens, and dozens of versions of himself.

Because he's somehow back inside the mirror house. At the carnival.

"What—?"

"That's fucked up, Briar."

Kai's voice now.

Adrenaline surges through Finn's veins. He doesn't even think before launching into a run, tearing through the mirrored tunnel. He couldn't say why, but he knows with fierce certainty—this isn't a memory. This isn't a dream. This is now.

They're here. They're *right* here.

"Kai!" Finn yells as he careens around the corner. "Briar! K—"

Pain ricochets through his body as he slams directly into glass. Stars burst along his peripheral vision. But it's barely a second before Finn spins and tries another corridor, their voices the map guiding him.

Finn runs faster.

"So you can dish it but you just can't take it?"

And faster.

"Call me tomorrow if the aliens return my actual friend."

And—

Finn's heart leaps at the exit sign's beckoning crimson glow. He yanks the handle, bracing himself for the wooden steps down to the beach—

But he crashes into another mirrored dead end instead.

Galaxies explode behind his eyes. A groan of pain tears from his throat as the glass cracks and spider-webs, despair crushing him.

It was never an exit. It was always a trick. Everything in this place is a fucking trick. A maze of missed chances and almosts. Getting right to the finish line but never close enough. A phone call that just won't connect. Friends he once had but can't ever find again.

A girl he tried to save but never could.

Frustration crackling, Finn slams his fist into the mirror. Glass bites his skin, but he doesn't care. The pain feels better than sadness, better than defeat.

So he pounds again and again, barely registering the ruby soaking his skin or the silent tears against his cheeks. All he can hear is endless shattering, everything breaking and falling apart around him.

And then something snaps him to attention.

Astrid's voice, clear as day.

As if she's directly on the other side.

"What the hell is that sound?"

Finn freezes. The fractured mirror fogs with his breath. Was she talking about—?

He bangs on the glass again.

Kai this time. "*Is someone in there?*"

Incredulous wild laughter bubbles at the back of Finn's throat. His lashes sting with fresh tears, and he scrambles to hold on to this moment. To the flimsiest thread of hope that maybe he isn't out of chances after all.

That maybe—just maybe—*lost doesn't mean gone.*

He raises his fist again. And suddenly remembers—

Kai beneath his window, with a flashlight. Dots and dashes. Morse code.

Finn slams the broken mirror. Two short smacks with his fist. Two long ones. Three short. One long. More and more until he finally works out: *I'm—still—here.*

He can't say how long he bangs the wall. It could be minutes; it could be hours. But he does it over and over until his hands are raw and aching, until his lungs are so full of hope that he imagines they could explode into a cluster of burning stars.

But when Finn opens his eyes again, the mirror house has gone dark. There are no voices echoing in the walls.

Just shadows and cold.

And mirror Finn staring and staring.

But this time, he looks different.

Finn gasps, rearing back. His reflection's white shirt is soaked through with blood. His face is sunken and grotesque, rotten flesh sliding off the bone. His hand clenches around a protruding dagger—buried in his stomach all the way to the black-colored hilt.

"What the f—?"

Panic flashes in Finn's rib cage, and he breaks into a run. His breath comes in sharp gasps as he careens down the mirrored corridor, until—

He skids to a halt.

Because he's right back in the distorted cottage. He looks over his shoulder as though he might find the mirror house again, but all he sees is a long tunnel of shadows instead.

Wiping a film of sweat from his brow, he flies down the corridor toward the sitting room before snatching the phone. He dials. It rings, and Briar's voicemail clicks on.

He dials again. His heart hammers as he eyes the window. The moon swells like a red balloon; the shore licks at black seagrass. A king tide. The highest one he's ever seen.

He dials again. *Pick up. Pick up, pick up, pick up.* Voicemail, voicemail, voice—

But then, on what has to be the fiftieth try, it clicks.

And Briar's voice erupts into a sob around his name.

"Finn. *Finn.*"

His name. Like the first thing he ever heard her say.

But this time, Finn's chest tightens at the sound: the roughness of her cries, the sheer *alarm* of them. Something is wrong.

Something is so, so wrong.

"What day is it?" he asks, the words rushing together. "How many days until your b—?"

"Today," she cries. "Finn. *Today is my birthday.*"

PART FIVE
KING TIDE

The waves now have a redder glow—
The hours are breathing faint and low—
And when, amid no earthly moans,
Down, down that town shall settle hence,
Hell, rising from a thousand thrones,
Shall do it reverence.

EDGAR ALLAN POE, "The City in the Sea"

CHAPTER TWENTY-EIGHT
BRIAR

6 Hours Until Briar's Birthday Party

Briar rips through the front door of her house, nearly smashing it into the wall.

"Mom? Dad?" she cries, dropping her keys in the dish with a clatter. But the entryway is dark, the entire house quiet. Adrenaline seizes her, and she starts for the foyer, desperately hoping she'll find her mother upstairs.

There's no way they can have this party tonight. Briar doesn't give a shit how much money her parents spent, how many people will be there.

They have to cancel. There's no other choice.

"Mom!" Briar yells again, flying up the steps. "I need to talk to you—"

Her words are swallowed by the terrifying realization that the carpeted stairs are drenched in water. Each step squelches beneath her flip-flops, icy liquid biting her toes.

Panic ensnares her. The leak in her room. What if—?

Briar kicks off her shoes and sprints, careening into the corridor.

And gasps at the sight of an inky substance spilling from beneath her closed bedroom door.

"No, *no*—"

Briar lunges for the doorknob with a wail.

Her room is flooded from the ground up. Blackened water rushes her ankles, pooling around her desk, devouring stray items of clothing. Photographs float like lily pads; her favorite stuffed bunny is face down, its fur matted and stained. The book she was reading last week, destroyed; the diary she keeps hidden beneath her bed, consumed.

All Briar can do is stare in horror as everything she owns drowns right in front of her.

But before she can decide what to do, her right eye bursts into blinding pain.

Briar folds at the waist, a groan spilling from her lips. Her eye has been hurting since she left Nerissa's cottage but *this*—this is new.

She imagines a blade poking at her retina until it pops, spilling viscera down her face. Heart slamming with panic, she presses her palm to her lashes—and whimpers when she finds them sticky with something thick and gelatinous.

Briar blinks through a wet blur. Her hand is smeared with a liquid so dark, it might as well be onyx. *Blood as black as midnight.*

"No," Briar groans. She staggers across the room through the pool of standing water, and before she can talk herself out of it, she rips the sheet from her vanity—

Where she explodes into an anguished scream.

Her right eye is partially dislodged from its socket, hanging from fleshy tendrils and weeping ink. The syrupy black fluid leaks down her cheekbone and the side of her nose, staining her skin.

But it's not her wraith this time. It's just *her*: Briar Winters, Loch Creek's favorite. Briar Winters, who dies at nineteen. Who dies *today*. This is how she will look as she leaves the world: covered in demonic blood and choking on all the things she never got to fix.

Consumed with an overwhelming mix of furious rage and despair, Briar grabs a cheerleading trophy from her bureau. Angles it behind her shoulders.

And smashes it into the mirror with a keening howl.

Glass rains down on her water-covered feet like dust, but the shattering sound only stirs her veins with fierce rebellion. Perhaps destiny can be dented.

Being damned doesn't mean you can't fight back.

So she swings the trophy again. And again. And again. Until the mirror is broken straight through, its edges like teeth, and Briar turns her attention to the window. Without thinking twice, Briar smashes that too, screaming through the crash. Rain sprays onto her face, drenching her skin, but she doesn't fucking care. Grief rages inside her with every swing, taking the shape of Finn's hand in hers, Riley's laugh, her broken friendships. And just as she's about to fly into the bathroom to demolish that mirror next, something warm ensnares her waist. Almost like a restraint.

But more like an embrace.

She freezes.

You can stop, Winters girl, purrs that voice in her skull. *You're safe with me.*

The Hell Prince. Here in her room.

Maybe he's been here the whole time.

As if in a trance, Briar sinks to her bed. The wind hisses through broken glass, and the cheerleading trophy slips from her bloodied fingers. But when she touches her lashes again, they're only wet with tears. Suddenly overcome with exhaustion, Briar lies atop the drenched comforter, rain spilling from the fragmented window. She should get up, call Professor Quill. Astrid. Kai. But in this moment, all she can think about is how peaceful it feels to close her eyes beneath a spray of mist. Like she's lying in an open casket, buried at sea.

You deserve to rest. A flutter of breath against her cheek. *I'm the only one you can trust, remember? I've been with you from the beginning.*

Yes, Briar thinks, *I know.*

A low growl vibrates in her ear, and Briar relaxes at the sensation of a firm hand along her lower back. Eyes still closed, she arches into the touch, imagining a broad palm enclosed in leather curving around the triangle of her hip bone. Sliding across the soft plane of her stomach. Possessively stroking. Claiming. A confusing heat gathers between her thighs, and she imagines her resolve like a crumbling dam against a turbulent wave.

Perhaps she's just as wretched as this evil voice inside her.

Perhaps they've always been the same.

I can give you anything you want, Winters girl. I can make all the pain stop. The Hell Prince's whisper brushes the curve of her neck. *I just need to hear you say it.*

Say what? Briar thinks.

His words have a smile in them. *That you're mine.*

Tears sting her lashes at the thought of a world without this splitting ache in her chest. Where she'd never think about Riley again. Finn. Morgan. She'd be numb forever instead. Silent and at peace. She's out of choices, hurtling closer to the hour of her death.

Maybe she should just let him take her.

The acquiescence is on the tip of her tongue when the room darkens. That grip tightens around her, and the mattress dips, as though there's actually someone behind her in the bed. Or some*thing*.

Briar freezes. She opens her eyes.

And her breath catches at the sight of a strong gloved hand splayed across her belly. Without turning, she tracks her gaze higher, tracing up a muscular arm swathed in black armor.

She sees him for only a moment before leaping from the bed, terror ripping through her.

But in the next blink, he's gone.

"What the *fuck*?" Briar hisses, raking a trembling hand through her hair. There was just a *man* in her *bed*. A man with silver-white hair and eyes the color of crystals. A man in all black, holding her. *Touching* her.

But was it . . . even human?

That face—those terrifying opal eyes, the knife cut of his cheekbones. Skeletal. Glowing with death. And beauty.

Something about that infuriates her. This voice—the one that purred while she stared blankly at a struggling Riley in the waves—it should be attached to something grotesque. Not an alluring creature with soft lips that can graze her throat and stoke the fire of her surrender.

Flushed, Briar snatches her phone, remembering what she set out to do when she arrived here. Call Kai. Astrid. Professor Quill.

Use the compass as an amulet.

Find Finn.

Briar grabs Ryland's business card from her bag. Her heart hammers as it rings and r—

"Hawthorne College Department of Anthropology and Religious Studies," someone with a smooth voice says. "How may I direct your call?"

"Hi." Briar sniffs. "Can you connect me with Professor Quill, please?"

A silence shifts on the other end, and goose bumps prickle on Briar's skin.

"I'm sorry, did you say Professor Quill?"

"Yeah. Ryland Quill? Department Head?"

"Uh . . . hold on." A muffled conversation cracks like static in the background. "I apologize, but Ryland Quill is no longer with us."

"What?" she breathes, wide-eyed. "No, that's impossible. I—"

"Unless we're talking about two different people," he continues, "Ryland Quill passed away about eighteen years ago."

Briar's phone screen cracks down the center as she drops it with a thud on the side table.

She snatches it before tearing from the room, heart thrashing in her chest. She races down the stairs, feet squelching with every step. Professor Quill is dead? How? She saw him *yesterday*. He gave her his *business card*. He—

Briar skids to a halt at the bottom of the stairs, Morgan's words echoing in her mind.

The original thread is trying to right itself.

She looks down at the violet veins snaking up her wrists. The original thread, the one where Finn's father is dead.

The one where she's dead too.

Then, just as she's certain this panic will wrench every ounce of air from her lungs, she spies a light from her mother's craft room. Desperation rockets through her, and she flings herself toward the door.

"Mom," Briar calls, knocking. "Mom—I need to talk to you about tonight."

A clacking sound drifts out from beneath the door. The loom, rotating and lurching.

But no one responds.

"Mom!" Briar yells louder. "Mom, we have to cancel my party. Mom, please—*please* open the door."

She tries the handle. Locked. But the sound continues, as if her mother has headphones in.

Or she's unable to answer. Because something got to her first.

I'm the only one you need, remember?

Despair pools in Briar's stomach. She imagines her mother slumped over her loom, blood leaking from her mouth. Her father, crumpled in the corner, his face frozen in a wail. Leaving her alone in this drowning house with the dark thing that's been waiting to devour her for years.

"Mom!"

Gritting her teeth, she grips the door handle and leans, hard, with her whole body. She rears back, shuddering the wood with her shoulder. She feels ridiculous. But she does it again.

On the third try, the door finally bursts open.

And Briar screams and screams at what she finds inside.

CHAPTER TWENTY-NINE
BRIAR

5 Hours and 30 Minutes Until Briar's Birthday Party

Briar circles her mother's craft studio, her breath coming in jagged waves. Fear and confusion boil inside her at once as she stares. She has to be dreaming. This cannot, cannot, cannot be real.

The walls are covered in photos of herself.

School photos, camp photos, pictures printed from her Instagram. Vacation to Paris, eighth grade. A formal picture at a cheer competition, tenth.

And her senior portrait. The one that's been missing from the frame in the basement.

The one that's now marked with a fat daisy wheel, drawn in thick, black ink.

Just like all the other photos.

The symbols defile various parts of her body: her stomach, her neck. The curve of her clavicle, the swell of her shoulder.

But in her senior portrait, the symbol conceals her entire face. Her eyes are completely covered in ink, petals obscuring her lashes, making it hard to tell there's even a girl in this photo at all.

Briar has barely a second to register it before she notices the smell.

A rotten odor consumes her, crowding her nostrils. She fights back a gag and turns toward her mother's loom—

Her chest lurches. Bile rises in her throat.

Because there's no yarn threaded between the warp.

Instead, it looks like the skin of a squid or an octopus, the pigment pale and splotchy. Daisy wheels punctuate the rubbery texture—a tapestry composed of dead sea creatures, menacing with decaying scales and foul-smelling brine.

Briar staggers into a shelf and dislodges a handful of glass vials holding fish innards, urchins, and severed tentacles. They shatter on the floor, the slithery contents coating her bare toes. She tears from the craft room, a scream ripping through her throat.

She races without purpose out the back door, flying flying flying into the rain-drenched yard. Lightning sizzles overhead as she sucks in shallow breaths.

Her *parents*.

The daisy wheels on her face in the craft room.

Daisy wheels in the spell book.

Daisy wheels on the lighthouse proposal.

The daisy wheels she finally, *finally* remembers seeing as a child: On a necklace her mother used to wear. Embedded in the leather of her father's belt. Drawn with chalk by Briar's own hands on the playground.

Scraped into the sand the day Riley died.

A terrible new thought occurs to her, and she rolls up her soaked leggings. Rain cascades down her shoulders, matting her hair, as she peels the bandage away. How did she not realize it before? It was right in front of her face—

There, carved into her flesh, are two brand-new ovals. There are six now, arranged in a perfect circle.

But, of course, they aren't ovals. They never were.

They're the petals of a—

"*Daisy wheel*," she whispers.

The marking on her leg was always evolving into this: the symbol of aether magic, of the spirit whispering in her skull since she was a little girl.

It was never just the town officials, the mayor, everyone in charge of Loch Creek. This whole time—

This *whole fucking time*—

The people who bargained with that evil, the ones who want to sacrifice her—

They've been right here, *inside her house.*

Riley's death wasn't an accident. It was a plan. A *prophecy*. Her own parents—pretending to grieve the loss of their son, pumping Briar full of medication so she wouldn't suspect. Letting her believe it was her fault, letting her drown in that guilt. And all along, they were the ones who planned to bury her at sea in exchange for power and magic. Just like they did to Riley.

A pair of twins.

Briar was never a person to them.

She was always a sacrifice.

Briar's sobs rise into grief-stricken wails, and she sinks into the mud-drenched grass. She cries so hard that she's sure her lungs will explode, that her whole body will disintegrate into sand right here in this yard.

Winters girl.

"No," she howls into the rain. "Leave me alone."

But the rattling voice only grows sharper.

Now you know the truth. You're mine, Winters girl. You always have been.

Rage thrashes behind her ribs. She thinks of the photos in her mother's craft room, the black ink covering her face. Her entire existence has been spoken for since she took her first breath, wrapped in ribbons and delivered to a dead thing that already owns her. She suddenly feels detached from herself, like she's hovering in the stormy clouds, high above a body that never belonged to her in the first place. Despair and dread roil inside her as she presses her palms to her ears.

"Fuck you," she yells into the wind. "I'll *never* be yours."

An unseen force suddenly fists her hair, dragging her to her knees. She cries out at the swift splitting pain on her scalp.

Do I need to test your loyalty again? Send you on a little mouse hunt to see how well you can listen?

Briar gasps as she recalls the dead mice that appeared over and over in her middle school backpack. She'd reach into the front pocket for a pencil and squeal at the sensation of the cold, stiff rodent. All this time, she'd been certain Morgan planted them to torment her.

It was never Morgan at all.

Little Briar, catching mice in the grass behind her house. Little Briar, squeezing life from their tiny bodies and tucking them in her pocket with a whisper of praise in her ear. Like an eager kitten bringing home mangled presents with pride.

"I hate you," Briar growls, as the Hell Prince's invisible grip tightens on her curls.

You don't, he purrs. *You only hate how much you need me.* She can hear the malicious smile in his words. *But perhaps we need a bigger test to prove it. Like that day on the beach.*

"Shut up," she whispers, squeezing her eyes shut before she imagines the things this monster could force her to do next.

How he could poison her thoughts until her hands become covered with the blood of someone else she loves.

That invisible grasp tugs her hair again, now at a terrifying angle that feels like it could snap her neck. Panic and fury sink into her throat, growing pointed and sharp. And as she struggles and gasps for air, she thinks of Finn.

Finn, standing outside Loch Creek Primary, screaming into the salt-bitten wind. The way the sound consumed every nerve in her body, wrenching loose the grief that had been trapped inside her for months. The look on his face when she screamed back.

The ocean of unspoken words between them now, things she may never get to say at all.

Winters girl. Are you going to be good?

She grits her teeth. "No."

That death-cold grip suddenly drops to her throat, and she corkscrews out a gasp.

Then the next time you need my help, you're going to beg for it.

Briar curls her fingers into fists. She slams them into the earth.

And empties a new scream into the storm.

Just like that day in kindergarten, the sound is raw and wild, keening and torn. It rises above the thunder, above the streaks of wind, piercing the air like a knife. Like a reckoning.

Those hands on her neck loosen, but Briar doesn't stop screaming. She drowns out the gravelly voice in her skull; the blood-soaked nightmares of the craft room; her mounting, unrelenting despair. And it's like she's five again, screaming for Riley, for the gaping hole in her heart that will never fully close. For the small, identical hand that used to fit inside hers but is forever gone now. Her pulse races so fast that it turns into a buzz, a hum, a—

No—

Her *phone* is the thing that's buzzing.

Briar couldn't say why, but somehow, she knows—

She yanks it from the waistband of her leggings.

And her scream tapers into a disbelieving sob.

"Finn!" Her throat is raw around his name. She closes her eyes, relief and confusion and terror all blustering like a tidal wave inside her lungs. "*Finn.*"

And then, his voice. Just as she remembers it: honey warm and deep and perfect, right in her ear, asking—

"What day is it? How many days until—?"

"*Today*," she wails. "Finn. *Today* is my birthday."

"No—no, your party, are you—?" His words come in incoherent bursts, a tornado of confusion and panic. "Briar, you *cannot* go to your party tonight. Get out of Loch Creek *now*."

"Where *are* you?" she demands instead.

"Briar, please, I'm begging you—"

"Tell me. Please, Finn. Tell me how to find you."

She can picture him clenching his jaw, squeezing the bridge of his nose under his glasses. Her heart fractures inside her chest, and she cries harder, the cracked phone screen slick with rain and tears.

"No. Briar—you can't come here."

"Finn," she says again. She wants to say his name over and over, wants it to be the last thing she ever breathes. *Finn, Finn, Finn.*

"I won't *let* you come here," he says. "It's not safe, Briar."

"I can. Finn, I will. I'll find you. I'm going to bring you home." She stares at the graying afternoon sun. The last one she'll ever see. "Whatever that place is—we'll leave it together."

But as the words leave her mouth, Briar knows they're a lie. Even if she finds Finn—even if she saves him.

She won't be coming back alive.

CHAPTER THIRTY
BRIAR

1 Hour Until Briar's Birthday Party

On the evening of her nineteenth birthday party, Briar Winters wears the white dress her mother picked out for her to die in.

It's a simple dress, with straps that crisscross up the back, a low V-neck, and an empire waist. The bottom spills around her thighs and billows in the wind. She leaves her hair down and wild, secured on one side with a starfish pin. Her palms' mutated veins are out of sight, hidden beneath white lace gloves from an old costume trunk.

The dress does little to keep her warm as she sits on the edge of the lifeguard tower, staring at the darkening sky. The cut at her calf burns beneath a bandage, devoid of medicine now. She won't need it where she's going.

Briar studies the ocean's raging crests, its mysterious darkness, and wonders how something could be at once so beautiful and so soulless. Alluring yet indifferent.

The waves, a calming sound that puts so many to sleep peacefully at night.

The waves, the last thing she's sure she'll ever hear.

~

When Astrid and Kai arrive at the lifeguard tower, the sky has turned a deep blood orange. The rain has temporarily subsided, a layer of mist clinging to the horizon. There, Briar finally releases her secrets, one by one. But this time, there's no choking seawater, no claws around her throat—as if the Hell Prince owns her so completely that he'll grant one pocket of air as a parting gift.

For a moment, Astrid and Kai can only stare, their eyes glittering in the setting sun. Behind them, a crowd has gathered at the base of the dock. The party will be starting soon.

"Your *parents*?" Astrid murmurs in disbelief.

"Maybe not just hers," Kai adds. "My grandma's on some of those town committees. Your moms, Astrid."

"Unknowing participants," Briar says. "I'm sure of it. Your families are full of good people."

The unspoken part hangs between them.

Mine isn't.

"There's more," Briar says, reaching into her bag to hand stapled pages to Astrid. "After I talked to Finn, I searched my dad's office. This was on his computer."

"Are these . . . your medical records?" Astrid asks, flipping through the papers.

"He's been sending them to Mayor Caldwell." Briar swallows, bile rising in her stomach. "Once a year, since I was born."

"*What?*" Kai's breath rushes out.

"All my blood work, dental records, psych reports, my *period cycle*—god." Briar grinds her teeth. "They've been studying me for years. Grooming me for this fucked-up prophecy. That's what they do at their secret leadership meetings. Analyze the girl they plan to sacrifice for immortality and magic. They've been waiting my entire life to kill me."

Her words linger in the salt-drenched air. Briar can feel Astrid and Kai wrestling with the reminder that family can be nothing more than blood, that parents aren't inherently good, a lesson they learned over and over from knowing Finn. A parent can trap you forever by clipping your wings and calling it love. Distorting your world so you never question what it would feel like to fly free.

Briar reaches into her bag to pull out a square of graph paper covered in Finn's scratchy handwriting.

In the beginning, there was a girl who talked to the water.

"This was at the bottom of Finn's backpack," Briar says, offering it to Kai and Astrid. "When I first saw it, I thought it was about me." She swallows. "But after talking with Professor Quill, I read it again. It's the history of Loch Creek. Read the part Finn underlined."

Astrid glances at the paper. "The harvests will continue every thirteen years to maintain the prosperity of our haven, until a pair of tw—" She halts, swinging her gaze up to Briar's.

"It's okay," she whispers, surprised to find that she means it. That, for once, her body doesn't clench upon hearing the word. She takes a steady breath. "Keep reading."

Astrid nods, her dark eyes swooping down. "The harvests will continue every thirteen years until a pair of twins in flames extinguish each other's light in a sacrifice to the dark," she recites. "Then, and only then, can Our Savior break free of His sea-bound chains and bring eternal celestial power to the aether coven."

No one has to speak to know they're all thinking the same thing: Thirteen years ago, Riley was sacrificed to an ancient evil in the ocean.

Briar's parents meant for her to die that day too.

And tonight, they're going to try again.

"I'm sorry," Briar finally adds, sliding her gaze to Kai. "For shoving you earlier." She looks at Astrid. "For the bitchy things I said to you. I didn't mean them."

"Yes, you did," Astrid replies, but there's a kindness to her words. "I meant what I said too. And that's okay. We're a *real* family, remember? Sometimes we aren't careful with one another. But we can always survive together."

Briar nods, clenching her jaw so she doesn't cry. For all the words that just tumbled loose, she didn't tell them one important thing. . . .

After tonight, she won't be around to survive with them any longer.

Bass thrums under the sand—music from the yacht, lit up with a fairy's den of bulbs. The sound seizes Briar's awareness. The boat will be leaving the dock soon.

"I have a plan to reach Finn," she says, wrapping her gloved fingers around Finn's compass. "It's a long shot, but it might work with your help."

"Whatever it is, it might not be as much of a long shot as you think," Kai says. At Briar's arched brow, he adds, "Do you remember when we found Finn's backpack and we heard those sounds from the mirror house? Like a pattern?" He raps a few times on the wooden railing of the lifeguard tower—short knocks. Long ones. "I think it was Morse code."

A chill scrapes the back of Briar's neck as she realizes. "Finn?"

"We used to do it with flashlights as kids." A muscle knots along the side of Kai's jaw. "One time, in seventh grade, he signaled something that made no sense. I asked him about it the next day, and he didn't know what I was talking about. But I'm positive: it's the same pattern we heard that night."

"What is it? What does it mean?"

Kai swallows, his dark eyes glittering. "'I'm still here.'"

"Holy shit," Astrid breathes, intertwining her fingers with Briar's, matching bracelets kissing at their wrists.

"Professor Quill said he's stuck between the folds of time, right?" Kai says. "Maybe light and sound have their own rules. Maybe they're stronger than time itself."

"Or maybe we are," Briar offers, taking Kai's hand with her free palm. "Maybe it's like Finn's dad said. Our love crosses galaxies. Defies the laws of physics." Her throat works to swallow. "Maybe we're stronger than magic too."

Astrid smiles, silent tears dampening her cheeks as Briar pulls her and Kai into a hug. Kai's arms fold around them both, and for a moment, they stay that way, listening to gulls' cries on the wind. Briar tracks her friends' steady heartbeats, her ribs aching with the awareness that this embrace feels like a final goodbye.

The music gets louder, and Briar leans back, swiping at her lashes. She thinks, fleetingly, of whispering secrets in the bunk after dark with Astrid at camp, of curling in a sleeping bag on Kai's deck to watch the sunrise. If she'd known how little time they'd all have together, she would have paid more attention to the details: the soft sound of Astrid's voice in her ear, the firmness of Kai's hand in hers.

She simply would have paid more attention to her life.

"Okay," Briar whispers. "Here's the plan."

~

The evening sky swells with lavender as Briar boards the yacht alone.

She smiles at a cluster of girls from the cheer squad, adorned with their rainbow of sundresses. Toward the stern, Mika Baisho stands with Jessamyn and Inez Hoffman: Kai's grandma and Astrid's moms, all holding plastic cups of rosé.

The yacht is draped in twinkling lights, and aproned staff members circle the deck, offering delicately plated appetizers. Everything glows gold beneath the setting sun, igniting a fresh wave of anger inside Briar's chest. A flawless celebration for a flawless girl. But this party's perfection is as illusory as her own—one careless crack would surely reveal the rotten parts underneath. What would everyone think if they knew the food they're so mindlessly consuming was paid for with the blood of their own neighbors?

Pulse thrumming, Briar searches the party for flashes of white.

Mayor Caldwell, in a suit the same shade as his hair.

Patrice Weatherstone, in an ivory dress.

The city attorney, the county manager, all of Loch Creek's officials. Each one dressed in white.

Just like Briar.

Her throat tightens, fingers itching inside their gloves as she recalls Mayor Caldwell's penetrating stare at the art gallery. The syrupy-slick way he talked about her working in his office, when he knew the entire time that she'd never live long enough to start. How both he and Patrice have hovered for years, filling her house with flowers after Riley's funeral, asking questions at dinner parties about school and cheerleading. As if they gave a single fuck about her future.

As if they believed she'd have one at all.

A knot tightens in Briar's stomach, but it loosens a little when she spots

Astrid and Kai on opposite sides of the bow. Just like they planned.

Another slip of white snags her attention—Briar's parents moving swiftly across the hull toward the stairs that lead below deck.

Briar's chest clenches.

She hasn't seen them since she returned home from Morgan's, shooting off another lie over text about doing her hair at Astrid's instead of the salon. She wouldn't have been able to stomach looking at their faces. But the sight of them now puts a new wave of fury inside her. All those times she felt safe in her mother's arms, all those times she was soothed by her father's deep voice in her ear... all of it, a trick. Their affection might as well have been an orange bottle of pills, meant to keep her quiet until she served her purpose.

Briar squeezes her fists and darts a glance to her friends.

They all nod. It's time.

It happens fast. Kai and Astrid scramble up to the highest point of the bow as Briar yanks the cord from the sound system. The guests buzz in protest as silence replaces the steady pop beat, and Briar slinks toward the staircase unnoticed.

"I know you're here tonight to celebrate Briar Winters's nineteenth birthday," Kai calls, wind-whipped as he holds on to the flagpole. "But there's something you need to know about the people in charge of Loch Creek. What they've been doing to this town for decades. Centuries, even. What they're planning to do next. And"—he angles a glance toward Mayor Caldwell—"we have proof."

Briar pauses to wait for their agreed-upon cue, her satisfied smile twitching as the guests appraise the mayor. A sea of brows, all knit in confusion.

"Lance Nottingham, 1947," Astrid calls out.

"Evelyn Baker," Kai says next. "1960."

"Perrie Vale. 1973."

Caldwell's face turns ashen as he exchanges glances with the other members of the Cultural Council. Recognition sparks on the guests' expressions like television static, the crowd's collective memory flickering to life at the names of people who have met tragic ends along Sorrow's Shore.

The names of Loch Creek's harvests.

"1986. Kenneth Evans."

"1999. Genevieve McMannis."

Kai's eyes find Briar's across the boat. She nods, knowing whose name is next.

"2012," he says, his jaw knotting. "Riley Winters."

A hush falls over the crowd, but Briar ignores the way the guests search the deck for her reaction. Because it doesn't hurt this time to hear Riley's name. Not like it used to. It's like her body has been hollowed out, her heart excavated and replaced with water hemlock and coral tentacles. No room left for pointless emotions like sorrow and grief—not when the worst things have already happened.

Yet there is one emotion that burns within her: determination. She wasn't able to protect Riley. She won't be able to save herself.

But Finn—Finn, she can still save.

That feeling hardens, swift and fierce, into vengeance. She imagines it like stardust coursing through her veins. Like fury. Like magic.

She tightens her fingers around Finn's compass, tucked beneath her dress.

At the end of all this, if she can say she rescued Finn, then her life will have been worth something. *She* will have been worth something.

"You may recognize these names," Astrid says, "as people who went missing or died on the north beach. One victim, every thirteen years. Contrary to what you might have been told, none of these were accidents."

"Coincidences come in twos," Kai chimes in, echoing Finn's words. "Anything over three is a sign. And I don't know about you, but I think this town has been ignoring the signs for far too long. Astrid? Want to show them?"

Astrid brandishes a remote, lighting up the screen meant to play a slideshow of Briar's childhood photos that are too painful to see. And Briar holds her breath as an image of Mayor Caldwell pops up instead—the photograph she snapped at Old Town Hall. Grotesque and soberingly real.

"Before anyone asks," Kai adds, "this is an authentic photo. Untouched. Unaltered. *This* is the man in charge of Loch Creek."

Horrified buzzing pulsates through the crowd at the sight of the mayor's peeling skin, the nightmarish veins erupting around his eyes. Looming over the boat in full color, the mayor looks every bit the hideous monster Briar knows him to be.

A flash of white zips across the deck as Mayor Caldwell and Patrice start toward the exit.

But they don't get far because a barricade of guests thwarts their path. Briar rises on her tiptoes, and reassurance surges inside her to find Kai's grandmother Mika at the front of the throng. Blocking the mayor from leaving, waiting to hear what else her grandson has to say.

"We're going to tell you everything we know," Astrid continues from the bow. "And you can decide for yourselves if these are the people you want running your town."

"Then, as soon as we're done here, everyone will need to evacuate on our word." Kai stares at Briar over the heads of the crowd, their eyes locked in agreement. "Because in approximately twenty minutes, this entire boat will burn."

At that, the crowd erupts in chaos.

No one will notice Briar when she disappears.

Sucking in a breath of salt air, Briar takes one last look at her friends. Her family. Her chest crushes beneath the weight of a goodbye she's not ready to say.

But she races down the stairs anyway. Down, down, down to the bottom of the boat.

Where she opens the door to a candle-draped shrine built for her death.

CHAPTER THIRTY-ONE

BRIAR

Nothing could have prepared Briar for the hell-washed horrors of the basement cabin.

Black flames circle the floor. Photos from her mother's craft studio plaster the walls, some adorning tables littered with stones. Those squid-stitched tapestries hang over the porthole, blocking any light from the crystalline moon.

At the center of the floor waits a wide metal door with a latch. Vault-like and sinister, it's the kind of door that's not meant to be opened unless you don't plan on returning.

It's also exactly where she needs to go.

And standing on either side of the rusting hinges are Sabrina and Otto Winters, clothed in white robes and looking nothing like the parents Briar knows.

Her mother's strawberry curls are in a low braid, seashells stuffed throughout. Her eyes are rimmed in dark blue, lips painted like blood, and she's holding a small leather book. Her father's eyes are also heavy with blue shadow, his cheekbones dusted with cerulean glitter. Unfamiliar rings decorate his fingers as he clutches a chalice encrusted with black stones.

"Briar," her mother says, voice chilled. "You're early."

Briar stares at them and grasps for the threads of her plan: Confront her parents. Burn this boat that was meant to deliver her to her death. Leave Loch Creek in a cloud of ash.

Ignite the compass with her magic, disappear in the water, and *get to Finn.*

She has no idea if that last part will work. All she has is flimsy, desperate hope.

But now that she's in front of her parents, everything feels tangled. What do you say to a mother who orchestrates the death of her children? A father who chooses ancient magic over his own daughter? And here they are, still holding her back. Obstacles between a dying girl and the one right thing she needs to do in her too-short life.

"How could you?" Briar finally whispers. "All these years, you let me think what happened to Riley was my fault. You convinced me that voice was *in my head*. And all this time, you were planning *this*?"

"Briar, darling," her mother coos. "You make it sound like we're horrible people."

"Because you are!" Her words erupt into an angry laugh. "You let Riley die! You left us at the edge of the water to play because you *knew what would happen*!" She swallows. "You thought I would die too, didn't you? But I lived, and it ruined your plans."

"Riley's mortal body might be gone, but *he* isn't," her father says. "His purpose lives on."

"His purpose? He was six years old! We *buried* him. In a tiny—" Briar's voice catches. "In a tiny coffin. It rained the whole time. I put his—I put his teddy bear in there with him. He's in the *ground* and gone forever, you *absolute monsters*!"

"Briar, please," her father says in a terrifyingly quiet tone, dripping with condescension. He extends the chalice. "It's your birthday. Why don't you sit and have a drink?"

She snaps her gaze to the cup. Fury overcomes her, the seconds ticking in her mind. She's low on time. She won't play this game.

"No way I'm drinking that," Briar bites.

"Darling, it's just wine," her mother answers. "We wanted to properly celebrate."

"Like hell it is!" Briar exclaims. "What should my birthday wish be? For my parents not to kill me?"

"You have things wrong, my dear," Briar's mother says. "We would never hurt you." She almost looks offended, a hand flattened against her heart. "You're the future, Briar."

"A legend. Destined to become a high priestess." Her father's eyes brim with a silver glow. "Just think—royalty, in our own family. After tonight, everyone in this town will bow to *us*."

"I'm not a high priestess," she hisses. "And this screwed-up family is anything but royalty."

"You were selected, Briar," her mother says. "Three hundred years ago, my ancestor, *your* ancestor, Harper, was the strongest witch on this great earth."

Her mother extends the leather book, and Briar takes it wordlessly. She flips through the crinkled pages, her stomach flattening as she catches sight of the drawings and symbols. And the dates on every entry—*1692.*

Harper's journal.

She thinks of Professor Quill. *It was once kept in the archives of Old Town Hall, though it hasn't been there for years. Someone must have moved it.*

"But," Briar's mother continues, "as powerful as she was, Harper couldn't bring celestial magic to her people. She made a grave error that started a feud with the water coven and forced ours into shadow. No one could unlock immortality for ten generations. Until you."

Her mother steps back, gesturing to the hatch in the floor.

"You'll see what we mean." Her mother tilts her head. "Death is not the end, Briar. You'll return to us, and you'll return anew. A renaissance will bless our coastal town. We can bend the edges of time so we never grow old nor ugly." Her eyes flare white as she gestures to the chalice. "All you need to do is drink and let the sea take you."

"Like it took Riley," Briar says. "A pair of twins in flames."

Her father's mouth peels in a dark smile. "We've been waiting years for this day."

Briar studies her father's face, the yellow stain to his usually veneer-white teeth. She cuts a glance to her mother's uncanny wrinkles, recalling that clump of hair she tugged loose. Past-due bills on the counter, crumbling art on the walls. The hills and valleys of Professor Quill's economy chart flicker in her mind, and anger blazes inside her.

"Waiting years," Briar echoes, "because the harvest cycle is up, isn't it? You'd rather kill me for magic than experience an ordinary life."

"Enough now," her mother says, taking the chalice. "It's time to start the ceremony."

"No." Briar backs up, thighs colliding with the table behind her. Frames topple like a row of fallen dominos.

"Briar." Her father's tone is a warning as he steps toward her. "This will be much easier if you don't resist."

"You're going to poison me!" she cries, stepping back. "And then bury me at sea!"

"It's not like that." He gestures to the hatch. "This corner of the ocean is a place without time. Without space."

Briar's determination hardens. She was right, then. That *is* the way to get to Finn. With her magic, and his compass as an amulet, she can—

"Come," her mother repeats, advancing too. "Have a sip. You won't feel a thing."

Briar whips her gaze around the cabin. The *candles*. She has to get to the candles—

Her father tracks her stare to the shimmering flames. Puzzlement flickers on his face before his expression flattens into understanding.

Adrenaline surges inside her. She has only seconds.

Briar lunges for the table, but her father blocks her path. In one startlingly smooth motion, he snatches her elbow and spins her, restraining her against his chest. The journal tumbles to the floor, and Briar shouts as he forces her wrists to her sides.

"Sabrina," he barks, "now."

"No, *no,* let go, let—!"

Briar's protest spirals into a keening yelp as her father grasps her hair, yanking her head back for her mother to bring the chalice to Briar's lips. Briar thrashes, but it's futile. Her father's grip is too tight, and rage-salted tears fall at the awareness that she might never see Finn again. His last words to her will be those terrible panicked ones on the phone, and she'll leave this world with nothing but ruined plans. Add this to the graveyard of almosts, everything she wishes she'd said and done before she lost the chance.

"We didn't want it to be this way." Briar's mother strokes her forehead. "I'm sorry, sweet girl."

"No—" Briar manages to say. "I'll die if I drink that—please, Mom, *please don't*—"

But her mother's eyes are wild and cold. Faraway and unreachable.

"There is no death," she whispers.

A defeated sob breaks in Briar's chest, and she thinks, inexplicably, of the smell of fresh linen—being wrapped in a warm towel after a bath, tucked into bed below a gauzy canopy of fairy lights and stars. This can't be the same mother. This can't be—

Warm liquid floods her mouth. At first, it's sweet, but then a burning taste scorches her tongue. Like fire. Like acid. She whines, but her mother holds her jaw open like she's a dog who lapped up chocolate. Tears stream down her face, her chest heaving as she sputters and gags. She can feel it. She's going to die in their arms, she's never going to make it to Finn, she's—

Well, well, well. You're in quite a mess.

Briar gasps as her hands burn underneath her gloves. A searing ache sizzles down her fingertips, ripping through her corrupted veins.

You told me to leave. But we need each other. I am not your damning, Winters girl. I am your salvation.

She squeezes her eyes, her resolve so close to crumbling. She's so close to agreeing, to climbing into this monster's arms and letting him have her any way he wants.

You're no use to me as a crumpled, lifeless thing, the Hell Prince purrs. *That's rat poison you're drinking. Calculated precisely for your weight.*

Briar's chest clenches. The scale in the guest bathroom. Her father.

He wasn't looking for the correct dose of medication to keep her healthy.

He was measuring the exact amount of poison to kill her.

Fresh fury ignites in her bones.

What will it take, the Hell Prince continues, *for you to admit who you belong to? What will it take to make you beg for me?*

She doesn't have time to consider. Doesn't have time to weigh the consequences.

Because Briar's mother empties the chalice in her mouth and holds her jaw until she swallows.

White foam bubbles at the corners of her lips. Her limbs jerk like electricity. She can feel herself slipping and slipping away, her deflating body an airless balloon. It would feel good, she thinks, to sleep forever.

But then she sharpens her thoughts on Finn.

Finn at ten years old, his chin in his hand as he evaluated chess pieces across from hers. Finn at fourteen, backpack slung over one shoulder while he bumped his fist into Kai's. Finn at seventeen, forehead pressed against Astrid's arm as he cried-laughed over a silly YouTube video.

Finn this very summer, his mouth against hers as he whispered how he'd wanted to kiss her for years.

Finn, never alone when he was with her. Finn, alone in the dark now.

Her life can still be worth something, she remembers. Her life can still be worth something. Her life can—

Please, Briar thinks, squeezing her eyes shut. *Help me, and I'll do anything you ask. If you let me reach Finn—if you don't hurt him—you can have me.* Tears burn her eyes. She summons all her strength to silently scream the terrible words. *You can have me forever.*

I'm yours.

And then that creature. That demon. That Prince of Hell.

He roars with satisfied laughter inside Briar's skull, and something wild shivers to life within her blood. She imagines claw-tipped fingers reaching down her throat, triggering her gag reflex. Briar's shoulders lurch as she expels the poison, splattering her mother's white dress.

It's just enough time for Briar to twist her wrists away and peel off her gloves.

Silver-blue crystals ignite in her veins as she flings herself at her mother. Briar's hands connect with her flesh, her cheeks, her neck—and then air. Just empty space.

A thud reverberates, followed by shattering glass. Someone screams—a wolfish, animalistic sound. By the time Briar realizes it's her own voice, her mother is clear across the room, slumped against the wall. Blood drips from her temple over the slope of her nose. But her mother doesn't move. Her eyes are frozen open, seeing nothing.

Despair creeps into Briar's throat. She sinks to her knees.

"I'm sorry," Briar whispers, crawling toward her. "Mommy, I'm sorry."

But the words have barely left her lips before her father flies at her from above, his expression ablaze with rage and grief.

"What the hell did you do, Briar?" he yells. "What—?"

His voice disappears into Briar's scream as she pushes back, palms throbbing. Celestial silver bursts between them, burning their flesh, and when she sends him flying across the yacht, she doesn't look away. She watches as his skull smashes into the wall, watches as he slides to the floor in a heap. Unmoving. No longer able to hurt her.

Briar bends her forehead to her knees, dry-heaving. Cruel, discordant memories flicker in her brain: twinkling lights on Christmas morning; her mother's high-pitched whistle from the stands at homecoming; her father teaching Finn how to knot a tie. But her parents are not the people from her memories. Those people wouldn't dress a boat with flowers and candles and prepare their only remaining child for death at sea.

Quiet fills the cabin, the upstairs emptying after Kai's warning. Such deep quiet.

Winters girl. That hissing voice curls in her ear. *You've improved.*

"I never wanted this," she rasps. "Take it back. Take the magic back."

The Hell Prince only laughs and laughs. Frost digs at her neck, like claws hooking beneath her chin. And for a second, she sees him again. That silver-haired man dressed in black. Grasping her throat with a possessive hand, his long fingers adorned with glittering rings. But he flickers in and out of her vision, teasing her with glimpses of hollowed cheekbones and burning opal eyes.

You don't get to pick and choose when your power is convenient, foolish girl. It's a part of you. I'm *a part of you.* The voice deepens, as if reverberating from the walls. Those fingers probe her jaw, her lips. *You said it yourself. You belong to me forever now.*

Briar once might have felt panic at this creature caressing her; now she's filled with eerie calm. When the only choice is surrender, it somehow arrives with numbing relief. She relaxes into the demon's broad palm, and his low growl of approval vibrates in her bones. His talons rake through her hair, a heavy hand stroking the top of her head. A dark prince petting his cat.

You and I are the same, he reminds her. *But you've known that for a long time, haven't you? You've known it since you first spoke to me that morning on the beach.*

Briar's eyes flip open, the words a pinprick jarring her awake.

"We're not," she works out. "*You* told me to hold Riley's hand. To keep walking into the water." A tear snakes its way down her cheek. "It was you who told me to let go."

I tested you. And I knew you were worthy of our bond.

"You tested me? You made me *drown my own twin*!" She snaps away from the icy claws, leaping to her feet. The world spins in a flash of silver and black. "We *aren't* the same. That wasn't me. *I* didn't do that. *You* did. You used my body, you possessed me, you—" A fear-soaked understanding rips into her. "Was *this* another test? To see if I could kill my parents? Who—who are you going to make me hurt next?"

When there's only silence in response, Briar realizes she knows the answer.

Because the Hell Prince already told her—on graduation night.

He hauled her awake as she slept peacefully in Finn's arms and whispered a threat that poisoned their final summer together before it even started—

You'll kill him one day too.

At the time, the words made Briar run. Made her shrink into herself, become smaller and smaller until she was nothing at all. But now, the memory puts a fight inside her. The Hell Prince brought her back to life twice—he just *said* she's no use to him dead. He needs her, needs her *body* for something else. Another death. His final test.

Finn.

Briar tightens her fists in determination and forms a silent promise: this moment, right now, is the last time that creature forces her to do anything ever again.

"You'll *never* make me hurt him," she seethes to the empty room, whirling. Daring the Hell Prince to reappear. "Do you hear me? I'd kill *myself* first,

I'd slit my own fucking throat, you can watch me *bleed out all over the—*"

Briar slams to a halt as the door flies open.

And Morgan Parker-Blake appears in the entryway, dressed in black.

For a moment, Morgan stares at the photos, the lifeless bodies of Briar's parents. A terrible déjà vu claws at Briar's bones. Here she is again, thirteen years later—blood on her hands, and Morgan is the only one around to see it.

But this time, Morgan doesn't run away.

This time, Morgan runs toward her.

And instead of shame, all Briar feels is a rush of unexpected comfort.

"Are you hurt?" Morgan demands, processing Briar's stained dress, the bruises along her throat and arms.

Briar shakes her head, clenching burning fingers.

Morgan's eyes fall to the compass tucked between her breasts, then to the hatch in the floor. Her breath hitches. "You're going down there, aren't you? To find Finn."

Briar swallows, remembering her father's words. *A place without time. Without space.*

"You know I have to," she says.

Morgan holds her gaze for a second, eyes darting in debate. Then she reaches inside her bag and produces a leather strap in one hand—

And a small elegant dagger in the other.

"You'll need this," she says.

Briar's eyes widen as Morgan unsheathes it, revealing a jet-black blade with a pointed tip, the hilt glistening with moonstones and dark seashells.

"This is obsidian," Morgan says, pointing to the blade. "It's activated by elemental power and can offer you protection. It can't impact mortals without magic—but it *can* defeat ancient evil beings." She reholsters the blade. "Like the one that's bound to you right now."

Briar snaps her gaze back to Morgan's. Renewed hope surges inside her. "It could really kill . . . *him*? The Hell Prince?"

"It's possible—if you do it exactly right." Morgan lowers to her knees, and Briar's breath catches as she lifts the torn hem of her dress to fasten the strap around her thigh. "The stabbing needs to be pure. The entity must be visible, in its own human or beast form. But you have to be careful—losing too much blood from an obsidian wound can be fatal for a witch." She glances up at Briar. "Don't let this dagger fall into the wrong hands."

Morgan's nails click as they work the buckle, her fingertips brushing the soft curve of Briar's inner thigh. She fleetingly wonders if Morgan is remembering touching her last night, if she's questioning if she'll ever get to touch Briar like this again.

If she knows deep down that she won't.

Rising, Morgan hands her the dagger; the gesture feels like a peace offering. Briar wraps her fingers around the hilt, transfixed by the possibility that she's holding the one thing that could destroy that wicked creature for good.

It seems too easy.

"Could something this simple really kill him?" Briar asks.

"It's a gamble," Morgan replies. "And it's not the only risk. You're tethered to the demon, remember? He's keeping you alive. So if he dies..."

"I die too," Briar understands.

"I mean..." Morgan swallows. "You've already died. But this could sever your life thread completely—which also completes the banishing spell's loophole. And then the demon could get free again."

Briar's pulse quickens with fresh anxiety. "Wait. If me dying supposedly completes the loophole, why isn't he free already? He has Riley. I'm the second half of the sacrifice. 'A pair of twins in flames.' "

Morgan shakes her head. "I don't know. That's partly why I was studying that spell book. Something's not right about that translation."

Briar narrows her eyes. "Professor Quill said the same thing."

"The point is," Morgan continues, tapping the dagger, "if you use this on that creature?" A knot forms in her jaw. "I don't know if you'll be able to come home."

Briar falls quiet, and something unspoken simmers between them. She watches Morgan's expression drop with solemn understanding.

"You never intended to come home anyway," Morgan whispers.

Briar shakes her head. "I made... a bargain."

Morgan's face turns ashen. "*Pom-Poms.*"

The ocean simmers beneath their feet, the boat eerily tranquil. The silence holds all their unsaid words, and an ache in Briar's chest takes hold. She doesn't know how to say goodbye to a girl she once thought she hated. A girl she realized, too late, that she didn't.

As if thinking the same, Morgan reaches for her hand. "I'd try to stop you," she whispers, "but I know I can't."

Briar tightens her grip and nods. Morgan sniffs, glancing away.

"But I'll need—" Morgan's voice is rough, like she's fighting not to cry. "I'll need something from you—an object. As an amulet. In case I need to come find you."

Morgan's words only sound hollow. As if they both know there might be nothing of Briar left to find.

Nodding anyway, Briar frees the starfish-shaped pin from her curls. White-blue magic crackles between their fingers, taking the shape of translucent butterfly wings.

"It's funny." Morgan's lips twist in a sad smile as she tucks the pin in her own hair. "I keep thinking of all the ways we're more alike than either of us realized. I hated you for so long, for nothing. Maybe we weren't ever going to be *together*. But we could have been friends." She pulls her bottom lip between her teeth. "Now there's no time left at all."

Briar searches for words to respond, and finding none, she folds Morgan into an embrace. This time, there's no anger, no desperate, breathless kissing—just salt air and death, and the lingering awareness that whatever they could have had together doesn't exist in this universe. Not under this blood-soaked moon. When they pull apart, Briar searches Morgan's gold eyes for any flutter of doubt. But she finds only acceptance.

Morgan swallows. "This is the part where I let you go, isn't it?"

"Wait," Briar says, pulling back. "Take this."

She bends, picking up the leather-bound book. Harper Clay's journal.

"I don't have time to read it," Briar continues, "but maybe you can keep it safe. Maybe there's something in there we missed. Just in case."

Morgan takes the book, eyelids rimmed in red.

"Pom-Poms, I hope you realize I wasn't ever going to make you confess what transpired on the beach." She slides her gaze to Briar's. "But I do need you to know one thing: what happened to your brother that day... that was *not* your fucking fault."

Tears spring to Briar's eyes, unexpected relief flooding her ribs. For the first time in her life, that stone of guilt feels a little less heavy.

Like something she can grow strong enough to carry alone.

As she stares at Morgan through blurry lashes, Briar inexplicably imagines her under a pool of light, wrapped in sequins and feathers, her hair tight in a bun. Ribbons lace up her calves, and she spins atop pointed toes, faster and faster until she's untethered and free from a world she never wanted to be a part of. Briar somehow knows with fierce certainty: Morgan will make it out of Loch Creek to chase every last dream.

Gritting her teeth, Briar bends and rips the bandage from her calf. After unsheathing the dagger, she guides the blade in a perfect circle around the pointed ovals in her skin, completing the daisy wheel. She doesn't cry out this time, doesn't even flinch as she carves open her leg.

It's a silent agreement—a signature on a contract. A recognition of the bond she'll endure for an eternity.

The demon growls with laughter. *Forever, Winters girl.*

She nods at Morgan one last time, watching her retreat from the room.

And then, Briar Winters grabs a candle and sets fire to the Loch Creek town yacht before lifting the hatch and disappearing through the floor.

Into the sea below.

~

The waves thunder around her. Salt stings Briar's nose, her eyes, her mouth. Finn's compass burns with her magic as she swims and swims in the empty dark.

For so long, there's only endless black. Her arms grow numb, the wound on her calf seared by seawater. Her lungs weaken, balloons about to burst.

She lets the voice beckon her down, kissing the edges of her consciousness. *To die is to wake. To sleep is to forget.*

Then the world underwater glimmers to life in the darkness. Torn sails of ships, the emerald whisper of a mermaid's tail, creatures with black fins and claws—everything somehow terrifying and beautiful at once. Bones of broken buildings quiver in and out of her view, alongside the cracked spindles of a Ferris wheel and mirrors covered in sea moss. Briar swims through countless abandoned worlds, sadness flooding her chest as she considers all the ways things can get lost.

She drifts through the water toward a crack of light, letting those heavy arms steer her. She can feel the Hell Prince's victory in her surrender, the way he's leading her toward the terrible violence he promised she'd do in his name. But every part of her battles for survival, heart pounding with desperation, with determination.

Her violet-warped hands hit a stretch of wet sand, and she sinks her nails in deep.

This place might be her grave, but it won't be Finn's.

Ahead, a small cottage waits on a blackened hilltop beneath the glow of the scarlet moon. A wolf howls into the salt-drenched wind.

And Briar, more dead than alive, crawls her way to the door.

CHAPTER THIRTY-TWO
FINN

The fierce grip of anxiety hasn't released Finn's ribs all day. He paces the cottage, feeling time slipping and slipping through his fist like silky black sand. Hours, minutes, seconds.

When the sun rises, his body will belong to the Death King. He *agreed* to that.

But that was before he heard Briar's sob-choked voice on the phone, a sound that stabbed straight to his heart and jolted him wide awake. *Today is my birthday*, she cried in his ear. Today *is my birthday.*

Without him, did it happen the way it could have the first time? Or was Morgan there to stop those fucking monsters from forcing poison down Briar's throat and casting her into the sea? Kai? Astrid? Did *anyone* stop them?

He sits on the floor. Claws at his hair. Imagines Briar's mouth overflowing with white foam, her convulsing on the floor alone. No one to hold her. No one to keep her safe.

Maybe Finn was always destined to fail. There's no equation, no spell, that guarantees plans will work. He couldn't protect her then, and he didn't protect her now. He's just a boy with a compass and ragged hope. He's nothing.

But if he gets his hands on that obsidian dagger and kills the Death King, he could still be something.

Just then, a blistering howl interrupts his thoughts. He snaps his head up. Neptune.

Finn scrambles to the window. The black ocean burns under the ruby moon, and a sharp breeze shuffles the onyx sand into a cloud. He almost turns away, but a flash of white snags his attention.

Neptune's growls get louder just as Finn registers the tangle of dark wet hair, the shape of a person. A white dress drenched against skin.

And then, his breath rushes out.

He tears through the hall, hardly noticing as debris slices his bare feet, and flings open the screen door with such force that it nearly bursts from its hinges—

As Briar Winters collapses in a heap on the front steps of the cottage.

Briar, here. In this place.

"Briar!" he exclaims, flying down to catch her, to hold her, to see if she's even alive.

Because she looks like she just crawled out of a grave.

Her limbs are kissed with plum bruises, and there are rough scratches all over her back, as though she had been ensnared in coarse twine. His heart plummets at the sight of the furious wound on her calf, streaks of inky blood running down to her ankle.

All this time, the desperate hope that he saved Briar has been his life support.

Seeing her now, he knows she isn't safe at all.

"Briar." Guilt churns inside him as he tries to hold her upright. "Briar, can you look at me?"

Her skin is ice-cold, and fear ignites his spine at the violet veins marring her hands. Her chest heaves in shallow breaths, and when her eyes drag to his, they're filled with wild panic.

Finn says her name again, his hands framing her face, pushing ropes of wet hair away from her mouth. A million questions spasm inside him. How did she get here? How long did it take?

What did she have to bargain in exchange?

Fresh worry gnaws at him, but he doesn't have time to dwell. Briar's breath is coming faster. Too fast—*way* too fast. Silently forming his name through blue-tinged lips.

Inhaler. She needs her—

"Where's your inhaler?" Finn demands, and the words immediately sound ridiculous. As if she'd *pack a bag* to come here. She's got nothing except this flimsy dress and a gold necklace tucked inside.

Briar shakes her head frantically, confirming.

"*Fuck.*" He drags a hand through his hair, fear skyrocketing, and gathers her in his arms to race past Neptune and back inside.

There's no time to think, no time to come up with a better plan.

Briar's breaths grow weaker as Finn barrels them into the bathroom at the end of the corridor. He nudges the light with his shoulder, wincing at the green glow of the fluorescent bulbs, and reaches into the shower to turn the dial all the way hot.

He sees the confusion on her face but doesn't explain—just shoves her inside and climbs in with her, sealing the curtain around a cloud of steam.

He's making her a sauna, and it better fucking work.

Because there's no way—*no goddamn way*—that Briar survived her birthday party only to die in his arms here. He won't allow it. Not for one second.

"Breathe." Finn places both hands on either side of her cold neck, bending his forehead to hers. He takes an exaggerated inhale, sweeping his thumbs along the bruised cords of her throat. "Breathe with me, Briar."

But she trembles violently instead, her lips turning a deeper shade of blue.

"Damn it, Briar, *breathe.*"

Finn articulates his own breath again, feigning calm over the absolute terror ripping through his core.

"Please," he begs, as she releases another strangled sound. "*Briar—*"

Finn clutches her hair, his voice catching on a sob. Hot water drenches his spine, burning his skin through his clothes, but he barely notices as Briar folds limply into his chest. Despair crushes him. She's dying, he realizes with renewed grief—she's dying *right now*, and everything he's done will be for nothing. That demon will come for him tomorrow and find there's nothing left of him to claim.

"Briar, no, no, *no.* Stay with me." Finn holds her face, pleading through a film of tears. "*Stay with me, Briar.*"

Just as he grows certain this is how everything ends, a puff of air slips from her mouth to land, soft, on his.

An incredulous laugh bubbles out of him.

"That's it," he coaxes, "keep going."

Finn's eyes drop to her clavicle, tracking the soft rise and fall of her chest. A grin splits his face, drenched in disbelief. It's working.

"That's my girl," he manages to say, blinking away panicked tears. "Just like that."

Briar's breathing deepens with each inhale, and he curves a palm over her rib cage. Relief pours through him as he feels her coming back to life, and he holds her, listening to the water and her breath. In his ear this time. Not through a phone, not in his dreams.

"Finn," she finally whispers, her gaze meeting his.

Too many words tangle at the base of his throat, heart torn at the sound of her voice. He pulls her tighter against him, certain he'll never be able to get close enough.

"Do I even want to know how you managed to get here?" he asks, his hands splayed on either side of her face. His fingertips ghost over her lashes, and his chest throbs with the memory of the gunshot. Salty tears spill onto his skin as he whispers, "Are you even real?"

Briar doesn't answer either question; she only strokes his cheekbones, as if she's wondering the same thing.

"I would have looked for you forever," she says, and something electric flares inside him. He rests his forehead against hers as the shower pelts the tile around them.

"I'm still here," Finn whispers over her lips.

Briar's eyes search his for a moment before she reaches toward the shower wall. Where she taps. And taps. And taps.

Short and long. Rapid and rhythmic. Dashes and dots.

I'm still here.

His throat tightens. All those hours spent wondering if he could ever cross oceans and time to get to her. If he'd ever calculate the right tide. If the strings of fate could be rethreaded where they were once torn apart. If anyone ever really got a second chance.

"Finn." Briar whispers his name like she's memorizing the way it feels in her mouth. Like she never thought she'd get to say it again. "I'm sorry. For avoiding you. For not picking up the phone. For—"

"It's okay," he says, but she sucks in a ragged breath to keep going.

"It's *not*." Her voice is raw at the edges. "I'd do it all differently if I could. I'd rewind time and—" Her face crumples in a soft sob. "I'm sorry. Finn—"

"Baby, I know." Finn brushes the pads of his fingers over Briar's lips, shushing her. Partly because of the way she's struggling to get the words out. But mostly because hearing them is breaking his heart.

He can't bear to listen to her pleading for more time when he knows there isn't any left.

Tomorrow Briar goes back to the world above. And Finn's body becomes a demon's vessel—until he locates that dagger and ends both the Death King and himself.

All they have is right now.

"No more talking," Finn adds. "I need you to catch your breath, okay?"

She nods and leans against the wall, and in the soft quiet, he laces his fingers with hers to study the jagged lines throbbing in her palms.

It's like her veins are ablaze, seething beneath her skin. On anyone else, these would be repulsive—monstrous, even—but it's Briar, *it's Briar*, and she's still somehow more beautiful than he remembers.

He can feel her stare, anticipating a string of questions, a hypothesis—*something*. But empty of theories, Finn just presses a kiss into her palm and hopes it says enough.

It must, because Briar's eyes drift closed, her face slack with relief.

In her silence, Finn contemplates the rest of her, frowning at the constellation of cuts along her throat, the layer of dark sand dusting her skin like poisonous glitter. He eyes the scratches along the dip of her neckline, and protective fury courses through him with each additional wound.

Grinding his teeth, Finn lowers the water temperature and tugs the showerhead loose.

"Okay?" he confirms, and Briar opens her eyes long enough to offer a gentle nod.

He holds her upright with one hand and works the stream with the other. Crimson and onyx swirl together, running down the tile in a bloody pool at their feet. Neither of them says a word in silent understanding.

He's going to cleanse and heal every inch of her.

Throat tight, Finn turns Briar until her head tips back toward his chest. He guides the water over her hair, soaking the shell-tangled strands. As he weaves his fingers through her curls, he can't help but recall the emptiness in his bones after she died, that all-consuming longing to touch her exactly like this.

And here he is now—defying logic, battling physics. Briar's hair in his hands should be a mathematical conjecture, but he aligned the numbers exactly right—and now she's his again. Touching her feels like this past summer, like salty moonlight and a kiss that wrecked him in ways she'll never know. It's also like being fifteen, electricity sparking inside him every time their knees brushed beneath desks. Like being six and hearing her voice for the first time.

It's as though they've lived a million lives in thirteen short years, a million stories threading them together. He's loved her since the beginning; he'll love her after it's all over.

Because they only have hours left.

Setting the showerhead at their feet, he creates three sections in Briar's damp curls before working them into a messy braid. He's not even sure how he knows the steps, but he moves without thinking through her perfect hair, perfect even like this, rough with seawater and salt. Briar is quiet the whole time, but he calculates each flutter in her face, and when he notices that her lashes are wet, he can't say for sure if it's water or tears.

For as much as he's wondered if he'd ever get the chance to be this close to her again, maybe she's been wondering the same.

Finn tears away a loose ruffle dangling from Briar's dress, then secures her braid in a makeshift ribbon. He lifts the spout again, spilling water down her arms, searching for her freckles amid the blood, the dirt. He lowers to his knees, aiming the stream at the backs of her legs, the—

Freezing, Finn blinks at the wound on Briar's calf. He spotted it when she first arrived, but up close, it's worse. His stomach turns at the sight of the purple-red circle, the six swollen petals sliced into her suntanned skin. This isn't like the other cuts—she didn't get this by swimming too close to a jagged cluster of coral.

Someone *carved* this into her flesh. Branded her.

A minute ago, he was imagining Briar returning to the world above, safe and unharmed—a vision that he'd cling to in his final moments before the Death King consumed his body for good. Instead, he has this image: Briar's body marked and claimed. Possessive anger grips his bones, followed swiftly by fresh panic.

He's not sure this is something he can fix.

"Briar," he works out, blinking through the steam. "Who did this to you?"

The second the words leave his mouth, he realizes he doesn't need to ask.

There's only one person—one *thing*—that could have done this.

Or could have gotten Briar to do it herself.

A memory surfaces: That day in kindergarten, before he heard Briar's voice, before he even guided her to the edge of the woods. She had been sitting on the blacktop, drawing a flower with blue chalk. But it wasn't a flower.

A daisy wheel.

A sour note of dread seeps into his stomach. An image of the Death King's long-taloned fingers around Briar's throat burns in Finn's mind. The demon's fangs sinking into that delicate spot below her ear, a place that should only belong to Finn. *Mine*, the Death King would say, his mouth slick with her blood. *She's always been mine.*

Finn clenches his jaw and snaps to his feet.

Not this time.

Maybe he can't fix it, but he'll try anyway. He won't let himself leave this world while she's hurt like this. Heart hammering, he turns off the faucet and drops the showerhead again. He peels the curtain and reaches for a towel, ignoring Briar's questioning gaze.

"Where are you going?" She suddenly sounds childlike and faraway.

He pulls in a steadying breath. "Briar, that cut is infected."

"I know." There's a weight to her voice that wasn't there before.

"We should treat it." He steps out of the shower, ignoring the pathetic sinking feeling that comes with the words.

Briar climbs out after him. "Finn. You won't be able to."

I know, he wants to yell. *I know, but I have to fucking try!*

Finn grinds his teeth instead, holding the towel out to her. "I'm gonna find something to use for stitches. Wait here. I'll come right back." His gaze drills into hers. "Promise."

He half expects her to argue. Half expects her to follow.

What he doesn't expect is the laugh that rips from her instead.

It's soft at first, then climbs in volume, rising like steam toward the ceiling. Briar tips her head back, laughter growing wild while he stares and stares, the towel hanging from his hand.

"*Stitches!*" she chokes out, tears pooling at the corners of her eyes. "Stitches, oh my god!"

"Briar."

Her untamed cackling just swirls around them.

Finn swallows. "I don't understand why that's funny."

"*Because I'm already dead!*" The words fly loose from her throat, the laughter gone. "I'm not really here, not in the same way you're here."

He freezes. "That's—that's not true. Morgan—she fixed it. She brought you back."

"It won't last," she whispers. "I don't feel like a person anymore."

Finn's entire body threatens to shut down at that. He thinks of everything he's done so far—the ritual, the blood, the waiting, the endless despair—and wonders if it's all been for nothing. If they brought Briar back but didn't bring her back whole. If somehow, being half-alive is worse than being fully gone. Just the thought of it makes him want to howl with grief, but he folds her into his arms instead.

"I've got you," he breathes, pressing a careful kiss to the top of her hair. "You're not dead, okay? You're alive, Briar. You're *alive*."

But something cold and lonely spreads in his chest at the possibility that Briar doesn't intend to live much longer either. He digs his fingertips into the soft curve of her waist, gathering as much of her as he can in his hands. As if to convince himself that it can't be true. That she's *real*. But Briar shivers beneath his hands, her cold skin prickling with goose bumps.

"Let's get you warm," he says, grasping for something—*anything*—he can do for her.

Briar takes the towel from him, her expression far-off and difficult to place. He trails behind her, waiting for her to realize that they're standing in a nightmarish version of the house where he used to live.

In his room, Briar studies the markings on the wall, the flimsy mattress and thin blanket on the floor. Finn stands at the door, staring at her silhouette in the dim light, and braces himself for the inevitable inquisition to come. He'll tell her anything she wants to know—anything to get her to stop looking at him like she's steeling herself for another goodbye.

But before Briar can launch a single question, a blistering cold seizes Finn's neck. It runs the length of his spinal cord, sinking into his bones. Like claws, like teeth.

A reminder of his lingering bargain.

Don't forget—the Death King's voice curls in his ear—*who owns you now.*

And Finn summons every ounce of his energy to silently bite back, *Not yet.*

CHAPTER THIRTY-THREE

BRIAR

Briar stands shivering in Finn's old bedroom and wonders if this is how it feels to fall apart.

She always imagined breaking down would be loud, like unleashing a scream that's been stuck for far too long. But perhaps it's a quiet crumbling. A glance at the person you love most in the world and the silent agony of knowing it can't last.

It hurts to even look at Finn. Everything about his appearance is a reminder of what he endured for her when she didn't deserve it, when her life is ending anyway. The bruises along his throat. His untrimmed hair, the gaunt, bony angles of his frame. The way something grief-stricken and somber has haunted his eyes since she arrived, as though he's biting down on another secret that he knows will ruin them both.

But mostly, it's how he studied the monstrous lines on her hands and kissed them like he didn't care. Like he loves her anyway.

She could have told Finn the truth from the start. She could have whispered every one of her secrets when they were kids, back when the world was a stretch of stars beneath their flashlights and the word *future* still glittered with hope. She could have, she could have, she could have—but she didn't. Seeing him now is like returning to a place that's been burned to the ground and finding a bouquet of matches in her own hand.

Finn Adler has always been her home.

And she's the runaway who realized it too late.

"Say *something*," Finn urges from the doorway.

Briar swipes at her lashes, gaze settling on the dates marking the walls. May 4. June 9. March 1.

Understanding snaps into place.

What's today's date?

Is it spring?

How many days until your birthday?

"Those calls late at night," she says. "You were *here* when you made them."

Finn nods, and Briar darts a glance to the bare mattress, the dark moss woven along the walls. She imagines Finn curled up in the frostbitten cold, frantically warning her while she sighed and rolled her eyes beneath her warm comforter. A new wave of guilt climbs her bones like ivy. She sucks in a breath, certain this one will crush her from the inside out.

"This whole time—you knew?" Briar asks, struggling for something else to replace this terrible regret. "All those conversations—you knew about my parents? About Loch Creek? About the harvests? And you didn't—you didn't say anything?"

Finn's eyes widen with pain. "Briar, I tried to tell you a million times after graduation. I tried here too, but it was like something wouldn't *let* me say it. You have to know I tried."

"Clearly not hard enough!" she cries. Her entire body aches from directing this fury at him when really, she's mostly angry at herself.

"Are you kidding?" Finn exclaims. "You didn't answer a single call or text for two months. Your parents told me to stop coming to your house. You wouldn't even *look* at me." His eyes burn. "Why did you shut me out like that?"

Briar's gaze swoops to the floor. A knot tightens in her chest as she thinks about the Hell Prince's voice on graduation night, threatening all the terrible things he'd make her do.

To *Finn.*

But to tell Finn about that now would also mean telling him about the bargain she made. About her secret plan, the dagger hiding beneath her dress. The way she's been imagining herself plunging the black blade into that creature's heart with a final wrenching scream. Ending this nightmare.

Ending her too.

Finn would never let her go through with it. So this has to be the one secret she keeps forever. He disappeared to the end of the world for her once. She won't let him do it again.

She'd rather he be angry than lost.

"I can't tell you that," she says, and his eyebrows shoot to his hairline.

Finn drags a hand through his tousled hair. "Jesus, Briar."

"Finn—"

"How can you come at me for keeping secrets when you're doing the same damn thing?"

"Maybe I'm trying to protect you!" she explodes. "Maybe it's something you don't want to know."

"No—*no*. We're done with that." Finn's eyes flash as he steps toward her. "I want to know *everything* about you. I want to know every thought you have, everything that's ever made you happy, everything that's ever made you cry. Everything you're scared of. Everything you dream about. Everything you think is too messed up to say out loud. You're trying to protect me from knowing these things? You don't understand—I want a fucking *archive* of them."

Briar's entire body burns at his words. Her breath thins. She wanted him to get mad, but not like *this*, not in a way that turns her blood to fire, making her hands itch to cling to him and never let go. "Finn—"

"*I'm* the one who's supposed to know you better than anyone," he continues, "but sometimes it's like you don't want me to know you at all. And, god, you're still doing it now! After everything." He shakes his head. "What's it gonna take for you to just let me see you?"

"Stop," she whispers. Her chest aches with remorse, each of his words prodding the wounds inside her heart. "It doesn't matter anymore."

"Doesn't *matter*?" Finn steps toward her. "Are you for real? There are so many things you could have trusted me with that I would have kept safe. I would have kept *you* safe. Instead, I had to figure out so much shit on my own, like—" His jaw knots, as if he's debating which painful card to pull. "Like *Riley*."

Briar scrambles to mask the hurt in her face, but it's too late. He sees it. He *wanted* it.

This isn't the Finn on the Ferris wheel, carefully holding her weak parts together.

This Finn is going to bait her until she shatters into pieces and gives him something real.

"You could've told me," Finn barrels on. "It wouldn't have changed how I felt about you. But all these secrets! Our whole lives!" He pauses, like he knows he's about to go too far. "Were you ever gonna tell me that *you* killed Riley?"

Something rage dusted and wild flares within Briar's chest.

Her palm collides with Finn's jaw, and the slap echoes through the darkened room.

Anger and embarrassment crash inside her as she searches for an equally soulless reply. She clutches her corrupted hands, as if the gift that horrible creature bestowed upon her might help her become more wicked.

"Okay," Finn starts, "I deserved that—"

"Don't," she chokes out. "I can't even look at you."

But it's not good enough. He tilts his head, calling her bluff.

"I hate you," she adds.

The phrase tastes especially wretched in her mouth, spoken here in this backward version of Finn's childhood bedroom. This place of tears and grief, wallpapered in Finn's doubt that he could ever be loved at all. Her palm stings with shame. Finn deserves better than her.

He steps closer, hurt shadowing his eyes. "You don't. That's the most ridiculous thing I've ever heard you say."

"I *do*. I—"

But Finn won't let her finish. His fingers find their way into her hair, drawing her forehead tight against his. "It's not true. You *love* me. Why else would you be in this miserable place?"

"I don't love you." The lie burns behind Briar's teeth like poison.

She twists away to the window. But he's right in front of her again, not letting her get away with this bullshit for a single moment.

"How can you say that with a straight face?" He backs her up, toward the mattress. "Are you really that ungrateful? I *saved* you. I sacrificed myself. I brought you back."

"You—" Briar trips over the words. "You brought me *back*?" She clutches at his shirt, letting the towel fall to a heap at their feet. "You brought me to a world where you don't exist, Finn! You brought me to *hell*. I'd rather be *dead* than live in that world for another goddamn *minute*."

Finn folds her hands in his, drawing her flat against him. Her back arches as she pushes and he pulls; they become a tangle of physics, a movable object and a stoppable force. Her foot twists with his ankle, and they both lose their balance, toppling to the mattress in a heap.

For a moment, neither of them says anything, their breaths heavy in the small space between their mouths.

"You *are* going back up there," Finn finally orders, his chest heaving against hers. "Alone."

She grinds her teeth, thinking of her parents' lifeless bodies, the burning yacht. "What even is there to go back *to*?"

"Astrid," Finn says. "Kai. They'll still be there. They'll protect you. But you have to—"

Briar twists against him. "No. I'll *never* be safe there."

Finn's expression flickers between anger and despair. "Tomorrow morning, at sunrise," he demands, "you're going back home, alive. It's *not* a choice."

"You don't understand. I *can't* go back. I—"

"Briar!"

She freezes at the way her name erupts from his mouth, like a dam just shattered inside him. Pain rages behind his eyes, and when he speaks again, his voice breaks.

"I saw you die," Finn wrenches out. "I saw a bullet—*a fucking bullet*—go through your face. Your perfect, beautiful face." He presses two fingers to her lashes, tears spilling onto his cheeks. "*Right here.*" He strokes the skin beneath her eye, as if convincing himself that she's truly whole. "So don't ever tell me that you'd rather be dead. 'Cause I can't think of anything—*anything*—worse than that."

Briar stares at this version of Finn she's never seen. Every one of his walls has come crashing down. He's not talking in hypotheticals or equations anymore. He's looking right at her and pleading with her to stay alive.

An ache floods her chest. How could she even begin to explain that she's promised to that horrible creature?

How could she ever tell him that she can't remain alive when she's already gone?

She can't. So she doesn't.

Instead, Briar reaches up to touch his jaw, right where she just hit him. Something about the contact breaks him, and all Briar can do is watch as Finn Adler unravels in front of her.

Their foreheads press together, lips grazing but not kissing because Finn clutches her and sobs as though he's making up for not getting to do it before. She imagines his horrified face after she went over the side of the boat, the scream that must have ripped through him at the thought of never holding her like this again.

Briar's eyes grow damp, her furious facade slipping away. Finn pulls back to look at her, sweeping his fingers beneath her lashes when he sees she's crying too.

"Tell me you hate me one more time," he challenges.

He says it like he knows she won't. Like he knows what will come out instead.

Briar shakes her head, fighting to keep the truth locked. Saying it aloud will only make this hurt more.

But Finn's hands are in her hair, his breath warm on her neck, and she feels the words dislodge, spilling from their hidden place, because it's Finn—it's *Finn*.

It's always been Finn.

"I love you." The phrase rushes out like one word—*Iloveyou*—and she sucks in air to replace the breath she's lost.

He stares at her as though he's not sure he heard her correctly. "Say that again."

So she does. She says it over and over until he silences her with his mouth, his lips crushing against hers.

"I love you, Briar Winters," Finn echoes, his whisper melting into a kiss that burns with salt and loss. "I love you so fucking much."

Her lungs feel like they're bursting at his words, the firm sweep of his tongue, the scrape of scruff at his jaw. Finn's hands trail up and down her body, charting every rise and dip and curve, as though trying to memorize what she feels like.

As though he also knows there won't be any more nights like this one.

Briar tangles her fingers in his overgrown hair before mapping the slope of his shoulders, the swell of his upper arms. Their kiss goes on forever as their hands work to explore and remember, heat blazing between them.

"I didn't think I'd get to kiss you again," she whispers into his mouth.

He lets out a low sound that vibrates against her tongue. "I don't ever want to stop."

"So don't." She scrapes her teeth over his lower lip. "Don't stop, Finn."

With another rough sound, Finn cages her against the mattress, his hips locked with hers. Briar reaches beneath his shirt, skimming the ridges of his lower back, and then higher.

Right to the faded cigarette-burn scars along his spine.

She feels him tense, and she breaks their kiss to search his gaze. "Is this—is this okay?"

Finn nods, guiding her mouth back to his. "It's you," he whispers. "It's okay."

Briar's nails leave a whispering echo as they ghost along his scars. Their kiss slows to a hypnotic lull as she flattens her palm, stroking her thumb in slow circles around the worst one—the burn from seventh grade that Finn only talked about once, right after it happened. Briar wonders if he's remembering how rage simmered visibly under her skin at the thought of anyone hurting him.

He must be, because he clings to her with renewed ferocity. Like she's something rare and wild. Something he's been searching for his entire life.

Finn's hand slips between them, hitching the hem of her dress toward her waist. As though he's suddenly desperate to touch her, to feel her fall apart for him.

And she remembers at the same time he freezes—with his palm flat over the dagger at her thigh.

He sits back, staring down at the weapon.

"Briar. What is that?"

Shit.

With her brain too frazzled to come up with a lie, she scrambles for a half-truth instead. Desperately hoping he believes it, because she needs him to not ask a million questions, needs to keep her plan to kill the Hell Prince secret. It's the only way she keeps Finn safe.

"It's a dagger. Made from obsidian. Morgan gave it to me, for protection."

Finn's storm-colored eyes cut back to hers with an expression she can't read at all.

"It can be used for spells, but the blade only works on magic." Briar lifts her marked palms, swallowing the unspoken part of her plan—the part Finn cannot, cannot, cannot know. "I... I have magic now. Aether magic."

She expects Finn to unleash a million questions. But instead, he peers intently at the dagger, as though he's working through a new series of equations in his head.

Unease creeps inside her. "Finn? What is it?"

"Can I take it off?" His gaze slides up to hers. "For now."

"Yeah, sure," she says, distracted, watching him work the buckle. "Finn, are you—?"

Finn shushes her with a quiet sound, his fingers hovering over her lips. "No more talking." His mouth dips to the soft spot below her ear. "I'm busy."

A nagging worry claws at her. Why doesn't he have more questions? Why was he staring at the dagger like he has a use for it too? Why—?

But Briar's thoughts fizzle as Finn presses a line of kisses down her throat, covering each bruise along her clavicle. Tracing the shape of every wound, as if he could heal them with his lips. His trajectory glides lower as he maps the plunging neckline of her dress—until his mouth hovers over the brass compass that has slipped out from the fabric.

His surprised gaze slides back up to hers.

"You found it," he whispers.

She shakes her head. "It wasn't ever lost."

Finn stares for a moment before kissing her mouth again—measured this time, his lips warm, patient. She burns everywhere, and he seems to know, his fingers ghosting over laces and buttons. She reaches for him too, tugging on fabric and buckles until there's nothing left between them except desperate shared breath.

"Can we . . . ?" he asks, and she nods.

"I haven't ever . . ." she replies. "Not with a guy, I mean."

Finn stares again, his gaze searching. But if he has questions, he doesn't ask them; instead, he leans back in to brush his lips against hers.

"I haven't either." Finn's mouth is warm as it drops to her jaw. "With anyone."

Briar's heart hammers. "Do you want to? With me?"

She can feel the curve of his smile as he nods.

"You're the only one I want," he whispers, voice low and soft.

Finn kisses her the whole time. Starlight crackles between them, and Briar fuses her mouth to his as though she's certain she won't remember the taste of him tomorrow. Finn is blue ocean and silver crests, onyx sand and glittering death. He is both treacherous sin and holy ground, and she'd give anything to feel this way for the rest of her life. She'd let him pull her through time and space; she'd let him take her anywhere he wanted.

But there's a cold awareness in the marrow of her bones: There's only tonight. No future waits beyond this stretch of moonlight and stars. They'll never have more than this hidden pocket of time.

It's enough to draw fresh tears to her lashes, but Finn kisses those too, which only makes the ache in her chest worse. Sorrow and euphoria erupt and collide within her. And it's only then—teetering on the edge of distant planets and lost oceans—that Briar finally stops fighting her own wild heart and lets every emotion wash over her instead.

Like a wave sweeping her away from the shore. Seeing only darkness, only midnight sky.

One last breath of air with him before she disappears beneath the sea.

CHAPTER THIRTY-FOUR
FINN

In the dark stretch of *after*, Finn holds Briar and counts all the ways running out of time feels worse than dying.

There are traces of her everywhere, like the little scratches from her nails along his shoulders and the orchid-pear taste of her kiss lingering on his mouth. He can register all the places they're still touching, can describe how soft she feels beneath his palms—and yet part of him feels like he's not even here. Like he's already somewhere else, each tick of the clock pulling him away. Toward an empty liminal space where his body is no longer his own.

Briar's lashes droop, and anxiety sparks in Finn's chest. He wants to drain every second they have left, stretch time in his fingers like clay.

He can't let her fall asleep.

"Briar," he whispers, thumbing over her cheekbone. "Stay awake with me. I want to hear your voice." *I want it to be the last thing I hear*, he silently adds.

She raises her head, turning so they're face-to-face. He pulls the thin blanket over them both, and suddenly they're fourteen again—him explaining the science behind thunder and trying not to stare at how pretty she was in the silver moonlight. His chest clenches. It all went too fast.

"What do you want to talk about?" Briar asks.

He brushes a strand of hair away from her eyes. "Everything. I'll go first."

Finn whispers nearly every recent memory—from the spark of fear when he heard Briar talking about disappearing into the sea on graduation night, right up until the gunshot. For a tiny moment, he wonders if the truth will make Briar hate him too. That maybe she won't think of his hands as a place of comfort, but merely the violent things that ended her life.

Instead, she moves even closer, the bridge of her nose brushing his.

"My turn," she says, and something stirs inside him. The same thing he felt that day at recess, an understanding that they've always been broken in matching places.

Finn's lungs ache when Briar laces her fingers through his and describes how it felt to wake up with him gone. How she, Astrid, and Kai unthreaded time to find him. He stares in stunned silence when she tells him about his own father, how they would be a perfect pair if they existed under the same sky. He pictures a man with gray eyes that crinkle at the corners, wearing a Berkeley sweatshirt and driving across the country while Pacific wind whips both their hair. His ribs suddenly burn, bursting with memories of a life he never got to claim.

But then Briar talks about her mother's craft studio, and he goes entirely still. His breath comes faster as she describes what happened at her version of her birthday party—and when she dissolves into wrenching sobs in his arms, he kisses her to quiet the sound. She clings to him too, until they're an electric tangle of grief, breathless and desperate for each other again.

Their words become lighter afterward, cycling through memories and inside jokes. Their conversation melts between years, between lifetimes. And all the while, his brain begs him to stay awake, stay awake, *stay awake*, knowing that if they fall asleep, their time ends forever.

Because once the Death King possesses him, Finn won't be able to touch her at all.

"Do you remember in fifth grade," he asks, to quiet his thoughts, "when you took home the class hamster? And then told Ms. Wood that you lost him?"

"She called him '*Mr. Jingles.*'" Briar snorts. "He was *begging* to be rescued with a name like that. But if you want to talk about lying to teachers, let's never forget the time you helped our entire history class cheat on the midterm."

"Hey, it's not my fault the answer key was right there on the desk." Finn cracks a small smile. "I was a hero after that though."

"You were," she admits. "Everyone's always loved you, Finn."

He falls quiet, searching her gaze until she continues—

"I've always loved you."

He brushes her lips with his. "I loved you first."

As the hours blur, Briar asks, "What's with the wolf outside?"

"His name is Neptune," Finn answers, caressing the dips of her rib cage. "And for your information, he's a *coy*wolf, actually. I've been feeding him. We're bonded now."

The second the words leave his mouth, a cold chill ensnares him.

Because Neptune isn't the only creature bonded to him.

He eyes the dusty window beyond Briar's head, knowing that sunrise can't be far away.

Finn imagines what will happen when the Death King comes for him, picturing that windswept cold, the shadows that will fall between his lashes as he retreats to a darkened corner of his soul.

The Death King thinks he'll use Finn's body as a weapon in the world above.

But Finn will extinguish them both before he gets the chance.

He eyes Briar's obsidian dagger on the floor. That damn dagger. Here, finally, in his possession. And Briar, with magic of her own.

Magic that will soon be his.

If he closes his eyes, he can nearly picture the exact page in the spell book, the translation he once worked out in the early blue of dawn. The plan has been growing roots since he found the dagger, the steps sprouting like a garden. Like a gift. It's almost too easy.

It will also break every last piece of her fragile heart.

Which is why he cannot tell her until it's done.

Briar's gaze droops again, and Finn nudges her with his nose. "Hey, wake up. Wake up." He sweeps the floor, reaching for the dagger. "There's something we have to do."

"Finn," she whimpers. "I'm tired."

He clenches his jaw at her sleepy little whisper. Just like on the phone.

He'll let her rest for an hour, he decides.

She deserves one last peaceful sleep—before he ruins them both.

Finn studies Briar's face as she drifts off, memorizing the constellations of her freckles, the gentle slope of her lashes. He sees every iteration of her all at once—from the girl he met at six years old to the woman he's been kissing tonight. The images collide, and for a moment he imagines what their future could have been.

A house on a different coast, a beach where he'd surf without fearing what's beneath the waves. Maybe she'd own an art shop, a bookstore, or both. He'd teach physics without being addicted to the certainty of numbers because he'd have her, something greater than infinity. Stronger than time.

Perhaps, somewhere else, it's happening. Somewhere else, he's bringing her coffee with too much sugar every morning. Somewhere else, she's slipping notes on torn graph paper into his pockets.

Somewhere else, they're growing old together and nothing has ever gone wrong.

Finn combs his fingers through her thick hair; he presses his cheek against her forehead. He holds on to every detail as if he could take it with him. As if he could save it for later, when there's nothing ahead but darkness and empty, vacant space.

An abyss meant only for him.

~

It's close to sunrise when Finn's eyes snap open.

He didn't mean to drift off, but he was lulled by Briar's steady breathing, the comforting rise and fall of her body against his.

He twists onto his elbows, gaze adjusting to the dim light outside his window.

Shit.

"Briar," he whispers, reaching for the dagger on the floor. "Baby, wake up."

Briar lifts her head, lids heavy with sleep. She presses her hands to her eyes. "Is it morning?"

His stomach knots at the sudden childlike fear of her voice. But before he can respond, a slick, icy cold enshrouds the room. Almost as if on cue.

Their eyes snap up in tandem as the walls splinter, as though the house is the epicenter of an earthquake. Inky water seeps from the corners of the ceiling, spilling in ominous rivers toward the shell-dusted ground. The floorboards vibrate beneath them; the bones of the cottage groan for their attention.

Minutes. They have only minutes.

"Finn." Briar tucks herself closer as he scrambles for their clothes. She tugs hard on his shoulder. "Finn, look at me."

"Briar, there's no time, listen—"

"*Finn*," she cries, grabbing his face. Her brows are drawn, pain etched in every line of her skin. "Finn Adler. I love you with my whole heart. Don't ever forget that, okay? I love you, I—"

"Stop that," he interrupts. Gritting his teeth, he practically shoves the sundress into her arms, the fabric stiff from dried seawater. "I have a crazy idea. But we need to move *now*."

She narrows her eyes. "What do you mean?"

Finn pauses, his pulse whirring as it hits him: Their final moments will be stained with betrayal if he does this. Whenever she hears his name, she won't remember the way he kissed every inch of her and told her he's loved her his whole life. She'll only remember him like this: lying through his teeth and willfully tearing them apart.

But he'd rather Briar hate him than be dead.

"Your body knows magic, right?" he presses, as they hurriedly dress. "Well, there's a spell—I remember it from the book at Old Town Hall. We need an obsidian blade, which we have. We need magic, which we have. It's a protection spell. Against all kinds of evil." He forces himself to meet her eyes, his fingers working the buttons on his shirt. Despair pools inside him and he swallows it like poison. "We have nothing to lose. Shouldn't we try?"

Fear tugs at Briar's face. She studies the cracked walls, the black water soaking the floor. Her jaw trembles, eyes red with tears. As though she's bracing herself for an impact he doesn't see coming. Her expression makes him want to rage against everyone and everything that's already hurt her, burn the world to ash so nothing could make her this scared again.

"Briar." He grips the hilt of the dagger. "Do you trust me?"

She flicks gaze to his and nods. His ribs feel like they're going to explode. She'd let him do anything to her. Briar's trust is a sacred thing.

And he's about to destroy it.

"Okay." Finn unsheathes the dagger, turning so they're sitting directly in front of each other, knees brushing. "Give me your hands."

She does, extending her wrists without a single question, and Finn fights back tears at how easy it is for her to offer herself to him.

"This might hurt," he warns, dragging the tip of the blade through her left palm.

Once, then twice. A tiny set of crosshairs in her skin.

Briar whimpers, and he grinds his teeth at the awareness that he's causing her pain. He does the same to her other palm before slicing his own hands down the center, barely registering the sting.

Finn drops the dagger and grabs both her hands in his. "A shallow cut with obsidian summons your magic, right?"

"Right," Briar whispers.

"You're protecting me." He bends his forehead to hers. "We're protecting each other."

He guides her closer until her knees fall on either side of his hips, blood-slick hands clasped between their bodies. Finn's throat constricts around his next words. "Briar. Tell me you love me again."

She breathes it into a soft kiss. "I love you."

Finn's heart twists. Because these aren't just words to a spell—they're *real.* He's never loved anyone the way he loves her, has never wanted to belong to anyone else. But these words—the ones he means with every ounce of his soul—are also a trick. A ruse. A betrayal.

He's never hated himself more than right now.

"Tell me," he says, as he interlaces their fingers, "that you're mine."

But Briar looks distracted now, watching the window over his shoulder.

"Briar," he says again, his voice a note sharper. "Say it."

Her gaze slides back. "Finn. Of course. *I'm yours.*"

"And me?" he whispers, guilt churning inside him.

She doesn't hesitate this time, kissing his forehead. "You're *mine.*"

"Forever, right?" Finn has to fight every muscle in his body not to break at these words—words that, in another lifetime, could be spoken on a different beach, with Briar in a different white dress. *Because it's not fair.*

If they hadn't grown up in Loch Creek—if they'd met somewhere else, *anywhere* else—maybe their ending wouldn't look like this, whispering wedding vows in a haunted room with weeping walls. He'd bend the entire ocean, unspool time, to find the tide that could take them back to the beginning so they could get it right.

"Forever," Briar echoes, her lips meeting his. But he isn't oblivious to the way her voice drops, as though there's something she isn't saying too.

But Finn doesn't have a second to decipher it because silver-blue electricity courses from Briar's hands, altering him from the inside. He imagines his airway filled with sea moss, urchin spines puncturing the chambers of his heart, and it's suddenly hard to breathe.

Is this, he wonders, what drowning feels like?

The answer might be yes. He loses himself in Briar's kiss as the first rays of dawn flutter to life behind them.

He could, he thinks, drown in her.

It's finally then that Finn surrenders to the impending darkness, the looming sea.

To the Death King himself.

Inviting him right into his soul. Just as he once predicted he would.

The ice flooding his throat is painless this time, as though his body has prepared itself for evil's arrival. Finn holds on to every last second of control, every taste of Briar's lips, her wet blood on his skin.

Then he lets go. Like inhaling black water.

Like vanishing.

Don't hurt her, he warns the monster inside his skull. *She's mine.*

Wrong, the rattling voice hisses back. *She's ours.*

CHAPTER THIRTY-FIVE
BRIAR

Briar's palms feel like they're on fire.

She opens her eyes and groans at the swollen ache in the center of her hands. She hadn't meant to fall asleep after Finn's protection spell, but the unfamiliar magic exhausted her. She feels drained, as though a tap has been left on inside her. It takes her several moments to realize she's alone in the room, that Finn is nowhere in sight.

And a jolt of adrenaline surges through her when she takes in the paling light. Daybreak.

Briar leaps to her feet, pausing to strap the dagger back to her thigh. She lingers with her fist around the hilt, briefly wondering what it will feel like to drive the blade through the Hell Prince's heart.

How much it will hurt when she dies along with him.

If she can somehow do it all without Finn having to watch.

"Finn?" she calls, unease corkscrewing inside her. He wouldn't have left her alone here. Unless something happened to him. Unless—

It's only when she snaps her head up that she registers her surroundings.

Gone are the cracked walls, the moss sprouting from the ceiling. This isn't the decaying room she saw last night. Instead, Finn's bedroom is spotless, velour curtains in place of crooked blinds. The bare mattress has been replaced by a canopy bed overflowing with velvet pillows and gold-trimmed blankets. An ornate side table holds long candles and a platter of fruit.

Confusion whips inside her. None of this was here an hour ago.

"What the hell—?"

Something snags the corner of her vision, and when she turns, it's to find Finn sitting across the room in a chair she hadn't noticed. Tucked beneath more candles, gold spilling around him like a halo.

Wild disbelief grips her as she registers his changed appearance. His hair is combed into a slick knot, face clean-shaven and free of bruises. His white shirt is ironed to a crisp, unbuttoned at the top, and tucked into trousers that disappear into high black boots. Partially rolled sleeves reveal sun-kissed skin corded with muscle, and he stares at her with a small knowing smile. Like he's waiting for her to realize they succeeded, that they're finally safe.

Briar braces for the growl in her skull, the winter-cold claws on her skin. But this time, there's only the comfort of silence.

Uncertain hope balloons inside her.

"Finn?" she cries, rushing toward him. "Did that—did it seriously work?" She slides into his lap and holds her blade-slashed hands up to his face. "Did—did my magic do all *this*? Finn!"

Delirious and exhilarated, she doesn't wait for him to respond before pressing her lips against his.

It's a kiss infused with impossible relief, a wordless thing of desperation and prayer. She exhales her fear, bunching his shirt in her fists, clinging to him like he's the only sturdy place in a windswept storm.

Finn's hands close around her waist, hauling her closer, as if he's thinking the same thing. His entire body is scorching hot against hers, feverish almost, and she warms her icy palms along his muscular chest.

But then Finn sweeps his tongue along the seam of her mouth, coaxing her open, and faint alarm bells trill in her ears. The taste of Finn's kiss is different somehow—too sweet, too sugary. Like foaming poison disguised as celebratory wine.

His tongue isn't soft and warm like last night. It's rough, like sandpaper, and covering far too much of her at once.

Almost like it's forked.

And when she parts her lips in a surprised gasp, Finn licks into her mouth with a sound she's never heard him make.

It's a half growl, half snarl. Low and guttural. Primal and deep. That untamed groan vibrates in her throat, at once filling her with terror and turning her insides to smoke. Bewildered heat spins in her stomach as he clutches her hips with a heavier grip than she remembers. She should stop this. She shouldn't be kissing him back, shouldn't be arching into his possessive hands. Something is wrong, *wrong*—

Briar wrenches her mouth away.

And Finn stares back at her with eyes that are completely black.

All the gray is gone from his irises. It's like his eyes are two portholes looking out into the abyssal zone of the ocean, a location that's never seen the sun. And when Finn's face splits into a wide cruel grin, the final understanding slips into place.

"No," Briar grinds out. "*No*. This wasn't part of the deal. You don't get to have him too!"

Deal? he echoes, and Briar's chest constricts at the sound of the Hell Prince's rattling voice coming from Finn's perfect mouth. *To which deal are you referring?*

Panicked confusion consumes her, but she shoves it aside.

"Get out of him," Briar commands, digging her nails into his hair. As if she could claw the Hell Prince loose from Finn's body. "I gave myself up—I *said* you could do whatever you wanted with me. Not *him*! Get out, *get out, get*—"

Perhaps we should talk about our *deal*, says the thing inside Finn. *You may have let that mortal boy defile you all night, but we both know who you really belong to, Winters girl. The truth was in that kiss.* He drags ring-adorned knuckles down the side of her throat and smirks at the way she flushes. *What would he think, if he knew how much you liked it?*

Briar twists away from his touch and swallows a wave of shame. Of course she liked it. She's just as vile, just as wretched. Broken in a thousand places. Of course, a monster's kiss would put a blazing heat inside her and make her want more.

But Briar grits her teeth. She won't let him get to her like this.

"You *said* you wouldn't hurt him. You lied!"

I did no such thing. I keep my promises, Winters girl. His smile is a blade in the candlelight. *Because* I *won't hurt him at all.* You *will. Or have you forgotten what I told you?*

Despair and rage swallow her as she's forced to think of graduation night again: Finn's hands on her skin and his whisper in her ear. Touching him felt like finding something she never even knew she lost, and every breath only made her wish she'd done it sooner. Even as they kissed, her body ached from all the *almosts* that had come before.

But the Hell Prince's voice crept into her skull at dawn and took Finn away from her with those six whispered words: *You'll kill him one day too.*

She left Finn's apartment minutes later with tears dampening her face and a blade lodged in her throat, one that sharpened every time he begged her to stay. She ran because she had to; she ran to keep him safe.

She ran because she loved him more than she loved herself.

Maybe that's why Finn left too.

Yet here they are. Entangled in this room at the end of the world, a beast possessing his body and claiming ownership over hers, all because they couldn't protect each other.

But failure, she thinks, can be a weapon too.

Something shatters inside her, fierce and destructive. Her entire life has been a fucking setup. Every breath she's taken has been by someone else's design, choreographed for a circus of tragedy and grief. *All eyes on Briar Winters! Watch as she dances across our tightrope! Observe carefully as she inches closer and closer to the blood-soaked fate that's already been written in the sand. Applause, applause!*

No more. *No more.*

She's not a prophecy. Not a legend or a high priestess or a loophole to a spell. She's not a person either. Not anymore. Not ever again. She played her role for far too long, and today—*today* it stops.

"You're wrong," she growls to the Hell Prince. "*I won't do it.*"

Briar wrenches herself off his lap, tumbling in a heap to the ground. This possessed version of Finn stands, and her stomach flips at his sudden massive height, towering over her.

You're disappointing me, Winters girl, the Hell Prince hisses from Finn's mouth. *You know I don't like it when you disobey.*

Electricity courses through Briar as she springs to her feet and races into the hall. Those heavy boots thunder behind her, and she pushes harder. With every step, her plan from last night crumbles, and a new one sprouts in its place: Run as fast as she can. Get to the water's edge.

Drive that obsidian dagger straight through her own flesh.

The Hell Prince needs her body alive; he said that himself. So maybe—just maybe—she has one bargaining chip left. A way to snap the tether.

And put an end to this once and for all.

A flash of brown catches her eye outside the kitchen screen door, and she skids toward it. Neptune. Finn's coywolf.

With her hands flying faster than her feet, she flings open the latch and waves into the salt air.

"Go on," she begs. "Run."

But Neptune sits on the deck with his chin tucked into his paws, eyes round. Leave it to Finn to turn a wolf into a clingy golden retriever looking for treats.

"Go!" she yells, bending and gripping the coywolf at the scruff of his neck. She guides Neptune to the stairs, and he listens this time, becoming a blur of brown against black sand.

At the same moment, Finn's tall silhouette looms in the doorway, and Briar sprints for the other corner of the kitchen. She topples a chair in front of his feet, buying herself only seconds. Terror consumes her at the sight of that wretched beast's feral hunger in Finn's eyes. Her best friend. The boy she loves. Her home, her sanctuary. Her *haven*. It's enough to make her want to sink to her knees and sob, but there's no time, no time—

Briar tears for the front door of the cottage. She makes it halfway down the stairs outside before she flies forward, tripping on a rock.

The wind escapes her as she tumbles down the remaining steps, each one finding a different part of her to bruise. Briar collapses, bleeding, in the dark sand. Finn strolls down the steps behind her, his movements languid and unhurried, as though the demon inside him knows she won't make it far.

She tries to stand, but her knees buckle—so she crawls instead. Dragging herself through dry sand and then into thick mud. The raven-colored waves crash in and out just ahead, beckoning. Her chest heaves in panic.

Perhaps it was always going to end like this. She recalls Morgan's words: *The original thread is trying to right itself.*

With a sob, Briar reaches to her thigh for the dagger. Will it hurt to die, she wonders distantly, if she's already dead?

Just as her fingers brush the leather strap, Finn seizes her waist from behind, flattening her into the ground until her teeth clack together. A mouthful of wet sand crunches between her lips, and she struggles with every remaining effort to twist away.

Winters girl, the Hell Prince snarls from inside him. *When will you learn that you can't run from me?*

He fists her hair, throwing her onto her back, and she desperately gasps for air. Those soulless eyes burn and burn, inky liquid seeping from his lashes. Horror fills her lungs as the onyx substance spills down Finn's cheeks, and despite everything, she wants to gather his face in her hands. Tell him she still loves him—that he's hers.

But then he ensnares her wrists with one palm, the other crushing her rib cage. Her bones audibly splinter, pain shooting through her as she unleashes an anguished scream.

"Finn," Briar begs, a weak, last-ditch effort. "Finn, *please*. Please—make him stop."

But he won't stop. She knows it with crushing certainty, with bleeding dread. She catches sight of his curved talons, carving the paper-thin skin on the inside of her wrist. When she screams again, the beast inside Finn laughs, fangs wet with saliva as he bends his head to hers. That forked black tongue slithers out to lick her throat, a predator moving in on his prey.

"*Finn*." Her voice breaks as she struggles and gasps. She thinks of being little, of sitting next to Finn on the hot cracked seats of the bus on the last day of school with humid air and summertime spilling through the windows. She thinks of silver snowfall, of wet orange leaves, of the first blossoms of spring. Dozens of seasons all colored by him, creating a life that was never built to last.

Something that was always designed to fall apart in the stretch of early morning, beneath this raging sea.

"Finn," she whispers, a prayer, a plea, an omen. Her last words will be his name. "Finn. Finn. Finn."

She freezes, suddenly thinking of dots and dashes. Short and long, long and short. Sound and light. She spits out a mouthful of blood to grind out—

"You're still here. Finn. *You're still here.*"

At that, the endless black of his eyes flickers to gray surrounded by bloodshot white. He makes a rough sound, like he's wrenching something loose from his mouth, before finally growling through clenched teeth in his normal voice, *his* voice—

"*Briar.*"

Tears sting her lashes at the grief-torn way he says her name. And a new possessive fury rips through her at the thought of this demon hurting him any longer.

Briar didn't want to do this in front of him, but there's no choice. No options left. No time. She has to save him. She has to do *just one thing* right.

"I love you," Briar whispers—then tugs the dagger loose and angles the blade directly at her own heart.

"No—!" Finn chokes out, snatching her hand before she can draw blood. "Briar, *no.*"

"I have to," she says through sobs, "it's the only way."

"*It's not.* It has to be me. I don't—I don't have magic." Finn gasps, like it's hard to breathe. Like his lungs are crowded, tentacles curling around his organs. "You'll kill it—if it's in here with me—but I'll—I'll be okay."

Briar's heart thrashes in her chest at the choice, the knowledge that she won't survive either way, the terrible awareness that Finn believes she will. She processes the desperation in his eyes as her brain buzzes with thoughts of blades sinking into flesh, draining magic and life. She doesn't know what to do. *She doesn't know what to do.*

"Briar," Finn pleads through gritted teeth. "*Trust me.*"

The comfort from Finn's hands lasts for only a split second before his eyes morph straight to black again, but it's long enough for her decision to snap into place.

Long enough for her to press the blade to his throat.

Ah, the Hell Prince purrs, *there's the Winters girl I know*.

She tightens her grip, the flat side of the dagger tracing the purple-black veins now climbing his neck. Finn's beautiful face cracks open in a terrifying grin.

Be a good girl—the voice of the demon rattles—*and end him*.

Briar stares at him and contemplates the words, not enough time to turn them over, not enough time to pick them apart. Finn said to trust him, Finn said, Finn *said*—

She sucks in a breath and squeezes her eyes shut.

And when Briar plunges the blade into Finn's chest, she has nothing in her heart but hope.

CHAPTER THIRTY-SIX
FINN

The first time Finn Adler saw Briar Winters, he thought to himself, *This is what an angel looks like.*

He knows now that he was right.

CHAPTER THIRTY-SEVEN
BRIAR

For a moment, nothing happens.

It's as though the world has been paused; the black waves become the only sound, along with the shrill of Briar's racing pulse. She drives the blade deeper and deeper until she realizes the ringing flooding her ears isn't her heartbeat at all.

It's a primal, demonic howl. Like a death knell.

It's working.

She twists the hilt with a satisfying squelch, and the thing inside Finn screeches again. Warm liquid sprays onto her face, but she barely notices through the adrenaline scorching her veins. Briar imagines the blade carving out every ounce of evil until he's purely Finn.

With her eyes still shut, she yanks the dagger out—and thrusts it back in, a few inches to the side. Another gush of warmth sprays onto her. She cracks her lashes against a film of red—

Just as Finn chokes out her name.

His normal voice, two syllables wrapped in a thick cough.

Briar wipes her eyes frantically, but her face is covered in blood.

Finn's blood.

She blinks until he comes into view, her own breaths stilted and raw.

A scream rips out of her at the sight of his white shirt completely soaked, blood pouring onto her, the two of them lying in a lake of endless crimson.

"*No!*" Briar wails, splaying her hands against his neck, finding only the faintest pulse.

Finn rolls off her, face up on the beach. She kneels over him, her hands shaking as she presses on the open wounds. It's fucking useless; blood streams from the gashes, running between her fingers, spilling onto the muddy sand below.

"How did . . . ?" Briar trails off, incoherent. "You don't have magic! The dagger only—"

Finn turns his head and coughs again. Blood leaks from the corner of his mouth. "You—you gave me yours."

An icy chill spreads through her lungs, and her hands freeze over his chest. "*What?*"

He doesn't answer, but his gray eyes find hers, shining with resolve.

And in his silence, she understands.

Finn was never going to let her rescue him. He told her that all along.

Briar's fists curl as the weight of his words sinks in. The world spins. *No one can take your magic from you, Winters. You'd have to give it willingly. Be careful who you trust.*

"You tricked me!" she seethes through clenched teeth. "That wasn't a protection spell, was it?"

He shakes his head. "It was—a bonding ritual." Finn winces around the words, each syllable drenched with pain. "When a witch bonds with—a regular mortal, she transfers her magic. She can—"

"*Finn!*" She roars his name. Clutches the blood-soaked collar of his shirt, buries her face in his neck. "How could you make me do this? Why *the fuck* would you make me do this?"

Panic and terror boil inside her; she wants to smash her fists into the earth until her hands are as bruised as her heart. She also wants to kiss him until there's nothing left. Until her breath runs out too.

"You never would've agreed," Finn chokes out. "I wasn't—" He coughs up another mouthful of blood; it trickles over his lips as he lets out a low groan. "I wasn't going to let you die twice. I had to get rid of it. Had to—*sever* it. It was the only way."

Briar raises her head, breath suddenly shallow. The air turns to murky liquid all around her—water in her lungs too. Thick inky-black seawater, filling her airway.

And that water will rise.

She glances down at her leg, at the daisy wheel that's already fading into a pale pink scar.

"Finn," she whispers. "I'm going to die anyway."

His own struggling breath slows, and he cuts his gaze to hers. "What?"

"I made—a bargain. And so did Morgan. When she did the spell." She swallows. "It's a double bond."

Finn's eyes narrow into slits. His voice darkens to frost. "*What?*"

Briar forces herself to say it. "That monster—it was the only thing keeping me alive."

"No." Finn strains to sit up, hands clenching around his wounds. "No, Briar. Tell me you're lying."

"It's true." She swallows again, feeling a wave of dizziness. "That voice. I've heard it all my life... since I was a little girl. It told me to let go of Riley's hand that day. It told me to kill my *parents*. It—Oh god." She whimpers as her chest constricts. "I think my lungs are going to burst. Everything hurts."

Finn splays his hands on either side of her face. His eyes search hers. "You're okay," he manages to say. "Promise me you're going to be okay, you—"

"That creature. It talked to me the night of graduation, after we—" Her chin trembles. The ache in her chest splits and splits. "It said it would make me kill you one day too. *That's* why I left that morning. I thought if I wasn't around, you'd be safe, you'd—"

Something bitter foams against her lips. She tries to cough around it, choking on sable liquid. Finn holds her with blood-damp hands as her back arches, and she spits mouthfuls of foul seawater, determined to get the rest of the words out before she drowns on dry land.

"Last night, I agreed. I promised an eternal bond, thinking—thinking that if it had me, it wouldn't hurt you too."

"*Briar.*" Finn attempts to sit up but collapses on the sand. He fists her dress instead and releases an anguished sound that's so drenched in grief, Briar nearly covers her ears to make it stop.

"Why would you do that?" he chokes out, fractured. "*Why—?*"

"You let it inside you—you sacrificed yourself to protect me." Her chest heaves. "*I* sacrificed *myself*... to protect *you*."

"Briar—"

"You made me destroy it." Her breaths are slower now, labored. "But *I'm* bound to it. I killed Riley. I killed my parents. I killed *you*. That monster is a part of me. So, when it dies, I do too." Her face crumples. "I deserve to die. You don't."

"No. *No.* Get up," Finn orders. "Get the fuck up." His blood-soaked palms weakly grasp for her shoulders. "You're not dying in this place. I won't let you."

"I am," she grinds out. "We are."

Finn goes quiet, reigniting the awareness that he's dying too. In minutes, he won't say anything else at all. She'll die alone on this shadowed beach, atop a cold, lifeless boy she once knew. Tears spill down her cheeks, and she works to tilt his head to hers.

"I'm sorry," she whispers. "Finn, I'm so sorry."

"Tell me," he says, "that you love me."

This is what people do when they say goodbye.

But Briar isn't ready. They weren't ready the first time, and maybe they never would be. Maybe no one is ever ready. Would it have been better if they'd had decades? If they were dying together with wrinkles and white hair, with decades of life and love behind them? Would that have been easier than being nineteen, hardly more than children, having barely lived at all? What would they have been, she wonders, if they'd just had more time?

Do you ever wish you could go back and fix something that's already gone wrong?

More tears push through her lashes. His forehead touches hers, lips blue and cold.

"Please," he whispers. "I want to hear you say it again."

"*I love you.*" But the admission is airless, nearly silent.

Finn folds his arms around her. There's surrender in the gesture. Defeat. "I've loved you forever." A quiet, broken sob shivers through him. "Briar, we could have been something great."

"We were," she murmurs, vision blurring. "We were something great."

There are no more words between them after that.

They hold each other as the waves lap the sand, unmoved, unforgiving. She strokes his hair, his cheek, all the parts of him she wants to remember. She maps every dip and angle with her fingers and lips, swallowing the knowledge that she's kissing a boy who is mostly dead.

When his hands finally fall limp around her, her surroundings swim in a starry mess of silver and black.

Because Finn—Finn is gone.

And Briar is alone.

Alone, alone, alone.

Taking her final breaths at this lonely sea's edge.

Lost within the folds of time exactly as she once predicted: trapped forever in Loch Creek.

~

Nothing about death will be easy for Briar Winters.

She clutches Finn's lifeless body for what feels like hours, impossibly still breathing through the sour liquid that swells with every painful gasp. It's like she's being punished twice over—first for disobeying that creature, and second for taking its life.

She tries to memorialize the years she had, cycling through sleepovers with Astrid, Kai's backyard at dusk, that day in kindergarten when she and Finn unleashed shared screams of grief. For that entire year when she didn't speak, nearly everyone assumed she'd forgotten how. But Finn gently made space for her to find the words when she was ready, all so he could know what she was thinking in the quiet.

Briar runs her hands over Finn's chest now, feeling the sticky wounds in his skin. Why did that creature want him? Why would it make a bargain with him too when it already had her and Riley? *A pair of twins in flames.*

And at that, Briar's eyes widen, suddenly thinking of Professor Quill's words.

Of what Morgan also said on the yacht.

Something's not right about that translation.

"Twins in flames?" Briar gasps, curling her fingers in fury that she didn't realize it sooner.

That was never the prophecy.

It had always been *twin flame*.

A mirrored soul. A celestial counterpart. People who finish each other's sentences, people whose wounds are matching shapes. People who are destined to find each other over and over, in every universe, in every timeline.

Of course, a high priestess would be smart enough to seal a banishing spell with something rare. The kind of love that's only described in stories, in poetry and art. The kind most people never get a chance to feel.

The kind of love between her and Finn.

There was more to the translation though. Briar squeezes her lashes, trying to picture the scrap of graph paper from Finn's backpack. Because it didn't just say twin flames; it said *twin flames who extinguish each other's light*. The key to freeing the Hell Prince was never something as common as twin siblings.

It's soul mates—who willingly sacrifice each other.

"No," Briar whispers, choking on another wave of water.

Dread plummets in her stomach as understanding floods her. But there's no way to fight what's already been done, nowhere to hide from this terrible truth:

She killed Finn, just as the Hell Prince told her she would. And Finn killed her in the original thread of their life. The one that's been rethreading stich by stich, because of Morgan's unpracticed magic.

Despair swallowing her, Briar swings her gaze up to find the sky darkening to tumultuous gray. Lightning splits the world above.

And just along the horizon, the sea starts to climb.

A menacing wave roars toward the shores of Loch Creek, and she realizes with her last bit of awareness that the screeching, keening sound she heard earlier wasn't a death knell—it was a celebration.

She didn't kill the Hell Prince.

No, Briar *just set him free.*

Winters girl, the wind seems to purr. The beach grows black as midnight, the sand suddenly frostbitten and slick like ice. *Winters girl. A goddess of the damned. When all the world is a shadow, statues will be erected in her name.*

If it weren't for the water in her lungs, Briar could almost laugh. She'd cackle the way she did in the shower. Raw and wild, untethered and feral. All this time, all this pain, all for *nothing*. Finn is gone. She failed, she failed, she failed.

But Briar can't laugh.

She can't cry.

She can't breathe.

And yet, she *still doesn't die.*

She languishes instead, in limbo between living and dying. Thunder cracks in the distance. The Hell Prince's laughter roars in her skull. The sound makes her think of buildings crumbling, fire cascading across stone. She pictures Loch Creek sinking brick by brick, swallowed by an ocean that never intended to keep its promises. There'd be a marble statue of her amid the wreckage, posed like a mermaid without tears. A tombstone beneath a sea-drenched sky.

Briar Winters, daughter, sister, and savior to demons.

New rage stirs inside her—but then, a streak of silver snags her vision: a small pistol nestled in a dune.

The gun Finn stole from Old Town Hall. The one he shot her with in their original thread.

It's here. Of course, it's here.

And just a few feet away stands her wraith.

She's silent as she always is, her dress pooling in the ravenous sea. Her scraggly hair hangs in front of her face, the lacuna in her eye glowing as she hovers. Waiting.

Because Briar was always going to die like this—the only way she can.

For the first time, Briar isn't afraid. Doesn't want to smash glass or rip her reflection to shreds. Her wraith isn't a threat, but an answer to an equation. A set of coordinates that could finally lead her to peace.

Briar crawls toward the weapon. Her fingers curl around the handle, testing its weight. Death whispers in her veins, beckoning.

Fixing the muzzle of the gun over her right eye, Briar squeezes both shut. She thinks of her parents. Of Riley. Of Astrid and Kai.

Of Finn.

Maybe she'll find him somewhere, after.

Her finger trembles over the trigger, breaths stilted and uneven.

She doesn't see the trio of figures running toward her. The girl with a flurry of braids, kicking sand with every desperate sprint. The boy with a messy ponytail and T-shirt whipping in the wind. And the second girl at the front, a starfish pin clasping her wild blue-streaked hair. She's the one screaming, a leather book raised to the tempestuous sky.

But right as Briar is about to squeeze her index finger, she hears the sound of her own name. It echoes through the rising winds, the air full of salt.

And a tide that's about to change again.

CHAPTER THIRTY-EIGHT

MORGAN

Morgan Parker-Blake never wanted to be a witch.

She never asked for magic. Never wanted to bend time or control the weather. If she could have it her way, she'd hide herself in mirrors and tulle. She'd pirouette faster than the speed of light, escape this world and all its demands, if only for a second.

But here in this monstrous place, she has no choice.

All of Loch Creek is drowning.

And it's taking the one girl who has ever made her feel alive down with it.

It started with a rumble close to dawn, like a roll of thunder that tore from the sand to the sky. Like something clawing its way out from the earth. By the time Morgan hauled herself up from the floor where she'd been studying Harper Clay's journal, the sea was a shadowed wall outside her window, its tip curving like talons to tear Loch Creek apart.

Something had gone wrong.

Stretching a muscle she hadn't used in ages, Morgan curled into herself, bending water in her mind, conjuring salt and mist. Commanding and beckoning. Imagining the ocean like a blue ribbon she could loop around her fist and ask to show her what it had done.

The town elders were first, their faces leaking inky water as their rotting skin sloughed off the bone. Mayor Caldwell, his eyes chewed out by a slithering thing with teeth that emerged from his own mouth. The others falling one by one, choking on the taste of magic they'd never be able to claim.

Then the buildings: Entire structures swallowed in minutes. Old Town Hall, the courthouse, the gallery—all underwater. Brass frames floating in a murky abyss, broken marble columns lost beneath waves. The art would be forgotten; the history would be buried.

Loch Creek would be consumed by the very thing it's been trying to free.

But it wasn't just the wicked elders and their brick-laced hideouts. Homes, schools, restaurants. Nerissa's cottage. Briar's house. Their entire town, border to border, would soon be lost at sea. Morgan could see it so clearly in her mind, brain overflowing with the screams that would eventually turn to gurgled silence.

The official welcome sign would be the last thing to drown, slipping beneath sea-foam until the words vanished like they were never there at all. *A haven since 1692.*

Loch Creek had never been a haven. It had always been a prison.

But it didn't have to be one anymore.

Morgan tore her way to the north beach, the one place she knew wouldn't be destroyed because it was already soaked in tragedy: Sorrow's Shore. She laid out the spell book and Harper's journal, frantically reading the ancient words as the sky opened up and unleashed silver hail from the deepening black.

And there, in the same spot where she ran to avoid her mother's conjuring lesson thirteen years ago, Morgan used her magic. She clutched Briar's starfish pin with desperation as if it were Briar's hand instead. Something she wished she grabbed sooner, something that could have made her feel a little less alone all these years.

But as Morgan races toward Briar's bloodied form here in the space between worlds, she's not alone at all.

Astrid Hoffman and Kai Baisho are at her side.

Morgan wasn't sure if they would come when she called earlier, but at the last minute, there they were. Running along the edge of Sorrow's Shore toward Morgan, a girl who stole their best friend's secrets, a girl they could have hated if they wanted to.

A girl they chose to trust instead.

It's Kai who reaches Briar first. He wrenches the gun from her hands and throws it into the tumultuous sea before gathering her into his arms. Astrid is at his heels, flinging herself atop Finn Adler's lifeless body.

Morgan kneels between them, at the epicenter of their grief. She flips through the math-laced spells in Harper's journal, arranges candles and stones in the sand.

She'll get it right this time. She has to.

"Don't," Briar protests through rattling teeth, as Kai lies her on the shoreline beside Finn.

Morgan ignores her, prying the dagger from Finn's chest to clean the blade in the water.

"That creature—it's tied to us both," Briar chokes out. "It'll all happen again. Over and over and—"

"We won't let it," Kai says, stroking her hair. "We're here now. We're here."

Astrid nods in agreement, still holding Finn.

"That demon will destroy the planet if I don't banish it," Morgan says, reaching for Briar's clammy hand. She drags the blade through Briar's already-sliced palm and grits her teeth. "Everyone meets their destiny eventually. This one is mine."

For the first time, Morgan doesn't feel a swell of resentment as she bends beneath the expectations laid out for her centuries ago. Because in a way, it's like dancing. Like crushing her feet into satin. Forcing her toes into just the right curl until her body changes shape, until she can leap into the sky and become a blur of ribbons and lace. Until she's more feather than girl, more air than blood.

She taught her body how to escape.

She can learn how to come home too.

"There's all kinds of evil in this world. But only one Briar Winters." Morgan slides her gaze to Finn's bloodstained chest. "Only one Finn Adler."

Her heart twists with the words, the truth about Briar's unrelenting love for Finn burning behind her teeth. She's known it all along, known it in the way Briar's eyes always blazed when she said Finn's name; how her cheeks always flushed when she talked about their past; how she'd travel to the ends of the earth for him, disrupt time and space just to see him once again.

But Morgan knows better than to follow those bitter feelings. Morgan Parker-Blake doesn't get jealous. She cares about balance. About order. About getting things right.

And maybe, just a little, she cares about a curly-haired girl who once kissed her and made her see stars.

Maybe she doesn't want to live in a world without Briar in it.

"You didn't—" Briar coughs; thick black liquid leaks from her mouth. Another trickle of it bleeds from her eyes. "You didn't call me 'Pom-Poms.' Just now. You said—you said my name."

Morgan answers with a sad gaze before grabbing Finn's stiffening hand. She extends the dagger to Astrid and nods. The other girl works the blade through Finn's palm, silent tears dampening her cheeks. Kai leads Briar's outstretched grasp to Finn's, and Morgan watches through blurred lashes as they fit Briar and Finn's fingers together. Laying their best friends down in their death, their hands intertwined.

A memorial, here, at the end of the world.

"Your life threads are already cut," Morgan explains, dragging her fingers through the sand. "To restore you both, the spell will cut your love threads. Your memory threads. For every action, an equal and opposite reaction. But you won't disappear. Neither will he. Not this time." She spreads a tendril of black sand across Briar's cheek, another on Finn's. "This time, love pays the sacrifice."

"What?" Kai asks, glancing up.

"When we did the first ritual, Finn traded his existence," Morgan says, recalling the desperation in his eyes, how quickly he agreed to vanish if it meant Briar would be safe. "But it wasn't enough, because our bodies are temporary homes. Fleeting things. *Love* is eternal. It's greater than life itself." She swallows. "That's what they'll need to give up now."

Briar's eyes flutter with approaching death. Morgan's pulse skips, traitorous tears stinging her eyes.

"You won't remember Finn," Morgan rushes to tell Briar. "Or he won't remember you. The spell will decide who loses the past and who retains it." Morgan turns to Astrid and Kai, finding their faces contorted with pain. Her throat constricts as she adds, "That goes for you too."

Kai shakes his head, eyes bloodshot and raw. "I—I don't understand."

"I do," Astrid whispers. "We won't be friends anymore. Not like we are now." Her voice breaks. "It won't ever be like this again."

Kai looks at Briar and Finn, his jaw knotted at the corners. Astrid stares too, her lips trembling. Grappling with what it will mean to lose their shared history. Measuring the ache their hearts will hold from missing something they'll never know they had.

Morgan studies them, wondering if they're silently trying to memorize their friends' voices. The sound will become a glimmer of déjà vu one day, a whisper that somewhere, in another life, they loved each other. Fiercely. Unapologetically. Like family. Like blood.

Messy and flawed. Real and beautiful. And *theirs*.

"Okay." Kai's voice fractures on a sob, and Astrid draws him against her. The embrace does him in, tears spilling onto his cheeks. "If it means they'll be safe. Then, okay."

For a moment, Morgan lets them hold each other and cry, lets them mourn the seasons they'll never live together. The inside jokes they won't ever make. The stories they would have woven over a lifetime, all about to unravel with a few ancient words.

A family who chose one another years ago.

A family choosing, now, to let one another go.

"Imagine," Morgan finally says, tracing a moonstone down the length of Briar's battered body, "if you'd never met. Imagine if nothing had ever gone wrong."

She stands, beckoning the tide. She imagines the water's surface fluttering, like little butterfly wings kissed at the tips with red.

Red—but not blood.

Magic.

"Imagine," Morgan whispers, "if you could change the smallest thing about the thread that led you here—and create a brand-new one in its place. Imagine if you could begin again."

PART SIX
RED TIDE

The wave—there is a movement there!
As if the towers had thrust aside,
In slightly sinking, the dull tide—
As if their tops had feebly given
A void within the filmy Heaven.

EDGAR ALLAN POE, "The City in the Sea"

CHAPTER THIRTY-NINE

THIRTEEN YEARS LATER

BRIAR

The bookstore tastes like salt.

There's no other way to describe it, and Briar winces as she flips on the lights. Salt in the air, so thick that it burns her tongue.

She throws her bag behind the counter for what's likely the last time. Glancing out the window, she studies the gray shoreline, the shadow of the Ferris wheel against the foggy horizon. The Loch Creek Lighthouse looms, spilling yolk-hued light onto the waves, and Briar briefly wonders if she'll miss anything about this town.

Certainly not the carnival. It means everyone from Loch Creek High is back for the weekend, an ensemble cast of the people who made her life *miserable* in school.

School. The place where no one ever talked to Briar Winters.

She must be a witch, the kids always said about her. *Everything she touches dies.*

Briar, a girl death clung to like a shadow. Her brother. Her parents. No one wanted to be next.

Tonight, all the people from her past will return to a place that's only offered them good memories. They'll be ready to make new ones, colored with neon lights and the sugary scent of fried dough. But not her.

There's something she knows she has to do tonight—the reason for the dread-soaked salt crunching between her teeth. Her time is receding like the pull of the tide. And if she's quiet enough, she can almost hear a familiar growl in her ear, ready to welcome her home.

Briar clenches her jaw to shut it out and continues opening the store.

Paint & Pages is the first thing she ever did on her own, the only part of Loch Creek she could almost love. More than the town's art gallery that she helped restore after it burned, taking both her parents with it. More than that lighthouse committee after graduation—a pointless venture, another garish flaunting of Loch Creek's wealth.

This tiny shop filled with novels and paint supplies—located on Rowan Street, the last street anyone cares to visit in Loch Creek—feels different from the rest of this town with all its expectations and demands.

Because *this* place is hers.

Briar twists her curls into a knot as she arranges shelves, straightening piles of fantasy novels and coordinating paint palettes. She works her way around the perimeter until she finds herself in front of the pamphlets near the checkout line. The tourist wall, she calls it. Souvenirs for people to take when they leave Loch Creek behind.

Something everyone gets to do, except her.

One pamphlet is out of order. Boston Ballet Company's summer season: *Swan Lake* and *Romeo and Juliet*. She snatches it, flicking her gaze to the glossy photo of the dark-haired dancer draped in tulle beneath a spill of light.

A girl she knew once. Morgan.

A girl who always stared across the cafeteria as though she knew a secret Briar wasn't in on, as though she longed to talk to Briar when no one else would.

But she never did.

The bell jingles; Briar slips back behind the counter. Two Loch Creek High alumni stroll in—Kai Baisho and Astrid Hoffman—holding coffees and buzzing with conversation. Briar busies herself with papers, a calendar that's half a year old. Anything so she doesn't have to—

"Briar Winters?"

She looks up to find Astrid with a warm smile spread across her face.

"This store is so cute," she adds, tucking a strand of glossy curls behind her ear. "I love what you've done with it."

She's just saying it to be kind, Briar reasons. Astrid lives in DC; she's always on the news talking about reproductive justice and giving viral speeches from the Capitol Building. And Kai—she's lost track of how many Emmys he's won. Why are they even bothering to talk to her, a girl who's never left their hometown?

"Thanks," Briar manages to say.

"You coming to the carnival tonight?" Kai asks, lifting a book and thumbing the pages.

Briar slides him a surprised glance at the question. Who would she even go *with*? She ate lunch alone every day in school, was picked last for everything. If she was even picked at all.

"I don't think so," she replies, digging her nails against her cuticles. "Not really into mirror mazes."

Kai meets her gaze, and something shifts in his stare.

"Never liked the mirror house either," he says. "I always skip that one. Too creepy."

Briar forces a small smile in agreement, but an unsettling feeling itches beneath her skin. She studies Kai's button-down shirt, his slicked-back hair, and for one bizarre moment, she imagines them huddling close amid neon and glass. His arm around her waist, comforting and secure. Like an older brother. Like a friend. Kai Baisho is essentially a stranger, but Briar is suddenly and inexplicably certain that being beside him in the dark would feel safer than most things she's ever known.

When she meets Kai's gaze again, it's to find him staring intently back. As though he's impossibly thinking the same thing about her.

But then he turns toward Astrid, making Briar question whether she imagined it. Briar eyes them as they browse and allows herself to wonder what it would feel like to be their friend too. An image winks to life—the shape of a moss-covered tree house beneath a storming sky—and a strange, lonely ache fills her chest.

"Maybe we'll catch you around before we leave," Kai says, as they stroll toward the door. He fixes Briar with another curious stare, as if he's trying to summon a word he's long forgotten. Finally, he shakes his head and lifts his hand in a wave. "It's good to see you, Briar."

"Yeah, you too," she replies.

She expects them to leave, but Astrid slows at the counter again. She gingerly lifts one of the woven friendship bracelets from a dish.

"Did you make these?" Astrid asks.

Briar's cheeks turn warm. "Yeah. Just a silly hobby."

Astrid falls quiet, studying the lavender and pink strands, the crystal beads between knots. "Funny," she murmurs, "I think I used to have one just like this."

The sight of her sudden wistful expression yanks the words out before Briar even realizes what she's saying—

"You can keep it if you want."

Astrid snaps her eyes back up. Kai turns his head, halfway out the door.

"I mean." Briar's face flushes hotter. "They don't really sell anyway, so you'd be doing me a favor. But—"

"I will," Astrid interrupts, and Briar lets out a breath. Astrid attempts to fasten the bracelet onto her narrow wrist but struggles with the clasp, frowning. "Do you mind?" She extends her hand.

Briar leans over the counter, looping the ending bead through the knot. Déjà vu dizzies her, and every thread of the bracelet seems to whisper, *It could have been. It could have been.*

"Thanks," Astrid says, but there's something sad woven in her smile.

Like she's wishing things had been different too.

When Astrid and Kai leave the bookstore, Briar stares after them for a long time. A sour loneliness fills her belly. It reminds her of being a kid and longing for something she's carelessly misplaced. Something she might not be able to find, no matter how hard she looks.

When the bells on the door jingle again, Briar bites down on her lip.

She recognizes this customer too.

He wasn't in any of her classes—but sometimes when Briar was at her locker, her skin would prickle with the awareness of being watched. She'd turn to find a tall golden-haired boy with gray eyes—and in the next moment, he'd always look away. Sometimes, he seemed angry that she caught him staring. Other times, it looked like he was about to cry.

She only spoke to him once. It was her nineteenth birthday, and she had no one to celebrate with. Long-dead parents. No friends. Briar spent most of the evening alone beneath the lifeguard tower, watching the sun sink behind the waves. Trying to shut out the guttural whisper that seemed to urge her closer. The sea called to her, beckoning her to disappear beneath the bottomless black. Just like Riley.

And right as the sound grew so loud that she had no choice but to stand and drift toward the shore, someone shouted her name.

That quiet boy with the stormy eyes from school. Meticulously studying her in the crisp moonlight. His presence was like a snap of cold air on her skin, silencing the sea's whisper.

How long have you been here? she asked, embarrassment creeping up her neck.

He didn't answer, though she saw words fighting for release inside him. He glanced at his watch. Stared at it for several moments. An infinite pause stretched between them, the only sound the crashing waves, until he turned to leave without any explanation. She flicked her gaze at her own watch—seconds after midnight. Her birthday, officially over. Confused sadness overcame her as she realized she didn't want him to go.

Hey, wait, she called. *Come back!*

He didn't.

Yet here he is in her store, all grown up, with tousled dark blonde hair, the hard angles of his jaw lined with scruff. He's wearing a white shirt and ripped jeans, and a gold compass hangs from a chain at his side. Unease stirs within her, but before either of them can speak, her gaze swings to the floor.

"You can't bring a dog in here." Briar frowns, scrunching her face. "Wait. Is that a *wolf*?"

Something hard to place flashes in his eyes. "He's a coywolf, actually."

"Okay, well, you can't bring a *coywolf* in here either," she says. "This is a bookstore."

"Can you make an exception? He's kinda old." He glances around. "We're the only ones here. You don't have to tell your boss."

Briar's eyebrows shoot into her hairline. "I own this store. *Actually*."

But her annoyance quickly softens at the way he smiles and huffs a soft laugh under his breath. The way he's looking at her, like he already knew.

"I'll be out of your way in a second," he says. "It's just... I lost something here once."

"What do you mean?" She shakes her head. "When?"

"It was a while ago. Over a decade, actually."

"A decade? This store is only two years old." Briar gestures to the framed photograph behind the counter. "Used to be an apartment building."

"That's right," he says. "It did."

She tips her head. "Did you live there?"

He hesitates, as though he's debating whether to answer. "Yeah. A long time ago."

There's something pointed about how he says it, something that puts a strange, inexplicable ache in her chest. And for a singular nonsensical moment, she can picture him differently: Not squinting above a locker, but his eyes crinkling at the corners with laughter. Sunlight spilling onto him through a school bus window. His face close to hers, his rough whisper grazing her skin.

She flicks her gaze to the coywolf in efforts to mask the blush heating her cheeks. "What's his name?"

He pauses again. "Neptune."

"That's a good name." She glances back at him and scrambles for something else to say. "So where do you live now?"

"Moved to California after graduation," he says, but his voice is strained around the words. "I work at Berkeley. Physics department."

"Physics," Briar echoes, and another image wedges itself in her mind. Her in a Berkeley sweatshirt. Him waiting for her in the driver's seat, parked beneath palm trees. She blinks to clear it, but the ache in her ribs lingers. "You in town for the carnival?"

He shakes his head. Something sad spreads across his face. "Not my scene."

"Mine either. Never liked it." She clears her throat. "Wait. You didn't tell me what you were looking for. You said you lost something?"

"Not exactly *here*." He gestures with the hand wrapped in Neptune's leash. "Out there."

Briar glances to the window, the choppy waves in the distance. *Me too*, she could say. She swallows, thinking of that August day when she was six, the slippery grip of her brother's hand in hers. The way Sorrow's Shore only reminds her that she'll disappear too.

Tonight.

She turns back, and her stomach flips at the way he's staring. It's the same heated expression he had on the beach thirteen years ago. Unease floods through her, and she knows with fierce certainty:

He didn't come in here to browse books or ask about a misplaced object.

"If you're not in Loch Creek for the carnival," she starts, "then why are you in town?"

"There's a girl I used to know." His jaw knots again. "Today is her birthday."

Briar holds his gaze, her thoughts racing with the question of how he could possibly know that today is *her* birthday. Her thirty-second. But he never spoke to her before this, always glared like she'd wronged him somehow. He must be talking about someone else, she thinks.

Swallowing the inexplicable hope that he could be talking about her.

"Well, do you need help finding a card or something?" she asks, gesturing.

"No." A sad smile tugs on his mouth. "She and I don't speak anymore. I just wanted to see her. Find out if she's happy." He pauses. "I'm not sure if she is."

A soft pause flutters between them. In the quiet, Briar contemplates all the things she could say. *Is this about me? Why did you always look at me like that? What were you doing on the beach that night?*

Do I know you from somewhere else?

But before she can say any of it, he takes a step toward the counter. "What if we went to the carnival? Together?"

Briar lifts her eyebrows, not just at the question but the way he asks it. The words all rushed together like they tumbled free no matter how hard he was holding them back.

"What?" she blurts. "The carnival? With me?"

"Yeah, I don't know." He shrugs. "I've actually never gone."

"But it's a Loch Creek tradition!" Briar clips with bright sarcasm, and he smiles.

"So are a lot of things," he says, "but it doesn't mean you gotta do any of 'em."

She nods, her eyes trailing to his hand resting on the counter. Vertigo hits her, dizzying and disorienting, and she's suddenly consumed with the nonsensical urge to drape her fingers over his.

Briar yanks her hands beneath the counter instead.

"Okay," she whispers, before she can stop herself. "What time?"

His eyes burn into hers. "Seven? At the Ferris wheel?"

"Alright."

"I'll give you my number," he adds, "in case you can't find me."

She hesitates for a tiny fraction of a second. Because she knows in her bones, she doesn't have time for the carnival.

She doesn't have time left for anything at all.

But he's looking at her with expectant eyes, inexplicably glittering with strange, anxious hope. So Briar reaches into her pocket and slides her phone to him. He loops Neptune's leash around his wrist and types, and she watches his fingers as they spell out his full name. Nine letters, each one pushing that blade of déjà vu deeper into her chest.

"Here," he says, tipping the phone back to her. His voice is thick around the next words, like they're the hardest ones for him to say yet. "My name is Finn."

~

It's nearly seven when Briar arrives at the sea's edge.

The carnival looms in the distance, the Ferris wheel sparkling against the softening red sky. But she's on a different part of the beach, a lonely, quiet part of the shore meant just for her.

She's wearing white, like she's supposed to. The dress pools around her thighs, billowing in the wind. Her pockets are heavy with moonstones, and a sharp obsidian blade fits neatly in her palm.

It's her thirty-second birthday. In another time, another place, maybe there would have been someone beside her. Maybe there would have even been a party.

But tonight there's only this: the sea and that voice that's haunted her mind since she was six years old and letting her twin brother slip beneath the waves. The voice that told her to douse her parents' art gallery in gasoline, drop a match, and lock the doors. The voice that told her to sit alone at school, to never talk to anyone else. *I'm all you need*, it whispered, invisible hands in her hair.

She somehow bargained for blocks of time in thirteen-year stretches, but her time has run out.

Tonight she fulfills the promise made by a woman ten generations ago. A promise that's pulled her like a magnet her entire life, leaving her no other choice but to stop fighting.

She'll carve an ancient symbol into her skin and step into the sea. She'll take her rightful place as the head of a coven forged in celestial magic and stars. Briar Winters, aether witch. Briar Winters, high priestess.

Briar Winters, savior of demons and goddess of the damned.

Everyone meets their destiny, someone once told her. This one is hers. Her entire body aches from avoiding what's been inevitable for so long. Sometimes it's easier to give in.

Sometimes, surrender can be a weapon too.

But first, a phone call.

To apologize to Finn, to tell him she can't come to the carnival after all, that he'll have to ride the Ferris wheel without her. That even though she'd love nothing more than to feel the wind rip through her hair high in the neon-drenched sky, she can't. She's double-booked. She won't make it in time.

She won't make it at all.

Briar taps a button on her screen before tucking the phone beneath her hair.

It rings four times, and then, Finn answers.

CHAPTER FORTY

FINN

Finn Adler has always been a damn good liar.

He lies the way other people breathe. Without thinking. Words string together until his mouth is spinning a story that slips further and further from the truth. Until he's not sure which parts are real.

He's lied to his teachers, to his mom. He's lied to his friends, to his coaches, to nearly everyone he's ever met.

But mostly, Finn has lied to himself.

He lied every time he passed her at school and pretended he didn't notice her wild curls, her sad blue eyes. He lied every time he had his class schedule rearranged, coming up with excuse after excuse so they wouldn't ever be in the same room. He lied when other kids said horrible things about her and he just shrugged, as if he didn't spend every minute of every day thinking about how to get her alone and ask if she remembered him too.

It didn't stop there.

Finn lied that night on the beach thirteen years ago, telling himself he would watch over her from a careful distance, that he wouldn't let her see him. But that was before she started walking toward the water like she didn't plan to return and his entire body seized with panic. He pretended it didn't make his heart splinter to say her name, that his bones weren't hollowed with grief when she asked him to stay and he walked away from her instead.

He moved to California the next day, spent the entire plane ride with red-rimmed eyes, and tried to convince himself that doing the right thing often hurts. That he could live with that maddening pain in his chest as long as she was safe.

That he wouldn't let it happen the same way twice.

Finn lied when he came back to Loch Creek this weekend. He told himself it was to visit his old apartment, a building that remembers its history even if everyone else forgets, and not a last-ditch effort to protect her *just one more time*.

And he lied today.

Finn lied in the bookstore when he looked right at her.

Briar Winters. *His* Briar.

He pretended they were first meeting, that he didn't know her better than he knows himself. Put his number in her phone like they could ever have a normal date, a normal life.

As if anything about them could be anything but broken.

Finn glances at his watch. The carnival buzzes with electricity, and his pulse is racing. He knows he shouldn't have done it. Shouldn't have wedged himself back into her world.

Because Finn remembers everything that happened back then on that liminal beach; his eyes were closed, his breath was gone, but he heard every word Morgan said.

The spell will decide who loses the past and who retains it.

He's not sure which is the crueler punishment. To forget the imperfect yet fiercely beautiful love they shared? Or to remember every second of it in silence?

Finn has spent his whole life thinking about her. Thinking about what could have been, if just one thing had been changed. Butterfly effect. Chaos theory.

He's also spent his whole life trying to avoid her, terrified of pulling them back into that dreadful place. That haunted shore at the edge of the world, drenched with blood and tears and loss and grief.

He refused to do it to them a third time.

But, as this summer drew nearer and Loch Creek's thirteen-year hourglass ran down, Finn felt like he was choking on an impending catastrophe. Remembering that phone call in the In-Between when he spoke to Briar *from this exact day*. Consumed by visions of her dragging a blade through her wrists at the shore's edge, Finn found himself booking a plane ticket east. Like he was compelled by something bigger than himself to come home.

He swore it would be one night. He'd make sure she wasn't in danger. Nothing more.

He'd leave the next day.

And she'd have more time.

But once Finn heard her voice this morning, once her eyes met his, it was like he was drowning. Drowning in a magnetic field, Briar's own gravity. In every universe, they'll drown in each other.

He never had a choice, and neither did she.

Finn looks back at his watch—7:30.

She's going to come, he assures himself. *She's going to come.*

But 7:30 turns into 8:00, and 8:00 turns into 9:00.

The sky grows darker, the air colder. The crowd starts to thin, jovial screams from the rides fading into ocean waves.

"Dude," says the teenage boy working the Ferris wheel. "You want a turn?"

"I'm waiting for someone," he answers, anxiety roiling in his stomach.

He remembers that phone call again, how he spoke with the Briar from today without realizing what it would eventually mean. How she cried with the waves in the background.

How she talked to him like she'd forgotten who he was.

Finn tried, without understanding anything, to keep her talking. He tried, he tried.

In the end, he'll say they both tried.

Briar, he asked that day, *do you ever feel like you lost something, but you can't remember what?*

He barely caught her response before the line went dead. But he's carried it with him his whole life, like a rabbit's foot of hope. *Yes*, she whispered.

I feel like that all the time.

An ache widens in Finn's chest as he tracks the stars overhead, the water beyond the Ferris wheel, the empty stretch of black sea.

Maybe it was always going to end this way. Maybe two people like them are only fit for goodbyes.

And maybe—maybe, it's better not to feel that pain again, that grief. He thinks once more of the onyx beach, the dreadful sounds that ripped from her throat as she kneeled in his blood. The splitting ache in his heart when he realized she was dying too.

Maybe they're not meant for this world; maybe they'll become something more like folklore. A song you can't quite remember the words to. A childhood memory that changes shape over the years. An island that you know exists but can never find on a map.

Finn swallows. He'll go back to his hotel, and he'll get on a plane tomorrow.

And he'll try—he'll try—to forget Briar Winters.

But then—a flash of light from the dunes. Finn's eyes widen; his pulse skips.

Briar is walking toward him, dressed in white.

He stares at her, charting the pull of her curls in the breeze, the way her skirt whips around her legs like she's a mermaid in human form. But then his eyes drift to the scar on her calf—a jagged daisy wheel, the same one looming from the lighthouse, the spell book, the horrible tapestries at her birthday party.

The same symbol that's been branded into Finn's chest since the start of his newest life. A reminder of where they've been. Of where they can only go again.

His heart twists; ice climbs his spine.

For a moment he contemplates telling her to forget the Ferris wheel. He could feign illness, a family emergency. He could be back on a flight to California tomorrow, save them both. Save them from themselves, from each other. From the darkness they'll always share.

From what will inevitably happen, over and over.

But which is worse, he wonders again, to forget their fiercely imperfect love? Or to remember every second of what it felt like?

"Finn," she says, when she reaches him.

Planets and stars collide behind his eyes. He should protect them both while he can. He should tell her to go, make up another lie, just one more lie, one more—

"I'm sorry I'm late," Briar adds, and his breath catches.

Because it's the *way* she says it.

Like she's not talking about just a couple of hours.

He stares at her as he unthreads every syllable. Salt air and moonlight spill between them; numbers flood his veins.

Equations can predict endings from beginnings.

He knows how this will end.

But, the middle. That uncertain space—a cursed, lonely beach; a neon loop against the darkening sky; a kiss in the early hours of dawn between high school and college. Between what came before and what comes next—

That space has always belonged to them.

Because math isn't just math. Math is also faith. It's knowing the numbers, knowing the odds, knowing the conclusion—and doing it anyway.

Choosing imperfect, fierce, always-too-short love. Knowing how it ends and choosing it anyway.

He steals a glance over his shoulder, catching the eye of the Ferris wheel operator who sighs and motions them forward.

Finn extends his hand to Briar, and her palm is warm and familiar. Like something he once lost and has been trying to find. She feels, he thinks, like home.

"That's okay," he says. "I think we have some time."

* * *

ACKNOWLEDGMENTS

The novel you're holding began with four words written in a notebook: *Lost doesn't mean gone*. Back then, I had only fractions of a story: a boy missing somewhere in the threads of time. A girl with a horrible secret that clung to her like a shadow. And the ending that you read moments ago.

I knew this book's conclusion before I wrote a single word of its beginning, and every sentence strung along the way was in service of getting there. To that final image of two people, broken in matching places, choosing fierce love in the face of everything that can, would, and did go wrong.

This Raging Sea doesn't shy away from its sharp edges, but there's softness underneath—much like the main characters. In many ways, this story is a tribute to horror as a means of comfort and healing. It's also a love letter to old friendships, to the echoes of grief, to all the girls who are tired of making themselves small. I've always said that if one person feels seen by this story, I will have done my job as an author. With that, I'm endlessly thankful for those who helped Briar and Finn find their way into readers' hands.

To my amazing agent, Samantha Fabien. I'll never forget the moment my life changed on a Thursday morning, reading your email asking for a call. Thank you for believing in me and my words, and for your wisdom, guidance, and endless encouragement. I've told you a million times you're the definition of a dream agent, but let's make it a million and one. To all of Root Literary, I couldn't ask for a better support system. I'm so happy to be part of this team. And to Gabrielle Greenstein, thank you for helping get this book ready for submission with such a careful read of that early draft.

To Kade Dishmon, my incredible editor. You saw into the heart and soul of this story from the very first iteration, and your masterful edits helped it evolve into the book it was truly meant to be. I'm so grateful for your talent, your (often brilliantly evil in all the best ways) ideas, and your teamwork. It's been such an honor and delight to work with you on this book. Thank you for loving Briar and Finn as much as I do.

So much gratitude to the entire Holiday House team for giving *This Raging Sea* its perfect home. Thank you to Mary Cash, Sara DiSalvo, Michelle Montague, Rebecca Godan, Manu Velasco, and Stephanie Cohen for getting this book ready to be on shelves. Thank you to Chelsea Hunter and Kerry Martin for bringing Loch Creek to life on the pages.

To Elena Masci—Thank you for capturing Briar and Finn's love in your cover illustration. It's an author's dream to work with you, and I am so appreciative of your time and your talent.

To Taylor Grothe—Where would I be without this safe harbor of a friendship? Who knew a DM slide would turn into writing retreats in the forest and galavanting around Paris with the books of our hearts. Thank you for being there for every high and low, and all the soft quiet in between.

To Kelly Andrew—It feels like yesterday we were swapping word documents and spamming one another with live commentary. Thank you for adoring Briar and Finn from that extremely chaotic first draft (RIP to *that* kissing scene), for all the 5 a.m. ramblings, and for the "passing the torch" metaphor about publishing that encouraged me to finish this book.

To Elizabeth Urso—Thank you for always listening to my podcast-length voice notes and sending equally long ones back. From lizard days to clown days to screaming into the void while in the trenches (not to mention all those manifestation croissants), I'm so glad we've had each other. Forever toasting to our haunted girls.

To Dana Choe-Murray Draper, Alysha Rameera, Molly O'Sullivan, and Katie Wilson—I'm beyond grateful that Root Lit brought us together. Thank you for the Zoom drafting sessions and the endless solidarity.

To Marilyn La Jeunesse—From writing *Teen Vogue* articles together to drafting our respective novels, your friendship has been a constant. Thank you for always reading my messy chapters and supporting my over-use of jawline descriptors.

To Molly W.—The internet may be a hellscape, but it brought you to me, so I guess it's good sometimes. Thank you for being one of the earliest readers of this story, for sending me your Act III crying selfies, and for believing in me when it wasn't easy to believe in myself.

To all of Team Samantha—It's not every day that your agent siblings really do feel like family. I'm so happy to be part of this one, and so grateful for such a safe place during the roller-coaster of publishing.

To all the '25 debuts and the many authors and friends who have supported me along this journey in some way—I'm so lucky to know you. To Kendall Annette, Molly Burford, Ella Cerón, Sari Hitchins, Kalie Holford, Jessica James, Jessica Joyce, Jac M., Davona Mapp, Kara Nesvig, Meg Smitherman, Nicole Ting, Riyana Straetker, Kendra Syrdal, Lydia Wang—thank you for reading, for being there, for listening.

To the amazing authors who blurbed this book—Kelly Andrew, Skyla Arndt, Lyndall Clipstone, Kamilah Cole, M.K. Lobb, Wen-yi Lee, Rachel Moore, Riss M. Neilson, Jenna Voris, Pascale Lacelle, I.V. Marie, CG Drews, and Claire Legrand—thank you for your generous time and gorgeous words.

To Juliana, Marcella, Eirlysa, Georgina, Nana, Corinne, Gaiatri—Thank you for your stunning illustrations of my characters, and to Arthur for *that* portrait of the Death King that all but broke the internet. Artists are magical, and I'm grateful for your talents.

To the Newton Brothers for the soundtracks that played in the background while I wrote and edited every word of this book, and to Mike Flanagan for inspiring me to create horror that hurts and heals. The rest is confetti.

To Lauren—You were one of the first people to read this book, and I'm so grateful for your friendship and excitement. Thank you for cheering me on, and for always supporting my unhinged villains.

To Roberta—I'm thankful all the time that our paths crossed during Spring Fling freshman year because I'd be lost without you. Thank you for being there during every season since, and for always seeing me as I truly am.

To my entire family, thank you for your endless support and encouragement. Dan, for lending me your horror-buff brain whenever I said "I need to make this scarier;" Kate, for reading every word; Mom, for being the loudest and fiercest cheerleader; Connor, for listening to my plot ramblings and always asking "What if you just put your characters in outer space?"; and Iz, for everything. Neptune can be yours now.

To all the bookstagrammers and booktokers who added *This Raging Sea* to roundups, who helped spread the word online, or generally expressed excitement over reading, thank you from the bottom of my heart.

And finally, to you, the reader. Thank you for picking up this book, and for choosing to spend time with Briar and Finn. They were mine for many years, first quietly existing in my head, then a word document—and here, finally, a book. It's the honor of my life to say that Briar and Finn's story officially now belongs to you.